AGNES

By

Roberta Agnes Seiwert Lampe

ISBN: 1-58597-356-4

Library of Congress Control Number: 2005906634

LEATHERS
PUBLISHING
4500 College Blvd.
Overland Park, KS 66211
1/888/888-7696
www.leatherspublishing.com

In memory of my grandmother,

AGNES PUDER LINNEBUR

Violets for Agnes

Sketch by Rebecca Sevart,
great-granddaughter of Agnes.

ACKNOWLEDGMENTS

My profound gratitude to my mother,
ESTHER LINNEBUR SEIWERT,
for sharing the story of her mother, Agnes.

Special recognition is accorded to my dear grandfather, Joseph Linnebur.

To his children, my aunts and uncles, thanks for the wonderful remembrances and fond memories they shared. Without them, there would not have been a story.

My utmost respect, admiration and gratitude to those who encouraged me in this endeavor:

- My mother and father, Esther and Ferdinand Seiwert;
- My kind, patient husband of 45 years, Roman Lampe;
- Our two daughters, Mary and Ramona, whose curiosity was piqued by the stories they heard of their especially interesting great-grandmother;
- My sisters, Ruth, Betty and Rita, who know Agnes mostly through the stories;
- My niece, Rebecca Sevart, for the sketch of her great-grandmother.

Special thanks to Rabbi Pincus Aloof for his most gracious explanations of the beautiful religious customs and ancient beliefs of Judaism. His help was invaluable.

My total profound gratitude is extended to my dear friend and mentor, Martha Dandurand, for her extensive support, astute constructive criticisms and suggestions. She literally lived every moment of Agnes' story with me.

Agnes boarded the train at this impressive railroad station, in Breslau, Germany, for her trip to Hamburg, Cuxhaven, and America.

The Oder River flows past a beautiful church in Breslau. The river was, at that time, the boundary between Germany and Poland, and emptied into the Baltic Sea.

TABLE OF CONTENTS

Foreword ix
1. Auf Wiedersehen 1
2. Reverie 3
3. Jilted 9
4. America 19
5. Leo House 25
6. New Home 31
7. Happiness 37
8. Changes 47
9. The Advertisement 55
10. Joseph 59
11. A Decision Made 69
12. Kansas 75
13. The Arrival 79
14. The Farm 87
15. Decision 95
16. Country Morning 99
17. Garden Time 105
18. Buttons, Buttons 111
19. The Sleeve Ordeal 119
20. Heart's Song 129
21. Shivaree 137
22. Homecoming 143
23. The Hired Hands 151
24. Gypsy Wagons 161
25. The War 167
26. A Baby 175
27. The Wedding 183
28. The Letter 191
29. Christmas 195
30. The Radio Show 203
31. Runaways 209
32. Target Practice 215

33. Graduation 223

34. A New Daughter 233

35. The Killer Car 241

36. Harsh Words 249

37. Favored Child... 253

38. The Leave-Taking 261

39. The School Stove 269

40. The Journey 279

41. The Slogans 289

42. The Secret 295

Epilogue 301

Author Biography 303

Photo courtesy Esther Linnebur Seiwert postcard collection.

A German dirigible aloft over the large city of Breslau. The Germans used dirigibles for transportation across Europe, to South America and North America.

FOREWORD

IN THE EARLY 1900s, mothers were lost because of birth complications. Families, primarily of small towns and agricultural areas, were often confronted with these scenarios. When the father remarried, it was difficult for the children to accept. The title "Step-Ma" seemed to provoke instant vilification among some families.

There appeared to be that immediate dislike, regardless if the stepmother was a lady bred and raised in the immediate area, or someone like Agnes, who came into the vicinity as an outsider.

In many instances, the intense hatred was introduced, developed, nurtured and force-fed, not within the family household, but by those outside the home. Whether it was because of familial ties, jealousy, resentment or just interference and unkindness, it still fostered the same effect, the attempt to discredit the woman who put her life into the difficult role of stepmother.

The life story of Agnes, my maternal grandmother, typifies the trials of countless women, who took it upon themselves to raise children from a previous marriage. Her German ancestry during the early 1900s was also cause for concern, according to others.

Born and raised in Breslau, Germany (now a part of Poland and renamed Wroclaw), she spent all her years living in large cities. In America, she worked in New York City, Milwaukee and Chicago. She relocated to the Kansas plains and a very small town to take the job as housekeeper for a widower and his children. Her broadminded, worldly mannerisms, stylishness and interest in political events were also cause for suspiciousness among the local female populace.

Presented here as a fictionalized version, particularly the dialogue, it is based upon actual events of that family. Poetic license has been taken to extol descriptions of some occurrences. Some of the incidents were made known by my mother, Agnes' daughter. But many, the majority of the incidents, were recalled by my mother's half-brothers and half-sisters.

Through the years family members reminded my mother how terrible Step-Ma (her mother) was. My mother never raised her voice in protest, however, as she and her brother always enjoyed the company and connection with the first family, despite the feelings toward their mother.

It was accepted knowledge, however, that Agnes was as hard on her own children as her stepchildren.

Throughout the story, the reader, hopefully, will realize that kind, generous, soft spoken Joseph bore the brunt of those tumultuous years. He had experienced the agony and sorrow of his first wife's death. His youthful, hopeful love died with Katherine. He searched for help, for answers. He must have seen Agnes coming into his life as the answer to his dilemma. He also, then, had to endure the situation between his children and, eventually, the second love of his life.

My grandfather, Joseph, passed away when I was twelve, and Agnes, when I was seventeen. Consequently, they both were very familiar to me. My parents took my sister and me to see them practically every Sunday. By that time, Joseph and Agnes had retired to the city.

Even in her late years, Agnes still read voraciously and kept up on the political and war scenes of the 1940s, as did my father. As my mother pointed out, both Agnes and my father were very vocal in their opinions, while Joseph and my mother sat meekly by, figuring none of the topics could be solved by any of them. The adults spoke German to each other. In that guttural language, we children interpreted it as constant arguing.

Agnes was a wonderful, kind grandmother to my sister and me. She definitely did not spoil us with material things. And we intuitively knew how to behave around her, and to respect her and Grandpa. With a smile, we recall she still demanded respect, especially when the neighbor children were too noisy or trespassing. She became especially protective as Joseph aged and his health began deteriorating. She also, almost single-handedly, cared for him in those years. My mother and her half-sister, busy with their families of small children, helped out when possible.

In her last years, Agnes was still very determined, resourceful and demanding, even of herself. A stroke left her bedfast and unable to feed herself. At that time, she came to stay at our home. My mother asked for a bit of patience when she told Agnes she was anticipating the birth of another child, an event that was not supposed to be medically possible. Agnes rose to the occasion, forcing herself to become able to do some things on her own, for herself. She also insisted on going to a nursing home. That was almost unheard of in those days, the early

1950s. Nursing homes were also frightfully inadequate back then.

Mom's oldest half-brother helped her through this difficult time with his financial expertise, his compassion and caring.

Agnes was bedfast for most of her remaining three years. But her determination was still intact. She willed herself to exercise and to walk again. Her goal was to visit her daughter's home one last time. I can still see her in our yard, standing by my parents' car, ready to return to the nursing home. Her smile was bright and warm, her demeanor cheerful. At 6:00 a.m. the next morning, the call came. Agnes had died in her sleep.

Step-Ma stories still abound within the relationship. However, as the number of interesting stories of events came to light, the inspiration to write this story became apparent. In researching the world political scene of the years 1910 to 1930, events were brought into focus. Thus, many of the explosive and divisive episodes that happened within the family could be explained.

Perhaps, just perhaps, Agnes' feelings about her homeland and the welfare of her immediate family still in Germany were not realized by the children. But because of the definite feelings and opinions of their vicinity, family and neighbors, it made an impact on the youngsters. Agnes was, after all, from Germany, the country that was seen as the villainous aggressor of World War I.

The world was in a terrific uproar and, because of it, Joseph, Agnes and the children felt the impact.

With this in mind, I have written this account of my loving grandmother, Agnes. I also present the story with respect to my grandfather, Joseph; my mother, Esther; her brother, Robert; and Ellen, William, Agnes, Irene, Wendell and Coletta, my aunts and uncles of Katherine's family.

To all the descendants of both families, these accounts have become our family legacy, regardless of how we view them and pass them on to our future descendants.

I have chosen to use the family names to make the events as authentic as possible. Other names in the story have been changed, however, to protect the privacy of those individuals.

Agnes with her young nephews, Alfred and Ervin Neumann, sons of her sister, Martha.

Agnes as a self-assured young woman, in her home city, Breslau, Germany.

1

AUF WIEDERSEHEN

THE SHIP LOOMED huge against the dock. Waves of the restless and icy cold North Sea lapped against its side.

Agnes held on tight to her woven bag as she pushed through the jostling crowds. Porters pushed large flat carts loaded with steamer trunks and heavy leather valises. She wondered if hers was among them somewhere.

Men's hard voices barked orders. The air hung heavy with salty spray and a fishy smell. Agnes tried not to breathe too deeply of the wharf odors.

A waft of sizzling bratwurst touched her nostrils from the small street stand. The thin slices of dark rye bread in the early October morning now left a hungry void in her stomach. The smell of the sausages reminded her it had been hours since she had eaten.

Women clung to their assortments of kinder. The little ones waddled like Russian dolls, round and padded in layers of clothing to keep them warm from the ocean coolness.

Agnes let the crowds carry her forward in the direction of the gangplank. She clutched her bag and boarding pass tightly in one hand and pulled her coat closer to her body with the other.

People inched their way up and onto the deck of the ship. Agnes looked around and found herself gazing down, far down at the dock where she stood only minutes before.

She edged along the railings and looked back at her beloved Germany. Breslau, her beautiful Breslau, was only a train ride away from Cuxhaven, Hamburg.

Her eyes filled with tears, and she wiped her nose to discourage a torrent. With a delicate piece of white linen, Agnes tried to hide her emotions from the others.

She glanced around at the other passengers, but there was no familiar face. There was absolutely no one on this ocean voyage she had ever seen before.

The final boarding bell clanged. The mighty steam whistle bellowed and shook the windows of the nearby village. Tugboats tightened the heavy ropes and pulled the massive seagoing vessel away from the dock. The *Amerika* vibrated and rocked as its enormous engines roared into life. Black smoke belched forth from the twin smokestacks.

Agnes leaned even harder against the iron rail. Lowering her eyes, she touched her fingertips to her soft lips and kissed them gently, blowing the kiss back to shore. "Auf Wiedersehen, my Fatherland."

Sobs wracked her body as she pulled her coat tighter about her small frame.

"Ich liebe dich, Wilhelm."

Her lips quivered, her heart beat hard against her rib cage. She felt her whole being would explode. Anger, frustration, sadness, unfaithfulness and rejection all meshed into one. The last years swirled through her mind and the visions bombarded every corner of her consciousness.

Agnes doubled over and fought faintness, "Auf Wiedersehen, my love."

2

REVERIE

AGNES LOOKED OUT across the icy gray of the Atlantic Ocean.

"Meine Mütter, what am I doing?"

Tears welled up in her eyes. She touched her linen handkerchief to her face and dabbed away the drops on her cheeks. "No, my dear Mama, it must be this way. I must look forward, not backward. My life in Deutschland is over. America will now be my home."

Agnes straightened the white lace collar of her navy blue dress and squared her shoulders with determination. A smile crept across her face and she laughed gently, "An adventure awaits."

The afternoon sun warmed her face and caused her cheeks to flush a light pink. A soft ocean breeze fanned the air around her. The hard wooden deck benches seemed to soften under her weight as her reverie slipped deeper and deeper into her past.

Her blue-gray eyes took on a faraway look. The soft mother's voice she loved so well spoke to her inner soul. "Agnes, it is a beautiful morning, please come," Anna had said.

"But it is only 5:30, Mama."

"Oh, but daughter, the fragrance of the flowers floats heavy on the Mai Luft. No other time of year is the air so sweet as in the early hours of a May morning."

"Is Martha going?"

"Yes, daughter, your sister and brothers are anxious to partake of the sweetness of the morning. Happy chatter and laughter are already filling the air. Our neighbors are out early this morning."

Agnes smiled to herself as she remembered. "Yes, the Mai Luft, the May air, of her country was thick with the perfume of the spring flowers."

A sadness crossed her face as other childhood memories flooded her innermost thoughts.

"Come here, my little fraulein." Her father took an awkward step across the floor, reaching out to Agnes with unsteady hands. His brown eyes had the vacant look of one who enjoyed the spirits too much. Liquor made his body and breath reek.

Seven-year-old Agnes backed closer to her mother's skirts. The older children, Conrad and Martha, pulled their younger brother, Constantine, back to the parlor wall. The skinny nine-year-old Conrad knelt down beside the little boy and wrapped his arms around his small brother. He whispered ever so softly to him, "Do not be afraid, it is your Papa."

"Now, Robert," chided Anna in a quiet calm voice, "You are frightening the children."

Papa glared at Mama for several long seconds. Slowly, he backed off and sat down on a kitchen chair. He looked around at his scared children. Refined, long straight fingers were raised from his knees. Robert cradled his head in his large hands as he looked down to the floor. Tears gathered and started to roll down his nose. He wiped the drops on his sleeve, then looked up at his family.

"I am so sorry, Anna." Stretching out his arms to the children, he whispered hoarsely, "I am sorry, my little ones."

Conrad rose to his feet. "It has been a long time, Papa, since we have seen you. The little ones do not remember you."

"Conrad, my son, you are such a smart young man. I am so proud of you." Robert shook his head, "You are good to be like a Papa to the children while I am away."

Conrad eased slowly across the room and put his hand on his father's shoulder. "I try, Papa, I try. It would be much nicer if you could be here with us."

Robert straightened up and took Conrad's arm. "I would like to do that, too, son, but I am a horse inspector. When there is not much of that work, there are always trainers needing a good groom. The rich people that raise horses are out in the German countryside and in Poland." He chucked the boy under the chin, then spread his lips in a crooked smile. "My son, do you know of any horse farms in this city of Breslau?"

"No, Papa," Conrad squeezed his father's shoulder gently as he looked at the others. "Come, my brother and sisters, give your Papa a hug. He has been away a long time taking care of beautiful horses."

Constantine ran into his father's arms, "Do they have long, shiny tails and black manes?"

"Ah, my small son, those horses are so shiny. Their coats are brushed and curried for hours every day."

"Why, Papa?"

Robert lifted his youngest son up on his knees. "They are very special horses, Constantine, beautiful fast race horses. Their owners take them all over to other countries to run in races. When a horse wins, the owners make lots of money." He brushed the young boy's blond hair from his eyes. "With that money, they can pay me. Then I send the money home to your Mama so she can take care of you." Papa looked at the other children now sitting on the floor around his chair. "Sometimes I do not get much work, so there is not much money left to send home."

Anna rolled her eyes, but stayed silent. What Robert said was not quite true. Her thoughts recoiled at the lies her husband spoke. "I know," she whispered within her mind, "He squanders most of his earnings drinking too much and trying to live like the rich people he works for." There never was much left for her and the children. All the dainty intricate handiwork she made and sold helped keep the family in food.

She touched the children's hands tenderly. "Come, your Papa needs his rest. He has to leave soon to go care for more horses."

Robert looked at her and sensed the snide tone in Anna's voice. She knew what he was up to; he could not hide it from her. A slight sigh escaped from his lips. He liked his vagabond way of life and he was not about to change it for his wife or the children. The ways of the wealthy were much more exciting than his way of life here.

Agnes' thoughts were broken by small feet running past her. A mother followed in a frenzy, "Come back here, do not get close to the railing."

The wind began to pick up. The waves were cresting higher. As she watched them, memories flooded her mind again.

Because of habit, Agnes pulled a small piece of frayed paper from her bag. Over the years, she had looked at it so often. But now it surprised her how worn the funeral card had become. No matter how hard she tried, the wrinkles would not smooth out. The words had become faint, but they could still be read, "Robert Puder, 1849-1894, 45 Years Old, Died and Buried in Poland."

Agnes wiped a lone tear from her cheek. "Papa, it has been so long. Fifteen years already since the accident." Another slow tear rolled down. "Oh, Papa, how I needed you these last months. How I needed you all my life, to know you, to love you. Why, Papa, were you not there for us like other fathers were?"

The tears flowed more freely. "I was only fourteen, Papa. Constantine hardly remembers you at all. I really have to squeeze my eyes and think very hard to see you in my thoughts. One thing I can remember, your brown eyes. And I can see Mama's sad face when she spoke of you. I can hear her sobs, still, when she learned you had been kicked by a horse. She never told you, but the horses scared her, and she worried and prayed for you."

Agnes turned her face so other passengers would not see the tears that came more profusely now. She put her head down low into her lap, and relived those days of so long ago.

"Papa, Mama had to beg for money from her family and friends so she would have enough to go to Poland to bury you. Conrad and Martha stayed home to take care of Constantine and me. We could not understand about you. Papa, Mama tried so hard to be brave when she explained to us there was not enough money for us children to go along to the funeral."

The agony in her face twisted into anger. "Papa, how could you have let us down? Poor Mama did not even have enough money to bring you home so we could stand by your grave and say our final good-byes to you. I do not know if I can ever forgive you for that."

Agnes rubbed her slender fingers. The cool breeze off the ocean was creeping into her joints.

Her mother's voice echoed through her subconscious. "You are fourteen now, Agnes, and old enough to help out. Your father never provided us with much, but with the embroidery I sell, we can have food for all of us. But now, you and Conrad must find work. Martha is already helping with her handiwork that is selling." She stroked Agnes' long dark hair and looked deep into her daughter's eyes. "A friend told me of a wealthy family that is looking for a young girl to take care of their children. The pay is not much, only about four marks a month, and all your meals. At least you will be able to get good meals every day."

Agnes smiled to herself, "Not so, Mama, not so. I remember coming home and eating all the dry bread crusts you had put aside for dressing. When I did that, you wondered if the rich family where I worked had enough food to feed their own children."

Brushing a strand of dark hair from her face, Agnes mumbled softly in an inaudible voice, "We all learned to work hard in those years, and we learned to work to the best of our ability. Oh, Mama, maybe that was Papa's legacy to us after all, to learn how to really work."

Agnes noticed a young woman about her age coming over to her. A wide smile spread across the lady's face, and Agnes found herself smiling in return.

"May I join you to enjoy the ocean breezes?"

"Yes, please do." Agnes patted the seat next to her.

3

JILTED

JOHANNA SAT DOWN and giggled, "So, Agnes, why are you on this ship?"

Agnes gasped. She had never been approached about her decision to go to America like that.

"It is very personal, very painful. I cannot talk about it just yet." She looked at Johanna. Tears welled up again in Agnes' eyes.

"I am so sorry, Agnes. I thought maybe you left for a new life like I did. Most of my relatives are already in America."

"No, I know no one there. I only know of America by all the books and stories I have read."

"You like to read?" Johanna pulled a small book from her bag. "Perhaps someday you would like to read this. These are stories by a man who calls himself Mark Twain. He was raised near the Mississippi River in the middle of America, in the state of Missouri."

Agnes took the book and flipped through the pages. "What an interesting name. It does not sound like a German or French name. What is his heritage?"

Johanna's sparkling laughter spread warmth around Agnes. "It is not his real name. That is Samuel Clemens. The name 'Mark Twain' comes from the days when he worked on a steamboat on the big river. Samuel liked to listen to the captain when the boatmen judged the depth of the river so the steamboat would not end up on a sandbar. When they called 'Mark Twain,' that meant the river was two fathoms deep." She giggled again, "Agnes, does not that river sound like a good place to go to?"

Agnes found herself smiling. "Who knows, one or either of us might see that big Mississippi River some day."

Johanna took Agnes' hand. "Are you traveling alone?"

"Yes, I am." Agnes looked at her then. "Me and my memories."

"Good, so am I. We can keep each other company. I need a friend, too, when we land over there. My family is spread all over the country, but I have to work in New York City for some money to go to them." A crooked smile lit up her face, "And I really do not know which relative I want to go and be near."

"At least I do not have that dilemma." Agnes laughed merrily. "And I think a nice friend in New York City would be quite helpful. That is such a big city, bigger than Breslau, I think." She looked at Johanna, "I need a friend, too."

The two leaned their heads together, then clasped hands. "This will never work," said Agnes as she straightened her big brimmed hat. Our hats are much too large."

Their laughter fell like shattering crystal to the floor.

"One of these days, before we get off this ship, I want you to tell me just why you are going to America. You need to get the sadness from your heart before then." Johanna squeezed Agnes' hand in a soft grip.

"You are right, my friend, you are right." Agnes stood and took her hand once more. "By the time on my timepiece, it is almost the dinner hour, and I am looking forward to a good meal."

The days turned into weeks as the large ship slid silently across the Atlantic. Johanna and Agnes spent hours on the second-class deck. They leaned against the railing and watched the porpoises glide along-side the ship.

"Oh, but that I could dance that gracefully," laughed Johanna. "Do you dance, Agnes?"

"I did once." She turned her face away. Johanna detected the sadness in her voice and put her hand ever so gently on Agnes' arm.

Early winter storms rolled across the ocean. The ship was small in comparison. Huge waves splashed up and over the decks in vicious torrents. No passengers were allowed out on those days for fear of being swept overboard. The young women sat in the lounge and watched the angry sea through heavy glass windows.

"Can you imagine what it must be like for the people in steerage class?" Agnes saw another huge wave rolling in. "They cannot see those mighty waves building, but only feel them crashing against the ship." She shook her head in wonder. "It must be so frightening for them, as the ship rolls from side to side. Those poor children – how sick they must be."

Dark curls framed Johanna's face and bounced delicately as she shook her head. "Oh Agnes, you are so much more compassionate than I. The thought never occurred to me."

"We can only imagine how many people they have packed together down in steerage." Agnes looked at Johanna directly, "Did you see those large families with all their young children on the wharf? They are not here in this class, so they have to be in steerage."

Johanna looked around the room. "So many, I have heard, can only afford the steerage passage. How sad."

"Someone told me the railroad travel agents paint a very colorful scenario and never tell most of the poorer people how much it is really going to cost them. The train fare to Hamburg actually is more than most of them expected. They have sold everything and have nothing to return to, so they can only go on and hope for their life to be much better in America."

Johanna took off her large hat and put it on a chair beside her. "I noticed so many of them carrying sacks of flour and potatoes onto the ship, and I was wondering why?"

"To get cheap fares, they have to bring on their own food and bedding, bowls and table service."

"In other words, there are no dining tables with snowy-white linens?" Johanna winced.

Just then an enormous wave came rolling, building across the water and hit the ship broadside. The vessel dipped under the force and tipped deep toward the angry, foaming, gray water.

The two women tried to stand, but the movement of the sea was too much. "We may just as well stay here until the dinner hour," Johanna laughed. "We cannot stand up to go anywhere else."

The ocean calmed after a long stormy night. In the morning, sunlight dappled the low swells and glistened off the water like a huge mirror all the way to the horizon. Passengers were able to walk on the decks again with grace and ease.

Another morning, Johanna and Agnes walked out on the deck for an early day stroll. A wall of fog hid the ocean. Even the railing of the deck disappeared in the gray moisture.

"Agnes, look at this fog." Johanna held her hand at arm's length. "I can hardly see my fingers," she gasped.

"It is thick as pea soup," Agnes announced merrily. "Now I know what they mean by pea soup. We cannot see the railing and it must be no more that ten feet from us." She looked at Johanna and grinned, "Should we walk and see if we bump into it?"

"Oh, but, Agnes," Johanna grabbed Agnes' hand. "What if it dissolved in this fog and we just walk right off the edge of the ship?"

Two dapper young men came strolling past, tapping their walking canes with each step. They gallantly tipped their hats. "Are you young ladies enjoying the early morning fog?" They stopped as if to make the women's acquaintance.

Agnes and Johanna nodded and smiled. No one spoke for a time. Agnes knew the men were waiting for an invitation, but she was not eager for that. Finally she spoke, "We are trying to find the benches so we can sit. The silence is so penetrating in the fog, we just want to relax and enjoy it. Our thoughts need time for reflection."

"Well then, good day, ladies." The taller of the two men tipped his hat again. "We will continue our stroll and leave you to your thoughts."

"Agnes, did you have to rebuff them that completely?" Johanna frowned. "They may have been good company." Then she tittered, "Maybe we could use some strong male protection when we dock in New York City."

Merriment sparkled in Agnes' eyes. "They did not look like the protective kind to me. We probably would have to protect them."

The two held their gloved hands to upturned lips and chuckled politely. Their giggles erupted into convulsions of laughter.

The loudspeaker crackled to life. A deep male voice spoke, "Ladies and gentlemen, this is the Captain speaking. We are two days out of New York City and the point of your destination. We are experiencing heavy fog that may last all morning and well into the later day. As we travel on, you will hear the deep-throated sound of foghorns from other ships that are passing. Those ships are our neighbors on the ocean.

Have a good day and enjoy the stillness and quiet of the fog."

Johanna and Agnes sat on a bench and watched the shadowy figures of others pass by in the thickening fog.

"It feels like the world ends just inches from us." Johanna strained to look through the gloom. "It is difficult to even try and imagine what is out beyond the fog." She sighed, "It really makes one forget about reality."

Agnes nodded, "Yes, it does." After a pause, she continued, "But then, perhaps, it helps put life into perspective." Her thoughts drifted off into long moments of silence. "Here I am, 28 years old and I am on a ship crossing a huge ocean. In search of what, I am not sure. My life should be about children, but this fog has succeeded in wiping out, at least for the moment, any thought of my past." A lump caught in her throat. The tears built to overflowing.

Johanna moved closer to Agnes. "Are you weeping?"

"Perhaps it is more the mist from the fog." Agnes dropped her linen piece to her lap.

"Why are you on this ship, Agnes?"

"The love of my life is gone." Agnes' thoughts tried to pierce through the dense fog to her Breslau home. "He is gone and I cannot understand why. Wilhelm told me he loved me with every fiber of his being."

"Oh, Agnes, I am so sorry."

Agnes continued speaking, not to Johanna, but more to hear the words she needed to say aloud.

"We met about six years ago, in 1903, at a Fasching celebration in a small village on the outskirts of Breslau. He was so tall and handsome. Our eyes met, and I knew in an instant we would mean so much to each other." She hesitated to untangle her thoughts.

"He courted me with every ounce of the gentleman that he was. We took long walks through the parks in early spring, and splashed through the rain, and made castles in the snow." Her fingers twisted the linen square into a tight roll until she could twist it no more.

Johanna sat quietly, knowing she could not, should not interrupt the other.

"Neither of us had much money. I was cooking for a wealthy family and he worked as a policeman. But we had our dreams and we began to save for the future." Another tear trickled down.

"Wilhelm. I can finally say his name aloud again." A second tear ridged her cheek. "Wilhelm loved me thoroughly. He gave me joy, so much to look forward to. I awoke with a smile in the early morning at the thought of him. I felt his tender kiss brush my cheek, even though he was not there."

Agnes took a deep breath. "My mother and sister did not like him because he was of a different religion. Just being with him clouded all thought of religious differences from my mind." She hesitated in thought once again.

"We professed our love for one another, and he gave me a beauti- ful, delicate ruby ring. Our days together after that were numbered. He had waited for his brother to return from the Army, so he could be there to help their mother. Wilhelm was so kind to her."

The fog began to lift, so the railing was now visible. Johanna reached over to touch Agnes' hand, but without saying a word. Her touch was comfort enough at the moment.

"Three years. Three years seemed such an eternity. But we knew we must wait until his three years of military service were over, other- wise we could not stand to be apart at all." Agnes smoothed her lace collar. "We exchanged photographs. He looked so handsome in his uniform." She smiled slightly. "Our letters would see us through. We promised to write every day or so. I knew that would be a difficult promise for him to keep in the Army, but I vowed to never let him feel lonely. He held me so close at the railroad station, then kissed me so tenderly. We waved to each other, until the train had taken him from my sight. I thought I would die from that moment on."

She turned away from Johanna as her eyes brimmed with tears. "Every day a letter, every day I wrote. And I waited for the post each day, but nothing. For months, day by day, I waited so patiently. My heart cried out in loneliness at first, then changed to anger. Anger at what, I was not sure. How could I be angry with my love? My heart screamed with bitterness. My mind was scorched to the breaking point. What had happened? No word from him. His mother and brother showed me their letters from him, but there were none for me."

Agnes dropped her head down into her lap and sobbed uncontrol- lably. "I just finally tore his picture to shreds."

Johanna wrapped her arms around Agnes and put her head against

Agnes' shoulder. She held her close. "I feel so helpless," whispered Johanna. "What can I say?"

She took Agnes' small hat and put it beside herself on the bench. "Cry, just cry, dear friend. Your heart is broken and bursting. Cry, so it may heal."

Tears flowed in torrents. All the heartbreak, the bitterness, the not knowing caused her dam of emotions to spill over. Slowly, then finally, her tears were spent. Agnes raised her head and wiped the drops from her red tear-stained face.

"I should not have let myself go like that, Johanna, please forgive me."

"Dear, dear Agnes, how could I not help you, not listen to you, not feel your heartrending cry for help? We two are here alone on this ship, on this huge ocean. We alone must be here for each other."

Johanna wiped a wandering tear from her friend's face. She stood up and held out her hand. "Come, let us go find a basin of cool water to take the tear stains from your cheeks."

Agnes broke into a forced smile. "Not just now. Let me tell you why I am on this ship." She took a deep breath. "After a long time, the realization dawned on me. I was not only very angry at Wilhelm for breaking my heart, but angry at my Fatherland also. It was my beloved country, my homeland, that took my true love from me. I could not bear to stay there any longer, either for my home or to wait for the man who probably never really loved me."

She picked up her hat and brushed the rolled brim absentmindedly. "Reading is so important to me, and stories about America started to entice me. The more I read, the more I felt America beckon to me. Then one day, I decided the savings for my marriage could pay for my fare." She smiled weakly. "It gave me hope, a purpose for my life, a healing for my being."

She stood up. "So here I am, on this ship, in the middle of this huge ocean, on my way to America." A touch of forced laughter, "Wilhelm, who is Wilhelm? He is not in my life anymore."

"Come," said Johanna, "the fog is lifting and I need a walk around the deck. We need to breathe in the salty spray of the ocean."

"Attention to all passengers of First and Second-class. This is the Captain speaking. The ship's crew invites each of you to come to our

15

Masquerade Ball, celebrating our journey across the Atlantic Ocean. Tomorrow will be a busy day as we prepare to dock in New York City. But, for this evening, we intend to celebrate. Come in costume if you wish. The ship's wardrobe mistress has numerous masks and different types of character clothing for your use. The challenge will be to find whose face is behind each mask. We will see you there."

Johanna looked at Agnes. "How exciting. Are you willing to go? Could you feel like going to a party?"

"Perhaps. Give me several hours to sort through my thoughts of this day."

"Certainly." Johanna put her hand lightly upon Agnes' shoulder.

The dresses were carefully hung in her closet, but which one would she wear? It had been so long. Would she remember how to act at a party? Wilhelm never cared for large gatherings of people, and certainly not parties.

A light knock at the door broke her reverie. Johanna handed Agnes a black satin mask. "Are you ready?" Giggling, she sashayed around the room.

"I would be, but none of my gowns seem to fit the occasion. Can you help me choose?" Agnes looked so serious, Johanna did not want to laugh.

"Of course. Put on this pretty blue one with the tiny tucks. It matches your blue-gray eyes." Johanna motioned to the chair, "Sit down and let me wind up your hair."

Agnes sat down and brushed through her waist-length brown hair. Johanna twisted it in a long coil, then rolled it up into a large bun at the base of Agnes' neck.

"Now, put on your mask."

Agnes lifted the mask to her face and looked at her reflection in the mirror.

"Do you think we will meet up with those two good-looking men we saw on the deck this morning?"

Agnes smiled, "If so, I had better keep my mask on, or they will leave in a hurry."

Johanna placed some pretty pins in the other's hair. She checked Agnes' image in the mirror. "Stand up and let me look at you."

Agnes stood and smoothed the skirt of her dress.

"Look at you, look at yourself. You are beautiful, dear Agnes." Johanna turned Agnes toward the mirror.

A serious looked crossed Johanna's face. "Will you dance, Agnes?"

The other raised her eyebrows, then turned from side to side and surveyed herself in the looking glass. A wisp of hair drooped down along her cheek and she brushed it aside gently.

A slight smile crossed her face as she whispered, "Of course, I will dance." She turned to look at herself again in the mirror. "Yes, I will dance," she declared emphatically.

She held out the skirt of her gown and curtsied to her reflection in the mirror.

With a look of sadness and uncertainty, Agnes ponders her future.

4

AMERICA

BASS-THROATED FOGHORNS OF ships broke the silence of the early October 25th morning of 1908.

Off in the distance, belching, trailing smoke appeared ever so small. When passengers looked back several minutes later, the tops of smoke-stacks were visible. Soon a miniature ship appeared where the curve of the earth was round. The closer it came, the larger it appeared.

"Land, I see land," shouted a shriveled-up old man. He balanced against his cane with one hand, and pointed out across the water with the other.

"Calm down, Papa, do not strain your heart," his daughter cautioned.

As the morning mist cleared from the ocean, the skyline of New York City was visible on the far distant horizon.

"America, at last," breathed Johanna, almost religiously. "We are here, Agnes, we are here." She remembered they were still surrounded by miles of water, but let her exuberance grab the moment. "We are here, America, we are here," Johanna shouted.

Agnes grabbed her joyous friend and clasped her hand hard. "Oh, Johanna," was all Agnes could mutter. Tears and laughter intermingled in happy profusion.

Agnes sighed joyfully, "All the books I have read, all the times I dreamed of this, I never could have imagined this moment." Then a shower of tears deluged her cheeks and the front of her coat. "What joy awaits me here?" she whispered silently.

"Attention, all passengers," the Captain's voice boomed across the decks. "In the late afternoon, we will be docking in the harbor at

New York City. Tomorrow, First and Second-class passengers will be cleared for departure here on the ship by American immigration authorities. You will then disembark the ship directly into the city. Representatives from the city's immigrant centers will greet you. They will offer assistance in housing and jobs for anyone needing their services. Railroad ticket agents will help you if you are going on to other states."

He paused for a second, then continued, "Steerage passengers will board ferries for passage to Ellis Island. Immigration officials and medical personnel will clear you there."

Absolute stillness settled over the ship, as though the passengers feared this may all be a dream. It was as though no one wanted to break the spell, the courage and determination they had undertaken to come to this land. And there was the silent fear that authorities may not allow them to enter.

The Captain's voice blared again from the loudspeakers, "As we enter the harbor, on your left will be the Statue of Liberty, America's greeting to you. We wish you all health and happiness in your new lives in this country, no matter where you choose to settle." The message was repeated in French, German, Italian, Hungarian and Russian, for the different nationalities on the ship.

"Do you have everything packed, Johanna?"

"I am ready, more ready than I have ever been for anything in my whole life." Her green eyes twinkled, as she patted the powder puff lightly on her nose. "Oh, Agnes, do you know where you will go?"

Agnes shook her head. "I am not sure exactly. Perhaps one of the immigrant agencies can help me."

The two found an empty bench. "My relatives told me to go to the Leo House. The Sisters of Loretto staff it. All people are welcomed there, but especially young women traveling alone." Johanna sat down.

"Is that where you plan to go?"

"It seems like a very safe place, so I think that will be the place I choose."

"A nice clean bed in a room that does not rock sounds good to me; I do not care where it is." Agnes smiled, "Even now, I have a sense of happiness about America. My heart tells me I needed to come here."

"You will find another to love, Agnes. Maybe not here, but somewhere in this huge country, there will be someone for you."

Agnes grinned at the younger woman. "You are so optimistic about my future. I need to be as open and trusting about it as you are." She shook her head, "Johanna, you are a hopeless romantic."

The waters became crowded with ships. Their own vessel was moving slowly toward the port. Passengers crowded to the left deck.

"Oh my, do you think this ship will tip to one side?" Johanna tried to be serious, but her eyes twinkled in fun.

"I hope not," Agnes answered, amused. "Remember, all those cattle and horses and pigs that were loaded. They are all down in the hold and, for sure, they will not go out to see the Statue of Liberty. The poor creatures will all be pushed to the right side of the ship to balance out the people's weight," she chuckled.

"Agnes, do you really believe that?"

"I do not know, do you?" Agnes' eyes lit up with merriment.

"Dear friend, I have not seen you look so happy since we met." Johanna hugged her. "Perhaps Wilhelm did you a favor."

"Perhaps he did."

Others began to crowd the deck around them, so the two women stood up for a better view. Passengers leaned heavily against the railings, pushed there by others behind them. Young men climbed up on the steps and platforms of the ship. Girls clambered up on the benches, and daring boys leaned way out over the railing. Their ship, the *Amerika,* slowly maneuvered the Narrows.

"Is that Brooklyn?" asked one.

"I think that is an island," said another, pointing to Staten Island.

A light mist, with the threat of rain, had moved in and hung over the harbor. Then, through the mist, an opening broke. Standing tall and stately was the famous lady.

"The Statue," shouted a hefty, vibrant voice. "The Statue of Liberty."

A murmur arose across the crowd, and built into a crescendo of tongues, foreign tongues of many peoples. Shouts of joy erupted. Laughter built in peals and ripples that spread out over the ocean's waters.

"America," they shouted. "We are in America."

The mist closed in and a light rain spread over the ship. No one noticed. They twirled each other in dance and slapped each other on the shoulders. Faces smiled and toothy grins spread wide. They had crossed the ocean safely.

Tugboats bumped against the ship and guided it into the dock. One last whistle announced its arrival, and then the engines shut down.

People on the deck waved to those on the dock below. The clamor of voices rose in swells, then dropped to whispers. It was like a religious experience for each of them.

Big, brawny dock hands wrestled with heavy, thick coils of rope that tied the ocean liner fast to the pier.

Early the next morning, gangplanks dropped down in place. Longshoremen rushed to open the baggage hold areas of the ship. They literally bumped over each other with stacked, loaded carts full of valises and trunks.

"Oh, my," breathed Agnes, looking down. "That could be mine."

The Captain's voice broke over the clamor below. "First-class passengers to the dining room for immigration check. Second-class clearance inspection will begin in three hours in the dining hall. Passengers will be allowed to depart immediately after clearance."

"This is so exciting," swooned Johanna. "I have to squeeze myself to realize this is real." She tugged Agnes' arm. "Look at the welts on my arm just from pinching myself." Johanna's merry laugh split the brisk air and bounced through space to echo against the New York skyline. "I must quit or I will get blood poisoning before my feet ever touch American soil."

"More like American cement," chuckled Agnes. "There appears to be no soil around here anywhere, only cement."

Immigration clearance was swift. "Hurry, hurry, Agnes, I do not want to spend one more minute on this ship." Johanna carried her small hatbox close to herself. "I certainly do not want my best hats crushed."

"Hold on to your bags tightly, ladies," warned a steward. "There are thieves in the crowd, just waiting to see what they can grab and steal. You will probably be asked if you have any blankets and extra clothes to sell. The street vendors are always ready to take those things from unsuspecting travelers." He walked with them in the direction of the gangplank. "They especially target those in steerage class, since most of them cannot speak English or German. Before the passengers realize what has happened, the vendor has disappeared into the crowd and has not paid one cent for the bedding or clothes. Many passengers are glad to be free of the extra baggage, but they sure could use some money for the things."

"On second thought, Agnes, do we maybe want to return to Hamburg?" asked the startled Johanna.

"I think not," smiled Agnes. "We must be brave." She looked around the crowd and added with a mischievous grin, "Where are those two gentlemen we met earlier on deck?"

Johanna giggled then. "Agnes, they would not protect us from anyone so nervy as the street vendors. Truth is, neither of them could hardly kill a bug. Why, I doubt they ever got their hands dirty from anything except eating a chicken leg."

Agnes just nodded her head in amusement.

A horse-drawn trolley car waited down the street a distance, at the edge of the crowd. "LEO HOUSE" was painted in large letters on the side.

Johanna grabbed Agnes' arm. "The Leo House, that is where we want to go."

The two pushed through the milling throng to get to the trolley. As they rode down the streets, Agnes looked around and stared in amazement.

"What are all those women chewing? I have never seen anything like it."

The conductor grinned. "It is chewing gum, Ma'am. Just a new thing that has come on the market. It is making quite an impression on the people, especially the ladies."

Agnes sniffed to herself. "They look like cattle must, that are chewing their cud."

Others on the trolley nodded, obviously in agreement, and smiled. The conductor winked at Agnes. She blushed self-consciously.

Agnes turned back for one last look at the huge ship looming over the New York docks. The previous days were unbelievable for her. She shook her head in wonder, "Did I really leave my homeland?" she muttered.

Johanna noticed her and turned her gaze in that direction also. She touched Agnes' hand lightly. "That is such a big, beautiful ship, is it not? I can hardly believe I was on it."

Agnes agreed, "It is beautiful." Smiling at Johanna, she continued, "I am feeling the same way. Did I really come to America?"

Johanna laughed, "What amazes me, I find it hard to remember what it felt like, just seeing all that water, and no land. Can you remember, Agnes, not seeing any land for days?"

"No, right now, I cannot." She hesitated again and slipped into deep thought. Finally, she went on, more to herself than to Johanna. "That ship accomplished so much for me these last days." She searched quickly in her bag for her linen cloth, to touch at her eyes. "It helped me by its peacefulness. Just being in its patient silence, I was able to think through things. And then one day, I realized I had just dropped my sadness, my frustration and loneliness into the ocean. All those feelings were swimming down in that water, right alongside those porpoises." Then she laughed.

Johanna laughed with her. "America will be the better for you coming here, Agnes."

Agnes turned once more in the direction of the ship, her stabilizer. She touched her lips to her fingers and blew a kiss in its direction. "Thank you, *Amerika*," she whispered.

Photo courtesy Esther Linnebur Seiwert postcard collection.

The ocean liner, Amerika, that brought Agnes to America, belonged to a large German fleet, the Hamburg-Amerika Line. The twin smokestack concept the company used is mirrored on the ocean liner, the S.S. Deutschland, a sister ship of the Amerika.

5

LEO HOUSE

SISTER MARY ANTHONY opened the door and held out her hand, "Welcome to Leo House." She motioned to a parlor off to the right of the hallway.

"Please come in and sit down. We will get acquainted."

The dozen or so immigrants who had come on the trolley looked around at the austere furnishings of the room. Sister Mary Anthony saw the expressions on their faces and smiled. "Our beds are much more comfortable than our chairs, I assure you."

Nervous laughter circled the room, as each person found a straight-backed chair.

"Just a little information about our immigrant house," she began. "The Sisters of Loretto founded Leo House and have opened our doors to foreigners coming to America for years. Many have found permanent housing and employment in the city through our placement service. Numerous businesses and individuals come to us, looking for dependable workers. Leo House has an outstanding reputation for job services, and the assistance we give to our clients."

She paused for a few seconds, "Most of our immigrants only stay two or three weeks before they feel confident going out into the city. Our Sisters can also help you learn basic English." Her smile dispelled their fears. "We will teach you enough to at least help you cope at first." Her warmth made them feel more secure. "Are there any questions?" she asked as she looked at each individual.

"We can settle you in now. Single women will be in one room, married women and children in the largest dormitory and men in a smaller dormitory. Beds and clothes lockers are provided for each. Curtains between the beds will assure you of privacy." Smiling, she continued, "After you are settled, come back to the main floor and we shall see if there are any job possibilities for you available now."

The nun lifted her chart from a small table and pointed to Agnes and Johanna first. "We will begin with you, ladies." Another nun entered the parlor. "Sister Mary Bernard will escort you to your accommodations. Let me record your name and the city where you are from."

"My name is Agnes Puder, from Breslau, Germany."

"I am Johanna Schmitz, from Bonn, Germany."

They followed Sister Mary Bernard up two flights of steep stairs. "Your trunks and valises will be delivered here late this afternoon," Sister Mary Bernard explained. "Our drayman, Jacob, is at the docks now collecting all the baggage."

"What a relief that is," breathed Agnes. "I wondered how I could transport that huge trunk." She looked at the nun, then at Johanna. "For a long time I thought most of my clothes could have been left behind." She laughed lightly as she continued, "Do all travelers pack like they cannot buy clothes where they are going, or do I just feel that way?"

"Hardly, Agnes, the majority of travelers feel likewise." Sister Mary Bernard's hazel eyes twinkled, and she pushed a stray curl of dark hair back under her tight fitting headpiece. "We see it all the time. Many women leave their extra, unneeded clothing here for us to donate to the needy."

The nun opened the door to the single women's dormitory. "The women who can afford it see the different clothing fashions here in America, and decide to dispose of their European clothes."

"How exciting," gushed Johanna. "How near is the largest department store, Sister? I can hardly wait to see how the fashionable ladies dress here in New York City."

"Do not forget, Johanna, we will have to learn to chew gum, too." Agnes touched her friend's shoulder in jest. "It will be difficult for me, I fear. My false teeth will probably not stay in with that sticky gum."

"You sure do not have false teeth, Agnes. You are much too young." The nun turned to look at her.

"When I was seventeen, a bout with pyorrhea alveolaris caused all my teeth to loosen and fall out."

"How sad." Sister reached over to pull back the privacy curtain and motioned to Agnes that the bed was assigned to her.

Agnes pushed on the thin mattress and pulled back the heavy woven blanket. "After a rocking bed on the ship, I am ready to sleep in a bed that stands completely still." The three of them smiled and nodded.

"The sounds of New York will be different from anything you have probably ever heard." Sister grinned, "This city never sleeps. Deliveries are made during the night and garbage cans bang all around. If you ever notice, you will see there are no alleys on Manhattan Island. All deliveries have to be made through the front doors of all the buildings. That causes an interesting dilemma." She fluffed up the covers. "The streets are almost as busy during the nights as they are during the days. And the night workers make sure not to let you forget they are working."

Johanna put her hatbox down on the bed next to Agnes. "New York sounds so thrilling and exciting. I think this is where my next home is to be."

"What about your relatives here in America?" Agnes reminded her.

Johanna flopped down on the bed next to her hatbox and sprawled her arms off over the sides. "They will just have to be content with my visits to them." Her silvery tittering rang through the long room.

"The city can always use especially happy people," Sister Mary Bernard smiled.

She pulled the privacy curtains together. "Agnes and Johanna, you may want to rest awhile. The women's bathroom is just down the hall, so if you would like to refresh yourselves and redo your hair. Later, you may like to come downstairs and see if we have work opportunities you might consider."

Sister checked the insides of the lockers, and then turned to the two. "Dinner is served here at six, in the first floor dining room, or you can find an eating house in the city. There are several reasonably priced delicatessens up and down this street, that are operated by vendors of various nationalities. So you can try cuisine from all over the world. Some of them have tables, so you can eat there. We do allow you to bring in breads, cheese and meats, and a few sweets, but only small amounts."

"I do not know how you feel, Agnes, but for this evening, I would rather eat here." Johanna narrowed her eyes. "I am not brave enough just now to venture up and down these unknown streets."

Sister Mary Bernard nodded, "You have made a wise decision. It is better that you take some time in the next few days to acquaint yourself with this part of the city." She turned to go, "I will see you ladies downstairs later, either at the employment registry or at dinner."

Agnes slipped off her high-topped shoes and wiggled her toes. "How wonderful. Just to lie back and rest."

Johanna lay down on the other bed and closed her eyes. "Oh, Agnes, if I fall asleep, please just let me be." Her eyes opened wide and sparkled with humor. "That is, unless my snoring is too disturbing."

Agnes laughed lightly, then rolled over so her back was to Johanna. "If I am not here when you awake, you will probably find me downstairs. I need to look for employment as soon as possible."

After thirty minutes, Agnes stood and rubbed her hands down her skirt to smooth the folds. Johanna was still fast asleep.

Agnes hurried down the stairs to the main floor. Sister Mary Anthony looked up from her desk when she knocked, and motioned for her to enter.

"I have come to see if there is work for me somewhere."

The Leo House, New York City, where Agnes stayed when she first entered the United States.

6

NEW HOME

THE STERN BUTLER opened the two wide, heavy oak doors and bowed low.

"Welcome, Miss Puder." He stepped aside and extended his hand back toward the long hallway. "I will announce you to Madame Levy. Please follow."

He walked stiff and tall through the wide hall to the small informal parlor. Agnes was overwhelmed. Of all the families she had worked for in Breslau, she had never seen such an elaborate display of wealth.

Long, beveled hall mirrors reflected the crystal prisms and gold branches of huge chandeliers. Rich-hued woven tapestries hung from the high ceilings and ended just above the carved backs of the Louis the XIV chairs. Persian rugs muffled the sounds of footsteps on the polished parquet floors. Tall, intricately colored and lacquered vases of various sizes were placed on marble-topped tables, tucked in between the velvet covered chairs and settees.

Agnes marveled and, wistfully, looked about. Her mind whirled in wonder, "This must be what the royal palaces of Europe were like." She shuddered slightly. "Is this the house of American royalty?" Wrestling with her thoughts, it occurred to her, "But America has no Kaisers or Queens." A slight smile crossed her face. "Johanna would be completely flabbergasted by all of this."

The butler stood before the empty doorway, waiting for her. He saw her look of amazement, as well as apprehension. Ever so slightly, he made eye contact with Agnes and nodded his head. She detected a touch of warmth in his otherwise austere manner.

"Miss Puder to see you, Madame. Mrs. Levy, Miss Puder."

"Thank you, Harrison." He bowed his head in respect, then backed out of the room, closing the door.

Agnes was left standing alone, quietly being inspected by the Madame. The regal looking middle-aged woman sat in a royal blue velvet high-backed chair that reminded Agnes of a throne. She leaned forward with her small hands resting upon the gold knob of her walking stick.

For several seconds, the woman looked at her. No smile was on her face. Dark brown eyes seemed to drill right through Agnes, looking at the very core of her being. Agnes had never felt this torn-bare in front of anyone before. But she kept her composure and looked Madame square in the eye. Neither woman flinched. Both were trying to find approval of the other.

Mrs. Levy relaxed and leaned back in her chair. She put the walking stick to the side, and rested her hands gently upon the ornately carved armrests. A slight smile crossed her lips. Her eyes softened to a twinkle.

"I like you, Agnes Puder. You are direct. There is no lack of confidence in you." The older lady motioned to a chair nearby. "Come sit, Agnes, I would like to learn more about you."

Agnes sat at the edge of the chair, a bit apprehensive. For a few moments she closed her eyes, fearful of recalling the last months of indecision. The woman became aware of her uneasiness. "Is it so painful to speak of yourself, Agnes?"

The younger woman opened her eyes and tilted her head downward. She brushed away a stray tear that bubbled up from inside her. Then she straightened up, clenched her jaws, narrowed her eyes and shut off any other possible drops from her eyes.

"I am sorry, Madame. Just for a moment, you caught me unaware. By asking me about the past, a swarm of pent-up emotions overwhelmed me." Agnes took a small handkerchief from inside her long sleeve and wiped across her face.

Madame smiled and began to speak German. "Ah, but that is good, Agnes. You have a heart. I see before me a young woman of great caring and warmth, and one who possibly hides some great sorrow." She reached over to pat Agnes' hand. "Some other time, perhaps, you will feel more comfortable sharing your previous life." Her gaze had softened and became warm and reassuring. "I see by your resume you have cooked in various homes in Breslau. I know of several of these families, and if you were employed there, that is satisfactory for me."

Madame leaned back in her chair. Agnes looked at her and took time to notice the silvery strands of gray in the other's hair, her kind eyes and the smile lines around her lips. Agnes relaxed and returned the smile. "This woman has understanding and compassion. It shows in her face," she thought.

"Let me tell you about us, Agnes. You will want to know as much about us as you can, so you will begin to feel as part of our household and family.

"We are Ashkenazic Jews, and our ancestors came primarily from Germany. We keep a kosher kitchen and, looking at your credentials, I see you are knowledgeable of food preparation for us. We observe the Sabbath faithfully and have the appropriate celebrations for the high holy days, Rosh Hashana, Yom Kippur, Hannukkah and the others. My family and my husband's family congregate here for these special days, and that means lots of extra food."

Agnes nodded her head in acknowledgment.

Mrs. Levy continued, "We have two daughters, Ruth and Rachel. Within two or three years, they will be married. Both are expected to be betrothed within the year." She smiled. "In the meantime, their governess teaches them the appropriate ways of presenting themselves and educates them in the arts. Ruth loves the ballet and painting. Rachel's interest centers around music. She is an accomplished pianist." Mr. Levy pursed her lips. "Both have become very involved in the suffragette movement. Their father does not favor the idea and frowns on their participation." The woman touched a small linen cloth to her lips to hide a wicked grin. Her eyes twinkled, "But, personally, I am very proud of them." She looked at Agnes, "Are you acquainted with the suffragette cause?"

"No, Madame, I am not."

"It is the cause to champion the right of women to vote in this country's political elections."

Agnes made a mental note for herself, "That is something I need to read about."

"Do you read English, Agnes?"

"Somewhat, Madame. I am learning to speak more English every day, and can recognize some of the written words. Recently, I purchased a cookbook giving the recipes in German in one column, and beside it, the same recipe in English. It is a good comparison and helps me learn the correct way to speak and read."

"Our daughters will be willing to tutor you if you choose. They have helped some of our other staff, and derive great joy in teaching the English language." She leaned nearer to Agnes, "If you do not feel comfortable asking, I will gladly seek their help for you." She shook her head in a knowing gesture, "Somehow, I sense you are not too shy to ask."

"Thank you, Madame."

"Our household staff speaks various languages but, basically, they try to speak English amongst themselves. We have eight full-time servants, including your position. Miss Sophie is the girls' governess, and stays in a small apartment next to our daughters' rooms. You have already met Harrison, the butler. Leonardo has not been our chauffeur long." Her eyes sparkled. "Right now he is trying to find his way around the city. Our new limousine is presenting him with quite a challenge, and he is trying to master driving it among the cabs and delivery wagons.

"Maria is our cleaning lady, and keeping our home tidy is very time-consuming. She also makes all the beds every morning and changes the bedding once a week."

Mrs. Levy stopped to count on her fingers and think. "Luigi, how could I forget Luigi?" She smiled. "Luigi is our gardener in the summer and our general maintenance man. In the fall, he helps Maria with heavy cleaning. He takes real pride in making our tall windows shine when they are washed, and also helps move the furniture." She smiled again. "Luigi can envision a complete room and always suggests nice arrangements when we change the furniture setting." Her eyes shone with merriment. "He always seems to know the right placement of furniture so we can display his beautiful flowers from the greenhouse. Luigi is so proud of his green thumb." She motioned to the chrysanthemums in a heavy lead crystal vase. "He likes us to use as many blossoms as possible in the house. One of his greatest joys is having our first spring flowers bloom so much earlier than those of our friends.

He works miracles in the greenhouse."

"Green thumb, Madame? Exactly what is that?"

"An American colloquialism, Agnes. It means a person who is able to grow beautiful plants and flowers."

Agnes grinned, "Another new English word."

Mrs. Levy lifted a small bell and its silvery tinkle sounded throughout the house. Harrison appeared in the doorway. "You rang, Madame."

"Harrison, please bring two glasses of cool water."

"Yes, Madame."

"We have two other full-time maids, Rosa and Anna. Rosa does all the washing and ironing, including the servants' bedding and clothing. If you prefer keeping your personal clothing clean, that can be arranged. Anna will help you in the kitchen and serves our family at mealtime."

Harrison came in carrying a silver tray. He placed a linen napkin and a crystal glass of ice water beside Mrs. Levy, then one beside Agnes. The woman lifted her glass to drink and motioned for Agnes to do the same.

"On the days of parties and celebrations, when we have guests, all the servants will help to make them comfortable. If it is a very large gathering, we order the desserts and breads from the bakery. You will order all food supplies, with my approval, of course. The orders will be telephoned in to the appropriate vendors, who will make the deliveries. We like to buy as much fresh fruit and vegetables as possible from the farmers who make their own deliveries in the city. Our fresh seafood and fowl are ordered from the vendors along the docks. Goose and duck are special favorites of ours."

She stopped to take a sip from her glass, then continued, "All our wines are purchased from local vendors and stored in our wine cellars. We prefer the French wines."

She hesitated, "Do you have any questions, Agnes?"

Agnes shifted in her chair, a bit nervously. "Not at this time, Madame. Perhaps as the days pass."

"Fine, Agnes." Mrs. Levy reached over to touch her hand. "We are here to help you at any time. Never hesitate to ask."

She stood to go. "We will contact the Leo House and they will deliver your trunks and personal things, or they can store your things there, if you desire. The Leo House does that for immigrants who have not decided on their final destination. Then the people can reclaim their things when they move on.

"I will contact Sister Mary Anthony then," said Agnes.

"Our other cook will leave us in four days, but I would like for you to work with her beginning tomorrow, so you can get acquainted with the kitchen and our preferences."

The woman lifted the little bell and rang again. "Harrison, would you please show Agnes to her quarters?"

Agnes followed him up the back stairs to the servants' area. He opened the door to a small bedroom, complete with wardrobe, a chair and a writing desk. He closed the door behind himself, as Agnes sat down on the high bed. She patted the mound of feather comforters and fluffed the goose down pillows.

For a moment, she looked around the room, much like others she had stayed in when she worked for the wealthy in Germany. "But they were never this wealthy," she mumbled to herself. "They even have a maid to do all the washing and ironing." She shook her head in amazement. "In Germany, there were washerwomen who went around to the different houses to do the laundry and ironing, but here they have their very own laundress." She shook her head again, unbelievingly. "I can hardly wait to write and tell Martha and Mama about that. How will I ever describe this city and this house to them?"

She leaned back against the pillow and raised her feet up on the bed. In a few minutes, she dozed off.

A knock at the door aroused her. "Agnes, your things have arrived from the Leo House."

7

HAPPINESS

LUIGI BROUGHT ANOTHER huge flower arrangement of pink and white tulips, lavender lilacs and golden forsythia through the door into the large oblong sitting room. The gardener carefully placed the tall, round crystal vase on the marble-topped end table. His smile spread from ear to ear as he looked around the room to survey his handiwork.

"Another beautiful room, thanks to you and your flowers. Ruth will be so pleased."

"Thank you, Madame." He bowed low to Mrs. Levy. "My pleasure always, to bring flowers into your elegant house."

She smiled at him. "Yes, and in six months we can do this all over again when Rachel marries."

"Certainly, Madame, but only then we will have the flowers of fall."

"I do so love the fall flowers, the heavy pungent smell of the chrysanthemums." She gazed around the room. "Our guests will certainly enjoy themselves surrounded by nature's beauty." She glanced at the diamond-studded timepiece hung on her rose-gold necklace. "Time waits not. I must see to the chupah. It is to be delivered soon."

Luigi brought in another bouquet of spring flowers. "We will need several bouquets in the main hallway, and also up in the ballroom where the party and dance will be."

"As you wish, Madame. Will you need me to help with the canopy?"

"Mr. Levy and his brothers will see to the canopy, Luigi. Flowers at each corner of the chupah would be especially beautiful."

She walked out into the hall and summoned the butler. "Please,

Harrison, invite our staff to join us for the wedding." Smiling warmly, she went on, "They are all like family to our daughters." After a pause, she added, "I am going to check the mezuzah one more time. It is possible I missed a spot when I polished it this morning."

The chimes of the tall grandfather clock struck twelve. The spring sun spread dapples of light across the Persian rugs and parquet hardwood floors.

The wide double doors stood open. The pleasant spring air filled the hallway with the fragrance of the season's blossoms. Mrs. Levy walked out onto the wide veranda and down the walkway. Copper pots of pink tulips brightened the edge of each step. Deep purple violets and miniature violet iris with velvety throats followed the curving brick walk to the circular drive.

Across the drive, Mrs. Levy turned to stand and look back at their elegantly carved doors, and saw the reflection of the yard's trees in the stained glass windows. It all seemed perfect, her doors would welcome the bridal couple's guests. With her arms wrapped around herself, the mother swayed along with the soft midday breeze. "My daughter's wedding day." She shook her head and felt her cheeks pucker into a wide smile and blush a tingly pink.

With slow, deliberate steps, the lady returned to the porch and paused at the doorpost. "Ah, our beautiful silver mezuzah." Touching it gently with a soft silver polish cloth, she rubbed away a hidden blemish of tarnish. "The silver glows like the joy in our hearts. *'Hear, O Israel: The Lord our God is one Lord. Thou shalt love the Lord thy God with thy whole heart, and with thy whole soul, and with thy whole strength. And these words which I command thee this day, shall be in thy heart.'* "

A tear crept out of her eye and slid slowly down her cheek. "The words of the parchment within the mezuzah are our life and our being," she whispered to herself. "I have polished the dullness of the mezuzah and the silver of the wine goblet and tray with the love for my daughter and those in my house." Another tear fell gently onto her cheek. "Ah, the blessings of the Lord come upon this house today."

A delivery wagon came up the drive, followed by a shiny black Cadillac.

"Oh, Mr. Levy, you have the chupah?" She clutched her chest with excitement. Walking closer, she waited for his answer.

Her husband and his brothers emerged from the automobile. Mr. Levy turned to brush the tufted leather seats. "We do, my love." His impish smile was always reserved for his wife. Before others, he was the serious, stern businessman who could challenge and outwit the staunchest competitor. "You know we would never trust our beloved chupah to any but the best." He winked at her. "And my new automobile is definitely the best."

Mrs. Levy blushed slightly and giggled like a schoolgirl. "Yes, dear Isaac, but your automobile or not, the time doth flee quickly, and we have a wedding to prepare for."

"Yes, love." His brothers took out the snowy white velvet canopy and carried it carefully up the steps. "Careful there, brothers, we cannot have one spot on the canopy for my daughter's important day."

Brother Benjamin chuckled, "We will take good care of this. Isaac, you bring the chairs from the delivery wagon." Guffaws filled the air.

Mrs. Levy looked at her timepiece, "Three and a half hours to go. Luigi is waiting to put the flowers in place." She turned to go back inside. "I want to check with Agnes about the meal, especially the goose. She fixes the most delicious baked goose."

"Rebekah, did you say Agnes is fixing that splendid goose she always serves?" asked Jonathan.

Mrs. Levy nodded.

"That makes me doubly proud to be an uncle of the bride, just to feast on Agnes' scrumptious goose. I do not need any other food, just her juicy, succulent goose." Jonathan smacked his lips. "I hope there is lots of her apple and raisin dressing, too."

"That makes two of us, brother Jonathan," grinned Benjamin.

"Isaac, has Jacob signed the ketubah?" Jonathan winked at Benjamin.

Benjamin winked back, "We need to know, Isaac, if Jacob has agreed to be your son-in-law."

Isaac answered happily, "My brothers, have no fear, there will be a wedding." A big grin spread ever wider across his face. "And you will be fed a big slice of baked goose."

A serious look crossed Benjamin's face. "When did they sign the marriage contract?"

"Last evening, at the synagogue. Jacob and Ruth have so many relatives among their friends, it was difficult for them to find two men witnesses who were not related to one or the other. Jacob asked Joseph and David, his friends from the university, to be his witnesses. They signed the contract in impeccable Hebrew." Isaac chuckled and shook his head in mock disbelief. "Our young people do quite well with our ancient language."

"I will always remember when my bride-to-be and I signed the ketubah." Benjamin sat down on a nearby chair and rubbed his chin with serious thought. "That is one of the most significant parts of the marriage ceremony."

Isaac's eyes twinkled, "It gave me special joy when my daughter signed her signature, 'Ruth, daughter of Isaac and Rebekah.'" He beckoned them, "Come, my brothers, we must not waste any more time. The hours are passing quickly."

The Levy men carried the rolled canopy to the far side of the room. "Isaac, this is the east wall, is it not?"

"Yes, Benjamin, the chupah must be along the east side of the room. The Rabbi will stand under it and face west to the people. Everyone else must face east, toward Jerusalem and the Temple Mount. This is the ancient Hebrew tradition."

Jonathan lifted one end of the rolled chupah. "Our traditions are so beautiful, and steeped in the continuity of our forefathers. What a wonderful way for a young couple to begin their wedded life together."

Luigi and Leonardo carried the chairs into the sitting room, while the Levy brothers put up the canopy. Mrs. Levy came in and draped the long white aisle runner over several chairs.

"Luigi and Leonardo, when you are finished with the chairs and the flowers in here, would you please put down this white runner from the canopy to the door. It is for the bridal party to walk on."

"Yes, Madame, gladly." Luigi gave her a toothy grin. "This is so exciting."

She looked around the room and nodded her approval. "Lovely, just beautiful." The mother then walked out into the wide hallway, gathered her skirts about her, and glided gracefully up the stairway. Garlands of flowers and greens had been wound around the highly polished banister.

Agnes came toward her. "Agnes, have the maids carried the clean rainwater from the cistern upstairs for Ruth?"

"Yes, Madame, Ruth is preparing for her bath now."

Mrs. Levy heard merry laughter coming from the huge dressing room. Just as she opened the door, Ruth let out a gasp, "This water is very cold."

Madame stood for a minute until her daughters noticed her and the expression on her face.

"Sorry, Mother," Ruth shrugged, "but the cold water took my breath away, just for a second."

"I know, dear." A smile broke across the mother's face. "How well I remember my mikhvah before I married your father." She lifted a thick, soft towel from the dressing room chair. "This ceremonial bathing is a tradition of Judaism that began in ancient times. Every bride since has bathed before her wedding. The pure, clean rainwater of nature is collected in the cistern for this ceremony. You, my dear Ruth, as the bride, must completely immerse your body under the water. It signifies your purity and your cleanliness as you prepare yourself to meet your bridegroom."

Gingerly, Ruth entered the water and let the coolness wash over her. As she stepped from the tub, her mother handed her the snow-white towel.

Mrs. Levy felt her body quiver with the pending joy and excitement. "My goodness," she whispered to herself, "the bride is supposed to be the nervous one, not me."

Rosa and Maria knocked at the door. "Ruth will be in her room in a few minutes. Will you please assist her with her toilette?"

They curtsied slightly, "Yes, Madame."

"Her wedding clothes need to be put out. Please see to that." She turned to go, then stopped again. "Ask Anna to help Rachel, and please call Sophie to help me. It will soon be time for the guests to arrive."

Mrs. Levy chose the brilliant sapphire necklace and earrings. How she loved them. Isaac had given the pieces to her when they first married, and she saved them for very special occasions. Today was certainly one of those memorable days. How she had waited for this blessed day, to see one of her daughters marry.

She rose from her chair and stood tall before her mirror. From side to side she turned. Every fold of her gown must be just right. She caught herself twisting and rubbing her hands. A slight "Oh, my," escaped her lips as a tiny smile broke across her face. "I need to go outside and breathe the spring air. Perhaps that will calm my nerves." She turned to see herself once more in the looking glass. The eyes of her reflection smiled back at her.

Her silk dress floated gracefully as she swept down the staircase, through the hallway, and out into the sunshine. A carriage pulled by four fine white horses entered through the tall stone portal gates. A wide smile brightened her face.

"Ah, the groom arrives." She waited at the front doors and held out her arms to him, "Welcome, Jacob, my son."

He cleared his throat nervously, "May I see my bride beforehand, Mrs. Levy?"

"Of course, that is our way, my son. We do not want to trick you into marrying the wrong sister as Jacob did in the Scriptures." The light in her eyes and the warmth in her voice relaxed him.

The mother took him by the arm, and together they entered the house. "Harrison, would you please see if Ruth is dressed in her bridal finery, and ready to meet her beloved Jacob?"

Ruth stood at the top of the wide curved stairway, a vision in white. Jacob gasped and put his hand to his mouth. "You are so beautiful, so lovely, my dear Ruth. What a blessed day this is for me."

"For both of you," whispered his mother-in-law to be, "and for her father and me."

Mrs. Levy walked up the steps to meet her daughter. The musicians readied their violins, violas and cellos and sorted through their musical arrangements. Beautiful chamber music from Ravel and Debussy soon filled the house and welcomed the arriving guests. Vivaldi's *Four Seasons* echoed throughout the wide hallway and out onto the veranda, followed by Handel's *Water Music Suite*.

"I love Vivaldi's *Spring*. Do you, Mother?" Ruth touched her mother's cheek with her fingertips. "I love you, Mama."

Her mother embraced her. "It is almost time, my daughter." They descended the wide stairway and met Mr. Levy at the bottom step.

"I am ready, Father, to become a wife."

"May God's blessing be upon you, my dear daughter." He leaned over to kiss her on the cheek. Her eyes lit up with joy as he whispered in her ear, "My little girl is a bride."

Ruth's bridesmaid, her sister, Rachel, and Jacob's best man, his brother, Joshua, walked slowly down the white aisle cloth, behind the other attendants. The men turned to the left of the canopy and the ladies to the right. Rabbi Goldman waited for them under the canopy. Then he nodded to the groom and his parents.

Jacob and his parents took their places to the left, under the chupah. He turned to smile at Ruth, as she and her mother and father walked toward the others.

Her heart skipped a beat. Jacob's white gown and yarmulke made him ever so handsome. Their eyes met in love and longing. She felt her cheeks color.

The couple and their parents took their places next to the Rabbi. Jacob's family was seated to the left, Ruth's to the right. The white silky tassels of the velvet chupah swayed gently from the soft breeze coming through the tall open windows.

The Rabbi raised his hands and prayed in the age-old Hebrew language for blessings upon Ruth and Jacob. His deep rich voice filled the room with ancient Hebrew-German melodies.

At the back of the room, Agnes sat with the family's other servants. The old German music touched her deeply, for it reminded her of a life not too long past, of melodies her mother hummed while she cooked for her children. Agnes felt a knot of emotion begin to build within herself. She squeezed her fingers tightly together to control her feelings and longing for the Fatherland she had left behind.

"We are reminded today," began the Rabbi, "of our ancient Jewish roots and the teachings taught us in our Torah. The wedding ceremony has virtually been unchanged through all these centuries. Couples become as one to show their love as husband and wife and, together, they give their love to the Lord."

He paused to look at the families, then continued, "Their witnesses have already signed the ketubah, the marriage contract that Ruth and Jacob agreed upon, the responsibilities and roles given to the wife and the husband. They gather together for their marriage under their chupah. Before their God, they now take leave of their parents' houses to establish a home and enter into a relationship that is totally theirs."

In accordance with the ancient Jewish custom, Ruth circled Jacob seven times. Her mother and mother-in-law walked behind to hold her long trailing skirt, and to signify their acceptance of her part as a new wife.

"This ritual is symbolic of Ruth's desire to build a permanent, lasting and loving marriage, and a home filled with the laws and beliefs of her ancestors." The Rabbi then looked to the groom. "Jacob, the ring."

The bridegroom took Ruth's right hand and slid the single gold band on her index finger. She coupled her finger to signify her acceptance. Her eyes filled with happy tears, as one slid down her blushed cheek.

Jacob looked deep into her eyes and recited the ancient declaration, "Behold, thou art consecrated unto me with this ring, according to the Law of Moses and Israel."

Rabbi Goldman unrolled the ketubah and read from it. "Jacob, will you provide for your beloved, Ruth, consider her personal gratification and assure her support?"

"In the presence of the Lord, my answer is yes."

"Do you take this bride, Ruth, to be your lawful wedded wife?"

Jacob smiled at his blushing bride, "In the presence of the Lord, my answer is yes."

The Rabbi then resealed the ketubah, and handed it to Ruth. "I give to you this signed contract, attested and sealed, to be held forever in your possession." She tucked the precious contract under her left arm for safekeeping. Her smile embraced her new husband with love.

Agnes remembered what might have been at this time in her life, if only her betrothed had been faithful. "Oh, that I might be a wife and mother this day," she whispered to herself. Anna heard the words, leaned close to Agnes and touched her hand kindly. The other looked at her and smiled feebly. Anna saw her friend's tears welling in sad eyes.

The Rabbi's rich baritone voice soared in crescendos as he chanted the seven traditional benedictions. Agnes remembered. Oh, how she had loved to listen to the cantor when she passed by the synagogue near her Breslau home. Her reveries were shattered when the chanting stopped.

Jacob took a hefty gulp of wine from the crystal goblet, then turned to Ruth. Her smile radiated with happiness, as she took the glass from him. The bouquet of the Burgundy smarted her senses as she took the tiny remaining sip. Jacob knew Ruth was not overly fond of the spirits.

"You are now husband and wife," intoned the Rabbi.

He handed Jacob another glass, wrapped in a silk kerchief. "This glass, to be broken, reminds us not only of this joyous occasion, but that we are still to mourn the destruction of the Temple in Israel."

With great aplomb, Jacob dropped the glass to the floor and with his heel, ground it to fragments.

"Mazal Tov," everyone shouted. Peals of joyous laughter swept through the room, "Mazal Tov."

"Best wishes," whispered Agnes.

The ballroom was loud with gaiety and merrymaking. Toast after toast of best wishes were hosted to Jacob and Ruth, as the wine loosened the reserves of the guests. Mr. Levy grabbed his wife and danced her around the ballroom floor.

The serving tables were loaded with food of all sorts and rich sweets. Agnes stood watch as Luigi, Leonardo and Harrison carried the large trays of baked goose out into the room.

"Lift them up, lift them up," shouted one of Ruth's uncles. "It is time to do the dance." Up, up they went, Ruth on one chair and Jacob on another.

"The groom called out, "I have waited so long for this day."

Ruth bit her lip and hung on tight to the seat of the chair. "Oh, my, oh, my," was all she could say, as her chair swayed on the shoulders of her cousins.

The rhythm of the old Jewish melodies beat upon the consciousness of the guests and stirred excitement among the crowd. The men circled and circled the couple hoisted in the air.

"Oh, gracious." Ruth looked at Jacob with pleading eyes. "I am ready to be put down."

He smiled and blew her a kiss.

Benjamin and Jonathan looked at the food-laden tables. "I can smell the aroma of that baked goose from here," Benjamin shouted over the clamor. He glanced up at Ruth and Jacob. "It is time to eat. Are you in agreement?"

"Oh, please, yes," Ruth pleaded.

8

CHANGES

"AGNES, KOMMEN SIE hier, bitte." Alarm filled Mrs. Levy's voice. She hardly ever spoke to her cook in German anymore. "Come quick," she shouted in English."

Agnes rushed into the main hallway. Near the informal parlor, Mrs. Levy was down on her knees over the lifeless form of her husband. She beat upon his chest and cried out in anguish, "He is gone, Agnes, my Isaac is gone."

The woman wailed and wept, and kissed her husband's cooling cheek time and again in desperation. Agnes watched in horror as the lady tried so hard to will life back into her mate.

Harrison had heard the cries and came rushing out into the hall. "I heard your alarm, Madame, and have called the doctor. He is coming right over. Your daughters are coming, too."

"It is no use, Harrison, he cannot help my Isaac anymore."

"Come, Madame, let me help you." Agnes leaned over to touch the woman's shoulder. "Let us go into the parlor so you may sit."

"No, please, I must stay by my Isaac. I must recite the vidui for him. He is no longer able to make his own confession."

Maria and the other servants heard her cries and gathered in the hall.

"Maria, get a blanket, please, to cover Mr. Levy. We must keep him warm if there is still life," Agnes ordered.

Maria rushed out, then came back several minutes later. Harrison helped her cover their master's body. Mrs. Levy stood then, but her shoulders heaved as the grief cascaded totally upon her.

Rachel and Ruth burst through the door and flung themselves on the floor beside their beloved father. "Papa, oh, Papa." Their heart-stricken, wrenching sobs filled the cold silence of the room.

Ruth pressed her cheek against her father's still heart and begged and pleaded to hear a heartbeat. "Breathe, Papa, breathe," she insisted.

Rachel brushed her hand across his cheeks, then over his unseeing eyes. Tenderly, she smoothed his silvery-gray hair back from his forehead. "Papa, please do not leave us. Oh, please," she cried.

Luke, husband of Rachel, and Jacob, husband of Ruth, stood back, respectfully, near the hall entrance.

Mrs. Levy touched her daughters' shoulders lightly and motioned them aside. They stood then, beside their mother.

The doctor came with his satchel in hand and knelt down on his knees. He lifted Isaac's wrist and felt for the man's pulse. Looking in the wife's direction, he shook his head. Gently, he closed Mr. Levy's eyes and mouth, and covered his face.

"He is gone, Rebekah. Isaac is gone." He stood and put his arm around the wife to comfort her.

"Why, Doctor, why?" she sobbed. He held her for a long time. Rachel and Ruth wrapped their arms around each other and swayed in sorrow. When her weeping calmed, the doctor held Mrs. Levy at arm's length. "Rebekah, there is not time. The hour is past three. We must call Rabbi Goldman now. He must cleanse the body and prepare Isaac for his burial."

She again leaned heavily into the doctor's shoulder, "Yes, yes, it must be so. Please call Rabbi." She paused, "Call his brothers. We have not much time to prepare for the burial. It will be almost sundown if we wait too long."

Agnes took her hand and led her to a chair nearby. "What else can we do, Madame?" she asked in German.

Mrs. Levy answered in the foreign tongue, "Please, Agnes, you know the ways of our people. We need to open a window so his soul may escape this mortal world and enter into the realm of our Lord."

Agnes nodded to Luigi and translated the widow's request.

"And the mirrors, Agnes," the lady continued in her native tongue, "the mirrors of the house must all be covered, for we are now in mourning and must not see our own reflections."

Again, Agnes translated her orders to the others. "We will do that after the Rabbi has departed with the remains." She walked closer to the others and whispered, "Out of respect, we will stay until then. For now, Jewish custom dictates that all who are in the deceased one's presence can ask for his forgiveness if they feel they have caused him pain." She looked at each one directly. The others nodded and bowed their heads. His widow felt the comfort and strength of their closeness. She bowed to acknowledge them, then smiled at each meekly.

"Rabbi Goldman is here, Madame." Harrison ushered him and the Hevra Kaddisha, the members of the holy burial society, into the hall.

Rabbi extended his hands to the widow, and gently rubbed her cool fingers. His eyes searched hers and calmed her pain. Finally he spoke, "Shalom, Mrs. Levy, we have come to prepare your husband, Isaac, for his burial." He turned to Rachel and Ruth and nodded with sympathy. One of the burial society members handed a leather box back to the Rabbi that he had carried into the house. He opened the box and took out the white hand-stitched shroud. "Mrs. Levy, have you ready his yarmulke and prayer shawl?" She looked again to Agnes, who motioned to one of the other servants.

Mrs. Levy nodded to the Rabbi. He continued, "His skullcap will be placed on his head and we will wrap him in a shroud. His prayer shawl will cover the shroud. First, we will cut the threads of a corner fringe. That is to remind everyone that Isaac's duties to this life are over. The shroud is to remind us that, in death, all of us are equal." He nodded to Mrs. Levy.

"Yes, Rabbi." The widow paused to think through the happenings, and then spoke in a calm voice, "We wish the service to be at the synagogue."

"So be it," the Rabbi answered. "In three hours, we will be prepared. The aninut will give you and your daughters ample time to notify Isaac's family and others. Also, the cemetery needs to open his final resting place. Is there any Levy family plot for him?"

"Yes, Rabbi." She hesitated, then asked quietly, "And the wooden box?"

"The pine box will be brought to the cleansing room and the Hevra Kaddisha will ready it there. A bit of soil from Israel will be placed in the casket beside Isaac." He took her by the arm. "Do your daughters realize once the casket is sealed, they cannot view their father's remains?"

"They know, Rabbi, they know," she answered softly. Rachel and Ruth returned her gaze.

The men of the burial society lifted Isaac and carried him away. A hushed silence fell over the house.

Mrs. Levy took Agnes aside. "We will need certain things prepared for our return."

"Yes, Madame. Everything will be made ready for the shiva. Do you wish that to be in the informal parlor?"

"Yes, Agnes." Mrs. Levy spoke again in German, "Harrison knows where the low seats are stored for the family to use."

"We will take care of the details, Madame. Please, go prepare yourself for the funeral."

"Very well." Mrs. Levy looked pale as she walked upstairs.

"Sophie, perhaps she could use some assistance." Agnes motioned for the maid to follow the widow upstairs. Ruth and Rachel stood rigid, still in shock. Their husbands came to wrap them in gentle embraces. Then, pale and with tear-stained faces, the daughters walked quickly up the stairs to be with their mother. At the appointed time, the three women came downstairs and went out the great doors. The servants bowed their heads in respect to them. When Agnes turned around, she saw the others were waiting for her directions.

"Luigi and Leonardo, would you please cover the long mirrors here in the hall and the ballroom upstairs with dark cloth? You can also help Rosa and Maria with the smaller mirrors throughout the house." She turned to look at Anna. "The tall silver pitcher and bowl in the cabinet should be filled with cool water. Please put it on the table near the door. Small towels will be needed also."

Anna, a shy girl, smiled and quietly asked, "What is the purpose for that?"

Agnes realized Anna knew very little about the Jewish customs. "I am sorry, Anna, let me explain." She touched the girl's arm lightly. "Each family member who comes into the house after the burial will pour water over their hands to cleanse them. They will do that to purify themselves after being near someone who has died."

Anna cringed, "I will do that right away." She bit her lip as she turned to go.

"Anna, there is another custom. During the shiva, the Jewish people do not wear leather shoes. Mrs. Levy and the daughters will wear cloth slippers. Mrs. Levy said they are kept in the linen closet." Agnes paused to remember other Jewish families' funerals in Germany. "Also, shiva lasts for seven days. During that time, Madame and her children will receive friends and family who wish to pay their respects and share their memories of Mr. Levy. Their custom of mourning is stated in the Scriptures."

Anna nodded, anxious to go. "I will take care of those things, Agnes."

The servants finished the tasks and prepared for the family's return, as they gathered in the main hall.

"Since we are all here," Agnes told the others, "There are several customs that will be observed by the family in the next month. When Madame returns, the right shoulder of her dress will be rent. At the memorial service, Rabbi Goldman will rend the garment and she will tear it more. That is to tell everyone she is in mourning. In the next seven days, she and her daughters will wear the same clothing each day. They will not go about their regular social or business affairs. The sons-in-law will not be in mourning, a sign of respect for their parents who are still living."

"Are there other customs?" Sophie asked.

"Cooking will certainly be different." She stopped to think for a few moments. "During shiva, the family does not come into the kitchen to touch or help prepare their meals. Much of the kosher food will be brought in by other members of the synagogue. The first women to come will bring them hard-boiled eggs and, perhaps, bagels."

"Hard-boiled eggs?" Anna was surprised.

"Yes," Agnes answered, as she formed her thumb and index finger in a circle. "The round shape of the egg and the bagel reminds the mourners that God is omnipresent, all around the world at once." She paused, "After shiva, the mourning period, called sheloshim, lasts another twenty-three days. During that time, the family's life will gradually return to normal. For a year, however, they will not attend any events where there is music."

The front doors opened and the widow and her daughters, Ruth and Rachel, came into the house. They slipped off their shoes and put on the lightweight cloth slippers.

The servants parted, some on either side of the hallway, as the family walked in silence to the back informal parlor. Stillness settled upon the house in mourning. The staff returned quietly to their duties. Mrs. Levy lit the special candle that would burn in the mourning room during the next seven days.

With all the details ready, the weight of the day's happenings settled at last, heavily, on Agnes' mind. Taking soft steps down the hall of the servants' quarters, she knew the time had come for much needed quiet rest for herself.

Agnes closed the door of her tiny room and sat down on the bed. The springs squeaked as she did. "Silence, there must be silence," she spoke aloud. It seemed necessary even to require respect from the bedsprings.

She put her feet up and laid back upon the bed. The unexpected events settled around her like a cloud of unending heaviness. Unlike her usual self, she drifted off into a fitful sleep. It was not in her nature to rest her head upon her pillow before sundown.

Dreams and visions swirled through her mind. She saw Mrs. Levy wailing and leaning over her dead husband. Another vision appeared, one she had not allowed herself to remember in years. The memory came back to her with sudden swiftness, with a harsh thrust that sent chills through her being. In her mind's eye, she relived that moment when the knock sounded at the door.

She was only a very young girl then, but now she felt again as she had then. A messenger had handed her mother, Anna, the note. Agnes watched helplessly as Anna crumpled and held the note to her bosom, "No, no, not my Robert."

Agnes came up out of bed with a jolt. She rubbed her eyes and tried to clear her mind. The walls of the small room crowded even closer. They squeezed her within their confines. Confusion.

"My Papa, why am I dreaming of my Papa?" She rubbed her temples. "Why now, not for all these years have I remembered that day, the day Mama received that message?"

Agnes put her feet on the floor and cradled her head down in her upraised hands. Tears swelled from the depths of her bosom and spilled in a torrent upon her hands and down the folds of her skirt. Agnes wept and rocked rhythmically from a force within herself. The words and sobs fell from her lips and echoed against the bedroom walls.

"Meine Papa, meine Papa. Oh, my Papa. All these years. I have been so angry all these years." She clenched and re-clenched her fists, holding them tight to her bosom. "I hated all the things you did, your drinking, your gambling, your being away so much. I hated you when Mama cried. How I hated you when you died and deserted us for good. How I hated you, never being there for me as a child, for missing out on so much with me. Oh, Papa, I hated you until now."

Agnes tried to curb the emotions, but the heart would not stop; the mind could not control.

"Oh, Papa, now I understand. You did not mean to die like that, so soon. Now I know. Mr. Levy did not mean to die so soon, but he did. You did. Oh, Papa, I loved you so. And you never knew. I never got the chance to tell you. You robbed me, Papa, you robbed me. If only I had seen you one last time. But please, Papa, know it now."

Agnes rested back against her pillow, her energy and tears spent.

Sleep came, for the women of the synagogue would be there with food for the distraught, nourishment for the hungry, comfort for the mourning.

The months passed. The stillness of the big house was unyielding. Agnes knew she must move on.

"Mrs. Levy, the time for me to see more of America has come."

"But, Agnes, you cannot."

"Madame, please, I feel the need to go, to discover what this country holds for me."

"Agnes, I plead with you." Mrs. Levy's eyes begged, beseeched her. She reached over to touch Agnes' hand.

"Of all the servants, you are the one I hold closest in my heart. We are countrymen, of the same hearty Germanic stock. Our roots grow from the same region, the same soil."

"I am sorry, Madame."

"We are fortunate to have wealth. My Isaac worked hard for us, to provide for me, for Ruth and Rachel." She smiled to herself, "How he loved his daughters. He wanted to give them the very best he could." A slight chuckle escaped her lips. "How surprised the girls were when he presented each of them with $80,000 on their wedding days."

Then sadness crossed her face and a tear slid down. Silent thoughts swarmed and meshed, until she could speak again. "He always managed everything for us." A soft look of love filled her eyes. "Yes, he managed so completely." She became silent again for a moment. "His business enterprises will provide well for me. Please, Agnes, stay on with me for the years I have remaining."

The cook began to speak, but was silenced. Words, there were no words.

Mrs. Levy moved her chair closer to Agnes. "Please, stay with me and you will be rewarded handsomely in my will; you will be provided for the rest of your own life. I will make you a beneficiary for your faithfulness." She squeezed Agnes' hand with affection. "Please, Agnes, consider it." Her eyes searched Agnes' face.

Agnes flinched. She lifted her hand up to her face to hide her erupting emotions. Gently, she rubbed Mrs. Levy's hand in return. "I must go. Somewhere in this big country is my future. I feel it in my heart." She bit her lip to tide her feelings. "It is now that I must go," she whispered.

Mrs. Levy lifted her linen napkin to dab at moist eyes. Ever so softly she asked, "Where do you plan to go, Agnes?"

"Milwaukee, perhaps. Or Chicago, it is a big city. Much like Breslau, I think."

Mrs. Levy leaned toward Agnes. "I have friends in both cities." Hesitating in thought, she finally continued, "My friends in Chicago have inquired if I know of an excellent cook they could employ. They would appreciate you, Agnes, and help you in their city."

"That would be so kind of you. It would make my journey more restful to know there is a place for me there." Agnes stood up, extending her hand to the other. "I must go now, Madame. There is a train to Chicago departing Pennsylvania Station in a few hours." She smiled slightly at the older lady. "And if I do not go today, I may never see more of America."

Mrs. Levy was quiet for so long, Agnes feared for her.

Quietly she spoke, "Yes, Agnes, I understand." She stood then and lifted her hand to stroke Agnes' cheek kindly. "Godspeed, dear Agnes, Godspeed."

9

THE ADVERTISEMENT

AGNES PICKED UP the morning newspaper. She liked to read through the Help Wanted advertisements in the German paper published in Chicago.

"One never knows what interesting positions might be available," she often thought to herself. "Oh my, the wanderlust is setting in again. My next destination is unknown, but it will be known soon. And it does not take long to pack my valise once more."

She looked at her small room in the large house where she worked. Then she stood and went to the window to look out at the Chicago skyline and Lake Michigan, off in the distance. "It is about time to go," she muttered, "there is nothing here for me. Just like Milwaukee was, this has only been a stopping place for me."

One entry in the classified section stood out. "Domestic Help Wanted: Cook and housekeeper needed to help care for a farm family of six young, motherless children in small German village of Garden Plain, Kansas. Catholic lady preferred, ages 25-35. Train fare will be paid by employer. Write references to Joseph Linnebur."

The small, insignificant advertisement was like many others listed. There was something about it, though, that haunted Agnes. She read the rest of the column, but the plea of the farmer intrigued her. She tore that section out of the newspaper and put it aside.

Each day, Agnes scanned the Help Wanted section. Still, none of the other notices seemed to interest her. Almost every hour, there was a tug at her heart, a nagging in her mind. Finally, one day, she threw all caution and reason to the side and sat down and drafted a letter of inquiry and interest to the father in Kansas.

"Dear Mr. Joseph Linnebur." That sounded very formal. "How should I address him?" she wondered. "Dear Sir," might be more appropriate. She sat for a long time and studied the greeting of her letter. "How does one address a farmer?" she questioned herself. "What on earth do I know about farming? Do they call them 'Farmer' or, maybe, 'Mister?'" She wanted to ask her present employer, but doubted that the rich Mrs. Anderson would know any more about farming than she did. "Maybe I should just begin this with 'Mr. Linnebur.'"

Agnes posted her letter and heard it as it slid down the mail chute. "What am I doing? I almost feel possessed." Shrugging her shoulders in indecision, she walked on down the sidewalk. "If he answers, I should know something about Kansas. Surely, the library has a book on that state."

She and her friend, Helena, took the bus down to the main library on their next day off. "We do have several books on Kansas, and the atlas," the librarian told her. "But I see no place called Garden Plain."

Agnes looked at Helena and smiled. "But what a charming name for a place – Garden Plain. It must just be like a huge garden." Dimples deepened in her cheeks. "It sounds like it could be the Garden of America."

"It must be," laughed Helena. "A huge vegetable garden out in the middle of the prairie. No trees, no flowers, nothing but wild grasses, and probably not much of that. The buffalo once were very numerous out there, so there may not be much grass left. Those huge animals ate it all."

"Oh, Helena, do you think so?" Agnes was aghast. "You are not serious, are you? Do you really know anything about Kansas?"

"Not much, except most of the people moving there are trying to be farmers. And, Agnes, just what do you know about a farm?" Helena looked at her friend with amusement.

"Nothing, nothing at all," laughed Agnes. "But I have learned many things in the last years, and farm life cannot be that different."

"Oh, dear friend, I do believe you are in for a big surprise. You have lived all your life in large cities, first Breslau, then New York, Milwaukee and now, Chicago. That small town cannot possibly have all the nicer luxuries of the cities. There will be no large libraries, and you know how you like to read."

The librarian had become interested in the exchange. "I can check what libraries are in Kansas, but I am sure none of them equal Chicago's libraries."

Agnes nodded her head. Reading was one of the most important things of life to her.

Helena kept up with her litany of things. "Will they have electric lights, oil heat and big stores?" She shook her head and her eyes twinkled with merriment. "I would wager they have never seen an automobile."

"Oh, Helena, you are trying too hard to change my mind." Agnes put her hand on her friend's shoulder. "But if Mr. Joseph Linnebur answers me, I may just answer back. This whole situation could be very interesting."

Helena snickered, "The day will come, dear Agnes, that I will be able to say, 'I told you so.' "

Agnes suddenly turned very serious. "Yes, Helena, I will be sure to tell you when you can tell me, 'I told you so.' But, for now, my intuition is very strong. The plains of Kansas are calling." She paused and her gaze wandered far off into the deep reaches of the library's many shelves.

Finally, she looked back at Helena and jokingly commented,"I have been in America four years now, since 1908, and have gotten older. It has been interesting, learning about the suffragette movement in New York City. And here in Chicago, getting educated about Lake Michigan and shipping on the Great Lakes."

She pointed to the Kansas map in the atlas and laughed. "Thirty-two years old. I think that is a good age for me to learn about farming in Kansas."

Helena winked at Agnes and touched her arm lightly."If you say so, Agnes, if you say so."

Agnes, in white, and a friend in Chicago.

10

JOSEPH

IT WAS SO quiet in the house. The children were sound asleep. The softness of their breathing took away the dead silence of the evening.

Their father leaned hard against the wooden spindles of the straight-backed chair. He looked around the small kitchen in a half daze. The shrill cry of a coyote sent shivers through him.

The staring gaze of his hazel eyes drifted to the tattered cotton curtain at the long, narrow window. Ellen had forgotten to pull it closed before she went off to bed. But, at her young age, that was not unusual.

In the bright moonlight, the tree outside the house was easy to see. Most of the fall leaves had drifted to the ground and were already rotting around the trunk. The last remnants of the tree's glory swayed slightly in the soft whispers of the breeze.

The big hunk of log was almost gone, so he had to put another armload of kindling into the huge black wood-burning cookstove. He needed the extra warmth for an hour or so. A dark blue and white speckled graniteware coffeepot sat off to the side of the stove. The heat kept the supper coffee good and hot. The father could not allow himself to get too cool and take the risk of catching a serious cold. He needed to stay healthy for his children.

In the flickering light from the kerosene lamp, he looked at the letter. He shifted the thin sheets of paper back and forth with his strong fingers, as he read and reread the words. A decision had to be made now.

"I have put this off much too long," Joseph mumbled. He took pencil in hand and was about to write, when he noticed the lamp's light was not very bright. He rubbed his eyes, thinking his sight had become blurred. As he looked up, he realized the glass chimney of the kerosene lamp was gray and coated with an oily film. Joseph sighed audibly, then spoke a bit louder to himself. "Aw shucks, I really do need an older housekeeper around here." A heavy sigh escaped him, as he looked around the room and noticed things in disarray he had not noticed for months.

In the downstairs bedroom, he heard the youngest son stirring. Wendell came shuffling through the dining room door and into the kitchen.

"Are you all right, Son?"

"Yea, Pop, I just need to make a trip to the outhouse."

Joseph chuckled as the boy shuffled on through the screened-in back porch and out into the crisp night air. "That boy is going to be a handful as he gets older. I will need a lady with a stern hand to keep him in line."

Wendell's untied shoes clumped louder as he hurried back in from the cold, through the kitchen, into the living room and back to the bedroom. The boy snuggled down into the warm bed. Soon all was quiet once more.

Joseph stood up and walked over to the small wooden cabinet along the west wall. He opened the top door and took out an old heavy ceramic mug. The hot liquid squished and gurgled as he poured it through the coffee pot spout. The warmth of the cup felt good on his cool hands, and the strong coffee soothed his confused feelings.

The man pulled his chair closer under the table. With nervous hands, he picked up the letter once more. "Agnes Puder, that is a good German name," he whispered. "I never thought anyone would answer my advertisement. I wonder why she did?" He put the thin sheets down on the table once more and pushed them closer to the lamp. The early December coolness made his strong hands and fingers stiff, so he rubbed them to get the blood circulating. After a time, he propped his elbows on the table and rested his chin in his upturned hands.

For a long time, he stared at the woman's letter. Finally, Joseph picked up the yellow stub pencil and wet the tip on his tongue. He rolled the pencil around between his fingers, and then took out his pocketknife. "This could use a little work. The lead is so short." With easy strokes of his knife, he whittled the wood back. "Nothing is better than a sharp pencil."

The farmer pulled the lined writing tablet closer to himself and stared at the clean sheet. "How do I address this woman?" Joseph shrugged his shoulders and shook his head. "I cannot write 'Dear Miss Puder.' That sounds too personal." He watched the flickering flame of the lamp. "'Miss Puder,' I think that sounds the best."

"Miss Puder," he began. Joseph hated to write, and letters were the worst. He sighed, "I used to write to Henry Charles a long time ago, but that was different, writing to my brother."

With a deliberate movement, he pushed the paper around in front of himself. "I am not sure this was such a good idea. The priest never told me it would be this hard." Several more minutes passed, "But I need the help. Maybe her help."

With fierce determination, he forced himself to write, "Your letter arrived, and I have put it aside for a time." The words flowed onto the paper, filling line after line. "I am anxious to hear from you. Otherwise, I will have to find another way to care for the children."

Joseph looked at the page and read each word carefully. "I cannot be too forward, but, still, she needs to know how things are here."

The pencil lead needed to be whetted again, and then he signed, "Sincerely," and his name.

A sigh of relief escaped his lips. "Dearest Katherine, I hope this is the right thing to do." Tears formed in his eyes and rolled slowly down his cheek.

His body shuddered as the vivid memories of those days were re-lived in his mind. He saw himself lean against her bed and stroke the lifeless face of his wife. In the other room, the muted voices of family broke the stillness. A baby cried, Katherine's baby. What would happen now?

His mind took him back to that horrible realization, the wake the night before the funeral. He could still see the scene in their small parlor. Katherine rested in her coffin as the faces of her young ones peered over the edge and into the box. Sobs from older family members shattered the quiet scene. Little Agnes and Irene touched their mother's face with tenderness.

Their oldest child, Ellen, stood in the shadows and was not brave enough to caress her mother's cheek. Anger seared her heart, an anger of fear and disruption. Her mother had to have another child, and that child had robbed her of her mother's love. Ellen could not, would not cry for the one who had deserted her when she needed guidance the most. Angry lines creased Ellen's face, anger at the newborn sister that caused the pain. Wendell was too young to know the meaning of it all. William tried to understand, but the reasoning escaped him.

The soft morning light of that May day filtered through the colored windows of the small country church, St. Mary's. The haunting strains of the Gregorian funeral music soared through Joseph's subconscious. "Re-e-quiem," the choir sang, "ae-ter-nam, do-na e-is Domi-ne, Give them eternal rest, Lord."

In sadness, the father held tight to his children's hands as they walked down the long path to the country cemetery. The soft spring breeze whispered its own mournful song through the young cedar trees.

"In Pa-ra-di-sum, de-du-cant to An-ge-li, May the angels lead you into Paradise," the choir intoned at the grave. Joseph's face mirrored the cutting pain in his heart.

The casket was slowly lowered into the ground. Several sisters-in-law led the children away. Joseph was left standing alone. Sobs wracked his body. His tears fell in torrents upon the coffin of his wife. A brother, John, watched Joseph in his grief and, finally, walked to be beside him at the grave.

Joseph felt himself falling, falling into the hole beside Katherine. He caught himself slumping off the chair, then came to with a start. A semi-sleep had overtaken his conscious senses. He shook his head to awaken and looked around the shadowy room with unseeing eyes. It was here in this room, this kitchen, that he and Katherine had shared so many happy times. Now that was all in the past. "Am I doing the right thing wanting to bring a strange woman into this room?"

Joseph stretched as he stood, and carried his cup to the wood cookstove. He lifted the graniteware pot and poured more of the thick, black coffee. With several gulps, he emptied the cup, and then put it back on the table.

A sudden gust of wind made the old house quiver and groan in protest. Joseph instinctively moved closer to the window to look outside.

The moon had dipped lower to the horizon. The glittering stars of the wintry night looked to be within his reach, if he chose to pluck one from the sky. A sob slipped from his throat and surprised even him. Upstairs, the springs squeaked as one of his children squirmed around restlessly in bed.

Sleep had left him. The thought of going to his cold, empty bed gripped his consciousness. The overwhelming loneliness and quickening wind drilled through his body. He just could not go to that cold bed this night, not yet.

His fingertips felt numb. The room had cooled off. The big, old stove was too quiet. There was no sound of crackling, burning wood.

Goosebumps prickled his arms, and he rubbed over them vigorously with his strong hands. Joseph turned away from the window and took the few steps to the stove.

"Good for William." He smiled. "He remembered to fill the kindling basket." Bending over, he picked out several strips and small chunks of wood, lifted the heavy round plate on the top of the stove, and poked them down among the glowing embers. Gold and red flames spun and rose up to lick around the invading sticks.

Joseph held his chilly hands over the warmth, and then rubbed his aching knuckles to relax them. He stood there in a half daze, watching the flames dance in a colorful array. The crackling, popping sound awoke him from his reverie.

Outside the wind began to pick up. The moon had drifted below the horizon and blackness enveloped the world. Deep shadows from the small lamp bobbed across the room's walls in a distorted rhythm. The dancing light glanced off the silver crucifix of his rosary beads that hung down from the clock shelf. He reached for the beads and spoke aloud, " I need to pray; I need to pray for guidance."

Joseph sat down on the chair nearest the fire. He suddenly felt so much older than his 41st year.

"Our Father," he began. Random thoughts tumbled among the words of the prayer. His thick, gnarled fingers slipped over the small beads. Weariness caused his eyelids to droop. He remembered the soft, warm comfort of his grandmother's lap when he was a small child in Missouri. Memories from the far reaches of his mind drifted through his thoughts. The prayer chain slipped silently from his strong hands to the table.

Joseph returned to the big kitchen of his early years in the 1870s. Five older brothers and four sisters sat at the long dining room table. Grandmother Maria patiently held the spoon for him to eat. Laughter rose and swelled to high pitches at those family meals.

He saw himself running through the cornfields, and chasing the cows in the pasture. There were school days spent with his aunt in St. Charles. He could see the narrow streets of the village and the walks he took along the wide Missouri. There was always something interesting taking place on the big river. In those years, he grew into a tall, strong young man. With older brothers going their own ways, it was now up to him to help his aging father on the farm.

But the joy was not to last. The mighty rivers, the Missouri and the Mississippi, clawed and ate away at his father's farm. In a few years, the wild waters washed over two hundred acres downstream.

His father tried to fight it, but Joseph was restless.

"Seventeen," he shook his head. "It seems so long ago that I lived there, close to Portage Des Sioux. 1888 seems so many years ago.

The letters came back from his oldest brother in Kansas. Henry Charles worked in a dry goods store. "What an exciting place to be," he wrote. "Wichita is a thriving village, and there is a need for all kinds of people with different skills. Good farmland is always up for sale west of here. So many who homesteaded decided not to stay. I do not know why; the land is nice and flat, and there are no major rivers around to flood the farms and wash away the soil."

Joseph remembered the day well. His father, mother, two older brothers, Peter, 25, and John, 18, and himself boarded the train at St. Charles. The hills of Missouri leveled off to the plains of Kansas.

"Almost eighteen then," Joseph smiled. "Hardly dry behind the ears, as the old-timers would say. What a switch farming is out here," he mused. "No raging rivers, but the cruel north winter winds and the equally wicked south winds of summer." He rubbed his sore knuckles again and again. "We had to learn about wheat. It was so different from our river bottom fields of corn."

He thought about those times and wondered how his parents faced the differences between their adopted homeland in Missouri and their farms in the Province of Westphalia. "What courage that took," he mumbled.

More joyous thoughts crowded into his mind. He could still feel the excitement the day his brother, John, introduced him to Katherine. John was smitten by Katherine's sister. Joseph chuckled softly, "How well I remember. John was so smitten by that girl, and he knew the only sure way to Wilhemina's heart was to line me up with her sister. And it worked for both of us. He won Wilhemina, and I won Katherine."

Joseph had courted the lovely young woman, and she was quite taken by the nice-looking, gentlemanly, young man.

"Twenty-five, that is a good age to marry," his father had told Joseph. "You should be ready to settle down now. And you already own your farm." The older man shook his son's hand. "The family is close by, so we can help each other."

Joseph nodded as he squeezed his father's hand.

He took the arm of his beloved as they walked together to the high altar in the quaint little country church. "I do," he promised for life.

A tear slithered loose, and he wiped it away with the back of his rough, wind-chapped hand.

The children came and all was good. Soon, he would have help on the farm. Katherine loved the babies and knew their help would make the farm prosper in years to come. It was the way of farm families.

Two sons, three daughters. Maybe another son. But it was too much for her. Six children in thirteen years had been too big a burden for her frail frame.

"I cannot get all the afterbirth," said the country doctor, "but she will be fine."

But Katherine was not fine. Infection set in her uncleaned womb and snuffed out her young life. A five-day-old daughter cried in her cradle as her mother died in her bed.

Joseph wept now. The tears spilled down upon his calloused hands, but he made no attempt to stop them. He had to cleanse the hurt that remained in his heart.

Finally, the last tear spent, he remembered more. His own mother had already passed on. Katherine's family had helped out in the home as much as they could until, finally, one of her sisters took the baby into her own home. So many children there, too. Was his young daughter being treated well?

He thought of all the young neighbor girls he had hired to help cook and clean. Most of them were not much older than his own Ellen, just mere children themselves. Four, five, he lost count in the two and a half years or so.

"I do not know what else to do, Father," he recalled saying to the parish priest. "The neighbor girls are too young, and I want my family together again. I want Coletta back in our house with her own brothers and sisters."

"Have you considered remarrying, Joseph? Many men do it."

A shocked look crossed the widower's face. "I cannot, not just now." The priest put his hand on Joseph's shoulder for comfort. "My Katherine was so special to me."

"Perhaps, in time, Joseph." The priest's eyes were so kind.

The farmer nodded, then shrugged his shoulders and dipped his head to the side, questioningly. "I just do not know, Father, what to do," he answered with a heavy sigh.

The priest stood next to him in silence, thinking, trying to find some help for the other. An inspiration came. "There may be an answer, Joseph. The other day I was reading through a German newspaper published in Chicago. There were all kinds of advertisements – some looking for work, others looking for workers. Many immigrants are only too happy to find work, no matter where they need to go. There was quite a list of men in the same position as you, who needed a housekeeper. You would need to pay the woman's train fare from Chicago to here, however. That is the way it is done. But I think you can afford that. If you cannot, perhaps I can help you some, financially."

What kind of a housekeeper is one liable to get?" Joseph rubbed his hands together in anguish and desperation.

"What you probably need to do, Joseph, is put your requirements in the notice. If you have any responses, you need to write them several times and try to judge them by their answers. It is a gamble, Joseph, but it may be the answer to your prayers. I will help you draft the notice if you need help."

It had come to this. Joseph picked up the letter from Agnes Puder to reread it yet another time. Then he picked up his reply and read and reread it.

The cool air of the room and his own tension made Joseph very tired. He put his head down upon his clenched hands and dozed off into a fitful sleep. Visions of his children danced among the feathery sequences of his dreams.

Joseph's body relaxed into a deep sleep. He wrapped his arms around Katherine and held her close for a long time. She slipped from his embrace and stood before him. A sweet smile covered her face. Her eyes glowed with love. A soft hand caressed his cheek, then she seemed to speak, "It is good." With those words, she disappeared.

He sat bolt upright and rubbed his eyes. "A dream, it was all a dream." Joseph put his fingers to his temples and gently rubbed.

The lamp's light was dim. The wood had burned down. The room was uncomfortably cold.

Joseph stood slowly, stretching stiff legs and knees. With a slow limp, he climbed the narrow steps and checked in each room. Only soft breathing was heard. On tiptoe, he returned to his downstairs bedroom and brushed his hand lightly across Wendell's dark hair.

Stretched out on top of the thick featherbed mattress, sleep came quickly to the tired father.

11

A DECISION MADE

THE CRUMPLED ENVELOPE caught Agnes' eye immediately. The postmark was smudged, but she could still make out "Garden Plain, Kansas." The scribbled return address made her catch her breath.

She almost wished he had not replied. Second thoughts about answering the Help Wanted advertisement had begun to haunt her. She looked at the letter and wondered about its contents. Her whole future could be opened to her by what the letter said. Somewhat hesitant, Agnes opened the flap and took out the one page.

"*Miss Puder,*" she read. The thought occurred, "He probably does not feel comfortable addressing another woman as 'Dear' since his wife died." She brushed the back of her tightly coiled hair. "He does not even know me, or what I look like. Why should he address me as 'Dear?'" She forced herself to continue reading.

"*Miss Puder, Your letter arrived, and I have put it aside for a time. After much thought, I think you would fill the housekeeper position quite well. My children definitely need an older woman's hand and influence around the house. My farm work keeps me away from them so much during the summer. My daughters, especially, should have someone around to help them. Your qualifications are good.*

"*My oldest, Ellen, was eleven when my wife died. She is now almost thirteen. There are five younger children: William, Agnes, Irene, Wendell and the baby, Coletta. My wife's sister has cared for her the last two and a half years. As soon as I can get a dependable housekeeper, I am anxious to bring Coletta back to be with our family.*

"*If you are interested in coming to Kansas, we can discuss your wages then. The custom for travel arrangements is usually up to the employer, so I will provide the funds for your train fare.*

"I am anxious to hear from you. Otherwise, I will have to find another way to care for the children.

Sincerely, Joseph Linnebur"

Her heart skipped a beat. Agnes clutched her chest. "What is happening to me? It is only a letter."

Still, it was as though her intuition was opening a door to her. He had written a simple, straightforward letter, but for some reason, she sensed more. She sat down and reread the missive several times. It was now up to her.

A few days later, she showed the farmer's reply to Helena.

"So, my dear Agnes, what are you going to do? Are you going to toss this, or are you going to answer him?"

Agnes sighed, deeply. She folded and refolded the paper. "I am not sure. My better judgment tells me to forget about it, but the voice in my heart tells me to write again."

She opened the letter one more time and quickly scanned the words. Agnes had read the letter so many times, the words were printed indelibly upon her mind.

With a nervous laugh, she looked at Helena. "I have never read a letter so many times as I have read this one. It seems to compel my attention, my every waking moment." For several moments, her mind soared off to another time, another place. Pictures she had seen of the flat plains drifted through her subconscious. "I feel I must write another letter," she said more to herself than to Helena.

Helena took Agnes' hand and looked directly into her eyes. "Dear friend, you know absolutely nothing about this man, nothing about Kansas. Have you stopped to think what kind of situation you might be getting into?"

Agnes' face creased in a slight smile, "I know, Helena, but his letter is so sincere." She put her other hand on Helena's. "A father with six young children must certainly be sincere."

Helena smiled, "Please, Agnes, share his next letter with me. I do not want to see you make a mistake you may regret for the rest of your days."

Agnes' eyes sparkled, but with a hint of sternness, "You forget, Helena, I am not easily swayed. My life has taken some strange turns in the last years, and this might just be another one of those. If it is not to my liking there, I will move on."

Her friend spoke sternly, "You are one stubborn woman, Agnes."

"You have to remember, I am not a mail-order bride, Helena. I am just looking for employment as a housekeeper." A faint blush colored Agnes' cheeks. "He never wrote anything about marriage, and neither will I. That does not interest me much anymore, at my age."

"If you go, I will miss you, and your sage evaluation of life." Helena wrapped her arm around Agnes' shoulder, and brushed her cheek lightly with a kiss. "You are a special kind of woman."

Agnes and Joseph wrote several letters back and forth, making the necessary arrangement for her trip to Kansas. She wrote lengthy ones. His were short and direct. "A man of few words," she mused, "I like that." The whisper crossed her lips, "An honest man."

Joseph had written, "Could you come in the spring, late March or early April? I will have to begin with the field work and gardening then. The danger of hard frost will be over."

"Yes," she thought, "spring should be pretty on the prairie. Perhaps it is like the Mai Luft, the May air in Germany."

She sealed the letter. "I will come then," she had written.

Plans had to be made to move to Kansas. She wrote to the Sisters at the Leo House, "I will come to New York City the first part of March to visit, and to get my trunks ready to ship to Kansas. I have taken a housekeeper position there, for a farmer with six small children."

The rhythmic click of the train wheels on the rails soothed her mind. "Do I, do I not, do I go to Kansas, do I not?" She finally realized the recurring thoughts winding through her subconscious. Her reflection in the window caught the smile that crossed her brow.

"What am I thinking? There is no turning back now." The trip gave her time to put everything into perspective. "Yes, it is time for me to look for the next phase of my life, and maybe it is in Kansas."

The boroughs of New York came into view. The green fields and trees turned to oneness of cement and buildings of bricks.

Agnes stepped off the train and remembered her first day in this country. "It does not seem so foreign and strange to me anymore." She looked up and down the streets passionately, like seeing a dear one from an earlier life.

Sister Mary Anthony opened the door and spread her arms wide in greeting, "Agnes, you have come back."

"Yes, I have, Sister, but not for long. In a few days, I will be on my way again."

"Look who is here, Sister Mary Bernard." The nun came walking toward Agnes and Sister Mary Anthony. "You remember our friend from Breslau?"

"Ah, yes," laughed the second nun. "How could I forget? It is the lady who thought chewing gum was very unladylike, almost vulgar." Her eyes twinkled, "Have you started chewing gum, Agnes?"

"I think not." Agnes smiled as she took the nun's hand. "Right now, I am more interested in a comfortable bed. After a good night's rest, I want to go out and see the city again. I need to walk these streets and be revitalized by them. Perhaps I will be able to see Mrs. Levy, too."

"We heard she sold her beautiful home and now lives in an apartment near Central Park," Sister Mary Anthony told her.

The streets of the city wrapped their exciting cocoons around Agnes. She sauntered through the museums and drank in the inspirations of the artists. The cacophony of sounds were recorded in her mind. "Will I ever get back here from the plains?"

She wandered around the city, soaking up the atmosphere, rubbing elbows with people of all colors and speaking a chorus of strange tongues. She walked along the docks and sat in the parks watching the ocean liners that were berthed there.

The idea to return to Germany on one of the ships never took root in her thoughts, never jelled in her mind. "I am here now, and my homeland is a whole ocean away. It seems like a dream that I ever lived anywhere but here. A sob broke in her throat, "It is better that my days there are wrapped in silk and stored in the recesses of my thoughts." Slowly, she walked back to Leo House.

Agnes joined the nuns for one last meal.

"I cannot believe you are going to Kansas, of all places." Sister Mary Bernard handed Agnes the cream and sugar. "Are you sure, Agnes? I hear there is nothing out there but wide open spaces, lots of

72

wind and heat, and herds of buffalo."

Agnes, caught surprised, raised her eyelids in amusement. "I do not know about the wind and summer heat, but at least Joseph did say there were no buffalo. They are all gone from the plains of Kansas."

"Yes, but, Agnes, you are used to the big cities of the world. All they have in Kansas are little dinky villages with dirt streets, cobbled-up wooden stores and horse apples strewn all over the roads." Sister laughed, "just imagine crossing the street there after a big rainstorm, nothing but mud and ruts!"

Sister Mary Anthony added, "Oh, and do not forget the horse manure." Her eyes twinkled mischievously.

"My goodness, you two. What are you suggesting?"

Sister Mary Anthony chuckled, "We are trying to tell you, Agnes Puder, you are most certainly not the type of person to become a farmer's wife. Do you know about butchering animals and raising a big garden for winter food? And how many children did you say he had?" She gasped in shock, "Oh, dear Agnes."

"No, I do not." Agnes' face broke into a wide grin. "Quit trying to persuade me to change my mind. It is made up; I am going to Kansas. He expects a housekeeper to arrive there in several days, and I intend to honor my commitment." She shrugged her shoulders as she added, "He certainly does not expect a wife."

Sister Mary Bernard glanced at the other nun and winked. Then she looked at Agnes and giggled, "If you insist. But, before you go, we are going to make a wager, a bet with you that you will not last one year out on the dusty and dirty plains of Kansas." She grinned widely, and her dimples deepened. "Remember, dear friend, there is no electricity or gas for cooking; and worst of all, I hear the bacon is really hard!" The nun put her hand lightly on Agnes' arm. "You may as well leave your trunk here. You will be back real soon." Her eyes twinkled.

"A whole year. The two of you do not have much faith in me. Not much compassion, either." Agnes looked from one to the other in mock seriousness. Then she answered with a merry lilt in her voice, "But I accept your bet, and I will last at least one year in Kansas."

The three of them laughed until tears rolled down their cheeks. The two nuns lifted their water glasses in a toast to Agnes.

"Good fortune to our city friend out on the wind-swept plains."

Agnes bowed her head and smiled, "Thank you for the toast of good wishes."

Her eyes sparkled with merriment, and the laugh lines on her face widened, as she dabbed her lips delicately with a linen napkin.

Huge smiles spread across the faces of the nuns.

12

KANSAS

AGNES RUBBED SLEEP from her eyes. It had been a long, interesting journey from New York, back to Chicago, through Missouri and into Kansas. She always enjoyed traveling, and the Pullman car fare to Kansas City was well worth the extra.

Thoughts of the miles slipped through her mind, as if she had to review them for her memory. The hustle and bustle of New York City was etched upon her brain. How she loved that city. It reminded her of the lively and cultured Breslau from where she had come.

Milwaukee and Chicago were not as sophisticated as her home city, and the cities of the East Coast, but they worked hard to try and be so. The Mississippi and the Missouri Rivers were the widest she had ever seen. The conductor told her the rivers divided the country almost in half. She saw that, as the train slipped across the countryside, mile after mile.

The towns were smaller and appeared more provincial. Each region seemed to have its own culture, its own language, its own view of the outside world. It was as if they intended to cut themselves off from other societies.

The flat prairie plains of Kansas surprised her. Agnes had never envisioned anything like the wideness, the almost treeless plains. The sky loomed forever, upward and outward. It stretched endlessly into the horizon. The prairie foothills were ablaze with the flowers of spring.

"Ah," she breathed in, "it must be the Mai Luft of the plains, even though it is only April." She breathed in longingly through the slightly opened window. The faint perfumes and fragrances of the wildflowers and prairie grasses caressed her sense of smell. She leaned back hard against the seat, and basked in the profusion of the beauty that spread, mile after mile.

"These small hills are the Flint Hills of Kansas," the conductor told her. "They stretch almost the entire width of the state, from north to south."

"Why the name 'Flint Hills?'" she asked.

"Because of the flint rocks that are found here. The Indians used the rock to fashion their arrowheads."

The sunset washed across the prairie. "How beautiful," Agnes whispered aloud. She glanced around to see if the other passengers heard her. Very few of them seemed taken by the beauty in the western sky. The deep, royal purples mellowed into the rich blues that blended with the vibrant shades of pink and orange, all overlaid with the overwhelming brightness of solid gold. "Oh my," murmured Agnes. "I have never seen such beauty at sunset." She smiled to herself. "Every sunset in Kansas must be as colorful as a Monet painting."

The Atchison, Topeka and Santa Fe train slid into the city of Wichita at dusk.

"The Eaton Hotel is several blocks to the west," the ticket clerk told her. "It is considered the best in this city."

The hotel was small, but clean. Agnes glanced around the sparse room. But all she cared about were the fresh sheets on the iron bed.

She rolled to her side, and stroked the pillow smooth where her head had rested for the night. The thoughts of the prairies replayed in her mind's eye. "So many wide-open spaces," she muttered.

The bedsprings squeaked as she sat upright and eased over to the edge of the bed. The roofs of the neighboring buildings were visible from her third-story hotel room window. "So this is the thriving metropolis of Wichita, Kansas." She realized her voice had a ring of subtle sarcasm. For a few minutes, she closed her eyes and found herself shuddering. "Did I make a mistake in coming here?"

Bells clanged and horses' hooves clattered in rapid-fire syncopation on the brick street below her window. The horse-drawn fire wagon swung around the corner and headed west down Douglas Avenue.

Agnes rushed to the window and pulled aside the curtains. "Thank heavens," she sighed, "the buildings are brick." She closed the curtain and laughed at herself. "My nun friends did not really know what they were talking about. The buildings are not clapboard and the sidewalks are cement."

With relief, she sat down at the dressing table. Her long dark hair hung loosely to her waist. Agnes pulled the brush with slow, even strokes through the dark strands. A smile creased her cheeks as she remembered her mother saying, "What beautiful hair you have been blessed with, Agnes." Her mother's hair was as dark as her own. Agnes' hair had never been cut; her mother had seen to that.

Agnes brushed the silky tresses back from her face. With steady hand, she wound the hair into a long rope, then twisted it into a smooth, round coil at the nape of her neck. She held her pink framed looking glass, then turned to check her reflection in the dressing table mirror. Agnes smiled. Every hair was in place and her circular bun was perfect.

With patience, she pulled each strand of hair from her hairbrush and placed it into the small holder. At some later date, she would braid the long strands into a delicate rope of her own dark hair.

With dainty fingers, she flicked away the small bits of dark hair from her white Gibson-girl blouse. The narrow navy scarf was knotted at her neck. With a precise turn of her hand, she tied the long ribbons into a neat bow and pinned it into place with her favorite brooch.

Agnes picked up the neat white straw hat with an upturned brim to the right side. She looked at the hat and shook her head in approval. The silk navy underlining on the brim and the large crushed flower on the left brim matched her two-piece navy suit perfectly.

Her gold timepiece reminded the young woman the time was near. She stood and smoothed her skirt, then slipped into the fitted jacket. Agnes smiled approvingly as she turned to see her reflection better.

"I feel so elegant in this. I would like to personally thank the designer of the Gibson-girl style." She turned around for another look, and then giggled like a schoolgirl. "What will his impression be?" Her cheeks blushed a tinge of pink when she realized her words.

Shaking her head, she picked up the matching navy pocketbook and valise. "I am ready for the next adventure."

Agnes' white-gloved hand grasped the bronze railing as she descended the wide, curving staircase. Others, standing in the large lobby noticed, and turned to watch her deliberate, determined step. The hotel doorman rushed to open the glass door and motioned to the cabdriver parked at the curb.

In a few minutes, they arrived at the depot. The Wichita and Western train, a branch of the Santa Fe Railroad, would leave soon on its once-a-day round trip scheduled to Pratt, with stops in Goddard, Garden Plain and Cheney. She checked to see if her trunk and valise were on the baggage cart, then found the conductor to take her ticket.

He tipped his hat to her, " A fine day for a nice ride, Madam." Moving to the side, he offered his hand to her as she stepped up on the first step. "To your right, please."

His eyes followed her up the steps. Most of the ladies traveling on this route did not dress in the latest fashion. He wanted so to ask where she had come from, but knew how improper that would be. The conductor could only wonder and watch who would meet her at the depot in Garden Plain.

The very stylish Agnes arrives in Kansas
to assume the post of housekeeper.

13

THE ARRIVAL

JOSEPH AWOKE EARLY and pushed aside the old lace curtain in the small bedroom. The April sun danced sunbeams off the raindrops that had gathered on the grass from the showers the day before. Emerald green sprigs were sprouting all over the dry grass of last fall.

Along the driveway, small early iris opened in deep purple profusion. "If she likes flowers, she will be happy to see there are some near the house."

Joseph dressed quickly. The hogs needed feed. He also needed to check the cattle. The night before, he had noticed one of the cows was getting close to calving. "I hope the cow has that calf without any trouble." He combed through his dark curly hair. "I do not care to pull a calf this morning."

Tying his shoes, he muttered more, "The time is going to go fast today. The train should get into Garden Plain about eleven this morning."

Thirteen-year-old Ellen and twelve-year-old William came into the kitchen right after Joseph. The father filled the black cookstove with several chunks of wood and strips of kindling, then held a match to the kindling until a small flame took hold. The fire started to crack and pop. A cozy warmth spread around the kitchen.

"William, can you fill the water bucket?" The boy carried the three-gallon bucket out into the screened-in porch and put it under the tall pump. William liked to hear the handle squeak as he pumped it up and down, faster and faster. If he pumped it fast enough, a full round stream of cool well water splashed into the bucket. In no time at all, the bucket brimmed to the top. "Do not spill any and waste our water," his mother used to call to him in those days before she died. Her voice still echoed in his mind as he carefully carried the bucket inside.

"Thanks, Son, you are always so careful." Joseph smiled at the boy. Ellen raised her eyes in mock disgust. William always seemed to get the compliments.

Joseph took the long-handled cup and dipped water from the bucket and poured it into the large blue and white speckled graniteware coffeepot. In a few minutes, the hot wood fire had the water boiling. Joseph measured out the ground coffee and dumped it into the water. "Ah, coffee, the elixir of life." He winked at Ellen.

"He sure seems in a good mood this morning," Ellen whispered to William, as she made a face behind her father's back.

"This is the day our hired lady arrives," announced Joseph. He smiled at his daughter, eight-year-old Agnes, just as she walked into the warm kitchen.

"I will really need your help today. Ellen and Agnes, will you make the beds just as neat as you can, and then sweep the floors. I also want all the dishes washed, wiped and put away after dinner." He looked around the room a bit. "Would you also dust the furniture?"

"William, after you help me with the chores, I want you to fill the water bucket again, and bring in more wood and kindling." The boy nodded he would.

"And, girls, the iris are blooming so pretty. Do you remember how your mother loved them?" They nodded yes, smiling. "We have not had any flowers in the house for a long time. Would you please pick some and put them here on the kitchen table?" He walked over to the cabinet, reached up to the top shelf and took out a clear glass vase. "This should be about right for some of the iris."

"When will Miss Puder be here, Pa?" Agnes asked.

"It will be early this afternoon, before we get back from the train station. So you will have time to clean up around here. Irene can help a little, too." He smiled again. "We want to make a good impression on the lady, do we not? She is coming from Chicago, a long way from here, to help us and to take care of you children."

Ellen made sure he was not looking at her, when she curled her lip and wrinkled her nose into a big sneer. "Wonder what it will take for me to get rid of this one?" she mumbled. "None of the others stayed very long, and this one probably will not either."

Joseph looked at his shadow on the ground in front of him, and then glanced up at the sky. "Almost mealtime," he called to William. "Finish watering the chickens and geese. I need to go into the house and help the girls fix a meal." He hurried to the house, shaking his head, "I sure hope that lady is a good cook. We have not had a full meal since Maria left, and that has been six months ago." He chuckled, "That last one, Hendrina, could hardly boil water. Oh, dear Lord, make Miss Puder a good cook. What I have put up with these last months, no family should have to deal with."

The screen door banged behind him. "Ellen, bring the basket of eggs. We will fix some scrambled eggs. Agnes, get the milk from the porch cave. It should still be sweet."

Joseph broke egg after egg into a large bowl, then whipped them into a froth. Ellen dropped a huge dollop of rich homemade butter into the cast iron skillet. Her father lifted the huge bowl and poured. The foamy eggs sizzled when they hit the hot melted butter.

As they sat down to eat, Joseph glanced around the room. "Girls, you did your tasks very well. The house looks so clean." He moved the vase of iris to the center of the table and grinned. "It is so nice to see flowers in the house again. That was one of the favorite things your mother liked to do." Agnes and Ellen turned to him and smiled, "Thank you, Pa."

Joseph climbed the steps and went into William's room. His clothes now hung in the boy's closet. For the time being, he and Wendell would share the older son's room. "If this does not work out, I may be back downstairs in my old bedroom soon." He fluffed up the covers on the narrow bed for the smaller boy. "Miss Puder needs her own room," he told the boys.

He opened the wardrobe and sorted through his clothes. "This is a special day, I think. My heart tells me so." He grinned, then took the stiff clothes brush to his Sunday suit, and whisked away the lint and loose hair. He held it up to the window for a closer inspection.

"Other men have married their housekeepers, so who knows what might come about," he spoke softly to himself. "If she is anything as interesting as her letters ... My goodness," he felt his face flush, "what am I thinking? Ah, dear Katherine, help me through this. Our children miss you so, and so do I. Will there ever be anyone who can take your place?"

He slipped on the white shirt his sister-in-law had washed and pressed for him, then added his black bow tie. The black wool suit fit his work-hardened body perfectly. He brushed his dark hair into place, then grabbed his best black hat. A quick glance in the narrow mirror confirmed his feelings; Joseph was still quite a dashing, handsome man at 42.

Joseph took Agnes' well-read letter from the nightstand and ruffled through the pages. "Three months, she agreed to a three-month trial period. Sounds fair enough to me. By then, we will know if we like her, and maybe more important, is she likes us."

He slipped the letter back into his coat pocket, then walked down the narrow steps. "William, have you hitched Old Ben up to the carriage?"

"Sure have, Pa." His oldest son took Joseph's arm and squeezed it, "I hope she is a nice lady, Pa."

Joseph looked deep into the boy's eyes. "Me, too, William, me, too."

Way off in the distance, he could hear the train whistle. He had to go; there was no turning back at the moment. He would have to meet that train. "I cannot leave the lady stranded there, not after she has come all that distance."

He slapped the reins and the horse started slowly out of the yard. At the end of the drive, he turned to wave to the children, then tipped his hat. Their arms weaved back and forth in wide arcs. "They are good children. Lord, my children are good. Katherine saw to that."

He tried to hurry the horse along by snapping the reins. His thoughts tumbled around and around, but there were no easy answers for him. She had always lived in the cities. Would she like it in the country? Why had she answered his advertisement? What if she did not like it here at all? What if she did not work out with the children? Did she know what to do with a wood cookstove, how to build a good fire with kindling scraps? Had she ever been involved in butchering; could she cook? How come I never thought to ask her all those questions?" He marveled at his own inadequacy. "I guess the thought just never occurred to me."

He laughed awkwardly to himself, and talked out loud, "Can she darn my socks'?" His eyes twinkled. "Even more important, will she?" Subconsciously, he bent over, pulled up his trouser legs and checked his stockings to make sure there were no holes.

A tug at the reins, and the horse turned south. "Only a mile and a half to go," mused Joseph. Right at that moment, the train whistle sounded again. The air of the spring day was clear and crisp. On such days, the mournful whistle from the steam engine split the silence of the countryside and could be heard for several miles. Its low shrill sound rumbled against his chest and quickened the beat of his heart. Never in all the past had he ever noticed the whistle as he did this day.

His mind raced. The horse seemed so slow. The carriage swung from side to side on the rutted road. Would this woman be shy, so shy she would not talk? "I hardly doubt that," he mumbled.

Would she be sloppy or neat in appearance? His breath caught, " I sure hope she is somewhat neat." He pushed his hat down close on his head. "I wonder what color her eyes are?" Joseph touched his right hand to his face and rubbed his chin seriously. He blew into his hand, as if to let off steam.

The mournful whistle sounded again, coming nearer. A bit of excitement stirred in Joseph. Was there, could there be a chance for something beyond the housekeeper and employer stage? Others had lost wives in childbirth and had chances at happy second marriages.

He had to hurry.

The steam engine hissed as it came into the farming community from the east. The engineer tooted the whistle at the main road on the east side of the village. The huge wheels ground down, slower and slower until the brakes locked and grabbed at the rails. Steam billowed out from under the cattle guard.

Joseph walked back and forth on the brick platform in front of the depot. He stood out in the crowd of farmers, dressed in his Sunday best suit and sharp black hat.

Joseph thought about his children at home. He blew his breath between his teeth. "Fortunately, they are not any older, or they might be plotting horrible things to pull on her." A deep sigh slipped from his lips, "But, I have to take that chance."

The conductor opened the back side door of the passenger car, and offered his hand to the ladies. Joseph knew all of them, they were ladies of the village, or farm wives. Most of them carried bundles from shopping in the city. Then, near the end, a neat lady in a smart suit of navy and white stood at the top of the platform. She looked over the crowd, then took the conductor's hand delicately. With graceful step, she came down the steps.

"That has to be Agnes." Joseph's heart skipped a beat and he felt himself feeling weak. His knees almost buckled under him as he took the first step to greet her.

Others on the platform stopped to stare, but Joseph did not see them. He saw only a smart-looking young woman. He approached her, tipped his hat, bowed his head and smiled. "Miss Puder, I believe."

A wide smile creased her cheeks. "Mr. Linnebur, I presume."

He took her by the arm, and escorted her to his carriage. It was then he noticed William had tied a wide red ribbon on Old Ben's harness. He motioned to the sash fluttering in the light breeze and spoke, "Looks like William dressed up the horse especially for the occasion."

Agnes nodded and smiled. He returned to the depot to get her luggage, then swung it up into the carriage. With all the grace his mother had ever taught him, Joseph offered his hand to Agnes, and graciously took her hand to help her in the carriage.

Heads turned as the carriage left the depot. Joseph knew there were whispers, but he could not hear them, nor did he care. He felt proud of the elegant young woman seated beside him. Words were not easy for Joseph, but Agnes did not lack for the use of them. In the three-mile trip back to the farm, Agnes took him mentally by the hand and helped him travel from her homeland, through the streets of New York, and the rowdiness of Chicago. He felt like he had traveled the world in that 45-minute ride back home.

Joseph turned the horse into the drive, and became fully aware for the first time ever, how small his house really was. He dared not look at Agnes, for fear of what her reaction would be.

He pulled up near the screened-in back porch, and as Old Ben stopped, Joseph's children came out the door. They shielded their eyes to get a better look at the new woman, while their father helped her from the carriage.

"Children, meet Miss Puder." They nodded and tried to curtsy.

Agnes smiled, "Hello, children."

Joseph walked around behind them. "Miss Puder, please meet Ellen, William, Agnes, Irene and Wendell."

Agnes walked closer to them and held out her hand, "It is my pleasure to meet each of you."

Ellen lowered her eyes in disgust. William looked at his sister, Agnes, and winked. The little girl grinned.

"This lady is certainly different, isn't she?" the oldest brother whispered to the others.

Photo courtesy Souders Historical Farm Museum, Cheney, KS.

Agnes rode this steam-engine train to her destination at Garden Plain, Kansas. The Wichita and Western train line was a branch of the Santa Fe Railroad. Here it chugs into the depot at Garden Plain. As early as February 1884, the railroad served residents who lived west of Wichita. People in the area rode the train to Wichita, where they shopped. They stayed in the city and returned the following day. Merchandise and the U.S. mail were regularly hauled on the daily round-trip run, from the city to the towns west, stopping at Goddard, Garden Plain and Cheney. Over a period of time, the line extended to Kingman, then to Pratt, Kansas, about 60 miles west of Garden Plain. The excitement of the day included meeting the train. Consequently, the crowd also witnessed Agnes' arrival. In the cities, she never encountered the attention she must have garnered upon her arrival at this small town.

Photo courtesy Souders Historical Farm Museum, Cheney, KS.

Agnes' first view of Garden Plain was from the train window. Looking from the train depot north, this was the sight she would have seen. This picture shows the town, and was taken in 1907. Many businesses lined the short three-block dirt street. Trees almost covered the front of the hotel, on the near left side of the picture. Numerous horses were hitched to wagons or buggies, while their owners took advantage of the town's businesses. Off in the distance to the left was the bell tower of the first Catholic Church, St. Anthony of Padua, built in 1901. Barely visible over the roofs of buildings on the east side of the street she saw a windmill, a necessity out on the plains for pumping water. The nuns at Leo House were right – the street was a muddy mess when it rained! And it was strewn with horse apples!

14

THE FARM

AGNES LOOKED AT the small farmhouse and tried to keep her feelings hidden. She hoped her surprised emotion did not register on her face. Her grip tightened on the straps of her handbag.

Agnes' smile grew pinched as she looked at the children. They looked clean enough, but their clothes were in desperate need of care.

Thoughts tumbled one upon the other in rapid succession. "I know these dresses are hand-me-downs, but that is no excuse for their upkeep," she surmised. "The elbows are tattered and the sleeves are missing buttons." She started to ask if they had needle and thread in the house and a box of buttons, but thought better of it and held her tongue. Tomorrow would be soon enough.

"It will be hard," she thought, "the father seems so nice. All things will come in time, perhaps."

William smiled so nicely at her, she reached to take his hand. "And you are the oldest son?"

"Yes, Ma'am." He held the door open wide for her to enter the screened-in porch. The tall, rusty water pump stood to the left side, close to the warped, dirt-encrusted door on the floor.

Joseph noticed the frown on her brow. "The door covers the steps that lead down into the cellar. We keep our canned food down there. It is also cool enough to keep the milk and cream sweet."

She nodded.

He gave a half-hearted chuckle, wondering what she knew of the Kansas weather. "It is really nice to have the cellar so close, especially when the spring and summer storms happen. Tornadoes are the worst, and can ruin a house." He gave her a weak smile. "But it has never happened since I have lived here."

She raised her eyebrows a little, then caught her own reaction and managed a slight smile in return. "I hope it continues to be so."

Joseph pushed the door open into the long kitchen. The huge, black wood cookstove was the first thing that caught Agnes' eye. A narrow, tall cupboard stood along the west wall and looked like it could fall forward without any warning, save a large crash. The curtains inside its glass doors were dirty and torn.

The afternoon sunlight filtered through the hazy, dirty, west windows. She wondered how long the faded, ripped curtains had hung there. Joseph smiled so politely and seemed so happy for her to be there, she pretended not to notice.

"Our kitchen is small, but our table is big enough for our family and company. I guess that is all that really means anything." He brushed a lone, stray bread crumb from the old, cracked, red-and-white-checkered oilcloth covering the table. Long benches were pushed under it. At each end sat a high-backed chair.

Joseph motioned to little rooms at the north end of the kitchen. "The one on the east is our bathroom, and the one to the west is the pantry. You will be able to organize those however you like." He grinned, "I want you to feel as comfortable here as possible. I will not tell you what to do with the kitchen." With a soft chuckle, he added, "I like to eat too well to try and tell the cook how to run her kitchen."

Agnes smiled at him, "Agreed."

The children had pushed into the door and crowded around Joseph. They watched Agnes' every move. Daughters Irene and Agnes smiled at her; Ellen flinched. Wendell just stared at the strange lady. Daughter Agnes finally spoke up, "What should we call you?"

Before the older Agnes could respond, Joseph answered, "Her name is Miss Puder, and I want you to call her that."

"Yes, Pa," their voices blended as one.

"Ellen, would you please show her to the bedroom? William, come with me and we will bring in her trunk and valise."

The oldest daughter led the way through the parlor and into the small room to the left of it. A frazzled, ragged piece quilt, askew and wrinkled, was pulled over the bed. The feather bed under it was thin and threadbare. At least the pillow cover was reasonably clean, Agnes noticed.

She took off her hat and put it beside her purse on the dusty, scratched, narrow dresser. Her reflection gazed back at her in the dim, grayish, checked mirror. It was quite a shock to see her feelings portrayed so clearly on her face.

Just then, Joseph and William came through the door, struggling to get the heavy trunk into the room. They put it next to the dresser. Agnes stepped back to the head of the bed and bumped into the graniteware chamber pot that was sitting on the floor. A slight rose colored her cheeks. She had not seen one of those in years.

"With some fried-down sausage from the crocks in the cave, and a pan of fried potatoes and eggs, we will have a fast meal. That will be easy for your first meal here."

He started through the door, then turned to look at her again. "I think we will have an early supper; then towards evening, I can give you a tour of the farm."

She nodded, and then closed the door behind him. Sitting down on the bed, she untied her shoes and slipped them off her tired feet. Stretching out on the lumpy mattress, she closed her eyes. Thoughts crowded in on her, "Oh, my, what have I gotten into this time?" She kept trying to sort out the rational thoughts and separate them from the discordant ones.

Fatigue began edging out her consciousness, but she did not want to fall asleep on the job her first day here. Sighing heavily, she got up and took off her better clothes. A work dress was right on top in her valise. Just then, she was in no hurry to begin unpacking her trunk. She shook her head more than once in dismay and total shock. So this was what she had agreed to.

Ellen sat at the table with a sullen look on her face. "Would you dig some sausage out of the crock?" her father said to her. She looked at him with disdain, and then turned to look at Agnes in the same way.

"I guess, Pa." She scraped the chair back loudly from the table, and stomped past him to the screen-in porch and the cave.

"She is a bit edgy." Joseph looked at Agnes. "It has been hard for her these past years. Losing her mother was very difficult. And then, having all the other young neighbor girls coming in here to help, some not much older than her. It just has not been easy."

"I understand." Agnes moved to the cabinet to get out dishes for the meal. She opened the doors and was horrified to find mouse droppings and dead spiders in among the dishes. With a hand over her mouth, she turned to him. "How long has it been since these cupboards have been cleaned?"

He was taken aback by her question. For all the times he had reached in there for a cup, he had never taken notice of that. With an embarrassed smile, he replied, "It probably has been some time."

"My first project, it seems." She took plates, bowls and cups from there, and put them near the sink. With boiling hot water from the teakettle, she rinsed the dishes.

When she realized how rude her actions must have seemed to him, she blushed and stammered, "Forgive me." She shook her head in embarrassment, "My past is revealing itself. I must remember your situation here."

Grabbing what looked like a dishcloth, she quickly wiped off the table. Under her breath, she noted other concerns that needed to be remedied in the next day or two.

The potatoes and sausage sizzled in the huge cast-iron skillet. "Hmm, the sausage really smells good." Agnes smiled at the girls, "It has been a long time since I have eaten real German sausage. You know, the spices are what make the meat special."

She opened another cabinet door, then turned to Joseph, "Do you have a special place for spices?"

Again he looked at her in surprise.

"Do not worry about it; that will be another special project for me."

Joseph sat between the youngest children, and Agnes watched him with intense interest. "This will prove to me what he is really like," she thought, "the patience he shows the little ones." He filled one plate for Wendell, and then winked at his youngest son.

"Another piece of sausage, Pa." The small boy wiggled around on his chair.

"Push your plate closer." Joseph stabbed the meat with his fork, then slid it onto Wendell's plate. "How is that?" He laughed, then put his hand on the boy's arm. "When you finish that, you can have more."

In his quiet way, Joseph talked to the family. He would smile, and then answer their questions. In a fleeting instant, a warm feeling passed over Agnes. This was a man filled with love. He noticed her look, then smiled slightly at her. A faint blush passed over his cheeks and he forced himself to turn away from her. He became aware of her intense gaze, and without being able to help himself, he sought her face again. His kind eyes met hers once more, and she caught herself smiling in return.

Ellen and her sister, Agnes, gathered the dishes and took them to the sink. Joseph poured warm water over the white lye soap, and then swished the dishcloth around in the pan for soapy bubbles. "Would you girls please wash the dishes?" he asked kindly. "And William, it is time to feed the livestock."

"Come, Miss Puder, let me show you around the farm."

Joseph held the kitchen and porch doors for her, then took her arm and led her around the north side of the house. Chickens and ducks squawked and scattered. The geese waddled away, then turned back for another look. The ganders stretched their necks and hissed. The two stood there quietly and watched the barnyard fowl.

The chickens finally settled down, and started scratching the dirt with quick, jabbing movements. "They are looking for extra grain," Joseph explained. "The animals soon learn when there might be food for them and," he chuckled lightly, " they always seem to be hungry."

Agnes looked astonished. "I thought all chickens were white."

"No," Joseph tried to hide his amusement, "chickens come in several shades. Some are solid colors." He pointed to a large reddish hen. "That breed is called the Rhode Island Red and lays large brown eggs."

A monster black and white rooster strutted toward them. "How beautiful," breathed Agnes in wonderment. "His feathers, they appear to be in stripes." She walked a few steps forward to get a closer look. The rooster eyed her suspiciously, then turned and walked proudly back closer to the flock.

"He does not seem to think much of me," she decided with a smile. "Probably knows I am city-bred." Turning back to Joseph, she asked, "What breed is that rooster?"

"A Barred Plymouth Rock. Some of the prettiest chickens there are, and the hens also lay big brown eggs."

"Don't you have any that produce white eggs?"

"Look over there." Joseph pointed to a huge white chicken. "If you want white eggs, they will come from the White Plymouth Rocks."

Agnes turned in a circle to look at the chickens and ducks that now surrounded them, and heaved a big sigh. With an exasperated voice she asked, "How many chickens do you have here, and how do you remember all those breeds?"

Joseph smiled as he touched her arm. "Ah, Miss Puder, please do not let it overwhelm you. In a few days you will get used to all of this." Sheepishly, he took his hand away from her arm, and blushed softly.

"Do you really think so?" She said, awestruck, "First, I have to learn to know the roosters from the hens." A slight laugh broke from her lips.

Joseph grinned, "The roosters are more apt to come at you to scare you. The hens are not interested in playing games with people." He rubbed his hands together. "Although, they are very good at delivering a swift hard peck to one's hand when a person tries to gather the eggs from under them."

"Oh, my," she murmured.

"These are the old hens, and as far as I can tell, they are practically all still laying eggs. If I can ever catch one that is getting lazy, she goes into a pot for chicken and dumplings." His eyes appeared even more hazel as he looked at her. "You probably make quite a pot of chicken and dumplings."

She smiled, "With the right spices, I do."

"Yes, Miss Puder, we must get all the spices you need." He laughed merrily, then added, "Chicken and dumplings, or chicken and rice soup, are some of my favorite meals."

He motioned to a small building, "Over there is where we keep the hens that are sitting on eggs. It takes about three weeks after a hen starts to sit before the first chick breaks through the shell." He turned to her, "They are so interesting to watch. Once all the eggs are hatched, the hen will lead the small chicks around the yard in search of greens and grain to eat. She keeps them close in a group near her, and makes a soft 'cluck, cluck' sound. If they have strayed, they will come running. When the hen thinks the chicks are in danger, or it starts to rain, she will tuck them all under her feathers."

Joseph twisted his head in amusement, "You know, it is really something how Mother Nature takes care of her own. They just know all that by instinct. In a way, animals are much smarter than humans." His eyes twinkled in merriment, but then he turned serious again.

Pointing to a somewhat larger building, he continued, "Once the chicks are full-feathered and have grown big enough to fly some, they will get up on the roosts in that shed, and spend the nights there."

"What do you do with all the chicks?" Agnes wondered.

"We will have hens hatching eggs during the spring and way into the summer. The young roosters will be butchered, so there will be fresh meat all along. Most of the pullets, the young hens will be kept back for eggs. We do sell the surplus eggs to the mercantile in town. It helps buy the sugar, and the flour and coffee we need." Then he grinned, "And any spices you may want to buy for cooking."

She nodded, but stopped short of saying anything more. He looked at her so kindly; she waited for him to continue. "Once you get used to the chicken business, that will be mostly your area. The children and I will help clean the fryers when it is time, and William and I will keep the chicken house clean. That is not a job for a lady." A big smile crossed his face, "But when and how you want to do those jobs will be up to you."

"How many chicks do you have hatch in a summer?"

"Usually around 200 or so."

"What am I going to do with 200 chickens?" Agnes gasped. She shrugged her shoulders, and finally spoke, "I will certainly need guidance on when to do those jobs. I have cleaned foul before, but," she laughed, "I may need some help running them down."

His eyes twinkled, "That is no problem. We go into the brooder house the evening before, after the chickens have settled in for the night, and then catch them. They hardly move as we check them for size. One by one, we take them off the roost and put them in wire coops." A slight laugh escaped his lips, "Sorry to disappoint you, but you will not have to hike up your skirts and chase the chickens down."

"Pa, Pa, I need help," yelled William. Old Bessie is starting to calf, and it looks like she is going to have trouble. Either the calf is too big, or it is starting to come backwards."

"I better go check, Miss Puder. You can look over the rest of the

93

farm if you like." He waved his hand to the east. "The hogs are back over there, and the cattle and horses are by the barn." He started to hurry off, then turned back to her, "If you need to know anything more, step in the house and ask the girls. My daughter, Agnes, is especially good with the animals." A grin started on his face. "She tells me she wants to be a nurse, so guess that is why."

With a swift stride, he took off for the barn.

Joseph introduces Agnes to the farm chickens. Taking care of them will be one of her duties.

15

DECISION

AGNES SAT DOWN on a barrel that was turned on its side. The chickens gathered around her, squawking and clucking, looking for a handout of grain. She looked in one direction after another, and then her breath caught in her throat. A huge area was tilled, and small plants were already beginning to show their top leaves. "Oh, my heavens, is that his garden?" A terrific sigh forced its way from her throat. "Well, it looks as though that will be something else to learn about."

Numbness began in the tips of her toes, found its way up her legs, tightened her arms and cramped her stomach muscles. She closed her eyes to shut out the scene that surrounded her, and breathed hard. Slowly, Agnes opened her eyes, but the enormity of the reality hit home. She put her hands up to her face and covered her eyes with her fingertips. Perhaps, if she wished hard enough, this situation might really be just a dream. After a long time, she knew she had to move. The barrel was getting hard to sit on, and she needed to walk, to think, to look this place over. A decision had to be made, and made within the next few hours.

She stood, and then walked to the east to see the other animals. The pigs wallowed in the mud left by the April showers. The smell of their lot was overpowering. Their grunts could only be sounds of pig happiness. Their euphoria certainly did not match hers.

Spring flies were already finding the horses' tender spots, and their long ratted tails swished through the air to beat away the pests. One fly landed on Agnes, and she turned in surprise and alarm, then beat it off. "Oh, how awful."

The cattle looked at her with disinterest. Chewing their cud was of the utmost importance to them.

Agnes felt she had seen enough. She looked back at the little house. The whole house was smaller than some of the parlors and dining rooms in the previous homes where she had worked. "I will feel so confined in that tiny place. The walls will probably close right around me, and I will never be able to loosen myself from their grip." Another sigh followed. "And all the closeness to the others will almost suffocate me."

With a slow step, she started back to the screened-in porch. Then she realized rags were strewn all over the yard. "Did he never make his children pick up the garbage?" She was totally horrified. "They must have just thrown things down wherever they were."

She bent over to pick up a shred of a sleeve, and found the buttons still on the cuff. "There are buttons here to fix those children's clothes, where buttons are missing." Stuffing the rag into her pocket, she continued her walk.

The irises were so pretty, she found her way to the drive. "The only piece of beauty on this whole place," she muttered aloud.

The front porch was small, but inviting. The step was slightly askew. Cracks broke the cement floor. An old chair stood by the front door. As she walked over to it, she noticed the front door probably had not been opened for years. "We will put that door to use, if for no other reason than to air out the house and let the fresh air circulate. Wonder how long it has been since the house has had a good airing."

She leaned hard against one of the wooden pillars. Paint chipped away and fell in dry blobs at her feet. Dizziness caught her by surprise and she swayed a bit to the side. A faint breeze, sweet with the fragrance of the wild April flowers around the farm, fanned her face.

She looked beyond the driveway, to the road that ran past the place. "Oh, to take that road again, somewhere else," she mused.

Her gaze swept over the front yard, littered with broken tree limbs and clumps of dry grass and weeds. She turned to look back at the barns and the few animals Joseph had.

"I really wonder how much money he has?" Pressing her lips hard together, she felt the muscles in her taut fingertips respond to her anxiety. "How much of his savings did it take for him to send me the train ticket to come?" Her sight swept out to the pastures, just now beginning to green. She had no idea if all that land was his or not, or perhaps someone owned all of it and he was only a tenant. Right now, that question was not one she could ask Joseph.

Her stomach felt sick. "Much as I would like to return to Chicago, I doubt very much this man could afford my return ticket." She looked down at the cracked cement floor of the porch, then put her hands up to rub her cheeks again. "I wonder how old this house really is?"

Agnes stood there for a long time, knots growing tighter in her stomach. "I do not want to stay here, but what can I do? I am really in a situation this time. For the first time in my life, I do not know which way to turn."

Her thoughts swirled in all directions, until they returned to New York City and the Leo House. "We do not think you will stay in that forsaken place called Kansas for a year," Sister Mary Anthony had laughed. "We will make a wager with you that you are back here in the city within the year." Sister Mary Bernard's eyes glistened with mischief. "You will see, dear Miss Puder, you are not destined to go to that state. You are not meant to live on a farm."

Tears welled in Agnes' eyes. "I cannot let them prove me unworthy of a challenge. Friends or not, those nuns are not going to laugh at me because I could not do it." She straightened up tall. "A decision must be made by tomorrow morning. One way or the other, it has to be decided."

"Miss Puder, Miss Puder, where are you?" Joseph was calling.

She could not bring herself to answer. Agnes just wanted to disappear into the Kansas sunset that was slowly beginning. He called again and again until, finally, she could not refuse to answer him.

"Here, I am here," she called in a weak voice. "Here, on the front porch."

He came around the corner of the house, with a big smile on his face. "I thought you had gone into the house, but the girls said you had not come in." A serious look crossed his face, and his eyes took on a touch of sadness. "I thought, surely she has not left so soon."

"No, Mr. Linnebur, I was just here enjoying the April air. It smells so sweet of the spring flowers."

He touched her hand with his strong fingers. "Call me Joseph, please."

She nodded, "And you may call me Agnes."

His smile spread wider and wider across his face, and he laughed gently. "But only when the children are not around. In front of them, you will still be Miss Puder." A gentle squeeze enveloped her hand.

"As you choose." She hesitated, then added, "Joseph."

A photo of the Linnebur farm, taken years later, but looking much like Agnes first saw it. To the left of the house were the chicken houses. To the right of the second story of the house, behind the tree, is the screened-in porch and kitchen addition. Fenced-in corrals had been in the foreground. Joseph's cattle and horses filled the barnyard.

16

COUNTRY MORNING

THE EARLY MORNING sunrise stretched golden rays across the bed covers and splashed against the west wall. Agnes moved slightly, and then sat bolt upright in bed.

The big black and white rooster stood in the middle of the yard and thrust his head high into the air, reaching for the sky. The golden orange sun made his tall, jagged-edged comb glisten even redder. "Cock-a-doodle-doo," he crowed loud and clear, over and over. His cheerful morning message echoed off the buildings and the tree trunks.

"Oh, my goodness," Agnes breathed heavily, "that is the rooster." Slowly she tossed aside the bed covers. "There is no staying in bed any longer. He summons us to work."

The farmer was already stoking the fire in the wood cookstove, when she walked out into the kitchen. "Good morning, Agnes." He smiled ever so nicely at her. "Did you rest well?"

"Yes, I did." Soft laughter startled him. "That is, until the rooster decided it was time for me to rise." Dipping water from the large pail, she filled the blue and white graniteware coffeepot. "One certainly does not need an alarm clock when Mother Nature provides one." Her soft smile touched his heart.

Joseph leaned over the stove and turned the handle on the stovepipe. By doing so, he adjusted the damper on the flue to add more updraft so the fire would burn hotter.

"I like to hear him crow. It makes me feel ready to get up and meet the day." With a soft chuckle, he added, "The children have a name for him, 'Old Grump.' He can be a rather feisty fellow if he does not get his way in the chicken yard."

Joseph took down a large box from a shelf and poured oatmeal into a cookpot along with some water. "The children like hot cereal on cool mornings. Bacon and eggs are good for really warm weather, when they can work it off playing." He handed her the wooden spoon. "If you would not mind to stir this, I will get the milk and butter from the cellar." He started for the door, then turned back again. "But first, I had better rouse the older ones. A school day, you know."

Agnes cleared away the breakfast dishes, then put soap and hot water in the dishpan. In the other room, she could hear voices.

"Hurry up, Ellen, the Sisters at school will be mad at us again," William said. "The horse is all hitched up, ready to go."

"I am coming, just you wait." She stood in front of the little mirror in the bathroom. "Oooh, my hair bow does not look right."

"Come on," William hollered, "the wind is blowing anyway."

"All right, all right," Ellen growled. "Brothers, they just do not understand."

The housekeeper turned her back to the children and smiled. How well she remembered her own brothers, Conrad and Constantine, being the same way. Her sister, Martha, used to growl around, just like Ellen.

The doors banged behind them. "I want to go with them," wailed five-year-old Wendell.

"Your time will come, Son, your time will come in a few months." His father grabbed the little fellow by the shirtsleeve. "Come along with me. I need some good help out by the barn."

"What are we going to do?" Wendell wiggled free from his father's grasp. "I do not want to help with the horses' stalls again."

Joseph looked at him and squinted. "No, it is going to be more interesting than that. We need to clean out the chicken house."

"Oh, gosh, Pa, that place stinks terrible," grumbled the boy.

"I know, but the chickens like a clean house just like we do." He pulled on his heavy cotton jacket, then handed Wendell his. "Come on, the faster we get to this, the quicker it will be finished." He paused, "Or would you rather stay in the house and help Miss Puder?" Joseph smiled at Agnes. "Right now, she could use a good hand. She probably does not know where to begin with the work."

Agnes grinned slightly and nodded. To herself, she thought, "He is so right; where do I begin?"

"Come on, Pa, let's go, I am not going to do girls' work."

Joseph glanced over at Agnes as the two walked out of the kitchen. "You finally figured it out, Wendell; our work might be harder and smellier, but it is more interesting."

A bit of coffee remained in the pot. "I need to think." Agnes poured it in a cup, then sat down at the table. "Dear God, where do I start?"

She looked at the ragged curtains, then at the cupboard. The ceiling could stand a clean coat of whitewash. Tiny slivers of bark and sawdust drew an outline around the wood box. The windows, dim with smoke from the cookstove, looked gray. A small pile of laundry was building in the washroom.

"The cupboards." She stood and walked around the table. "The cupboards must be first." The plates, then the cups and glasses began piling high on the kitchen table. Pots and pans were lined up on the benches.

Agnes filled the teakettle and soon had it boiling. Grabbing a piece of homemade white lye soap, she dropped it in a deep graniteware roaster and poured the steaming water over it. She swished a small thick towel around in it, until soapy bubbles built to within an inch of the top of the roaster.

Agnes looked at the cupboard, pushed up her sleeves, and attacked the cabinet with a vengeance. The glass doors turned clear as the warm cloth swiped across them. She slapped soapy water on the outside and the inside. The shelves and outside soon became white. Years of soot from the stove, the candles and the kerosene lamp had turned the cupboard gray.

She stood back to survey her work, then glanced around the room. The wood wainscoting on the lower part of the walls and the doorframes suddenly looked even dirtier. Dark smudgy spots reminded her of the many grubby little hands that passed over the wood.

Agnes bowed her head low. Then with renewed energy, she plowed head-on over the rest of the room. As the grime disappeared from the woodwork, the room grew brighter and brighter. Soapy water splashed on the worn linoleum and made puddles on the floor.

Joseph walked in from outside, and took one look around. "Ah, shucks!" A broad smile crossed his face. "Miss Puder, what have you been doing in here?" Laughter started in the lower part of his throat and bubbled forth. "This room sure does not look as I left it."

Wendell had followed him in. "Gosh, Pa, is this our kitchen?"

"I think so, Son, I think so." His smile searched Agnes' face.

A feeling of pleasure coursed through her veins. "It just took a bit of soapy water and some elbow grease." Smiling, she raised her eyebrows questioningly, "That is a term farmers use, is it not – elbow grease?"

"Soon, you will forget you ever knew the ways of the city, Miss Puder."

"Somehow, I do not think so. Many times I will be reminded of the city ways." She smiled.

"The boy and I have worked up an appetite, and it looks like you have, too." He opened the warmer oven door above the wood cookstove and pulled out a cast-iron skillet. Joseph gasped in embarrassment, "I never noticed before, but it looks like the grease has really built up a thick coating on this." He scratched at the surface of the skillet, but the outside was baked hard. "I guess we can still use it. How about a meal of scrambled eggs and fried potatoes?" His eyes sparkled as he spoke. "We can have a heartier supper this evening when the children are here."

Plopping a lump of hog lard in the skillet, he continued, "I will help you for a few days until you find where everything is kept. Our supply of canned food is getting low, but I think there are several jars of canned beef left." He looked at her for a second. "That is always good."

"I appreciate your help," Agnes answered. She had found the box of potatoes in the pantry. "Just a few minutes and these can be fried." With a few quick turns of her wrist, the potatoes were peeled. The slices hit the hot, melted lard with a popping sizzle. The aroma of food filled the kitchen.

"I am really hungry, Pa." Wendell rubbed his stomach. "I really worked hard in the chicken house. I pitched lots of dirty straw out the door."

His father laughed, "You are a good worker, Son. We really finished that job in a hurry."

The boy beamed, "Miss Puder, I really worked. Now I am hungry."

Agnes scraped the potatoes out of one skillet and the eggs from another. "Dinner is on." She looked at Joseph, "That sounds strange for me to say. In the cities, dinner is the evening meal, and lunch is the noon meal."

Joseph grinned, "I guess we are not as fancy as some of those people, are we?"

She smiled a little, "I would not say that. It is just that customs differ. No one can really say which is the proper way." Agnes walked into the pantry and came back out with a loaf of bread. "Do you have yeast here, Joseph?"

He shrugged. "There may be some baker's yeast in there."

"Never mind, I can cook potatoes tonight, then save the water. It always makes a good yeast. For supper, I can make baking soda biscuits."

The hours of the day flew. Agnes wiped cobwebs from the ceiling. The faded kitchen curtains came down, stiff from dirt and greasy grime. With soapy water, she scrubbed at the inside of the windows until they shone. "I will have to get the outside another time."

Joseph came in for his mid-afternoon cup of coffee.

"Do you have a step-ladder?"

"Why yes," he answered. His eyes mirrored a surprised shock. He looked at her intently. "What do you plan to use it for?"

She opened her hand wide and lifted her arm above her head. Her eyes followed the curve of her arm upward. "To wash the ceiling and the upper wall."

He let out a heavy breath as he, too, looked up. "It does look awfully dirty." His eyes softened. "I think I have been too busy to notice."

"I know," she answered somewhat embarrassed by her own boldness, "I know."

Joseph's soft gaze made her relax. "You have cleaned so much already today; why not slow down and rest? The children will be home soon, and then it will be too noisy for you to take it easy." He added softly, "Miss Puder, I do not expect you to get everything in order the first day. You will have many days to get things organized to your satisfaction."

"I guess so." She smiled weakly.

"I need to do some other things outside, so you can rest." Joseph turned to go. "Come, Wendell, I need your good help."

Agnes sank down onto the wooden chair by the table, and put her head down on her crossed arms. Her eyes clouded with tears. "Whatever am I doing in this place?"

She bit her lip to control her emotions. Soon, her eyes closed and she drifted off into a light slumber.

17

GARDEN TIME

"YESTERDAY WAS A good day to harrow the rest of the garden, William." Joseph walked to the kitchen door and looked outside. "We are fortunate we plowed it before the early April rains." He turned back to the children. "Did all the seeds come yet that we ordered through your school's gardening sale?"

"I think so, Pa," Ellen answered. "I put the seeds in the upstairs closet, as you said."

"Good. They stayed dry there. Bring them down later this morning and we will check to see how much of everything we need. What is not there, Tenison's Market has extra seed." He sat down for a second cup of coffee.

"Miss Puder, have you ever made a garden?"

"My mother always planted just a few peas and beans. We only had a very small space, just a few square feet beside our back door." She poured herself some coffee and sat down across the table from him.

"Breslau had very little open space among the buildings, but there were many open air markets about the city. There were vegetable farms of all kinds outside the city. The farmers always arrived very early in the day, and brought fresh vegetables and fruits to the outside markets. All the produce was so colorful. There were many fruit trees along the roads, too."

She looked off into the distance, as her thoughts crossed the miles and the ocean. "When he was home, my papa would tell my two brothers, my sister and me all about the pretty fields of vegetables and fruit trees outside the city." She paused for a few long minutes, so much so that Joseph soon looked at her more closely.

"Are you all right, Miss Puder?"

Agnes jumped a bit in surprise, and rubbed a stray tear from her cheek. "Forgive me, my mind has wandered far from here. The unexpected thought of my father startled me. It has been so long since he came into my mind."

"Were there mountains around Breslau?"

"Oh, yes, about seventy kilometers to the southwest. There were many copper and coal mines all along in that area. And they also mined some iron ore and zinc. More to the south were the large steel foundries. But in the plains areas right around the city, farmers raised wheat, sugar beets and rye. Papa used to talk about the huge potato fields near Lodz in Poland. He traveled through those areas many times because he inspected horses on the large breeding farms all around Poland. Wealthy people owned the farms." She took a sip of her cooling coffee. "We did not see him much when I was a child, he was away from home so much doing his work."

"So you never were out of the city to see the farms?"

"No, he died when I was only fourteen, and my mother could never afford to take us on a holiday into the country." She paused again in thought, "It was only when I left Breslau to come to America that I saw the farms. Riding through farm fields on the train, I still could not see much."

Joseph smiled, "Miss Puder, since you are now in a farm area, you can see what this kind of life is like." He stopped thoughtfully, "I hope it is not too hard a change for you to make."

A slight smile creased her face. "One question, though, do women do most of the field work here?" She looked at him intently. "Papa always said the women in Germany and Poland did so much of the field work. They cut the wheat with huge scythes, and then built tall thin stacks. As Papa told it, the women then left it stand until the straw dried so they could beat the grain."

Joseph shook his head and laughed. "Sounds like the stories my parents told about Germany. My mother talked about the women going out into the fields, and how she had to help, too, when she was a young girl." He stood up, walked to the stove and refilled his cup. "My mother spoke of the old men sitting under a shade tree at the edge of the field, keeping track of the women. She always laughed when she said, 'Those men probably wanted to make sure the work was done right.'"

Sitting down again, he continued, "But once they came to America, things changed. Much of the land had to be cleared from trees before it could be cultivated, and that was definitely man's work. In the old country, the land had been tilled for centuries." He poured the hot coffee onto his saucer so it would cool. "If the men were not sitting under the trees, they were probably off fighting a war for their landlords, the lords of the castles."

Agnes pushed her cup to the side, and rubbed a spot from the red and white oilcloth on the table. Her face broadened into a smile and her eyes brightened. "Oh yes, that reminds me of something else. Papa talked about rows of haystacks marching across the fields and the farmers herding their sheep. In the background were the snow-capped mountains. He would say if one knew just where to look, old castles were perched all over on hilltops."

Joseph's daughter, Agnes, grew wide-eyed, "Castles, do you mean real castles, Miss Puder?" She moved closer to the elder Agnes, "Castles with real-life princesses and queens?" She put her hand timidly on the older woman's arm. "Did you ever see any of the kings and queens? What did they wear? Were they pretty?" She edged even closer. "Were the castles beautiful? We read in school they were very cold inside, and that is why the people had to wear so much clothes, to keep warm in the winter."

She was all ready to begin another litany of questions when Joseph held up his hand. "My goodness, child, give Miss Puder time to think. Haven't you asked enough questions?"

Agnes smiled at the child. "I never saw any castles, but I have read about the people who lived in them. Someday when we have more time, I will tell you about them."

Joseph jokingly said, "This began as a discussion about the garden. How ever did we get around to castles and fair maidens?" He laughed heartily. "I am sure the potatoes grew six inches just during this question and answer session alone." His eyes twinkled, "I did find the first potato tops sticking out of the straw mulch this morning. You all know what that means; garden time is here."

He stood up, stretched his long legs, and buttoned his jacket. "Come on, everyone, grab your coats and follow me outside. It is time to mark off where we want to plant the vegetables." He looked at the younger girls, "Agnes and Irene, you are now old enough to have your own little garden spot." He tugged at their long braids. "You can have first choice, just as long as it is not smack in the middle of the garden."

"Do I get a garden, Pa?" Wendell grabbed his father's hand.

"Are you ready for that, Son? Everyone who has their own garden has to get chicken manure and spread it around for fertilizer." An ornery grin spread across the father's face.

"Aw, Pa, I am not old enough for that." The youngster stomped out the door ahead of the others. "I think I can help you until I am older."

"Good thinking, Son, good thinking." Joseph turned to Agnes. "Miss Puder, will you join us, please?" He held the door open for her. "We have certain vegetables we plant every year, but if there is something special you would like to grow, we will see if we can get the seeds for you."

"How about asparagus; do you have asparagus?"

"We have a very small patch started, but I can talk to Mrs. Pippen, the neighbor lady to the east. She gave me the start last year; maybe she can give us more."

"That would be nice. Most of the people I cooked for through the years were always anxious for the fresh sprigs of asparagus in the spring." She stepped through the outside porch door ahead of him. "So, asparagus has come to mean spring for me." Her eyes twinkled.

"It has to grow for a year or more, so it can establish a good root base. A new patch cannot be harvested for that time, at least." He smiled, "So, that means one thing, Miss Puder, you will have to stay in Kansas long enough to cut the first stalks of our asparagus crop."

She shrugged her shoulders slightly, and followed the children around the house to the west. She stood there for a long time surveying the huge garden space.

"William, I forgot the ball of string. It is on the shelf by the clock in the kitchen. Run and get it."

"Sure, Pa."

Joseph searched around the spot for a short, fat twig. Then he sat down on his haunches and brushed a spot of soil flat with his hand. With the stick, he drew a rectangle in the dirt.

William barreled out of the house so fast, the porch screen door finally banged after he knelt down beside his father.

Joseph looked at him and winked, "Ready, Son?" William nodded. "Let me see, how about if we plant the lettuce right along the garden edge?" He drew a line the long way in the rectangle. "Hand me the package of lettuce seed, Ellen." He kept drawing line after line, until the rectangle was covered with long lines. Beside each line, he put a sack of seed.

Joseph looked at his children crowded around him and chuckled, "How does this garden look to you?"

They giggled and pushed each other around a bit. Wendell was caught in the middle of the shoving bodies and almost fell over Joseph's back.

"Careful here, all of you, stop the horseplay." The father's voice rang out merrily in the clear spring air. "Oh, I forgot one thing. We need to find a spot for a large patch of asparagus."

Agnes smiled. His warm gaze tugged at her womanly emotions. She hoped he did not notice.

"You did a nice job harrowing the garden, William. The soil looks good. You broke down all the clods."

William grinned, "Yea, Pa, good thing we used Old Star to pull the harrow. That horse was determined we would not miss one clod."

The youngsters giggled again. "Sure, William, we are glad you gave the horse credit for how the garden looks," laughed Ellen. "That way Pa can see every crooked line we make."

Joseph stood up and walked to one edge of the garden and pushed a stake in the ground. "Hand me the ball of string, William." Taking it, he tied the loose end around the stake, then handed the ball back to his son. "Wait until I put a stake at the other side. If you will unwind the string, we can tie it tight over there. Once the string is tightened, we can pull the hoe along the string and leave a little ditch beside it." He winked at the children. "Then we drop in the seeds."

"Ellen, as we mark each row, bring the packages of seed over. Put one at each marker just as we planned it on the little drawing. Agnes and Irene, you can help Ellen pick up the seed envelopes. Take your time and do it right." He turned to the older Agnes, "Would you please help plant, Miss Puder? I will show you how close the seeds should be spread. After we get all the seed in the ground, William and I will take a hoe and a rake and level out the small ditches."

"What can I do, Pa? I want to help." Wendell tugged on his father's pant leg.

"I tell you what, Son. When we get to the bigger seeds for the peas, beans, pumpkins and cucumbers, you can help Miss Puder drop in each seed. She will show you how far apart to spread them. We will make little hills for the pumpkins and cucumbers, and put several seeds in each hill."

"Oh good, Pa, I will be just like a real farmer." He ran back to the housekeeper. "I am going to be a farmer, Miss Puder, a farmer just like Pa."

She nodded slowly, then sighed, "Oh my, another adventure begins."

"Run those chickens out of here, girls." Joseph flapped his arms wildly and yelled at the squawking hens. Then he turned to Agnes and grinned sheepishly. "Those ornery chickens will eat this garden up before it even gets a chance to grow. William and I need to patch up the garden fence. It used to be much better, but the last years, I just could not seem to get around to it."

He looked at her an unusually long time, she noticed. "But things seem to be different now." Joseph reached over and tied another string.

She heard him mutter, "Much different now."

18

BUTTONS, BUTTONS

AGNES WALKED THROUGH the small house and carefully surveyed every detail. The ceilings had been swept clean of cobwebs. Grimy handprints had been washed from the woodwork and walls. The linoleum on the floors had been scrubbed to within a fraction of any remaining color.

"Later on," she muttered softly, "when Joseph can afford it, everything needs to be whitewashed." She looked around at the floor. "And he might even consider getting some new floor covering. This has had every bit of wear taken out of it."

Looking at the large rugs in the parlor and bedrooms, she grimaced. The dirt in them must have been several years' accumulation. "It was quite a fog of dust we beat out of them." She bent over to brush one of the flower bouquets on the well-worn parlor carpet. "I cannot believe how the pink of the roses has brightened after being cleaned." A glance in the downstairs bedroom met with her approval also. "The woven rag rugs look much brighter, too."

The mattresses had been taken outside and beaten, then wiped clean. The slats on the beds were washed with soapy water. Every piece of bedding and all the linens in the house had been boiled in lye soap and hot water, and then hung outside in the sun to bleach white. The wash lines sagged under the wet weight of it all, but tightened up again after the Kansas wind whipped the large sheets of muslin dry.

Joseph had looked at all the bedding flapping and swaying in the bright May sunlight and marveled, "Those sheets probably did not look that white the day Katherine made them." He grinned, "I have never

111

known a woman with such a penchant for cleanliness." He stepped into the kitchen surprised, staring in amazement. "The house even smells clean."

In the early morning coolness of the next day, Agnes opened the front door of the parlor. The soft whisper of the south breeze caused the curtains to sway. The gentle wind of the outdoors gently caressed her face.

"Ah, the sweetness of the May air." A wave of loneliness for her homeland swept over her. Tears filled her eyes. Just then, Joseph came in the room from the kitchen.

"It is such a beautiful morning," he said ever so softly. "The trees and bushes are all in bloom, and the meadowlarks are really singing."

She turned to look at him. He noticed a wayward tear, and reached over to brush it from her cheek.

"I was just thinking about the Mai Luft in Germany. The May air was always so full of the fragrances of the flowers and new growth. People went out walking very early in the morning to enjoy it. My mother always said the May air was the sweetest air of the whole year."

"I also remember my grandmother telling me a little about that when I was a child. But I had forgotten it, until now that you mentioned it." Joseph stepped back and sat down on the large wooden rocker. "I doubt the air smells much different in May here in Kansas, than it did in Germany." He rocked back and forth several times. "But there the similarity ends, especially when the Kansas heat comes in the summer months."

Sobs began to well up in her throat. Never before had the longing to be back in Germany surfaced with such persistence. She turned her head so Joseph would not see her feelings that seemed so apparent on her face. "If you excuse me, I do think I will take a walk around the farm, and just drink in the sweetness of the morning."

Joseph nodded as he watched her go out through the front door. He sensed her growing uneasiness around him. The rocker squeaked and groaned as he pushed it forward and back. His thoughts tumbled at random, from his early boyhood to the past few days. Thoughts of the new lady in his house stirred emotions he had not felt since Katherine's death.

Back and forth, back and forth he rocked. "What do I do? Agnes has only been here a few weeks, yet it feels like I have known her for years."

Joseph looked around the room again and again. Each time he saw another thing that Agnes had taken care of. "Such little details," he marveled, "but she has noticed them all." He finally got out of the chair and walked through the kitchen and into the screened-in porch. From there, he watched Agnes stroll slowly around the yard.

She stopped and bent over to pick up something he could not clearly see. He squinted his eyes to look harder. "What is she collecting? There are no flowers out there."

Agnes walked around in a daze. "What is there about Joseph's gaze that unsettles me?" A shudder ran through her body. "I must keep my emotions in control." The thought caused her reflexes to react and her fingers squeezed in a tight fist. "Remember, Agnes, you are here just as a housekeeper. That is all, nothing more."

A piece of cloth fluttered in the soft breeze. She bent over to pull it out of the purple blooms of henbit. "Another project for me someday." Agnes turned the tiny piece over and found small white buttons on the material. "Just what I can use."

A sudden explosion of colorful scraps of cloth seemed to erupt everywhere around her. "I wonder why these are strewn around?" The morning dew had settled on more buttons, and they sparkled like diamonds in the sun. Another scrap, more buttons. Soon Agnes was bobbing up and down, snatching at the grass.

Her apron pockets began to bulge with scraps, with and without buttons. With hurried step, Agnes started for the house. "This will keep me busy for several days." She caught herself smiling at her own words. "As though my work here is almost finished."

Wendell slammed the screen door open and stood there with his mouth wide open. Joseph stepped through the porch door just as she came to it. His eyes twinkled and a wide grin spread across his face. "Miss Puder, what did you find so interesting out there?"

Her eyebrows arched in surprise, then relaxed into a shy smile. "Bits of material with many buttons." She cleared her throat somewhat embarrassed. "Something I can use to repair the children's clothing."

A shocked look crossed the man's face. "I had no idea buttons were in such short supply in our house." He wiped his hand over his chin, "Katherine always seemed to have enough."

"But, Joseph, that was several years ago. I doubt Katherine would have tossed rags around that still had perfectly good buttons attached."

A faraway look crossed over Joseph's face and clouded his eyes. For several seconds, his thoughts slipped back into a life that had been. Then he became aware of Agnes' gaze. "I am sorry. It has been so hard these last years. When she passed away, a large part of my world died with her."

Agnes reached forward and put her hand on his arm. "Do not feel you have to explain, Joseph. You have no need to apologize to me. Katherine was your beloved wife and the mother of your children." She gently squeezed his arm. "Your love for her will never die. It will always hold a special place in your heart and in your life."

Joseph put his hand over hers, and smiled at her tenderly. "You are right. She will always be a part of me."

He slipped past Agnes and out into the morning sunlight. The bench under the big elm tree by the back door looked inviting. He sat down, and dropped his head down into his cupped hands. Quietly he sat there, in deep thought. Wendell scooted out the door and plopped himself down on the grass next to the bench. He looked up at his father, but kept quiet. The boy had never seen his father cry, but he now heard the stifled sobs.

Agnes leaned against the doorframe, and watched the scene between father and son. Her heart filled with sorrow for Joseph, but she had to keep her distance. This was a special moment for the widower. It was in May that his Katherine had died.

Agnes lowered her eyes in respect. Her heartstrings tugged for the man, but her thoughts reminded her, "Joseph must face this moment alone. If he is to face the future, he must feel his emotions now."

The three of them were there in each other's presence, but still totally within their own minds, their own worlds of thought. The silence intensified with each passing moment. Only nature spoke in that time.

A slight breeze rustled the new leaves of a nearby cottonwood tree. The buzz of eager bees seeking out spring blossoms grew louder. Meadowlarks sensed the scene and the stillness, and tried desperately to fill the interlude with their song. People-loving robins glided down from their leafy perches and looked in the grass for bugs near Joseph's feet.

But still, the silence of the man and his son, and the woman was deafening, save only by an escaping sob of the father. Wendell wrapped his small arm around his pa's ankle and looked up into his face. Never had the youngster been so silent.

Finally, Joseph dropped his hands from his face to ruffle the dark hair of his son. Wendell squeezed his ankle tightly and watched his father. The man raised the back of his hand to brush away tears that rolled down his puffed cheeks.

Father and son were in a separate world, completely oblivious to Agnes. In that moment, she deeply sensed the loss of her own former love and the sorrow of losing him. But, in her heart, she knew Joseph's loss was even greater, for he had felt not only Katherine's kiss, but also her close intimacy. Their children were the proof.

An eternity seemed to pass, at least for the woman. Slowly, Joseph raised his face to her and his soft hazel eyes spoke a multitude of feelings. He choked back another escaping sob. "I just never thought about buttons when Katherine was here." He shrugged his shoulders ever so slightly, then went on, "A man never thinks much about buttons, that is, until after his wife has gone."

She nodded knowingly.

Joseph loosened his son's arms from his own strong ankles and heaved his supple body from the wooden bench. Looking down at the young boy, he smiled slightly. "Wendell, that sounds like a good chore for you to do."

"What is that, Pa?" He stood up to be nearer to his father.

"See all those tiny pieces of cloth stuck in the grass?"

"Sure, Pa."

"Go around and pick them all up and bring them to Miss Puder, so she can use the buttons."

"Aw, Pa." The boy's voice rose in pitch to a whine. "Do I have to?"

The man put his hand on the boy's shoulder. "It should not take long. I will help. If we at least get most of the scraps gathered, it will help Miss Puder." He slid his hand down and patted his son on the back, then grinned. "If we can find enough buttons for her to sew on, our shirts will stay closed." He pinched Wendell's ear playfully. "Almost nothing is worse than a shirt that does not have all its buttons."

Wendell tugged at Joseph's arm. "A race, Pa, how about a race to see who finds the most scraps?" Joseph laughed out loud.

Agnes had turned to go into the house, but when she heard Joseph laugh, it surprised her. Startled, she turned around to look at the two. "What is so funny?"

Before the older one could answer, Wendell jumped up and down. "We are going to have a race to see who can find the most buttons." He looked up at his father. "And I will win, Pa, 'cause I can run around faster than you."

"The race is on, Son." The man and the boy sprinted out from under the shade of the big elm tree and across the yard.

Agnes stood there with her hand cupped over her mouth. "I never expected that kind of reaction." She walked on into the kitchen, chuckling to herself. With a new reverence for the dead woman, she took Katherine's old sewing basket down from the cupboard shelf.

The housekeeper looked at the basket's contents more closely. "I wonder what Katherine was like?" There was no semblance of order to the thread and needles. "This really does not tell me if she was neat or not. Who knows how many have rummaged through this basket since her death." With patient care, she untangled stray threads from a small, dull scissors, then began to snip buttons from the scraps of material. Methodically, she sorted the buttons into small piles, by size and color.

"Looks like most of these are either white or black." Agnes pushed several colored buttons to the side. "Guess I should not be surprised that there are no unusual ones here. Much too frugal for fancier buttons, I think."

As she cut more buttons, she looked closer at the material. "Only cottons," she mused, "no need for too many beautiful fabrics out here on the plains." Picking up a pink and white gingham piece, the thought occurred to her, "Or maybe Katherine just never sewed any of the nicer fabrics. Two expensive, perhaps."

Joseph and Wendell came in, carrying two large buckets, each almost full of colorful bits of material. "I do not think we missed one piece," laughed Joseph.

"And I picked up more than Pa," chimed in Wendell.

"Yes, Son." Joseph grinned and patted the young boy on the back. "You did not have so far to bend over to pick them up."

For several days, Agnes kept unusually busy. In between baking bread, cleaning young spring chickens for supper and working in the large garden, she sewed on buttons and mended the family's torn clothing.

"You have certainly fixed us up, Agnes." Joseph sat down at the kitchen table across from her. "I really appreciate all your work."

"Thank you," she smiled. "There are some of the girls' dresses here that I am not sure just what to do with." She held one up for him to see. "The elbows are really threadbare, but the rest of the dress is still very good." Putting the dress down on the table, she continued, "I do have an idea, but I am not sure how the girls will accept it."

"What is that?" The fatherly concern in his soft eyes twirled her emotions.

She squeezed the sleeve of the dress in her hands, hoping she hid her feelings.

Pushing the garment closer to him, she folded the sleeve under above the torn elbow. "If I cut the sleeves off about here and hem them under, the dress will still be good to wear." She cocked her head to the side, "But I do not know how the girls will feel about wearing short sleeves. In the cities, I have seen it occasionally."

Pulling the dress back to herself, she said, "In Chicago, I bought several dresses made that way, and still have them."

For several minutes, Joseph sat there and thought about what she proposed. Lifting his head slowly, he answered, "If it means the girls will be able to get more wear out of these, it is agreeable with me." Taking the dress back, he folded under the torn part of one of the sleeves. "That should be no problem; school will be out soon. The weather will also be getting warmer. Then when it gets closer to school starting in the fall, perhaps we could buy them several new dresses." He paused, then looked at her directly, "Or do you sew?"

She nodded, "Yes."

19

THE SLEEVE ORDEAL

THE PORCH SCREEN door banged shut as the children hurried in from school. It had taken them longer than usual to get home. Most of the time, Joseph had William take the horse and wagon. But with the spring work starting on the farm, he needed the wagon. "Walk home from school today," Joseph had told them.

With the flowers in bloom, and buzzing bees and colorful butterflies to pay attention to, the three-mile walk and the time grew longer. The creek that ran through the farm on the east side of the barn was always a good detour. Shiny, orange and purple pumpkinseed perch turned the water into gold. Large frogs hid among the weeds on the banks. To scare one up meant a large splash in the water.

Finally, they made it to the house. The four thirsty children walked in and dropped their books and syrup-bucket lunch pails on the table with a loud thud.

Agnes put the repaired dresses on the girls' beds and looked at them. She felt anxious, perhaps, because of the growing resentment she sensed building in Ellen. Agnes did not want to alienate the girl, but it seemed no matter what she did, the other took it wrong. Never in her life could she remember feeling this way. Her mind spun in circles.

"Why do I feel like this?" She wiped beads of perspiration from her forehead, although it was a pleasant day in May. "I actually feel queasy, and that is not normal." She rubbed her hands and fingers together nervously. "And all I did was shorten the sleeves on several dresses."

The thin springs of Ellen's bed squeaked under Agnes' weight as she sat down. The quiet of the room settled around her until the sound of the screen door banging broke her reverie. The laughter and bantering of the children's voices drifted up the staircase to her.

Agnes turned the rusty doorknob on the upstairs room, and slowly descended the narrow steps and walked into the kitchen. "Hello, everyone," she said with feigned gaiety. "How was your school day?" She took the books from the younger girls and put them at the corner of the table. "Your Pa found some nice fresh lemons at the market this morning. As soon as you change your clothes, come back downstairs. I will have a pitcher of cool lemonade waiting for you."

The stairs groaned as the children clomped up to their rooms. Agnes could hear the bedsprings squeak as each child flopped onto their beds.

Ellen picked up her dress from the bed and shrieked, "What is this? What has happened to my dress?"

She jumped up and scrambled over to Irene and Agnes Marie's bed and grabbed their folded dresses from the foot of their bed. Picking up each dress at the shoulders, she whipped them open and stared at them. "I can not believe this," Ellen thundered. "Look what she did. Your sleeves." She stomped her foot hard on the floorboards. "That woman has ruined your dresses, too. Will she never quit? She is not even our Ma, and she is already trying to change us."

The younger girls just sat there, with their eyes growing wider and wider. "What is wrong, Ellen?" Agnes Marie asked with a whimper.

"She cut the sleeves off our dresses." Ellen stomped around the room, holding a dress in each hand. "Why did she do that?" The oldest girl threw them down on the floor and shouted, "I will not wear a dress with short sleeves. The other girls will make fun of me." She threw down another dress, "I hate her, hate her."

The housekeeper heard the commotion and climbed the stairs. "May I come in, girls?"

"No," Ellen barked. "No, no."

"Please, may I come in? I want to talk to you."

"No, no, no!" snarled Ellen. "Go away."

Agnes Marie felt bad and started to cry. Finally, she decided to open the door. "Yes, Miss Puder." The girl slumped back down on the bed, and sniffed through her tears, "Ellen does not like short sleeves on her dress."

Agnes leaned against the door. "Please, girls, let me explain why I did that. Perhaps, when you hear the reason, you will understand."

Ellen turned her face to the wall. She did not want to hear a word the housekeeper had to say.

"Your father and I talked about the condition of your dresses. The elbows were so threadbare and torn; there was no way to mend them. I could not find matching material here in the house to fix them. And a different color print cloth would not have looked good." She moved to pick the dresses off the floor. "Since school is almost out for the summer, I decided to shorten the sleeves and hem them under. There is a little lace in the sewing basket, so if you like, perhaps we could add some to make the sleeves longer." She smiled at the two younger girls. "If I had more time, I could crochet lace for the sleeves, but right now, the garden and chickens need tending every day."

Ellen grumbled under her breath. She stared at the wall, but after a time, she finally rolled over to look at the older woman. With icy sarcasm, she asked, "So, Miss Puder, what will you do about our dresses when school starts in the fall?"

Agnes tried to smooth out the wrinkles on the dresses, and then hung them on hangers and put them in the girls' wardrobe. She turned around to face them. "Your father said he wants all of you to have some new dresses. During the summer, we will take you into the village, so each of you can pick out two or three pieces of fabric. Then I will make you new dresses for the coming school year." She paused for a few minutes, thinking when her three-month trial period would be over, then went on, "Perhaps, I can even teach each of you to sew a little."

Ellen sneered, "I would like boughten dresses."

"We can see about that, perhaps. That is up to your pa."

"I want a yellow one," Irene squealed. Agnes Marie added, "Make me a pale blue, Miss Puder."

The housekeeper laughed, "We will see what we can find." She turned to open the door, "Come down and have some nice cool lemonade."

Irene jumped up from the bed. "Wait for me, Miss Puder." Agnes held the door open for her, as the little girl reached up to take her hand.

The next morning came too quickly for Agnes. Breakfast time again. The smell of cured bacon and fried eggs filled the kitchen. The heat

121

from the wood-burning cookstove took the chill of the May morning out of the room. William had been out with Joseph feeding the livestock. The girls came bustling downstairs and pushed in around the table, finding their places by the long benches.

"It is Friday. I love Fridays at school. Sister Hermina always lets us have a spelling bee." Agnes Marie slipped along the length of the bench to her place at the table.

Irene giggled, "We always have to remember a little poem for Fridays, and get to get up in front of the class and recite it."

"I hate spelling bees, ciphering tests and reciting," Ellen growled. "I will be glad when school is over for the summer." She went into the parlor to look for her books.

Joseph came in the door, and Irene twirled around so he could see, "Look at my dress with the short sleeves, Pa. My arms feel so cool." He smiled at his young daughter.

Agnes Marie rubbed her bare arms, "I like them, too." She looked at Agnes. "I know none of the other girls will have sleeves like these."

Ellen walked back in the kitchen and banged her books down on the table with all the strength she could muster. "I just know what the other girls are going to say. I can hear it now." She wrinkled up her nose. "Snooty Susie will ask me if the scissors slipped. And then Marion will say in her nicey, nice way, 'Oh, Ellen, what happened to your sleeves? Why doesn't your dress have sleeves like the rest of ours?'"

"Now, Ellen, in a few weeks you will be out of school for the summer. Try not to be so upset." Joseph grinned at her.

She glared at him, and then Agnes. "I will try, Pa." Her voice was curt and cold. Joseph pretended not to notice.

He finished eating the last of his bacon, eggs and soda biscuits, and looked at Agnes. "That was a good breakfast, Miss Puder, as usual." He turned to the youngsters, "I will take you to school this morning, and you can walk home. The weather is getting warmer."

Joseph did not say anything on the way to school; he just liked to listen to his children talk. "They sure are not as quiet as their mother was; she was so shy." He stopped the wagon and let the children climb out. They all waved to him, then turned to run into the school. He turned the horse and wagon around in the churchyard and headed back to the farm.

The elderly school principal, Sister Philomenia, stood at the door and rang the brass school bell with a hefty swing. "Good morning, children. Put your lunch pails in the cloakroom and line up to go to morning Mass. Father Manz wants to begin early, so he can leave soon after."

Ellen and William hurried to the back of the line where the older pupils waited. He pushed in next to his best friend, Jake. Ellen tried to slip in among the girls hoping no one would notice her short sleeves.

One girl after another poked each other, and then pointed at Ellen's dress. The giggles began softly, then grew in volume. "Ellen, where are your sleeves?" laughed Lena.

Rosie pulled on Ellen's belt and untied it. "Who cut up your dress like that?"

Ellen twirled around in anger and grabbed the ends to tie her belt again.

"So, Ellen, who did that to your sleeves?" Pauline snickered.

Ellen glared at the girls, "It is that foreign woman Pa has in the house. She thought we needed the sleeves cut off, because she could not mend them." She stomped her foot. "That woman was even too lazy to look for leftover scrap material from our dresses to fix the sleeves." Ellen tugged at her sleeves. "She told Pa she could not find any. You would think that was too much work for her." She twisted around to keep up with the moving line. "Cutting off the sleeves was much easier," Ellen said sarcastically, as she tried to pull her sleeves down more. I hate that woman. All she does is boss us around, 'Do this, do that.'"

The class passed Sister Philomenia. "Quiet, girls," she demanded.

A tear slipped out and trickled down Ellen's cheek. She grumbled so those around her could hear, "I wish that woman would leave us. Oh, how I wish Mama was still here."

"Ellen," Sister spoke again. "Quiet."

"But, Sister."

"I will speak with you later." The nun hurried up to the front of the line where the younger children were.

"You almost got in trouble," hissed Lena. "Serves you right, coming to school with short sleeves. That is like half a dress. Wait until I tell my ma about this."

Ellen made a face and stuck out her tongue at Lena just as they entered the church. Sister Philomenia's spectacles had slipped down low on her nose as she looked over them at the girls. She did not catch Ellen, but she did hear the whispering. "There should be no talking." The girls did not dare utter another word. It would mean a slap across the knuckles with Sister's wooden ruler when they got back in the classroom.

It was time for school to take up, so the principal rang the school's brass bell once again. "Pupils, get in your seats quietly." She eyed the squirming boys to get her order across. "Take out your penmanship tablets and practice your circles. We will begin class in a few minutes."

Sister Philomenia motioned for Ellen to come into the small cloak-room next to the classroom. She looked at the girl sternly. "I want to know what all the commotion was about earlier."

"Nothing, Sister." Ellen tried to shrink closer to the wall, but a metal coat hanger poked her in the back.

"There was something, and I want to know what." The nun looked at her intently. "You are not going back into the classroom until I find out what it was." She brought her face closer to the girl's. Her spectacles had slipped down on her long, slender nose again. Her grimace was the most threatening Ellen had ever seen.

Ellen tried to stifle the big sob building in her throat.

"Well?" Sister questioned her impatiently.

"They made fun of me because the sleeves on my dress have been shortened."

"I see," said Sister. "And why is that?"

The words tumbled out in a rush as she spilled out the reason. "That foreign woman at our house cut them off." Ellen choked back the tears. "Oh, Sister, I wish Mama was still here. Why did she have to die?" Then her emotions broke and spewed forth like a crack in a long pent-up dam.

The old nun gently put her hands upon the girl's shoulder. "Cry, Ellen, just cry."

Ellen cried and cried and cried, like her heart would break. Sister wanted to cry for her, for she, too, had lost her mother when she was just a young girl. She held Ellen close. When the tears became fewer, she lifted the girl's face up so she could look into her eyes.

"You have every right to feel as you do about your mother. But you must also consider your father and how he has felt since your mother's death." She stroked the dampness from Ellen's cheek. "He does not love your mother any less than when she was alive. But, he has all you young children and needs help. This 'foreign woman,' as you call her, is most likely the help he needs." She smiled at Ellen. "Your short sleeves do not look bad. They are better to be that way than full of holes." Sister wiped Ellen's eyes with her own white handkerchief and pulled the girl close to her heavy bosom. "Come now, we need to begin ciphering class."

Ellen gave a weak smile and nodded.

Early the next week, Agnes had a visitor at the farm. She heard the dog bark, and looked out the kitchen door.

The woman's shrill voice split the air, "Whoa, Hannah." She gathered her skirts about her legs and jumped down from the wagon. With an angry twist, she tied the horses' reins around the wagon post. "Hmmph," she growled. "This place looks cleaner than it has been for years. Poor Joseph, that city woman is already telling him what to do." She stomped up the walk and banged on the porch screen door.

Agnes had already walked out into the porch. As she opened the screen door, an unexpected outburst greeted her.

The woman pushed past Agnes and stomped on into the kitchen. Then she turned around to confront the housekeeper. "Tell me, Miss Puder," stormed Lena's mother, "just what is your idea of shortening the girls' sleeves?"

Before Agnes had a chance to answer, Joseph came in the kitchen door. "Minnie, I saw your horse out there. What are you doing here?"

The woman backed up against the table and tried to find the seat of a nearby chair. "I came to see what she had done to Ellen's dress." She sniffed loudly. "My sisters and I do not like this being done. Our daughters should not go around exposing their arms."

Joseph's pleasant manner disarmed her for the moment. "Now, Minnie, I think you are all upset over a very small matter." He turned to Agnes. "This is Katherine's younger sister, Minnie. Minnie, meet Agnes Puder."

"Yes, I have seen you. I know who you are." Minnie brushed a strand of loose hair from her forehead defiantly. "It made me so angry when Lena told me about Ellen's sleeves. Don't you know, out here in

125

the harsh Kansas sun, we like for the girls to have long sleeves? It keeps their arms from getting brown. We like our girls to have milky white skin. No young man wants to marry a girl that has brown, shriveled-up skin. Don't you know those things?"

Agnes took a deep breath as she sat down at the table. "I understand. It is not common here, but in the cities, I have seen girls wear their sleeves shortened. I have even worn two dresses that way myself. I have them in my closet, and plan to wear them."

"Now, Minnie," Joseph said as he sat down also. "Before you go blaming all this on Miss Puder, I want you to know that she and I discussed the shape of the girls' dresses. The elbows were torn out and needed lots of repair. She could not find any matching material here in the house, and did not want to just patch them up with anything. That would not have looked good, and would have been even more embarrassing to the girls." He reached over to touch her hand. "You mean well, I know, but Miss Puder did that with my permission." He paused for a few seconds, "And I think you need to let your sisters know that also."

She sat there for a long time, very quietly. Finally, she looked at Joseph. "Maybe there is more to my anger than I want to admit." She lowered her head and looked down at her hands. Self-consciously, she rubbed and rubbed her fingers. Then she looked again at her former brother-in-law. "Joseph, it is hard for me to see someone else take Katherine's place." Then she looked at Agnes. In a cold hard voice, she went on, "I have seen you in church on Sundays." She cleared her throat before continuing, "Forgive me for not making your acquaintance. I should have, but I just could not."

"I am just the housekeeper," replied Agnes politely.

Minnie nodded solemnly, then gave a nervous chuckle. "Lena wants me to shorten the sleeves of her dresses."

Joseph laughed out loud. Agnes looked at him surprised, for she had not heard him do that often. "Agnes, look what you have instilled in these young girls' minds."

Agnes smiled at him, then stood and went to the cabinet where she kept the cookies. Putting them on the table in front of Minnie, she said, "I just baked a fresh batch of raisin cookies this morning. Be my guest, please."

"Thanks for the cookies, Agnes. Please forgive my actions." Minnie walked to the door. "I must go now, but I will probably see you at Mass, Sunday." She walked into the porch, then turned around and sort of laughed, "Lena might get her wish. Those short sleeves would make a dress much cooler in the heat of summer. She has one or two old ones that we might try first, and see how she likes them that way." She opened the porch screen door to go, but hesitated once again. "I have several older dresses, also. I might get scissor-happy with them, too." She laughed, and walked out to her wagon.

Sunday morning after Mass, Minnie walked out past the pew where Joseph and Agnes and the children still sat. She grinned as she went by.

After most everyone had gone, Agnes finally stood to go. She opened her white sun umbrella as she walked out of the small vestibule and out on the front church step. Waiting for her was Sister Philomenia.

"Miss Puder," the nun spoke in a soft voice as she extended her hand. "I would like to make your acquaintance."

Agnes stopped to greet her. "I am so pleased to meet you. The children talk about you so much."

The nun smiled, and then went on, "I had a most interesting talk with Ellen a week ago."

The housekeeper smiled and her eyes twinkled. "No doubt, about the shortened sleeves."

"Quite frankly, yes." Sister said. "I did not know Mr. Linnebur had another housekeeper. These last years he hired older girls, but usually neighboring farm girls." She stopped as if to find the right words. "It was very sad for him that none of them stayed very long."

Agnes nodded. "That would be quite difficult for a very young person to go in and try to take care of five children, plus all the chores. It has been most challenging even for me."

"But the last month or so, I wondered about the help he must have there." Sister suddenly found herself at a loss for words. She stammered and cleared her throat.

Agnes realized the nun's embarrassment. "Yes, Sister, it has been about six weeks ago that I came here from Chicago. I saw his advertisement in a German paper there, asking for a housekeeper."

"Oh," Sister smiled. "I have noticed the difference in the last few weeks."

"Why is that?"

"The children's clothing is so much cleaner." She smiled meekly. "And missing buttons have been replaced."

"Yes," laughed Agnes, "and sleeves have been shortened."

Sister then relaxed and gave her a wide smile. "You are doing a marvelous job." She cleared her throat, and then put her hand on Agnes' arm. "I knew there had to be an older woman in the house."

Agnes smiled. "Oh, yes, much to the chagrin of the oldest daughter."

"But, in time, she will realize the true situation," Sister Philomenia predicted.

20

HEART'S SONG

"COME IN, JOSEPH, come in."

Father Manz closed the rectory door behind Joseph and ushered him into the office. The priest motioned to a large leather chair for the farmer, while he sat in a tall wooden-back chair behind his desk.

"What can I help you with today, Joseph?"

Joseph pushed himself back further in the chair. He looked at the wrinkles of his large hands for a few moments; then, finally, up at the pastor.

"I need some advice, Father." He groped for words, "You probably have seen Miss Puder in church with us on Sundays?"

"Yes, I have. The lady who answered your advertisement for a housekeeper, is that right?"

Joseph nodded.

"Quite a comely lady, my friend." The priest leaned forward on his desk. "So, Joseph, has she become more than just a housekeeper to you?"

Joseph shuffled his feet nervously. "I never thought it would come to this, Father. I did not advertise for a 'mail-order bride,' and I certainly never had any intention of marrying again."

A look of uncertainty covered his face, "That is, until several weeks ago. Miss Puder came into my house the second week of April. At first, she was simply the housekeeper I hired. But, as the days passed, I became aware of feelings that have not been there for several years."

Joseph lifted his left hand and wiped his face, from his brow to his chin. A heavy sigh escaped his lips. "I am not quite sure of where my feelings should go. It has not been that long since I met her. And, yet, it is as though she has been in my life forever. Every waking moment seems centered around her. I hate to leave the house, and I hurry back to be by her side."

Father Manz leaned back in his chair. "Are you feeling guilty, Joseph?" He paused for several seconds, then continued. "Do you feel you are being untrue to Katherine by recognizing your feelings?"

"I think so, Father. These emotions were not in my thoughts at first. She was to be strictly my hired help. After Katherine died, I felt there was no life left for me. I did not want to think of the emptiness that would come later."

Father Manz nodded, but let Joseph continue.

"Agnes is so different from other women I have known. She reads a lot and is self-taught. She is interested in so many more things than most of the women is this area." Joseph laughed self-consciously, "Agnes is much better than I am about keeping up with what is going on in this country and the world." Joseph raised his eyebrows in a questioning way. "She certainly does not hold back her opinions and can, and will, argue politics with the best of men." He stopped to take a deep breath. "She thinks through her views and speaks her mind, whether one wants to hear it or not."

Joseph realized his ramblings and, somewhat embarrassed, looked down at his intertwined fingers clenched in his lap. Father Manz watched him intently, silently marveling at the farmer's thoughtfulness.

Joseph felt the priest's gaze and lifted his eyes to smile hesitantly. "Agnes is a very smart woman and she is certainly not shy about it." He hesitated once again, then smiled at the thought of her. "Her entire view of life is so very broad-minded and interesting. She challenges me to think more than I have for years." His gaze swept past the priest to look out the rectory window. His reverie lasted for a minute or two, when he slipped back to the present. "Father, she just makes me feel so alive again. Being with her opens a whole new world to me."

The priest did not say anything. Joseph was answering his own question.

Then Joseph stopped, embarrassed for talking on so. "Forgive me, Father. Perhaps what I am looking for is approval."

"Why do you say that?"

"Because of her forwardness and outspoken manner, many women do not like her. That is a worry to me."

"My good man, other women are actually jealous of her because of her ways." Father Manz leaned forward on his desk. "She has developed this sense of willpower and confidence because of her past. These other women have never wandered far from the mother that nurtured them. They have not left their homeland alone, or crossed the ocean to go to a land where they knew no one. And to learn a new language and live in the large cities of America."

His voice became louder to prove his point. "Why, Joseph, Agnes has accomplished more demanding challenges in her 33 years than all of these other women around here will ever do in their combined lifetimes. Of course, they are jealous. They feel threatened and inadequate, for they know her knowledge will never be theirs."

Joseph sighed. "Perhaps, what really matters is how Katherine's family will feel. One of her sisters has already made known to Agnes her opinion." He squirmed from side to side in his chair. "I do not want hard feelings."

The priest stood and came around in front of his desk to face Joseph.

"You are much too kind and too considerate, Joseph. This is your life, not theirs. This may sound hard, Joseph, but when Katherine died, so did any obligations you had toward her family. You loved your wife, Joseph, and it was always apparent. Your heart was always full of concern for her and her family. But that has changed now."

His voice softened, "You will always have a love and special fondness for her in your heart. But, by her death, God chose to end that physical love you had for her. He gave you six children to always remind you of your years together." The priest sat down in the other leather chair beside Joseph. "Katherine is no longer here for you or for her children. You must keep that in mind."

"Surely, there will be talk that Miss Puder and I have not known each other long enough, that we do not know each other well enough."

Father Manz put his hand on Joseph's arm. "Why do you trouble yourself with what others think? After three years of trying to manage a family with young, inexperienced housekeepers, God has seen fit to bring a mature, capable woman into your life, into your home." He paused. "Have you thought about why this has come about? She has come all this distance, into your house because of a series of interesting and unexplainable consequences."

He squeezed Joseph's arm. "Do you love her?" He leaned closer to the farmer and looked at him intently. "Can you give to her a love that is solely and completely for her?" The priest paused, then went on softly, "If you can, than so be it. But if you cannot, then it would be best to terminate her employment and ask her to leave your house."

Joseph nodded while the priest continued.

"You have lived these last few weeks with Agnes always there. If you have awakened in the night and imagined or wished for her to be beside you, then, Joseph, the short time that you have spent together is of no consequence." He paused. "Does she feel about you as you seem to feel about her?"

The widower rubbed his strong fingers together, and then looked directly at Father Manz. "I sense a warmth from her, a caring that was not there when she first came. There is something." Joseph shrugged. "A feeling of emotion has grown between us. I do not know if she feels love for me, but I must find out soon, or ... " He straightened his broad shoulders and leaned hard against the chair. "I will have to ask her to leave my house." A pained look crossed his face. "Father, that would be so difficult now. She is a good woman, and so caring in every way." He smiled, "And a good cook."

Father Manz laughed, "That is very important, to have a good cook."

Joseph grew solemn again. "She is such a strong woman in her ways and thinking, so unlike Katherine. But I like that about her." He stopped, slipped into deep thought, then spoke with conviction, "She gives my life an excitement I have never known."

"You have answered your own questions, Joseph."

He stood and shook the priest's hand, "Thank you, Father Manz, thank you many times."

Joseph climbed into the wagon and pulled on the horses' reins lightly.

"How do I approach Agnes with this? She may feel it is too soon. Maybe she will mistake my intentions as too forward." Even though his muscles twitched with nervousness, he whistled a little ditty. Then he broke into a bit of a song, "It has been a short time, maybe too short, but so be it." The sky suddenly seemed a much deeper blue to him.

The he realized it was her letters that first intrigued him. Her written word was the reason he chose her over the other women who had written. A smile crossed over his face and his hazel eyes twinkled. It had finally struck him, "Agnes became a part of me before we ever met in person."

Thoughts tumbled in rapid succession through his mind. The breeze seemed more brisk, the horses stepped higher and the song of the birds was sweeter. For the first time, he really noticed the flowers along the roadside. "Ah, the fragrance of the flowers in the May air." He laughed. "Or, as Agnes would say, the 'Mai Luft.' "

The three miles to the farm seemed to take longer than ever before. He could not seem to hurry the horses along fast enough. The team finally reached his farm and turned into the driveway without any direction from him. They could always be trusted to bring him safely home.

Snowy white sheets and lines of colored clothes flopped and swayed in the soft May air. Agnes stood among the rainbows of colored cloth. With her arms raised above her head, she hooked a wooden clothespin on the line to anchor another garment against the wind.

The sight of her thrilled him and sent a shiver through his body. Goosebumps rose on his arms under his long-sleeved shirt, even though the day was pleasant and warm. June was only a day away.

"Oh, Agnes, if you should turn away from my request ..." He shuddered to think what his reaction would be if she did so.

Agnes came around the house just as the horses stopped by the porch door. Joseph tipped his felt hat and grinned at her. "Good afternoon, Madam. Are you the lady of the manor? I have some nice vanilla today, and lots of new pots and pans for you to choose from." His eyes twinkled.

"Mr. Linnebur," she said, "since when have you become a peddler hawking your wares from farm to farm?" Her merry laughter filled the air and fell down around Joseph like sprinkles of crushed diamonds. She started to walk inside the house, then turned to look back at him.

He leapt out of the wagon with the agility of lost youth. In a smooth sequence of quick movements, he bowed gallantly to her, and bounded up the path to the porch entrance. He leaned over and swooped up his clean, dry shirt that had fallen from the clothesbasket she carried, and then swung open the screen door for her to enter.

She giggled like a schoolgirl as she moved past him. "Kind Sir, what ever is the cause of all of this?" Her eyes brimmed with glee. "You do have a touch of theatrics within you."

"Blame my Missouri River upbringing," he laughed. "The shows on the steamboats plying the river touched my soul and filled my head with fantasy and foolish dreams."

Agnes smiled to herself. She turned away from him so he would not see the delight she felt. With forced determination, she put the clothesbasket on the table and started to fold the clean wash.

"Oh, this smells so nice." She held a shirt up to her nose and sniffed. "Clothes dried in the city never had this fresh scent about them. The clean fragrance of the country seeps into every thread."

Joseph came up behind her and put his hands gently on her shoulders. "Is Wendell asleep, Agnes?"

"Sound asleep." She kept folding wash, although it took every ounce of her willpower to keep from turning around to him. Her breath came in short, disconnected gulps of air.

"Agnes." With gentle pressure, he turned her to face him. "Dear Agnes."

Joseph put his hands gently on her shoulders. "Agnes," he paused for what seemed a long time. "Agnes," he repeated, hesitating. "There is something I really need to ask."

Taking his hands from her shoulders, he rubbed them together. He smiled slightly, embarrassed. "Agnes, the children, my children, need you here." He blushed. "And I need you here." After a long pause, he continued, "Your three months of helping us will soon be over." With mumbled words, he added, "Please, please, do not leave them, do not leave me. I need a helpmate."

Agnes looked into his kind eyes. "Joseph, I am not a young woman anymore. I am 33."

"But, Agnes," Joseph chuckled softly, "I am not a young man either. I am an old 42 years."

She took his weathered hands in hers. "Oh, Joseph, you are a wonderful young man at heart. You are a good man, a good father."

Agnes strikes a pretty pose with Joseph, the handsome Kansas farmer, who has become more than a mere employer to her.

She stepped closer to him. "I will stay longer if you want me to, if you feel you need my help."

"Oh, Agnes," he touched her cheek kindly, gently, "will you, please? Will you, could you marry me, be my wife?" A look of pleading, of desperation, of needing, of sweetness filled his eyes. "I only have the farm life to offer you."

Agnes closed her eyes in thoughtfulness, then opened them to look at the dear man directly. "Yes, Joseph," she whispered. Then she responded louder, "Yes, Joseph, I, I would be honored."

She paused for a moment, then melted into his strong embrace.

Agnes and Joseph on their wedding day, July 29, 1913.

Her head nestled against his wide chest. She could hear his heart beating as fast as her own. Joseph felt a sense of longing, of fulfillment.

For a long time they stood, no word passing between them. He raised her chin gently so he could search her face, to read an answer in her eyes. Like a whisper, he touched his lips to her cheek.

She smiled. He closed his eyes to relish the moment, as he softly touched his lips to hers.

"My dear, dear Agnes."

21

SHIVAREE

"DO YOU TAKE this woman … ?"

Joseph never really heard the words. He looked at Agnes and their mist-filled eyes met.

"Joseph, answer 'I do.'" Father Manz tried not to be too obvious when the grin spread across his face. "The ring."

Joseph's older brother by two years, John, handed it to the priest. A sprinkle of holy water and a prayer by Father Manz blessed the marriage symbol.

"With this ring, I thee wed." Joseph slipped the plain wide gold band on Agnes' finger. She lifted her hand to touch the ring to her lips, then smiled at him.

The bright glow of the candles and the sunbeams streaming through the stained glass windows bathed everything inside St. Mary's with soft, rainbow-hued colors. Joseph could never remember seeing the little country church so calming. It was as though a bit of heaven entered his heart. His thoughts swirled. The Lord had now smiled on him in a way he could never have imagined during his last three years of hardship. It was July 29, 1913.

The Mass came to a close with the priest's words, "Ite, missa est. Go, the Mass is ended." The servers answered "Deo gratias. Thanks be to God." Father Manz grabbed one of the acolytes by the arm and motioned to the church steeple, "Go, ring the bells loud and long. This is a special wedding day."

Sister Philomenia pulled out every stop on the high-backed organ, squinted hard at the notes, then hit the keyboard with every ounce of energy she could muster. The bellows of the 30-year-old organ wheezed as the elderly nun pumped the well-worn pedals that supplied the air for the sound. The pedal hinges groaned and squeaked loud to the rhythm of the recessional, and it only fired her enthusiasm more. Sister leaned forward so she could read the complicated music easier.

As the "Fine" neared, a wide smile came over her normally calm face. She had already planned to pump faster and harder to end the composition with a sweeping flourish and a mighty crescendo. To finish, she would lift her hands from the keys and let the notes hang there, suspended forever in time. "Just as the composer meant for it to be," she whispered. Her body quivered in anticipation of the grand finale and each fiber of her being trembled with the excitement of the music.

Joseph took Agnes' hand as they walked away from the altar, passing his family and friends.

Agnes felt a sudden twinge of sadness and self-pity, for there was no family there for her that special day. She could only envision their smiles and best wishes in her mind, and feel their happiness for her in her own heart. She would write to them of this day, and hope they could know of her joy in the words of the letter.

The couple walked out into the warmth of that sunny July day. Joseph put his arm around her and squeezed her waist gently. She leaned against his shoulder lightly and whispered, "Hello, my husband."

"And good day to you, my beloved wife." They looked into each other's eyes with affection that spoke volumes. There was no need for more words.

Long tables had been set under the shade of the huge elms in Joseph's front yard. His family and some of the closest neighbors gathered for the celebration.

The wives of Joseph's brothers spread out platters of fried chicken and fresh tomatoes on the kitchen table. Mounds of crusty homemade bread and bowls of creamy churned butter were set in amongst the dishes of mashed potatoes, brown gravy and snapped green beans and large white onions from the garden.

His sister-in-law, Margaret, brought a rich chocolate cake made from the old Linnebur family recipe. "Since your mother is no longer with us, Henry and I thought we would bring this special cake. He said it had always been a favorite of yours." She smiled at Joseph and squeezed his arm affectionately.

The wedding guests crowded into the kitchen to pile plates full of good food, and then found their way outside to enjoy the feast. Bottles of homemade grape wine passed from one to the other and helped enliven the party. Some of the men toasted the couple and serenaded them with song.

The sunset of reds, blues and golds brought a close to the happy day. Agnes looked at the western sky and remembered her first view of its beauty, only several months before. "This has to be the prettiest sunset ever," she whispered to herself, "for it shines upon my happiest day."

The warm summer evening closed in around the couple. Huge brown June bugs hit against the window screens. Fireflies' tails flashed their lights into the dark night. The exhausted children lay with their heads close to the open windows to catch a faint whisper of breeze.

Just as the house noises settled down, and faint snores were heard from the other rooms, the most horrible clatter broke loose out in the yard. Men beat on large washtubs, and women banged cook pots and lids together. The younger people whistled and called the newlyweds by name, "Agnes, Joseph, come out, come out."

Agnes bolted upright in bed. A cold sweat broke out on her brow. The racket grew louder. Lantern lights moved around the yard. Never had she heard such commotion. The frightened woman shook Joseph hard, and screamed, "Joseph, Joseph, what is going on? There is so much noise."

Joseph stirred, then sat up and rubbed his eyes. His laughter in the room carried over the din and revelry outside. "I cannot believe this." He leaned over to his bride and felt the nervousness in her body. "Relax, my dear Agnes, we are being shivareed."

"What is that?" her voice trembled. "I do not know that."

He stood up, and then sat down again beside her. She felt more secure with his arm around her shoulders.

"It is our friends and neighbors who have come to serenade us on our wedding night." More laughter, "We did not ask them to come to the wedding feast, but they are not going to let our marriage pass without some celebration for themselves."

"What do they want?" demanded Agnes.

Joseph still shook with merriment. "Mainly, they just came over to interrupt our wedding night and rest. They want us to come outside and join them in the party." He held Agnes tighter. "And they also want any food and drink we have left."

"What do we do to get them to stop? They will wake the children."

Joseph chuckled, "The children are probably already outside banging pots and pans with the rest of them. No doubt, William and Ellen knew of this beforehand."

"And they never told us?"

"What, and spoil their fun? They would not spoil the surprise by spilling the beans, so to speak."

The noise continued. "They must be getting tired. What do we do, Joseph?" She lit the candle on the nightstand.

"Slip on a dress, and we will go outside and join the fun. All the leftovers from the meal can be shared with them." He put his hand to his mouth and chuckled more. "We will have to bring out the little wine we have left, and see how much home brew is still in the cellar. I am not sure it will be enough for all, but if each one gets a taste, they will probably be satisfied."

Joseph and Agnes tried to hurry and slip on other clothes to go and meet the crowd. He chuckled again, "Do not be surprised, Agnes, if they stay here until the light of dawn. We have some folks around here who never know when to go home and go to bed."

Agnes finally settled down from the shock and smiled, "I understand, I think." Before they left the bedroom, she held the candle to the alarm clock to read the time. "It is already midnight, so there are not too many hours of the night left."

Joseph took the candle, stood by the window and waved to those outside. They screamed and banged their tubs even louder.

"We better hurry, Joseph, before they get too tired, or break each other's eardrums." Agnes finally laughed.

He led his bride from their bedroom, through the kitchen and porch and out to meet the well-wishers. "Food and drinks are in the house. Come help yourselves."

"Best wishes, best wishes," yelled the crowd. "Many years of happiness."

Josie Peppen, a neighbor's wife, set her lantern down on one of the tables by the back door, still left there from the wedding meal. "Joseph, let me carry the food out here. We do not want to make your kitchen any dirtier that it already is." She turned to her husband, Hal. "Get the boys and come help me. Joseph, where do you hide the home brew?" Her hearty laugh rolled through the night air.

"Josie, you know where." Joseph grinned, ""Nothing is a secret in this neighborhood."

Josie took Agnes by the arm and looked at Joseph. A hearty chuckle slipped from her lips. "I do not know about that, Joseph, this shivaree was a well-kept secret." She squeezed Agnes' hand. "Not even the women let the secret slip."

The early light of the new day was breaking in the east when Agnes and Joseph shut the door to their bedroom. "What a night," chuckled Joseph. "That shivaree was a complete surprise for me."

"Do they do that with every couple that marries?"

"No, most of the couples have a wedding dance that everyone goes to. But if there is no dance, one can almost expect a shivaree." He laughed loudly in merriment. "But that is usually for the younger folks, not someone our age."

Agnes rubbed his back and giggled, "After I got over the shock, it was rather nice. In a way, Joseph, it makes me feel welcomed into your world."

He leaned to kiss her on the cheek. "Yes, all of them coming was nice."

He wrapped his strong arms around her. "Perhaps we can get an hour or two of sleep. We do have a busy day ahead of us."

22

HOMECOMING

TWO DAYS AFTER the wedding, Joseph came in for his morning lunch. "I have been thinking, Agnes. I am ready to bring Coletta home from Katherine's sister. How would you feel if we did it soon?"

She sat down across the table from him, reached over with her hand and rubbed his hand gently. "Whenever you wish, Joseph. She needs to be here with you and the other children."

"This afternoon then, I will go see Rosie and bring my little girl home."

Joseph's heart sang, and he put his happiness into song. His mother had always told him he could not sing, but, today, he had no concern about that. His words rang forth, "My baby will soon be with me." He twirled his hat in the air, and tried to urge the horses to hurry. Finally, he came to the drive, and called, "Whoa," to the horses in his merriest voice. He jumped down from the wagon, and hurried to the door.

"Hello, Rosie, beautiful day. I have come to take Coletta home with me."

Coletta peeked around her aunt Rosie's skirt and watched the strange man. He smiled at the child and held out his hand, "I have come to take you home with me." Her fat thumb slipped deeper between her pink lips, and a scowl pushed together plump, chubby cheeks.

Rosie spread her feet apart, propped her hands on her broad hips and looked Joseph square in the eye. "I do not think so. This child needs to stay here. We are the only family she knows."

Joseph looked at her shocked, then sputtered, "What did you say?"

"Coletta is not going anywhere but here. I promised my sister on

143

her deathbed I would take care of her baby, and I intend to do just that."

"But, Rosie, I am her father."

"I always keep my promises." With that, she reached down to grab the little three-year-old girl's hand, turned and literally pulled the child back into the house.

Joseph was dumbfounded. Finally, he turned around, crawled up into the wagon, and slowly guided the horses out of the driveway.

Agnes heard the team coming and went to meet her husband at the door.

"Whoa." The wagon stopped. Joseph put his head down into his upturned hands and silently sobbed.

"Joseph?" she called out. Then, suddenly frightened, "Joseph, what is it?" She could hear his sobs, and ran to the wagon to look up at him. Agnes lowered her voice and spoke more calmly, "Joseph, where is the child?"

After a time, the distraught father rubbed strong fingers over his face, then looked down at his wife.

"Rosie says the girl needs to stay there with her. Something about the only family the child has known, and a promise she made to Katherine on her deathbed." He wiped the back of his hand across his face, brushing the tears from his cheeks. "I never knew of such a promise made to Katherine until today."

"Oh, Joseph, no. Are you certain that is what she meant?"

"Rosie is a stubborn woman, Agnes. She always means what she says."

"Joseph, come down, come in the house. We need to think what we must do." He followed her into the house, and sat down by the table. She sat down beside him.

He twisted his strong fingers and rubbed his hands again and again. "I have waited for how long to get my little girl back home. And I never expected this."

"Joseph, we must be just as stubborn. Coletta is your child, and deathbed promise or not, that child belongs in your home."

He sat silent for a long time, thinking, and then suddenly spoke, "In a few days, I will go to her again."

"If this is because of me, then I will go along. There is a stubborn streak in me, too, Joseph, and we are not going to let that woman push you around like that." She stood and propped her hands on her hips just as Rosie had done. Tomorrow morning, when it is cool, Joseph, we will go. You cannot continue to go on this way."

The two sat side by side in the carriage. Old Ben's hooves kicked up little puffs of dust on the dry dirt road. A mockingbird sitting in a tall tree mimicked other early morning songsters. Yellow-breasted meadowlarks perched on fence posts greeted the couple with their merry serenade.

Joseph held the reins easily. His mind wandered far from the beauty of the day.

Agnes sensed the agitation in his heart. "He is such a kind, quiet man. How will he convince this woman to return his child?" Somehow, she thought, she must be there, strong, for him, yet not too forceful. "Since I am the new stepmother, anything I say will only anger Rosie more."

Joseph did not speak for the five-mile drive, except to say, "We are here."

Agnes looked at the house, in dire need of paint and fixing. All kinds of things were strewn around the yard. This place did not look at all like Joseph's, where everything was more orderly and neat. The dog came from behind the decrepit, old granary and barked furiously.

Rosie finally came to see what the racket was about. She stood in the doorway, with her hands on her hips and stared. "So, you have come back, Joseph." A scowl crossed her face. "I never expected to see you so soon again."

Joseph stepped down from the carriage, and then turned and helped Agnes down, and escorted her to the door. "Rosie, I would like to introduce you to Agnes.

"I know you married her. You do not have to introduce her. Everyone in the parish knows about her cutting the girls' sleeves short." She snorted, "What a disgrace." Her angry gaze shifted to Agnes, "Just who are you to come into a community and cause such a fuss and rile everybody up?"

Agnes merely stood there. Joseph's face turned red with fury. "Rosie, you have no right," he stammered.

"I have every right to disapprove of the woman who you think is going to raise Katherine's children. Katherine never would have allowed her children to be ridiculed like you did, Joseph."

"Rosie." Joseph's voice rose in an angry pitch, "I have come to take my little girl home." Coletta peeked out the torn old screen door.

"That is not a good idea, Joseph. Are you sure this prissy woman will take care of Coletta, or push her off to the side when her own babies come?" She thrust her shoulders back and snorted, "You married this woman and you hardly know her. You do not know where she came from, and you do not know how long she will stay. And you want her to take care of your little girl. I think, Joseph, you had better think that over long and hard." She stared at him.

"Rosie, that is not fair. You judge Agnes and know nothing about her."

"I have heard plenty."

"From who?"

"Yes, Rosie, from who?" Just then, Rosie's husband, Ollie, came around the house from the barn. He repeated the question, "From who, Rosie?"

"You stay out of this, you old geezer. I do not need your help here." The irritated woman shot him a glance of disdain.

Joseph stepped closer to her. "I want my daughter back now. I always told you Coletta would come back to live with me when I was able to care for her." He looked at Agnes and reached back for her hand. "Now we are able to care for the girl."

The woman noticed the child peeking out the door past her. "Get back in there, Coletta. Emma, come get her and keep her in the bedroom."

"But, Mama."

"Now, do as I say." Her eyes narrowed to dark slits, and her face became even more contorted.

Agnes could not be silent any longer. "It would be nice for Joseph to have the child back with him."

"What makes you think you can raise a child?" Rosie's scornful look would have made most people wither, but not Agnes.

She stepped closer and put her hands on her hips, just like Rosie did. "I have taken care of many children in the homes where I worked over the years."

146

"But they were not yours," sniffed Rosie.

"I cooked in their homes and took care of the children when the governess was gone. They played around where I worked."

Rosie sneered, "What highfalutin talk is that? Governess?" The woman's face turned red. "You are a snob, just like other people said you are."

"Now, Rosie." Ollie stepped next to Agnes. "Do not talk to her like that. She is Joseph's wife."

"Or thinks she is. She is some kind of mail-order bride who was just looking to marry some rich farmer."

By then, Agnes was beginning to seethe. "The discussion here is not about who I am or where I came from. We are here to take the girl back to our home."

"Our home, is it?" Contempt covered Rosie's face.

"Rosie, you must know that I answered Joseph's advertisement because he needed a housekeeper to help him and his children, not because he was looking for a wife." Agnes paused to let Rosie accept the words. "And I certainly was not looking for a husband.

The woman snickered.

"I did not come with any intentions of marrying him, nor did he have any intentions to marry me. But we have married, and he can now take his child home because there is a mother there."

"Stepmother, you mean," sneered the other.

"Yes, stepmother." Agnes's voice rose in pitch, "That is what I am to this child. That is the situation." She stopped then, to calm herself, "But, Rosie, Joseph is her flesh and blood father."

"I do not like it. Katherine, I made a promise to her, my sister, Katherine."

Agnes' face softened. "No doubt you did. At the time of death, things are said to be comforting. You wanted Katherine to know her child would be cared for. And that you did."

Rosie half turned to go back into the house.

"Do not turn your back to me," pleaded Joseph. "I want my baby, Katherine's baby, home with me." He hesitated, "If this is so difficult for you, perhaps we all need to go speak with Father Manz and ask for his help."

The woman stood there for a long time. Slowly, her stubbornness melted and she relaxed her arms.

"For crying out loud, Rosie, I cannot figure you out." Ollie went to put his hand on her shoulder. "For how long you have been complaining how you could not wait to get rid of that child. She took extra care and so much of your time." He paused for a few seconds. "Ever since Katherine died, you and your sisters have been trying to run everything Joseph did at his house. Then, when Agnes came, you tried to run her too. Is it not about time you all let Joseph live his life in his own house?" He squeezed her shoulder gently, and looked directly into her eyes. "Especially now, since he and Agnes are married."

"Be quiet," she whispered hoarsely at him.

"You know it is time." Ollie moved closer to his wife and put his arm around her waist. She tried to squirm away, but he held firm. "Rosie, you kept your promise to Katherine and took care of her baby. For three long years, you were the girl's mother and I was her papa. But remember, Rosie, how many times you rocked her to sleep and sang that little song to her."

Rosie gave him an angry look.

"Remember, Rosie, the song, 'Your papa will come someday, to take you to his home faraway.'" He hugged her tighter, "Her papa has come, and now it is time to let her go." Ollie chuckled softly, "And she sure is not going far away, just a few miles down the road. You can always see her."

Rosie leaned her head into his shoulder and softly sobbed. Ollie held his wife tightly, but tenderly, in his arms. Joseph and Agnes stood by watching, silently waiting. Finally, Rosie pulled back from him. But, still, she looked down, not able to look at the others. "You are right, Ollie." She lifted her head. "We must get her clothes."

"Emma, come out here," Ollie called. The shy girl came to the door. "Go pack all of Coletta's things. She is going to live with her papa."

The child watched from inside the door. "Come, Coletta." Ollie held out his hand to the youngster.

The little girl pushed open the rickety screen door and almost stumbled. Looking up at Ollie with bright eyes, she broke into childish giggles. As fast as her chubby little legs would carry her, she ran to him and threw herself into his arms.

He lifted her high in the air and rubbed her cheek with his bushy mustache. Her high-pitched little giggles broke the air. "See that man there, my little pet. He is your papa, and you are going home with him and your new mama." Ollie hugged her tightly and whispered in her ear, "Remember, we always told you your papa would come for you someday, and he has now come."

The blond-headed child looked at Joseph, then shyly smiled.

"Come to me, daughter." Joseph held out his arms.

Rosie turned and bumped headlong into the door, trying to get into the house away from the others. "My sister, Katherine, has been replaced. But I tried, oh, I tried." She slumped on a nearby chair. "Now, just get that child out of my house."

The others heard her words. Ollie felt for Joseph; he had already been through so much.

Joseph rubbed his chin and tried to pretend he had not heard. "Tell Rosie she will never know how much this has meant to me, these last years.

He reached out to shake the other man's hand. "Thank her for me, Ollie, thank her for me."

The children of Joseph and his first wife, Katherine, gather together in 1913 for a pretty family portrait. Back, L to R: Irene, Agnes, William and Elnora (Ellen). Front, L to R: Coletta and Wendell. Coletta's brothers and sisters welcomed her back into the family. Now they were one again, two brothers and four sisters.

Coletta's laughter and good-natured ways spread happiness in the household. Her papa, Joseph, revelled in her joy of life.

23

THE HIRED HANDS

THAT LATE MAY day of 1914 was pleasant and cool. There was always so much to do every day. The hours just never seemed to stretch far enough.

For several weeks, Agnes' stomach churned each morning. "Could it be? Who can I ask?"

One Sunday afternoon, Joseph's brother, Henry, and his wife, Margaret, came to call.

"Oh, Margaret, is it possible?" Agnes smiled wistfully.

Margaret smiled knowingly and nodded, without speaking.

Agnes thought about it all that evening and caught herself squeezing her arms or clinching her fists. "I must be sure before I tell Joseph. Oh please, Lord, let him be as happy as this makes me. For so many years, it has been my dream, and now … " She caught her smiling reflection in the mirror as she passed by.

"Meine Mütter, my mother, how joyful she will be."

Two weeks had now passed, and it was the beginning of the second week of June. The long, hard weeks of summer work were about to begin in earnest. Thoughts of the last weeks occupied every waking moment.

She looked at the eight headless chickens flopping around the yard. "No time to think about anything else now, except all these chickens."

The two girls, Agnes Marie and Irene, gathered up the birds and piled them near the big black kettle. William dipped out a bucket of boiling water from the huge old iron kettle and put it on the ground next to the chickens, so they could dip each chicken. The scalding hot water matted the feathers against the birds' sides. Drips of the steaming water dropped from the wings onto Agnes' feet. "Come, children, help me pluck the feathers while the water is still hot. We must be quick about it."

"Oooh, I do not like to do this." Ellen curled her lip up to the side.

William looked at his older sister and laughed, "Come on, Ellen, I will race you to see which of us can pick the most chickens."

Ellen growled at him under her breath, "That is not fair; your hands are bigger than mine." She made a face at him. "Boys, you are all alike, always want to win." She made sure Agnes was not looking, then stuck out her tongue out at her brother. "Show-off," she sneered.

William winked at her and sang in a singsong way, "I can pick more feathers than you." He picked up a huge fryer and wrapped his long, narrow fingers around the bird. With one swipe, he had a handful of feathers and left a large patch of yellowish-white skin showing. "Can you do that, Ellen?"

She tugged at the longest wing feather until finally she got it loose, and then threw it at him. After that, she was only too content to pull just a few feathers at a time. Anything to keep her from having to pluck more chickens.

"Look at William, girls. Maybe we should just let him be our official chicken plucker." Agnes grinned, and then dipped her chicken into the pail again to loosen the feathers more.

The boy's eyes sparkled. "It is not that I like to pluck chickens that well, but I always like the final results, a big plate of the crusty-fried bird." He looked at Agnes, "And, Ma, you make the best fried chicken of any woman in the neighborhood."

A wide smile spread over her face. The children were beginning to accept her, she hoped.

"Girls, we must really practice the plucking. When it is time for your pa to get the wheat threshed, William will have to be working out there, so that will leave just us to get the chickens ready to eat. Pa is going to need William's help more and more, as he gets older."

William puffed up his chest. "Did you hear that, Ellen? I am going to be the water boy for the threshing crew. And that leaves you to pluck these chickens." He rolled his eyes at her and laughed long and loud.

"I would rather be out doing that than pulling feathers off these dumb chickens," declared Ellen.

"That is only because there might be a good-looking man out there, Ellen. You will not find one here."

"You said that, William; no good-looking man here, only pesky boys."

Agnes' mind wandered from the banter of the two. Her dinner menu was taking shape in her mind. Chicken was always good to serve. It did not seem to warm the body like beef or pork did on hot summer days. The men would be coming in from the field very hungry. It was harvest time, but she still could not get used to all the rush of the farm work.

Joseph was now cutting the wheat with the binder. She had watched the binding last summer and was fascinated with the process. The machine gathered so much of the pale yellow wheat and tied it into bundles. Joseph's hired men would follow along behind and stand the bundles upright into shocks, so the grain could dry completely. That was not only a hot and tiring job; it made the men really hungry and thirsty.

No matter how much food Agnes put on the table, it never seemed to be enough. All the men like her chicken and vegetables, smothered in a rich cream gravy. A smile crossed her face when she remembered how angry Joseph had become the first time she fixed a heaping bowl of rice to go with the chicken dish.

"These men are used to potatoes," he told her in a voice harsher than he had ever used with her. "They will never eat rice." But once they sampled her spicy, creamed chicken, or sometimes duck, the rice disappeared just like potatoes.

A wisp of dark hair slid down across her forehead. With a turn of her hand, she brushed it away. It was already getting warm, and it was still only morning. "This afternoon, girls, we will have to pluck the down and feathers from the last of the geese and ducks." She stopped to look over another chicken for missed feathers. "The feather beds are getting thin. And if this coming winter is anything like the last one, I sure do not want any of you freezing." A merry chuckle made the younger girls smile. "When the comforts are fat and fluffy, everyone snuggles way down deep under them, and only your noses show. Reminds me of a bunch of bunnies tucked in a snow bank."

"Ma," Irene giggled, "do you and Pa tuck your noses way under the covers like we do?"

The woman smiled, "Come to think of it, we do." She looked up at the sky to check the position of the sun. "It is time for us to begin dinner. William, help Ellen carry the chickens into the kitchen. Pump cool water to soak them until I get there. She looked at the two other girls. "Come with me. We might find enough nice lettuce for a salad."

The girls made baskets by pulling their apron skirts up and holding onto the ends, while Agnes picked large handfuls of leaf lettuce. "We will really have to watch when this is washed. Little bugs are liking this, too."

Back in the kitchen, she quickly cut up the chickens. "Ellen, please look over the lettuce and watch for the small green worms."

"Ma," William jokingly snickered, "if we leave those worms in there, the men will not eat so much chicken."

"You may be right, Son." She winked at the boy.

The chicken was crackling and popping in the heavy cast iron skillets. Rice was set on to boil. A jar of last year's dill pickles was opened. Home-canned apple pie sat on the sideboard.

"William, will you start pumping cold water from the pump? Ellen, I want you to squeeze the lemons." Agnes set the glasses next to the pies. "Cool lemonade is the best thirst quencher there is."

Agnes lifted the lids to check the sizzling chicken. The wood-burning stove was really heating up the kitchen. She lifted the corner of her long white apron and wiped the sweat from her brow. She turned to watch the smaller girls set the table.

"I have cooked for hundreds of people through the years, but never for anybody who eats like these hired men." She filled the sugar bowl and put it on the table. "Your pa says that is because most of these hoboes he hires for the summer have not had a square meal for days. So they eat enough to tide them over when they are without a job." She grinned, wondering if any of the children caught the meaning of what she just said.

"Oh, Ma, that cannot be true." Young Agnes Marie's dark eyes sparkled. "No matter how much a person eats, they always are hungry again the next day."

"I can see why you want to be a nurse, Agnes. You already think like one." The older Agnes put her hand on the girl's shoulder. "That is good."

The six hired men came trouping in the back porch after Joseph.

"Hurry, Irene, go check if the washbowl has clean water in it. Also make sure the bar of soap is still big enough. And take clean towels out there also." The girl hurried out into the porch.

"Hello there, little one." Luke, one of the hoboes, moved closer to Irene. His mouth spread wide in a crooked, toothy grin. Four missing front teeth left a big gap and caused his voice to whistle when he talked. "You remind me of my Susie at home. She is about your age. Eight, maybe? Am I right?"

Irene backed away from him, and shyly shook her head up and down. She almost bumped into Joseph trying to get back into the kitchen.

"Ma," the girl was white as a sheet. "Ma, he said I looked like his little girl." Irene stopped for a few minutes and stared at Agnes. "Who would want a papa who is a hobo?"

Agnes stepped closer to Irene and whispered close to her ear, " He travels all over the country on the trains, looking for work so he can send money home for his wife and children." Agnes then moved over to the stove, lifted a heavy lid from one of the skillets, then filled a huge platter with creamed chicken. She put it on the table beside the bowls of vegetables and rice.

"I sure am glad they stay out in the bunkhouse," Irene shuddered. "Some of Pa's hired men scare me."

"I am, too," chimed in her sister, Agnes Marie. "Just going in to help Ellen put clean sheets on their bunk beds scares me. I just know they are going to catch us and do bad things to us."

Agnes finished filling a huge bowl with fresh, buttered peas, and handed it to Ellen to put on the table. "Just remember, girls, your pa always tries to pick the best hoboes to work for him. That is why he looks for the same ones each year, the men he can trust." She lowered her voice so the men washing up on the porch would not hear. "Your pa said to remind you to stay away from the hired men. He does not want to lose a good worker because one of his daughters is flirting with the man."

"Ma, I do not know how to flirt," giggled Ellen.

"Oh, but you will learn soon enough." Agnes sliced into the tall, long loaf of homemade bread.

The men's chairs scratched the faded linoleum on the kitchen floor as they pulled themselves close to the table.

"Ah, Mrs. Linnebur, your delicious creamed chicken." Timothy's booming voice filled the room with laughter. "I was so glad your husband looked for me in the pool hall and offered me a job right off. I did not want to wait any place else, cause I figured he would know I would be indulging in a few drinks of the hard stuff before going to work." He piled his plate half-full of rice. "Yessireee, Ma'am, you make the best food of any I ever tasted, no matter where I was. Much better cook than my Sarah." He guffawed, "But then, I sure did not marry her for her cooking abilities."

"Sir?" Agnes raised her eyebrows to look at him.

"Sorry, sure am sorry." He ladled on the creamed gravy. "Always tell my Sarah when I am away, to keep her eyes open for any tramp that comes around. Them fellas are up to no good. All they want is a meal for no work. Sure cannot trust them either. Those fellas will con anybody out of anything. If they cannot do that, they will just haul off and steal it. I have watched them do it."

He filled his mouth with food and chewed loudly. "Most of the tramps I have seen are so slick, you never know they are around until they show up right in front of you, out of nowhere." He reached past one of the other men to grab two thick slices of bread. "They also put chalk X-marks on steps and foundations of houses so other tramps know they can get a handout there." He looked at Agnes. "They ever bother you?"

Joseph laughed, "Most of the tramps I have seen are really rough-looking characters. Just the other day in town, I heard that one like that was around. Guess he had a scraggly, dirty, gray beard that hung clear to his belt. As the story goes, he was almost to the porch door when the woman of the house came out. She did not see him come up the drive. Did he ever scare her!" Joseph grinned, "The townspeople said they could hear her scream three blocks away."

The mantle clock struck one. "Well, men, we do not have many more bundles to shock. Since it is Saturday, when we finish that field, I will pay you and you can go into town for the weekend."

They pushed back their chairs with a terrible scraping noise. Luke turned around to pick up one more piece of chicken. Lifting it up as a salute to Agnes, he grunted, "Need that extra strength to go into town." He grinned and she nodded.

The men hurried back out to the field. The remaining shocks went together in a big hurry. Joseph was amazed how fast the men could work so they could get off early. He handed out their wages, and then watched them rush down the drive, walking as fast as they could for town. Wearily, he walked into the shade of the house.

"The men have gone." Joseph sat down at the table, then took out his huge red handkerchief and wiped his brow. Agnes handed him a plate and the pie. "It is really getting warm out there for this time of year." Coletta came and snuggled under his arm and looked up at him with big eyes. "Would you like to drink some cool lemonade with me?" he said as he smiled down at her.

"Do you think they will be back Monday?"

"Never can tell, Agnes. Most of them will come back if there is a job. Others, if they have any money left, are just as liable to hop on the next freight train out of town, heading for someplace else." He smiled at her, "But I think your good food keeps them coming back." He finished off the slice of pie, "Sure good, Agnes, sure good."

He tweaked Coletta's little nose, then stood. Reaching over to grab his hat, he turned to go. "Need to check the cattle in the pasture, and the hogs. William, you want to come with me?"

"Glad to, Pa."

"Thanks for all your help, girls." Agnes sank into the rocking chair. "My ankles are swelling, so let me sit here for about 30 minutes and prop up my feet. We will do the dishes then."

Joseph turned to glance back at her. He had never known her to leave the dishwashing until later. "Is she sick?" he wondered.

Ellen was only too happy to slip upstairs to her room. The three young girls hurried outside to their playhouse. "We need to try that new mud pie recipe Nettie taught us." Irene leaned down to pick up heavy clods of dried dirt. "We need some of that straw Pa's binder dumped in the yard. Coletta, can you find an old can and fill it with water?"

Agnes relaxed while her subconscious opened its vault of memories from the past year. The events passed through her conscious mind like a veritable parade. First, she remembered her impression of this small house without the conveniences of big city homes. The smell of smoke caused her nostrils to twitch. She laughed softly, thinking of those first attempts to start a fire in the wood-burning cookstove. "The piles of wood that have to be carried in everyday is unbelievable," she had written to her mother.

She tried to picture her mother's face in her mind. How she wished she could talk to her mother once again, and tell her of her life here. "My Mütter must really wonder what kind of backwoods life I live." She smiled, "It would have been interesting to see her face when she read about the baby calves and piglets we kept in the kitchen overnight." Remembering back, she bit her lip in a thoughtful way. "I can only hope Mütter realizes Joseph brought them in the house and next to the wood stove to keep the little creatures from getting too cold and freezing."

Agnes rubbed her cheeks with long slow strokes, until more memories surfaced. "No books could have taught me as much as I have learned about animals. Who could have predicted that raising chickens and plucking geese and ducks would be in my future?" She closed her eyes to see the images clearer in her mind. "And all that butchering and slick, greasy lard."

Leaning forward to rub her sore ankles, she thought about the years past. "How much easier it used to be, just to go to the markets and select the meats we needed. Ah," she shook her head in wonder, "so much work, so many hours canning all that beef, and scraping yards of casings to use for the sausage." A frown crossed her brow, "I never really knew they cooked the hog's head, and all the other organs to make the head cheese. But it is rather good for breakfast, and the children eat piles of it at a meal." She thought about all the cooking and grinding that went in to making a huge batch of scrapple, and scrubbing those ugly, dirty hog ears to put in it. "Such nonsense," she said, "there was not enough meat on those ears to feed a bird. What a waste of time."

Shifting around in the rocking chair, Agnes remembered how good the house smelled when she fixed all that pork from the five hogs Joseph butchered last winter. All that meat had to be fried down, put in big crocks and melted lard poured over it to preserve it. She sighed heavily, just thinking of all those hours of work.

But then, her nose wrinkled as her sense of smell magnified and she thought of all those hams and shoulders they cured. "Joseph put that wonderful smelling pickling salt on all the hams so they would keep. Then he hung them in his little cement block shed to smoke them. What a delicious smell that was. Hmm."

She rubbed her temples with stiff fingers. Thoughts drifted back to her young years in Germany. "Oh, Mütter, how hard it must have been for you to always find food for us." Her mind saw the beloved face. "You would have felt so rich just to have a small portion of the food I put away this last year." Tears peaked in her eyes. "Mütter, you cannot imagine the amount of meat we have here." A sob slipped from Agnes' throat. "If I could just send you some of the roasts and hams." A touch of her fingers wiped away an errant tear from her cheek.

She caught herself talking out loud, "I must remember to write Mütter that Joseph helped me make blut wurst, blood sausage. I am quite proud of myself at the results. Tastes just like what I remember from when I was a girl."

"I must tell her, too, that I never dreamed someday I would be a farmer's wife. What twists one's life can take."

Agnes rubbed her tight ankles again to relieve the pain and pressure. As she relaxed, that sickening feeling in her abdomen returned. She tried to readjust her body in the rocker, but no matter which way she turned, it made no difference.

Her thoughts turned in another direction. "Perhaps, soon, I can write meine Mütter of my possible good news." She clutched at her body again. But still, a touch of happiness entered her soul. "What will meine Mütter say about having one of her grandchildren born in America?"

"I must tell Joseph, too." Agnes sighed, wondering. "What will he think, becoming a new father at his age?" Another sickening spell grabbed her being. "I only hope and pray that is what my condition is. If not, then what could it be? Oh, dear God, please do not let me get sick. There is much too much work around here for a sick wife and mother."

She tilted her head upward, hard, against the top of the rocking chair back. Thoughts upon thoughts piled up in her mind, like new mounds erupting and building into mountains. Either way, she had to think of the future. She had to begin planning for the outcome. "I must think of the positive and happy side of what might be happening to me. Yes, I cannot think negative thoughts."

"I must sew and crochet baby things. Is there a baby crib still in the house, or did Joseph discard it after Katherine's death? Are there still baby blankets hidden somewhere? If so, I have not found them. Dear Lord, guide my mind to face the future. And Joseph, help him to understand."

"Yes, I must tell Joseph. I cannot try to keep that secret from him." Agnes sighed again, a long, lengthy sigh. "But he understands these things."

She smiled then. "Yes, my dear husband does understand."

24

GYPSY WAGONS

THE SCREEN DOOR banged hard and three pale white breathless girls came rushing into the parlor.

"Ma, Ma," they shouted. "Ma, they are coming."

Ellen ran down the stairway from her bedroom on the second floor. Ashen-faced, she screamed, "We have to hide."

Agnes dropped her feet to the floor and quickly sat upright. "Who is coming? Who has to hide?"

"They are, they are." Irene's hands flew about in the air like windmills.

"Wait, wait," demanded Agnes, "who is coming?"

"The gypsy wagons," sputtered Agnes Marie out of breath.

"Wait a minute, how do you know they are gypsy wagons?" Agnes pushed herself up out of the rocking chair. "I never heard about any gypsies coming around here." Her thoughts raced, then she looked at them questioningly. "Are those your imaginary gypsies?"

"No, no, come quick. They are almost here." Irene tugged at her hand. "Their wagons are all pretty and painted in bright colors."

When the girl said that, Agnes decided to check for herself. No seven-year-old girl raised in these parts could imagine those wagons unless she had seen them.

Shep, their old farm dog, was unusually nervous, jumping up and down, then running back and forth close to the porch door. He howled, then barked and howled again. Sure enough, two gypsy wagons turned in the driveway.

"I cannot believe this, gypsies here on the Kansas plains." Agnes opened the screen door to step outside.

Ellen tugged on Agnes's skirt. "Do not go out there, Ma. They are bad people."

"How do you know?" Agnes turned to look at the oldest daughter. "None of them came last year."

"I know, but they stopped at other farms last year. And they are bad. They steal chickens and pigs. Anything they want, they take." Ellen pulled on Agnes' apron strings, "Please, Ma, come back inside."

"No, I have to talk to them and see what they do want. Maybe if we give them a few chickens and some eggs, they will go on their way and not bother us anymore."

"But you can not be sure," pleaded Ellen.

"No, that I can not. But Ellen, there were gypsies that lived in the countryside close to Breslau where I was raised. They would come and ask for food. Mostly, they would be thankful for any kind of food, and then be on their way." She touched Ellen's arm. "At least, it is worth a try." Take the younger girls and go back into the house and be quiet."

"Yes, Ma."

A dirty-looking little boy of about six jumped out of the first of the two colorful wagons before it even stopped rolling. His black, bushy hair hung long around the nape of his neck.

"Got anything here for us to eat?" he demanded in a thick, heavy Romanian accent. Deep, coal black eyes darted around the farm, surveying every inch of it in one quick glance. "You have anything of value here we can trade for?"

A dark-skinned middle-aged man drove the first team of horses. He moistened two fingers on his right hand, then curled up the edges of his long, droopy mustache. "Quiet, child," he rumbled in a low, throaty voice. He looked at Agnes and squinted his eyes very narrowly.

Agnes stared back. "I know his type. Just wants to see how much he can frighten me." The two eyed each other suspiciously, while the boy walked back and forth in front of the porch.

The raggedy curtain inside the wagon moved aside slightly. A shriveled-up old woman peered out the side window of the wagon and watched Agnes. "Ah-ha, one of those brave ones, that one is."

Agnes noticed the curtain at the window move, but she straightened her stance. "This is to be a war of the eyes, it seems," she thought.

Finally, the stooped, old crone could stand it no longer and opened the back door of the wagon. "Petter, Petter, come here." Still, the boy strolled back and forth. A few minutes passed. She hobbled down the steps. "Come here, you young ruffian." A long, skinny finger was pointed at him, "Get back here."

The boy scowled at the woman, then turned back to glare at Agnes. Step by step, scowl by scowl, slowly, he retreated back to the old lady. But he never let Agnes forget that he was watching her, too.

"Any luck, boy?"

"This one does not even seem to be afraid. I am not sure what to think of her, Grandma."

"You watch me and learn." Her stringy, matted, gray hair hung limp around thin shoulders. A black frayed scarf clung loosely over her bony frame and partially hid her full black skirt. She intentionally measured her steps toward the farm wife.

Agnes muttered to herself, "Just like all of them, pockets hidden in that skirt big enough to hold anything from chickens to turkeys and, maybe, watermelons and full-length coats." She had seen gypsies carry off all sorts of things in those pockets.

The gypsy woman stood before Agnes. "Food, we need food."

Agnes just stood there, looking at her.

"We want food," she demanded. The two stared into each other's eyes, hardly blinking. The woman finally could stand it no longer, and stomped her foot hard on the path. "Did you not hear?" She leaned forward, toward Agnes' left ear and shouted, "We want food."

Agnes stepped closer to stand right in front of the gypsy. "I did hear. You do not need to shout; my hearing is very good." After a long silence, followed by a disgusted sigh, she looked directly at the old woman and said in a soft voice, "Now, what do you want, eggs, bread, what?"

"Meat, meat. We need meat."

"On one condition. I give you two chickens and a dozen eggs, and then you be on your way and leave our farm alone."

Minutes ticked by, the silence was deafening. The withered old woman just stood there. Then she parted her dried, cracked lips in a crooked smile. Hardly any teeth remained in her mouth. "You know gypsies well. We will do."

"Ellen," Agnes called. The girl peeked around the kitchen door. "You and Agnes Marie take the hooked wire and go catch two hens out of the scratching pen and bring them here. Tell Irene to put a dozen eggs in a small box."

"Ma, we need help," Ellen begged.

"Do it now." Agnes stood firm in front of the woman. "As soon as you get the chickens and eggs, I want you out of here and down the road."

The old woman babbled something in a strange language to the drivers of the two wagons. The first driver slapped the reins on the horses' backs and turned the wagon around in the yard. The second wagon followed.

Ellen and Agnes Marie carried two squawking chickens out at arm's length. The beating wings scratched the girls' arms as they carried them to the woman.

"Petter, Petter, come, take the chickens."

The boy grabbed at the chickens and caught them by the feet. "You could have cleaned them for us," he growled to the frightened girls. His shrill laugh made them shrink back and race into the porch.

"The eggs, Ellen, bring me the eggs."

The girl rushed out and handed the small box to Ma. Agnes then held out the box of eggs to the gypsy, who snatched the box and shouted to the boy again, "Petter, Petter, the eggs. Come get the eggs."

"I will, I will," he snarled in return. "These chickens are too hard for me to tie up to the wagon. Their wings are scratching my arms, and they are trying to peck at me." The hens squawked and flapped their wings even more. "Help me, somebody," the boy hollered.

The head wagon driver cleared his throat with a long, noisy gurgle, and then spit a huge glob on the ground close to Agnes. Each one of the drivers stomped their feet on the wagon boxes and let loose with a round of raucous laughter. "You let a little chicken beat you, boy," one of them bellowed.

"Quiet," yelled the old woman. "Petter, Petter, hurry."

Blood ran from the scratches on his arms. "They are the meanest, orneriest chickens I ever handled," he growled, "but some of the fattest."

The gypsy woman turned and followed the boy back to the wagon. She flagged her arms at the drivers, and the horses started to move.

164

With a quick deft step, she swung her foot up on the wagon ladder and disappeared inside.

"Just as I thought," Agnes grumbled to herself. "That old gypsy was nowhere as old as she wanted me to believe. A likely scenario with them."

The wagons turned out onto the road. Four very relieved girls rushed out of the house and circled Agnes. "Ma, were you scared?"

The five shuffled back into the house, giggling and laughing. They were still all trying to talk at once, when Joseph and William came back into the house from checking the cattle and hogs.

"Oh, Pa," Irene screeched, "you should have seen Ma. She was so brave. The gypsies came."

Excited voices filled the kitchen. Joseph finally looked at his wife and shrugged his shoulders. "What is going on?" He winked at her.

She laughed lightly. "It was nothing, just two wagons of gypsies."

Joseph pushed his way past the children and put his hand on her shoulder. "Oh, my dear, dear Agnes."

"It could have been much worse, you know. It might have been a tramp instead of gypsies. The only problem would have been, could I have screamed as loud as the lady in town?" She laughed gaily.

He marveled, amazed, then pinched her cheek tenderly.

25

THE WAR

"WASHING AGAIN TODAY, Agnes?"

"Oh, Joseph, always so many clothes to wash, it seems."

William brought in another bucket of well water from the porch pump. Agnes lifted the bucket and emptied it into the copper boiler sitting on top of the wood-burning cookstove. The coal, combined with the wood, made such a hot fire that the water came to a boil in little time at all.

"Now, Agnes, you know why there are so many dirty clothes. You insist we all change often, especially when it is hot." Joseph squeezed her elbow affectionately.

"Clean clothes are cooler," she smiled. "The air circulates better around the body."

Joseph laughed, "And in a few days it will be bath time again, and more towels."

"Everyone really should bathe every day or two." She moved over to the kitchen table and put down a thick wooden cutting board. Reaching into a small box, she took out a piece of homemade lye soap and put it on the board. Then, with a sharp butcher knife, she deftly cut the strong-smelling lye soap into small slivers so it would suds up more. With a quick swoop, the chopped soap was scooped into a small muslin bag, so none of it would stick to the wash.

"Now, Agnes," her husband chuckled, "we would get absolutely nothing done around here except sitting in the bathtub if that were the situation. Are you sure you would have enough towels for all those baths?" He touched her shoulder lightly, and then started for the door.

"I need some supplies from Garden Plain. Should be back around dinner time." At the screen door, he paused and called out, "Please, Agnes, go easy on the pump today. It has been a long time since we had a good rain; the well might be going dry. The water level could be lower than normal."

Agnes carried the bag with the soap shavings out to the porch and dumped it in the old washing machine. Picking up two empty buckets, she hurried back into the kitchen. With special care not to spill any on herself and the children, she dipped boiling water out of the copper boiler, and then carried the full buckets out to the screened-in porch. Part of the scalding water was poured into a small washtub and the rest into the large washer. The lye soap shavings melted and dissolved into fluffy suds as the hot water was poured over it.

"Ellen, will you turn the crank on this washing machine?" Agnes gave the handle a few turns. "If you do this, I will scrub out the dirtier stains on the scrub board." She slipped the wide ridged board into the small tub, and lathered up the rough metal sheet with a thick, square bar of homemade soap. Picking up one of Wendell's shirts, she rubbed and rubbed a dirty spot, up and down, up and down, until her knuckles turned red.

Agnes straightened up to rest her back, and then paused to look at Ellen and William. "Every time I do this, it reminds me of the washerwomen who came to the big city houses. I do not know how they did it, but hour after hour they stood, with their arms in hot, sudsy water up to the elbows." She laughed lightly, "Watching them, I just knew some day they were going to pull their arms out of that water and have all the skin peeled completely off." She soaped the board more. "It always surprised me they still had knuckles and fingers. So many clothes, those wealthy people always had so many clothes and bedding to wash. Every day or two, the maids had to put clean sheets on each bed."

Stretching, she bent from side to side to ease her aching muscles. But, she kept scrubbing stain after stain. When each shirt and pants was clean enough for her satisfaction, it was tossed into the washer. "Ellen, start turning the crank now."

"Why not William?" the girl wrinkled her nose.

"The copper boiler has to be filled again, then the rinse tubs. That is his job. He also has to carry the soapy rinse water out and put it in the garden. We cannot waste a precious drop of water."

Ellen made a face and stuck out her lip in an angry pout. Agnes glanced at her, but did not say anything. Finally, the girl realized there was no way out for her. Grumbling under her breath, she grabbed the handle and rotated it back and forth as fast as possible. When she slowed down, so did the paddle. When another streak of angry ambition struck, the paddle beat up a froth of soapy bubbles. There was no stopping until the clothes were clean enough for Agnes' standards. Only then could the wash be run through the hand-cranked wringer into the tubs of cool rinse water.

Soap suds floated on top of the rinse tubs. "Empty these tubs and pump clear water in them, William. I want everything rinsed enough so there is no soapy scum left at all." Agnes turned to go back into the house for more things to wash.

"'Pump, William, pump. You have to keep clear water in there. We certainly cannot have any bubbles left in the rinse water, or the clothes are not clean.' Is everybody as clean crazy as she is?" Ellen made another face. The more her job irked her, the faster she cranked. As she did so, the bubbles multiplied.

"I think if you cranked a little slower, there would not be so many bubbles, and we would not have to use so much water to get the soap out." William winked at his sister.

"My brother, William, I do think you are very smart." Ellen slowed way down until Agnes walked back out. "These clothes are very clean now. I think they are ready to be rinsed out," the girl told her.

Agnes looked in the washtub, spread some of the things apart and announced, "Another ten minutes will be good." Ellen could not help herself. She raised her eyebrows and rolled her eyes. William bit his lip to keep from laughing.

He pumped and pumped bucket after bucket, until no more water came from the spout. "Ma, Ma, the well has gone dry."

"Oh, my. Go turn on the windmill, William, and fill the buckets there and bring them in here." William began to say something, but decided against it. "Perhaps we can get all the wash through before your pa comes home."

"We had better," thought William. "Especially since we pumped the well dry again. One of these days, I hope Ma learns we cannot keep pumping water and more water from this porch well." The boy sighed to himself, "Pa always said this was a shallow well."

As Joseph neared the farm, he marveled at the lines of white wash flapping in the breeze. "Clean, clean, white as the new fallen snow," he sang in a monotone. "My Agnes has the whitest wash around." Irene and Agnes Marie were hanging the last of the dish towels on the line. The sun sparkled off the wash like white sails at sea.

"I wonder if they pumped the well dry again. I just wish Agnes would realize a few soap bubbles in the clothes are not going to hurt anything. Next week it will be washed all over again, anyway."

He jumped down from the wagon and walked into the house carrying a copy of the June 20, 1914, Wichita newspaper. "Agnes, I brought a paper for you to read. The men at the barbershop were talking about the message that came over the telegraph into the railroad depot, day before yesterday. Something about an Archduke from Austria-Hungary getting assassinated." He put the paper down on the table. "The article sounds like this could cause all of Europe to explode into war."

Agnes wiped her hands on her apron and followed him into the kitchen. "Austrian Archduke Killed," the headline screamed. "Threat of War Looms," declared the subtitle.

"Oh, dear," her face turned ashen-gray. "My family." She struggled to choke back the sobs. Staggering against the table, her body slid slowly onto the chair. "Oh, Joseph, my family."

Coming around behind her, he leaned down and put his cheek alongside hers. His hands clasped her shoulders tightly. "Now, now, Agnes, it does not say a war has begun."

"Joseph, you do not know how the leaders over there think. That whole area of Europe has been restless since the 1870s, when the French and the Prussians fought. The French lost the rich coal areas of Alsace and Lorraine to Germany in the war. Our Chancellor Bismarck took advantage of the loss and demanded the provinces be controlled by the Germans.

She picked up the paper, then bowed her head slowly in shock. "My country became a very strong country because of that war. Our Kaiser Wilhelm the Second saw to that. He is a good man, a good ruler."

A quick reader, she scanned through the article way ahead of Joseph. "Oh, Joseph, if this just does not cause war again. So many alliances were formed back then, countries against countries. And there is so much hatred among the countries."

She pulled away from Joseph's grasp and rested her head upon her hands. "Oh no, Meine Mütter wrote several letters ago that Constantine had to begin his military duty soon." Reaching for Joseph's hand, she grasped it and held it to her lips. "We must pray, Joseph, we must pray so there is no war, so Germany does not go to war." She sobbed, "My brother, Joseph, my brother could get killed." Tears came rapidly, "Oh, Joseph."

He felt her agony, so every two or three days, he made a special trip into town to buy the big city newspaper. She read and reread the news about her beloved country, holding her breath and praying so Germany would not become actively involved. But, the fifth day of August she knew, the inevitable had happened. Her husband returned from Garden Plain. Without a word, he unrolled the newspaper and showed her the front page, "Germany Declares War on Russia."

Agnes grasped the paper to her bosom, then sank down onto the nearest chair. The paper fell to the floor. The tears came in torrents, "Oh, dear God, no."

Joseph knelt beside her and wrapped her in his arms. Her wrenching sobs tore at her chest and caught her breath in turmoil. Her weary body sagged heavily against Joseph's shoulder. His strength was strong, but anxious. She felt his support and let is seep completely into her being.

Finally, the tears were spent and she became aware of how exhausted she really was. "Joseph, the paper, I must read the paper."

He lifted its pages and tenderly handed them to her. "Agnes, are you sure you should do this? Are you sure you need to read all of this?"

"Please, yes. I have to know all that I can, Joseph. I have to know all that there is to know."

The fall school term was about to begin. Agnes approached Joseph one day, wondering how he would react to her suggestion.

"Joseph, I think we need to talk. I know you have not given this a lot of thought, but perhaps we need to send the children to the public school at Garden Plain. The nuns have a good school at St. Mary's, but all their teaching is in German. Mrs. Peppen's children go to the town school. She told me the county superintendent of schools has ordered English spoken in all the public schools. They are trying to enforce that all across the state, because of the situation with Germany and America." She paused for a few minutes to think.

"So, what are you saying, Agnes?"

"Joseph, the children really need their education to be in the English language. Once they get out of school, they will need to be able to read and write properly in English. We need to give them the opportunity to learn all of that." She paused momentarily. "We can transfer the younger children over to the Catholic school when they learn English. The Dominican nuns will be glad to teach the children then, for their First Communion. They are planning to go to the English instruction directive also, eventually. But the public school has been teaching English ever since they began. There are other families going there, not all Germans, so that will help the children learn to speak English quicker."

Joseph sat silently for a time. Finally, he looked directly at Agnes. "If we are going to do that, then we will also transfer to the Catholic church there. The town is a mile closer to our farm than the village of St. Mary's." He frowned, deep in thought. "And we do all our business there, so we may as well be involved in the church and schools there, too. That might be a good idea," he smiled. "Our children already know some of the neighbor children, like the Peppens. They have so many activities there that now our children do not get to participate in." He chuckled. "I hear the public grade school has a fairly good football team year after year. The men in town talk about it all the time. And as much energy as Wendell has now, just wait until he gets several years older. We might have to find a release for him like that, to get him to slow down."

"Oh, but, Joseph, is that that brutal game?"

Joseph laughed, shaking his head. "It is, and if any boy is made for that game, it is definitely Wendell. He is not afraid of a huge bull; why would he be afraid of some kid trying to tackle him?"

Agnes almost regretted saying anything about the education issue. But it was settled. Joseph arranged for his children to further their education in town.

The war news became glummer with each passing day. Joseph made the trip to town every few days, just to buy the daily newspaper for Agnes. He knew she was anxious to keep up with world events. His heart bled for her. He could only try to imagine her feelings and her anxiety for the family she had left behind.

One Sunday following the sad war news, Joseph, Agnes and the family arrived early at St. Anthony Church as had become their custom. It gave them the chance to get one of the very front pews for their family. Agnes insisted they be close to the front so there would be less distraction.

Father Silas cleared his throat to begin his sermon. "Kaiser Wilhelm the Second of Germany is an evil, greedy man. He is leading his country and all of Europe into war." On and on his tirade continued.

Joseph saw Agnes flinch, and reached to take her hand. After a long time, the priest tired and went back to saying the Mass. Agnes said nothing about the sermon, but Joseph knew it was painful for her.

The next Sunday and the Sundays after, the family took their seats near the pulpit. And Sunday after Sunday, Father Silas denounced the German leader in fiery speeches. Still, Agnes made no comment.

But one Sunday, she'd had enough. Joseph saw her body stiffen and watched her wipe the tears from her eyes. Then, he watched a look come over her face he had never seen before, a look of defiance. The woman could stand no more. She rose to her feet and looked the priest directly in the eye.

"Stop," she demanded. But he kept spewing his vehement words.

"Stop," she yelled. "You have no right to talk about my Fatherland that way."

Father Silas glared at her. "How dare you interrupt my sermon."

Agnes was not going to be put down. Her anger had become too great. He did not know of what he was speaking. She wagged her finger at the priest. Stretching her body tall and planting her feet firmly together, she glowered at him, for what seemed an eternity to Joseph.

Finally, in a most authoritative voice, she spoke, "You will not speak of Germany and the Kaiser in that way. He is a good man, an honorable man. He has led Germany into good times, prosperity for all the people. His countrymen respect him as their God-chosen leader."

The priest tried to speak, but she would not hear of it. "You have no right." Her voice was now calm, but firm, "You were not born in the Fatherland. You do not understand the German people. And you certainly will never understand the Kaiser or the love his countrymen have for him."

With that, she turned, picked up her handbag, looked at Joseph and the children, and then stepped out into the aisle. Looking hard at the priest for several minutes, she turned and walked up the aisle to the front door.

Joseph stood up in the pew and turned to watch her go, but he hesitated to follow.

"Go ahead. Go with her," said the priest in a shocked, but quiet voice. Joseph stood and held out his hand to his children. Together, the family followed Agnes out of the church.

Father Silas stood there aghast, dumbfounded. Slowly, he returned to the altar and continued the Mass.

Agnes spoke not a word all the way home, and neither did the others. In their bedroom, she finally spoke. "Joseph, I will certainly be the laughingstock of the community." She paused, then softly added, "And to embarrass you and the children so."

Joseph put his arms around her and grinned, "No doubt you will, my dear Agnes." Then he laughed softly, "But, in thinking about it, I am quite proud of you. He deserved that. He could not possibly have known how you and the other parishioners from Germany felt." Joseph pinched her chin gently. "But, you were the only one with enough nerve to tell him. I am proud of my wife."

Father Silas never mentioned the Kaiser again when Agnes was in Mass. Joseph readily reminded her with a twinkle in his eye, "He knows better."

Several months later, the news Agnes dreaded arrived. She slowly opened the letter edged in black, holding off for several minutes longer the horrible reality she knew it would reveal.

Her mother's harsh words spanned the thousands of miles. "Your brother, Constantine, died in the fighting," she had written. "Please pray for his eternal rest."

26

A BABY

"Do I HAVE to come home, Pa?"

"Ellen, it is about time for the baby to come."

She groaned under her breath, "A baby. Surely not, that woman is going to have a baby." She took Joseph's hand, "But, Pa, I like working here. Aunt Maggie is so nice." She paused a bit, thinking, then added in a quiet voice, "I do not want to come home and help Ma. She is always yelling at me. I can never please her."

"Oh, Ellen, you know that is not true. I know Ma expects a lot of you, but she works hard. She needs your help now. I need your help." He looked at her more sternly than she ever remembered. "Go get your clothes together, now."

"Yes, Pa." She took her time gathering her things, while Pa talked to Aunt Maggie. Finally, she came out of the house and climbed in the buggy.

Ellen rode home with him in silence. How she dreaded going home to help Agnes. She remembered that first time the housekeeper walked into the house. It was as clear in her mind as if yesterday. "That woman walked over to the cookstove and banged the oven door shut," she recalled.

"This door must be kept shut all the time, unless I leave it open. It is too dangerous down like this. Someone will hurt themselves." Agnes had looked at each one like she wanted to drill it into their heads.

"I hate her, I hate her," rumbled through the girl's mind. "Work, work, work – that is all she thinks about."

"You are very quiet, Ellen." Pa patted her hand, "What are you thinking about?"

"Not much, Pa." But in her thoughts she replayed what her aunts had said about Step-Ma.

Just the day before, Aunt Maggie was talking to her. "Your step-ma is much too strict with you and the others." The woman wrapped her arms around Ellen's shoulders. "Your mother was not like that. She was much nicer and so much easier to get along with."

Then Ellen thought about Aunt Nora. She could still see her mother's other sister shake her head and say, "That woman makes all of you work too much. You should not have to do all that work. All those chickens, and ducks and geese."

"Yea, and now she wants to get turkeys too, yet. Will she never quit?" Ellen had shuffled around on the seat. "Is she trying to make Pa think she is really special? And we have to do all that work. Just like her. We do the dirty work, she gets the credit."

"We are here," said Pa, much too merrily for the girl. "Try to be nice, Ellen. For me." He smiled at her so nicely she could not help herself, but to smile in return.

The next morning, Agnes told Joseph, "I think the time has come; we need to call the doctor."

"I will get Mrs. Peppen to come over and help. She is the neighborhood mid-wife." He winked at her. "And I will go get the doctor to come right away."

The house was soon bustling with extra people. Pots of water cooked furiously on the cookstove. Steam frosted the windows and carved winter fairies on the panes of glass.

"Ellen, you keep Coletta in the kitchen, will you?" said Joseph. "We need for her to be out of the way and as quiet as possible."

"Sure, Pa." Ellen took the little girl's hand. "Come, do you want to play a game with your doll?" Ellen spread the doll clothes out on the table.

Soon, the cry of a newborn was heard coming from the bedroom. Coletta's eyes grew big, and she turned to Ellen, "What was that?"

"I am not sure," the oldest sister said. "It sounded like a baby kitty crying."

Coletta laughed, then went back to playing with her dolls.

February 3, 1915, Agnes was fulfilled in a way she thought was no longer possible for a woman of her age. At 35, she had almost given up hope, the thrill of holding her own child.

She looked at the tiny little being the doctor placed in her outstretched arms. Joseph bent over to kiss Agnes tenderly on the cheek. "My lovely wife," he whispered. Strong fingers caressed the pink cheek of his newborn child. "My beautiful daughter." With unbounded gentleness, the father uncurled the small fist and wrapped the short, fat fingers around his own massive one. Tears welled in the 44-year-old farmer's eyes and rolled down his leathery cheeks.

"What name shall our child be called?" A shining smile broke through the fall of tears and brought his true emotions to light.

"Esther Anna Elizabeth, I think. 'Elizabeth' is for your mother, and the 'Anna' in honor of my mother."

That is a fine name, for there are no other Esthers in my family that I know of."

She grasped his hand and looked into his eyes kindly. "Neither in mine that I am aware of. But the story of Queen Esther in the Bible has always been my favorite." A smile curved her lips upward. "Esther was such a strong person with so much courage and integrity."

"Not unlike you at all, Agnes," he laughed, "not unlike you at all."

Squeezing his hand, "I always like to think my life paralleled hers somewhat."

Joseph leaned to kiss her cheek again. "I see a definite resemblance. Queen Esther stood up to her king, and you challenged the priest." His eyes twinkled, "Esther it is. Our daughter is Esther." He cleared his throat kidding, "Should I explain to Father Silas your choice of her name?"

They laughed together. "That does not sound like a good idea."

Very early spring storms lashed out at Kansas. Agnes protected her child with fierceness. She rushed in to check on the little one and Coletta, by now almost five. "Call me if she cries," the mother instructed the older one.

Agnes still trembled when the weather of the plains erupted into its awesome display of power. The glare of lightning could be seen even through closed eyelids. Determined, however, she brought herself to watch the tremendous brilliance of the bolts as they slashed the atmosphere, from the uppermost clouds to the horizon. The vibrations of the thunder no longer unnerved her, for she now listened to the musical variations and deep-throated rumbles of each clap as it raced across the earth's face. In her homeland, the earth was gently blessed with the sweetness of the rain. Hardly ever was the land replenished with such a violent display, as it was here in Kansas.

But then, the rains stopped and the clouds seemed to evaporate from the face of the earth. The intense heat and dryness of the prairies was so unlike the coolness of Germany. The sweat rolled from her brow in a way she had never known. Windows were opened so the heat of the cookstove could escape, but it only mingled with the unusually hot May and June breezes rushing to come in.

Prayers were said for rain. But in the meantime, the endless buckets of rinse water from the washings were carried out to keep life in the garden. Other days, water was carried from the windmill. When the winds stilled and did not touch the wind wheel and vanes of the prairie's pumps, the plants of man suffered. On those days, the pump in the porch was put into use. Mother Nature took care of her own plantings, but those of man suffered from her harshness.

The work still had to be done. There was no rest; it was endless. One burning hot July day, Agnes remembered it was time for hatching the ducklings.

"Irene, Agnes, bring those duck eggs over here."

"What are you going to do with them, Ma?" Irene carried three eggs over to her. Agnes Marie picked up two more she found and brought them over to Agnes.

"This hen has laid several eggs of her own, and is starting to sit on the nest. We will just put these duck eggs under her, and she can sit on them until they hatch. Our ducks are not very good about sitting still that long."

The girls carefully placed the eggs in the straw. Agnes put the hen back on the nest. The chicken gently pushed the extra eggs under her and spread her wings over all the eggs. "I sure like to watch them do that," laughed Irene. "That hen just knows what to do."

"Now, in a few weeks, we should have nice fat baby ducks." Agnes stepped back from the nest.

"They will be so cute." Coletta stroked the hen's rich red feathers. "Will the ducks have feathers the same color as hers?"

"I hope not," laughed Agnes. "If they do, they will be funny-looking ducks."

In just a few weeks, there were new baby chicks and five ducklings tagging along after the mother hen. Whenever they strayed, she would "cluck, cluck" loudly and call them all back to her. Soon, the little group was going all over the farm. The small creek east of the barn was so inviting. The hen seemed to know the ducks needed to find water for a swim.

Five-year-old Coletta had taken to following the babies all around. They were her playmates. Soon, she tamed them enough so they would eat grain from her outstretched hand. Coletta even named each one of them. The little girl was convinced the small babies knew their names and came when she called.

An enormous bank of clouds built up in the western sky one hot, sultry afternoon. The wind began to stir, and then turned into forceful, violent gusts. Huge scattered raindrops hit the dry dust of the yard. Small puffs of dust erupted from the impact. The fresh smell of rain on the parched earth filled the nostrils with unexpected pleasure.

"Coletta, bring the chicks and the ducks home," yelled Agnes out the back door. "Hurry, hurry. They will get sick if they get wet."

The little girl ran after them, trying to get them to follow the mother hen. But no matter how hard she tried, they kept scattering. The thunder frightened them, and only made them run more. She was getting so tired. The wind was getting stronger. Finally, she got behind the ones she could, and headed them for the house. She did not notice two little ducks had hidden under the grass along the creek bed.

By the time they all got to the house, Agnes was waiting for them, screaming to get the chickens over to the hen house. Coletta had a hard time getting them to go in that direction. Then Agnes realized two of her ducklings were missing.

"Where are they?" she yelled at the little girl. "Where are the other two baby ducks?"

Coletta turned around to her, "I do not know, Ma. I tried to get all of them."

"You should have brought them all. You know that." Agnes was beside herself. Those ducks were worth money. They could sell them for extra cash, money they would need if the dry season did not change.

In her haste and anger, she grabbed a branch off a nearby bush and hit Coletta across the legs, breaking the skin enough to bleed. "Next time, you keep better watch over them."

William came running up to the house when he heard Coletta cry. "Ma, Ma, what are you doing to her?"

She turned and walked back into the house, muttering, "Those ducks are worth money to us."

"Come here, let me look at your skin." He rubbed his little sister's legs and took her inside the porch. With cool water from the pump, he washed off her legs.

The spring and summer passed in quick succession. There was the gardening to do; spring chickens to be cleaned; ducks, geese and turkeys to be butchered; duck and goose feathers to be stripped for pillows; school clothes to be made.

Preserving the garden produce was an almost daily, long, hot, tedious job. Agnes was totally amazed with her gardening. Joseph always made sure the richest manure from the chicken house was spread thin. Straw mulched most of the garden to keep the moisture in, and the majority of weeds out. With this special care, the vegetables flourished.

Corn, peas, carrots, beans and tomatoes had to be canned in glass jars, and cooked in boiling water. Cabbage was chopped and put into large crocks. Covered in vinegar and salt brine, it turned into sauerkraut. Small cucumbers were canned for sweet pickles. Larger cucumbers were covered with dill weed and salt brine for dill pickles. Fruit purchased from fruit stands in the city also was canned.

By summer's end, the shelves in the cellar had to be brimming with row upon row of colored jars. If not, the family would not eat properly for the long winter months.

Sandwiched in between was the endless washing, ironing, cleaning and bread to be baked every day or two. And the hired farmhands who stayed in the bunkhouse needed three huge meals a day. When extra men from the neighborhood were needed, mountains of extra food were needed.

After one frustrating day, she asked her sister-in-law, Margaret, "How do you keep the hired hands from eating so much bread?" Agnes sighed loudly. "It seems all I get done is setting dough, kneading it and baking the bread. Just for a few days at a time, I would like the kitchen to be a bit cooler."

Margaret laughed. "The secret is, you do not feed them the freshest bread you baked, but some that is several days old." She winked at Agnes, "The older the bread, the tougher and drier it gets. That means it takes them longer to chew it."

"Good advice, Margaret; I never thought of that." Agnes stashed her latest batch of bread back in the pantry and pulled out some that was several days old. "We will see if that works with our bunch of men." The ladies giggled like schoolgirls.

"Our secret," repeated Margaret. "And if my husband says anything about the bread being dry, just act like you do not hear it." She grinned, "He knows."

It was also hard to keep her baby comfortable and cool. Agnes marveled at the changes in Esther. She had watched other people's children grow, but it was not like seeing her own. Numerous times, the mother counted fingers and toes, and made sounds to see if the baby could hear.

The months hurried by. A hint of fall touched the air. The hard red wheat planting was finished by mid-October, and the prairie hay had all been cut and stacked. Pumpkins were ripe and late apples were picked. Pies were baked often during the week.

"I cannot believe how many pies this family eats in a week," she told Joseph. He cut another huge piece and put it on his plate.

"But this is so good. No wonder the children eat a lot of pie." He smiled at Agnes. "I talked to the neighbor men and my brothers about butchering here next week. The four hogs and the steer are all nice and fat." He took a huge bite of pie. "Just looking at all that meat on the hoof makes me hungry for fresh beef and pork."

Agnes poured him a hot cup of coffee, then sat down across the table from him. "I used to think it took a lot of food at the rich people where I worked, but nothing like this." She laughed, "I just never realized how much farm men eat."

"They have to eat like that, to keep up with all the hard work."

"I can understand that. They work harder than anyone I ever knew." A smile stretched across her face, "That is, except for kitchen help and the cooks."

"You certainly do work hard, my dear wife, and in this hot kitchen with hardly any breeze. Without all your hours in the garden, and tending the chickens, ducks and geese, we would not have such good meals on the table." He reached over to touch her hand. "You have no idea how many of the men said they like to come here to eat. The meals are always better and more interesting than anywhere else."

He winked at her. "Even the hoboes are getting the word. They would do almost anything, even pay me, to get hired for our farm."

27

THE WEDDING

"AGNES AND IRENE are getting to be quite good help now. That has really made it easier for me these last years. I know it has been hard for them, especially Ellen, losing Katherine at such a difficult age in a girl's life. She missed out on learning so many things in those early years." Agnes stood up to refill Joseph's coffee cup.

She sat back down, and relaxed in deep thought for a time. "I may have been very hard on the girls, but I wanted them to learn so much for later on. And I know they never liked me pushing that way. I just hope they understand why I demanded so much of them."

"You do well with them, Agnes. They probably do not appreciate your efforts now, but give them a few years when they have families of their own. Hopefully, then, they will know why you asked so much of them." Joseph rubbed her hand again, "Only then, will they realize what you did for them, coming in and taking care of them." He lifted her hand to his lips. "I will always remember and love you for what you have given to me and my children."

She closed her eyes and nodded. In a soft voice barely heard by Joseph, she whispered, "Thank you. I love you, too."

Her mind drifted off to the future. "It will not be the same without Ellen around anymore after November. She came to me the other day and asked me to help her prepare for her wedding." She hesitated, "I was really hard on Ellen. But, Joseph, that made me feel so good that she asked me to help." She pushed the half-empty pie plate closer to him and motioned for him to take more. "1916 is going to be an exciting year; I can feel it. My intuition never is too wrong, it seems."

The winter storms blew with fury. Snows were at the mercy of the north winds. Country roads were blocked. The farmyard was piled high with towering drifts. Spring finally conquered the onslaught of winter.

By March 17th, the garden was plowed and harrowed. Chunks of seed potatoes were dropped into ridges and covered with mounds of straw mulch. Early peas, onions and beans came next, followed by radish and lettuce seeds. The busy, hot cycle of canning vegetables would soon begin again.

Agnes felt her body tighten and change, and she knew the seed of hope once again grew within her. The months would go fast because of all the work that needed to be taken care of.

"I will really need to lean on the girls this summer," the 36-year-old mother-to-be confided to her 45-year-old husband.

He held her close. "I never thought another child would come into my life at this age. But it makes me very happy, Agnes." His embrace tightened, "I only hope it will not be too hard on you." He shuddered as he remembered that Katherine was expecting with her last child at that age. Under his breath, a whispered prayer was said.

The summer months quickly turned into early fall. "How the days are going, Joseph. Ellen asked about getting ready for her wedding. She told me there was a dress she might like to have. She brought home her wedding veil the other day. Such a lovely headpiece it has. Ellen does have good taste."

Joseph pulled out a chair and sat down at the table. Agnes brought him a cup, and then walked to the stove to get the coffeepot.

"Whatever dress she would like to have, tell her we will get it for her." Joseph smiled a bit, "It is hard for me to believe that my oldest daughter is ready to get married."

"She is eighteen, Joseph. That is a good age for a girl to marry. She will be strong enough to have children and still do all the work she needs to do. Is August going to farm?"

"He talked about moving to Topeka after they marry. It sounds like there might be more carpenter work there for him."

"That will be a long way from here for Ellen, will it not? She is not used to being so far away from home."

Joseph grinned, "Sometimes that is best for a young couple, to be far away from the relatives. They have to make the best of it and get along." He poured some of the steaming hot coffee onto his saucer so it would cool. "I will miss her though."

"In the next few days, I will talk to the neighbor ladies about helping fix the meal for the guests. The two of you need to decide how many friends and relatives to invite, so I can tell the ladies." Agnes poured herself a fresh cup of coffee.

"Usually, it is just the immediate family, brothers, sisters, grandparents, aunts and uncles. My papa is the only grandparent still living. And the aunts and uncles, we will just have to count those. Maybe a few friends." He took a sip of his cooled coffee. "August, being from here, and most of his relatives around, that will mean more people. Joseph broke his oatmeal-raisin cookie in half. "Since it will be in November, and we cannot be sure just what the weather will be like, there is no way they can invite too many. The house just is not big enough." He thought for a few minutes, "If it is not too cold, we can put a few tables and chairs in the garage. It opens on the south, and the sun would warm it up somewhat."

"Ellen said she and August will go around Sunday and start inviting the aunts and uncles. That is a nice custom. It makes a wedding much more personal." Agnes took a cookie from the plate.

"Are you sure this will not be too hard on you, Agnes? Her wedding is less than two months before the baby is to come." Joseph reached over to take her hand and rubbed it gently.

"I am sure it will not be. There is a certain excitement about a wedding that seems to make everything else easier." She took several bites from the cookie, while deep in thought. "We have plenty of vegetables canned that we can use, and some of the fried-down sausage would be good for the meal. Ellen can decide what kind of desserts she wants, and if she needs help making her wedding cake, I will be glad to help with that."

"You are good to work with them. I just hope this is not too much for you, Agnes."

November 14th was a bright crisp day. The sky was an ice blue, and a few feathery clouds drifted across the sun.

"I sure hope it does not snow today," Ellen said to her sisters. "I want a beautiful, special day, all mine. And I do not want anything to happen to ruin it."

"It will be special, Ellen." Agnes Marie closed the buttons on the back of the bride's wedding dress. "Once the Mass is over and you two are married, nothing can ruin your day."

Ellen became very quiet as she looked longingly out the window. Quietly, she whispered, "If only my mama could be here with me today. I miss her so much." Her sisters wrapped their arms around her in a tight bear hug, so tight, that Ellen finally wiggled loose. "You are cutting off my breath."

The room filled with girlish giggles. "I feel like crying, though," said Ellen through a few tears. "I will be going so far away from home, and I do not know when I will be able to get back to see you."

"We will write to you," promised Irene. "We do know how to write, Ellen, remember." The girls hugged each other amid more giggling.

The church organist began to play the wedding march. Ellen and August looked at each other and smiled. He took her arm and crooked it around his own. Looking up at him, she blushed. "My, what a handsome, wonderful groom I have," she whispered to him.

"Do you take this woman? Do you take this man?" Ellen barely heard the words and could not remember answering, "I do." But then she heard the priest say, "In the eyes of God, you are now man and wife."

She pinched herself so she would remember it was not a dream.

The dust rose from the country dirt road as the parade of buggies and a few of the newfangled horseless carriages drove the miles back to the farm. Ellen looked back to see the long line following August's buggy and grabbed for his hand. "It is so exciting."

The guests assembled outside, under the leafless trees. Only a few dried leaves rattled in the soft, slight breeze. The men gathered in the garage where August and his pa had set up the home brew and the old man's favorite dandelion wine.

The golden wine shimmered in the glasses of some of the women. August's father said with a flourish, "This pretty wine is for the ladies, it is too light for a hardy man."

"I need to take Esther in for a nap," Agnes told Joseph. "She is getting much too tired and cranky."

"I think you had better rest awhile, too." Joseph took her arm. "You have been on your feet all day." He grinned, "That is not good for a woman in your condition."

"Do you mean expecting, or old?" Agnes touched his hand lightly.
"Both, I guess."

She took the little girl into their bedroom and put her down for a nap. Agnes slipped off her shoes and lay down on the bed for a rest also. "This does feel good." She wiggled her toes. "I am so thankful the neighbor ladies fixed the food for today. That would have been such a chore."

"Oh, no," said Agnes Marie to Irene, "I hear the 'baby waker' coming."

"Did Ellen invite him?"

"I am not sure, but if she did, there will be a price to pay. If he comes in here with that loud motorcycle of his and spins around the yard, Ma is going to get really mad. She just took Esther in the house for her nap."

Va-room, va-room! Closer and closer the noise came. With all the throttle he could manage, the neighbor boy wheeled his new motor-cycle into the yard, and skidded to a stop next to the house, right outside the window where Agnes was sleeping.

He pushed the throttle again and again to rev up the motor. *Va-room, va-room, va-room!*

"Oh, no, we need to get him out of here," Irene looked at Agnes Marie frantically.

"He is making so much noise, I don't think he would even hear us if we told him." Agnes Marie tried to get his attention to shut off the cycle.

"Waaa," Esther awoke with a scream. Agnes sat up in bed, still half asleep. "What is going on?"

Va-room, va-room! The noise seemed to get louder and louder each time he pushed the throttle.

"That fool, coming in here that way." Agnes was out of bed, trying to hush the baby. Esther only cried louder and louder. Agnes finally picked up the child, and headed into the kitchen. She rushed through the porch, screaming, "Joseph, Joseph!"

He hurried into the house and, even then, knew what the outcome would be.

"Joseph, Joseph, come in here."

"Yes, Agnes, what is it?" He tried to keep his voice soft to calm her.

"Did Ellen invite that boy with his motorcycle?"

"I am not sure." Joseph cringed.

"Get him out of here. He has scared Esther. That sound could make her deaf. Get him out of here." Agnes started back for the bedroom, then turned around again and growled, "Tell them all to go home. If they cannot behave around here, tell them to go home. If they cannot show a little respect, they should go home."

"But, Agnes, they were just having a little fun."

"Do as I say." She turned and stormed back into the bedroom.

Joseph hung his head and hesitated to walk out the porch door. All the guests were standing there, looking at him. Every one of them knew Agnes had an explosive temper. They felt for Joseph as they watched him in silence.

"I am sorry," he almost whispered, "but perhaps you had better leave. Agnes is not feeling very well. Her time is close." He leaned against the door frame. "Please, come in and get enough food to take back home for your families to eat this evening." He turned to go back inside, then looked back at those in the yard. "I am so sorry."

"Just like that woman," whispered Ellen's Aunt Maggie loud enough for all of Katherine's other sisters to hear. "She will never give that man any peace. I just do not know where he found her." She grumbled and mumbled, then spoke aloud to the others, "She just does not belong around here. Thinks she is too good for all of us."

"I feel sorry for Ellen," said another behind her hand. "That girl has had to put up with so much, and now this has to happen on her wedding day. I am just glad she has found a husband so she can get out of here this soon." She looked around at her other sisters, "Katherine should see this. She would never believe it."

Ellen stepped out from the crowd, and turned around to face them. "I do not like that woman; I do not like her."

August came walking up beside her and put his arm around her, "Shh, Ellen, do not get so upset."

"Did you see that? She just ruined my wedding day. That woman just ruined my wedding day. I will never forgive her for that."

Agnes with her beloved children, little rosy-cheeked, blond Esther, and baby son, Robert.

Anna Picke Puder, mother of Agnes.

28

THE LETTER

JUST BEFORE THE beginning of the new year, 1917, a son was born to Agnes and Joseph.

May we name him Robert, please, in memory of my father?"

"As you wish, Agnes."

Esther and Robert were the true joys of Agnes' life. Their smiles and antics erased all the hardships of the farm. Her biggest wish was to have her mother see these precious grandchildren of hers.

"Oh, Meine Mütter," she wrote to her mother, Anna. "My joy is complete. How I have been blessed." Agnes looked at the photo she had taken with her children. "See, Mütter, what butterball fat cheeks Esther has. Her hair is a soft yellow, like the beams of sunlight filtered through the trees. Two years, my little girl is two. Her laughter spreads stardust around the room for me."

She wiped the tears as the words formed upon her writing paper. "My baby, Robert, see what a fine child he is. His eyes sparkle when he looks at Esther. There is a special bond already. I look at the two of them and wonder how well I will be able to raise my children. But Joseph is such a good man, Mütter, and a gentle father. My children are so fortunate to have such a father as he."

The teardrops splattered upon the paper. "I know it will be very expensive for him, but Joseph has already told me I could take the children and return home to see you. They will have to be a year or so older to do that. But, oh, Meine Mütter, I can hardly wait to gaze upon your face once again, to put my children in your arms and have them standing by your knee. I want to see the continuation of the generations, the grandmother and the grandchildren."

Agnes touched the letter to her lips and sealed it with a kiss for her mother. "Oh, Mütter, sometimes I miss you so much I can hardly bear it. I hold your photo before me and look deep into your eyes. I try so hard to imagine the sound of your voice and to hear your laughter. Now, more than ever, Mütter, with the children here, I yearn to touch your cheek again."

She read and reread the letter many times before she gave it to Joseph to take to the post office. "My heart goes with this letter." He held her close and wiped the tears from her eyes. Never could he imagine the loneliness in her heart.

"Remember, Agnes, in a year or so, you will see your mother again."

"Thank you, Joseph. A faint smile broke through the tears.

She knew it would be a long time before she read the words from her beloved mother, who seldom wrote. But, in her heart, Agnes imagined the letter going by train to the docks of New York City, and then, stashed in the mail holds of an ocean liner, bound for Germany. She had to keep hope in her heart.

Some six months later, Joseph rushed into the house. "Agnes, a letter from Breslau."

She tore at the flap, anxious to read the words. But the excitement of Agnes' letter was not echoed in this one. "Wait until the children are much older," her mother wrote. "It is too hard to travel with such little children."

Agnes stared at the letter a long time. "She is right to suggest that, Joseph," she finally said. "I should have known better than to even consider it."

"Do not give up hope of seeing her, Agnes. In a few short years, then perhaps. I will see so you can go home again."

She stood and leaned her head against his shoulder. "Oh, my dear Joseph."

Christmas was two months away when Agnes wrote her mother a long letter, wishing her "Froehliche Weihnacten," "Merry Christmas." She drew a few stars and candles on the letter and wished she was a much better artist. "The children are growing up so. Esther will be four in February, and Robert will be three December 29th. You should see them, Mütter. Where one goes, so does the other. I never knew a brother and sister could be so close. Their laughter fills the rooms and gladdens my heart. What joy they will be on the Holy Night, when the candles of the Christmas tree sparkle in their eyes."

"Soon," she whispered to herself as she sealed the letter. "Soon they will be old enough to make the trip. How happy will be that day."

"Merry and Blessed Christmas to my daughter and her family," wrote Anna on a colorful Christmas postcard. "My love to all."

Several weeks into January, William rode Old Ben to the mailbox a half-mile from the farm driveway. Joseph happened to look up from feeding the hogs and noticed that William was riding home much faster than he went.

Joseph walked toward the house just as his son slid off the back of the horse.

"Pa, a letter came for Ma from Germany. Maybe you had better take it to her." He handed the envelope, edged in black, to his father.

Joseph turned it over slowly in his hands and looked at the return address: Breslau, Deutschland. "Yes, Son, I think I should."

"Agnes, come in the kitchen. There is a letter for you from your family." He handed her the letter, then put his hand on her shoulder. She slumped down on a chair by the table and held the letter in her hands for a long time. Joseph sat down beside her and said not a word.

"It is my mother," Agnes finally said. "Something has happened to Meine Mütter." With shaking hands, she ripped at the envelope flap.

A black-edged memorial card fell out. "Anna Picke Puder, Geboren September 30, 1850, Sterben November 27, 1919. May She Rest in Peace."

Agnes put her head down on the table. Long, torturous sobs racked her body with heaving.

"Oh, no, Meine Mütter, Meine Mütter, my mother."

Agnes' joys, Esther and Robert.

29

CHRISTMAS

"HURRY UP, ROBERT." Esther yelled at him from the kitchen. "I want to go to bed early. Maybe Saint Nick will come earlier then."

Coletta stood behind her and called to Robert, too. "If you do not hurry and get out of there, Christmas will be over and you will still be soaking." She stomped her foot. "Your fourth birthday might even pass by while you sit in the bathtub. Just think, then you will not even see your birthday presents."

Boyish giggles were his only reply.

"Now, girls," Agnes called them down. "I am heating more warm water for you."

"Good," ten-year-old Coletta answered. "It is always so cold in that little room." She looked back at Joseph, "Pa, is there any way we can get a bigger washtub?" He paid her no mind. "Maybe, could we get one that is not tin? And how about one that is long enough so my knees are not sticking up out of the water?" The girl thought she noticed her father smile just a trifle, but she could not be sure.

Wendell came into the room, "Harping again, Coletta? You hardly stay in there long enough to get wet."

She threw her towel at him.

"At least Esther and I have clean hair. Ma washed it this afternoon." She made a face at her brother. "And then she rinsed it with chamomile tea flowers, so it is pretty and light." Pointing to his head, "Look at you, your hair looks like you slicked it down with axle grease."

The 12-year-old took just a step to chase after Coletta, but Joseph's hand shot out and grabbed him by his bib overall strap.

"Hold it, Son. No chasing in the house. You know the rules."

"Yea," growled the boy. He shot Agnes a disgusted look.

Before the clock chimed eight, the family all had their turns in the small bathtub.

"Now everyone is nice and clean for the Christ Child's birthday." Agnes hung up the damp towels on the string line stretched across a corner of the kitchen. "Everybody to bed now. It is going to be a short night."

"Ma, can I stay up longer?" Wendell picked up a book and pretended to read.

Coletta looked back at him and snickered, "Yea, Wendell, put the book down. You know you hate to read."

He threw the book across the room at her. "That will be enough." When Joseph raised his voice, there were no more arguments. "The Christmas Mass will come early, six o'clock tomorrow morning. So, on to bed now, all of you."

Agnes turned back to hanging towels so she could hide the smile that spread across her face. "Wendell is anxious to know about Christmas, Joseph. Or do you think he already knows?"

"He is suspicious, that much I know," laughed Joseph. "Is the tree ready to be brought in?"

"It is. I put it in the hired men's room this year. Too many prying eyes." She wiped the bathtub dry. "You and William found a nice tree, so tall. Reminds me of those we found in the German forests."

William came in from checking the horses. "I will get the tree, Pa. Save you from putting your shoes back on."

"Thanks, Son," Joseph nodded. "Are you going to introduce your lady friend to us tomorrow?"

The young man grinned, "I suppose so. Ma, Pa, I really hope you like Alvina. She means a lot to me."

William left the house to get the tree. When he came back in, he banged the tree stand on the porch floor to shake off the few huge snowflakes that caught in the branches. Taking it in the parlor, he set the tree on a small square table in the corner. "Do you have the decorations here, Ma?"

Agnes went into her bedroom and pulled several small boxes out of the wardrobe. "Everything is here we need." Carefully, she unwrapped tiny, crocheted ornaments and long, silver strands of icicles. Another box was opened. "Here are the little metal candleholders. And in this other box, are new candles." Smiling at Joseph, she asked, "How long have you had these candle holders?"

"I think forever," he grinned. "You know, that is always something a woman remembers."

Soft laughter filled the room. She and William clipped the holders onto the tree branches. Ever so often, she would step back to see how the tree looked. "Another holder here, I think." Joseph watched in silence. How meticulous Agnes was, so unlike Katherine's relaxed view of details.

Joseph opened the box of candles, then walked over to the tree. Almost reverently, he stuck the slender five-inch white candles in the holders. "These candles remind me of the years when I was a child. My grandmother was not able to do much her last years, but putting the candles on the tree seemed to be her task. If was as if no one else was allowed to do it."

"Your grandmother must have been a very special person, Pa."

"Yes," he nodded. "Yes, she was, William. She used to tell me so many stories about when she was young. I learned so much from her about my family and their homeland."

Finally, the candles and decorations were all in place. It was time for a few hours rest.

Early the next morning, about four, Agnes rose out of her warm bed and tiptoed into the parlor and the kitchen. Hurrying as fast as possible, she spread plates of mixed nuts, a large orange and a box of candy for every one of the children and each of the adults, men and women, no matter how old or young they were. She also put out a plate for Joseph and herself. Several small gifts were arranged by each individual plate. She set a glass bowl, heaped with popcorn balls, in the middle of the table.

Agnes looked over the table and smiled. The gifts had been picked with care. "How happy Joseph is to have everyone here this Christmas morning." She checked each one's gift again. For Ellen's two young girls, there were pretty little dolls; and for her small son, blocks that would make a picture when put together right. There was also a cut glass flower vase for Ellen, a fountain pen for Agnes Marie for when

197

she went to nurses' training, and a photo album for Irene who liked to take pictures. For the younger ones, Saint Nick had found a game for Coletta, a football for Wendell, a doll buggy for Esther and a small copper horse for Robert. William and Ellen's husband had shaving sets. By Joseph's place was a new pair of socks. For herself, was a large book. "The drug store had a good selection of gifts this year," she mused.

She almost hated to interrupt the calm and beauty of the blessed morn. "1920 is almost over. This is my eighth Christmas here." With extreme care, she lit each candle on the tree. The light from the many tiny flames threw peaceful shadows upon the walls. She stood for a long time and remembered, "I wonder how my family is this special day?" A tear nudged at the corner of her eye, but with a gentle touch, it was brushed aside. "It is time to ring the bell."

The tiny bell tinkled its soft, merry song. The children were already waiting, quiet as mice, in their rooms. But then, when the bell sounded, all the doors opened at once. Eager faces glowed with excitement. Each had to be careful not to trip over the one before, for the candlelight did not cast enough brilliance to light the stairs.

No voices spoke as they gathered around the tree. The magic of it all cast a deep silence upon them. Then a voice whispered, partly in melody, "Stille Nacht, Silent Night." "Heilige Nacht, Holy Night," the others joined in sweet song. Agnes wanted so to sing along, but she had not been blessed with a song in her throat, only one in her heart. So she quietly listened and hummed in her mind.

"Ahh," each said when they found their gifts from the Christmas spirit. Voices rose in happy laughter as they showed their gifts to the others. Too soon, Joseph reminded them, "Time to dress and leave for the Christmas Mass. The church will be crowded this morning."

The horses stomped their hooves impatiently. The breath from their nostrils made wreaths of frost around their noses.

The older children, Joseph and Agnes, Ellen and her husband, August, got in first, and then pulled up the younger children and put them on their laps. Everyone crowded in and snuggled close together.

The early morning air was nippy. A few snowflakes swirled around the family as they started out the driveway. The festive red ribbons William had tied on the carriage light posts fluttered in the slight breeze.

"Wrap the comforts over everybody's legs," Agnes instructed. "We all need to keep warm, especially the little ones."

"Jingle bells," someone started to sing, and the others all joined in. The closer to town they got, the louder their songfest became.

"I think we should sing 'Silent Night' again." Agnes tried to start it, but her voice cracked and croaked. "If only I could sing. How I would love to sing along, but I just was never given a voice." She looked at the others, "Please, sing for me."

The church bells were ringing out loudly and clearly in the crisp morning air. Their deep-throated bongs sent vibrations throughout the town. Inside the church, the smell of cedar hung heavily. Shadows danced around the walls and rafters, as the glow of the candles flickered and fluttered from the breeze coming in the door and from around the old windows.

Off to the side, in front of one of the altars, stood the crib, atop make-believe rocks. The colorful statues sparkled like jewels on the fluffy wheat straw strewn around inside the lopsided little barn. The Virgin Mary knelt and St. Joseph stood, surrounded by the shepherds and the angels.

In the vestibule of the church, schoolgirls, dressed like angels in pink, blue, yellow and green gowns, pranced nervously. Their small wings jiggled as they moved about.

Floor-length, snowy-white gowns of the taller girls had long wide sleeves and hems, trimmed in silver garland. Their shiny, silvery wings cascaded from their shoulders to the floor. Wreaths of silvery garlands were placed on each angel's head. Soon, they would carry the statue of the Christ Child up to the crib and put him beside his mother, Mary.

The old organ wheezed and groaned until the straps on the bellows loosened up from the cold. The choir members, in the loft high up above the back of the church, shuffled their feet around to keep them from freezing. The warmth of the room finally reached a most comfortable temperature from all the people jammed inside the packed little church.

It did not take too long before Esther, Robert and Coletta were getting restless. The Mass was taking much too long for the children. Back home, their gifts and fruit and candy waited for them.

At long last, the priest sang, "Ite, missa est. Go, the Mass is ended." And the choir answered, "Deo gratias. Thanks be to God."

Huge snowflakes drifted lazily down, as the people left and hurried to their carriages and buggies. Coletta pushed Robert along, "Come on, walk faster, I am freezing."

By the time the family got back to the farm, a thick covering of snow made the countryside frosty white.

"Can we make a snowman this afternoon, Ma?" asked her young son.

"I do not think we will make a snowman today, maybe tomorrow." She tweaked his nose a bit, and he rubbed it with his finger and gave her a curious look.

"Did Aunt Martha send us presents from Germany this year, Ma?" Coletta inched up to Agnes and looked at her. "Esther and I are wanting to know if she did." Coletta looked at her younger sister, "Do you remember the pretty decorated gingerbread hearts she sent us last year? They were so good." She tugged on Agnes' apron strings, "Did Aunt Martha make some more of those in her bakery this year?" She looked at her older sisters, "Do you remember how pretty they were?" Then she looked back to Agnes, "Did she send them again this year?"

Agnes grinned at her. She marveled at how tall Coletta was getting, almost as tall as herself. "I think she did. Let me go in the parlor and see if there is anything there from her." Then she called to the others in the kitchen, "Come in here, there is a special surprise from Aunt Martha."

She lifted the cover on the box and took out enough wrapped gingerbread hearts for everyone. "Oh, and look, here in the bottom are little gifts. Let me see whose name she has put on each one."

The girls crowded around to receive their little gifts of crocheted ribbons, bookmarks for their prayer books. For the boys and men, she had sent leather pencil holders her son had made.

Coletta turned her gingerbread heart from side to side, front and back, inspecting each little picture that was frosted on the cookie. She finally took the tiniest bite, and then wrapped it back up.

Esther started to put the whole cookie in her mouth. "No, no," Coletta put out her hand to stop Esther. "Do not eat the whole cookie. Take just a very small bite, and then put the rest away for another day. We can put them in our room, and each day we will take just a bite. It will last so much longer that way."

"I will try," answered Esther.

"Robert, you do that, too," demanded Coletta. "I do not want you begging me for part of mine."

At the end of a long day, each of the smaller children sat at the kitchen table and waited for Joseph and Agnes to peel their big navel oranges. Slowly, they bit into the large pieces of the colorful, tangy, orange fruit and let the juice seep out the sides of their mouths and trickle down their chins.

"This is so good." Esther took the last bit of hers and licked the juice off her fingers. "Can I have another one of these?"

"They are a special treat from Saint Nick," her mother told her.

In the following days, Coletta was getting more and more curious. She snooped around the house until, finally, she found the secret she knew was there. She grabbed Esther by the hand, "Come with me; there is something to show you."

Esther followed her into the parents' bedroom. "Look up there." Coletta pointed to the top of the wardrobe. "There is the box that Saint Nick brings the extra popcorn balls in every year."

"Do you think there are more in there?" Esther was wide-eyed.

"Figure it out, Esther. Ma makes the popcorn balls, and then brings them out a few days after Christmas. She says they come from Saint Nick, but she is the one who makes them and pretends he brought them."

Esther stood a long time looking up at the box. "I do not care who brings them. They are the best popcorn balls. I love the dark sticky stuff that sticks in my teeth." Pulling a chair close to the wardrobe, she climbed up. "Can I have one now?"

"Get down from there. You will ruin it for all of us." Coletta tugged at her sister's belt.

"But you are the one who brought me in here."

"Quiet."

Esther climbed down off the chair and made a face at her sister. "But I am hungry for one now. All the ones from Christmas are gone."

"Well, you just have to wait. If you tattle one word to Ma, we will both be in trouble." The older girl pushed the chair back to where it had been. "We better get out of here before Ma comes in from hanging up the wash. She gets really upset when any of us are in their bedroom." She grabbed Esther by the arm. "Come on, the screen door just banged. It is probably her."

Coletta pulled the door closed as quietly as she could.

Esther stood there with a puzzled look on her face. "Why does Pa only get a pair of socks by his plate from Saint Nick? There are other things he could bring Pa, aren't there?"

"I am not sure." Coletta put her finger up to her lips to still Esther, then leaned over close to the youngster's ear. In a very soft whisper, she said, "You will just have to ask Saint Nick if you catch him when he brings the extra popcorn balls."

Esther's eyes grew wide as saucers. "Oh."

30

THE RADIO SHOW

JOSEPH PUT THE sacks of sugar and flour on the table. "The latest news in Garden Plain is the Cannon Ball Highway is going to be paved. I stopped by the City Hotel and Fred said the old wooden bridges will all be torn out and cement bridges put in. The dirt roadway is going to be cemented, too. From what he said, a lot more people are thinking about buying automobiles."

He sat down at the table and warmed his hands around the hot mug of coffee. The bitter cold January wind had stiffened the joints of his fingers.

"When are they supposed to start, Pa?" William asked. He had just come in from outside and heard his father talking about it.

"Around the first of March. They cannot run cement if there is a chance it will freeze." He poured some of the steaming black liquid out on his saucer and blew it enough so he could drink it. "Sure do not know what that is going to do to the area. With such a smooth road, it will not even be safe to cross the highway anymore. Talked to Sam Stone, too, and he thinks all the travelers going west from Wichita to Kingman will be good for his grocery business and the other businesses in town. But some of the other town men think it will get to be more like a race track, everybody in a hurry."

"What about horses, Pa?" William slid in on one of the benches and across the table from Joseph. "I heard talk it might be so slick for their hooves they could lose their footing and tip a wagon."

Joseph grinned, "I suppose that would depend on how fast they were going."

Agnes sat quietly during their discussion, but then added, "In the cities, horses did not seem to have any trouble on the brick streets. I do not remember too many cement streets, or I probably never paid any attention to them." She smiled.

"Most women do not," Joseph chuckled. "They just get in the carriage and go."

"Pa, do you think you will invest in a Model T?" William buttered a thick slice of homemade bread. Joseph just sat there quietly, pouring and blowing his coffee. "The reason is, Pa, I have been saving up and have enough in the bank for one."

Joseph winked at his son, "It would sure make your trip over to see Alvina faster."

"That it would." William shuffled around on the chair. "Another year or two, I will have enough saved to get married. There is even some land in her family that I will probably be able to rent. Looks like good wheat ground."

"Sounds good, Son." He dunked a cookie and ate it. "I still am not sold on automobiles. In a few years, they will make all kinds of improvements. Might even get them down in price so most people can afford them." He looked at his son for a few minutes, "But if that is what you want. You have worked hard here for me."

At the beginning of 1921, the small town experienced all kinds of exciting happenings. The Main Street was lengthened to the north to open onto the Cannon Ball Highway. The city council approved the installation of electric power. With its arrival, a tall streetlight was erected on the main thoroughfare. According to a new city ordinance, the few motorists and all horse-drawn modes of travel had to keep to the right side of the dirt streets.

In 1922, the excitement of the bridge and road construction crews brought extra people into the City Hotel. The local beauties tried to catch the roving eyes of the strange men. Competition was on to see who would be among the first to get electric power, so they could brag about just flipping a light switch. Several additional filling stations were planned because of the increase in gas-driven conveyances. With the projected money coming into the town, one or two new banks were in the planning stage.

Summertime had come and harvest was in full swing. Around the first week of June, William came home from hauling a load of wheat to one of the local elevators.

He called his sisters together to come hear some exciting news he had heard in Garden Plain. His eyes twinkled as he looked at them. "If it is agreeable with Ma and Pa, I would like to take you all into town July 21st." He furrowed his brow and raised an eyelid. "I think that will be a Monday evening."

"What, what is it?" Coletta jumped up and down anxiously. The family, and especially the girls, never were allowed to go into town much during the summer.

"Do you remember going to the picture show in March?"

"Another one, is there a new one they are showing?" Irene rubbed her hands together in anticipation. "Do you think Agnes Marie will come home from nurses' training to go with us?" She pushed her shoulder up against Coletta. "Wouldn't that be fun to see her again? She has been gone so long."

"I rather doubt Agnes Marie would be able to come, since she just started training," said her brother.

"Oh, William, are you sure?"

"I am sure. She has to stay there for quite awhile before she can come home, because Ma and Pa paid out a lot of money for her to go. So she just cannot be coming home every time you want her to."

"Oh, I was hoping." Then she turned to Coletta and Esther. "What do you think it is? Do you think Ma and Pa will let us go?" She shrugged her shoulders, "But you know how Ma is, she does not want us to go anywhere in the summer." She wrinkled her nose.

William stood still for a few minutes, listening to the younger ones' happy chatter. Finally, he held his hand up for silence. "This is even more exciting than a picture show. Some of the people are talking about a new invention called radio." He held his breath just for the sheer joy of making his sisters agonize over what he was about to say.

The brother straightened up tall, like an orator intending to speak, then cleared his throat. "Monday evening, July 21, 1922, promptly at eight o'clock, a free radio concert will be presented on the Garden Plain Main Street. The splendid program, as it is advertised on notices about the town, will be brought to the gathered public by wireless telephone. One of the most modern and up-to-date radio sets in the county will transmit a popular radio show." He grinned, "They hope people will come for miles around to hear this newfangled invention."

"All those boys," gushed Coletta.

"All those handsome young men," echoed sixteen-year-old Irene. As an afterthought, "All those tough, muscular, construction workers," she swooned. "Do you think Agnes Marie could come home from nursing school that weekend? She might meet her future sweetheart."

"I had better talk to Ma and Pa before you girls plan too many exciting things." William tugged at Esther's nose, "I will ask them later if you can go."

That evening at supper, William told his folks of the notices he had seen around town. "Could we all go," he asked. "This is the up and coming invention, and it sure would not hurt the girls to keep up with what is going on in the world." He winked at his sisters after he said that.

Ma laughed. "It will be a chore just to keep you girls in sight." Winking at Joseph, she went on, "It sounds like that evening might be educational." Moving closer to where her husband stood, she added, "It is always good for the young people to see what the newest inventions are."

"Please, oh, please, Pa," begged Esther and Robert. "We promise to be good."

Joseph pulled Robert's ear and chuckled, "We will plan on it. The wheat harvest should be slowing down by then, and an activity like that might be relaxing. It will give us all something to look forward to."

The July evening was perfect, wind still and moonlight. Fireflies flitted over the crowd. Young folks were seated on blankets spread over the dirt street. Older women sat on chairs near the edge of the street. Men straddled the wooden benches in front of the storefronts. William and the other debonair and eligible bachelors of the area leaned coyly against the pillars of the porches of some of the stores. With determined intensity, they surveyed the young ladies. Here and there, one of the pretty girls turned and smiled, showing their painted lips.

"Ooh, I love the bold red lips over there," the cocky, barely seventeen-year-old fellow next to William said.

"Sure makes one take notice." William reached up and straightened his bow tie. He punched the young blade lightly on the arm, "She is a bit old for you, is she not?"

"Age makes no difference. I will gladly give her a spin in my roadster any day." William just shook his head and snickered. "Cocky, young fool," he muttered.

Agnes held tight to the two smaller children. Esther saw some of her classmates nearby. "Please, Ma, can I go sit with them?"

"Only if you stay there. No running around."

"Can I go, too?" begged Robert.

"You sit down there at the edge of the porch, close to Pa."

"Wendell, where is Wendell? I want to go with him," wailed the boy.

"He is older." Agnes handed him two pieces of horehound candy. "Go, take Pa one of these. The other is for you."

She glanced across the crowd. Fourteen-year-old Wendell and his cousin, John, were in the middle of a bunch of boys about their age. A lot of jostling was going on.

"Typical boys," Agnes said to her neighbor lady, Mrs. Peppen.

The other woman laughed. "At least we know when boys are healthy. As long as they act up like that, we have no need to worry. Actually, I am more concerned when my boy is sitting still." She tapped Agnes' arm, "There is no need to worry about Wendell. He is just a live wire."

Several girls came sauntering by. Irene and Coletta giggled right along with the others. Skirts swirled with quick turns and braids twirled through the air. Lacy headbands ended in wide bows perched daintily above right or left ears.

Agnes noticed the girls made a special effort to avoid her gaze. "My girls are certainly ignoring me."

"So it goes with boys, so it goes with girls," chuckled Mrs. Peppen. "They are breaking away from Ma and Pa just as sure as you and I breathe."

"Yes, I guess. It is certainly different with young people these days." Agnes watched the girls pass and noticed Irene give something to Coletta. The young girl giggled, and hugged her older sister's arm. "Hmm, wonder what that was about?"

"Keep it in your pocket until we sit down. You know how Ma hates lip rouge. It is sinful, according to her." Irene held on to the tiny mirror. "This we cannot lose; we need it to see, so we get our lips colored just right."

"That was so much fun going into the drug store." Coletta pranced around like the older girls. "Irene, I just cannot wait until my sixteenth birthday."

Irene smiled at her, "No matter how hard you wish, it will still take four years."

The two sisters slipped and slithered through the multitude of feet and legs until they were far enough inside the gathering of other girls their age. Voices fell and rose in high-pitched giggles and silly chatter. A few of the more jaunty, self-assured young gentlemen of the town and countryside had plopped themselves there, too. Their total demeanor spoke volumes, as they looked about the sea of local beauties surrounding them.

"Bet the local plowboys can hardly stand us being in the middle of all of this," snickered one to the others.

The crowd quieted when the mayor stood to speak. "We are honored to have such a presentation in our town, the first of its kind in the area. Radio, you will discover, is the beacon of tomorrow. In the years ahead, every home will tune in to listen to the excitement shared with all our countrymen. Listen and enjoy. If you like what you hear, your order can be placed for one of these marvelous inventions right after the show. Be among the first to have a radio set. We want our town to lead the county in the number of home radio sets. He waved his arms above his head and shouted, "And now, on with the show."

Chuckles, giggles and loud heehaws filled the evening air. Mr. Peppen grabbed Joseph by the arm, "I think we are going to get one of the those."

"That is the greatest thing to come along that I know," proclaimed the haughty lad next to William. As soon as the program was over, a few men came forth to place their orders and put their money on the table.

31

RUNAWAYS

SEVERAL MONTHS LATER, Coletta stood and looked into Irene's special little box. Right in the center was the bright red case. Coletta smacked her lips. The sweet tasting, rosy-red lip rouge was such a temptation. She glanced at her reflection in the mirror and could just imagine how grown-up it would make her look.

"It will not hurt to take it to school today. Irene will be helping with the neighbor's children all day and never miss it." She picked it up and rolled the silky metal case through her fingers. Footsteps sounded on the stairs and she quickly put the case back and closed the small lid. "Oh, it is only you," she hissed at Esther. "Go back downstairs and wait. Just another minute or two and I am ready to leave for school. Is Wendell ready to go?"

"He is already in the wagon," shouted Esther.

"Hurry up, get out there." Esther jumped down every step. "Ooh, why does she do that? It hurts my head," moaned Coletta. "Why do little sisters have to be such an aggravation?"

Coletta could not resist. The lid of the little box was opened and the lip rouge was slipped into her skirt pocket. "This will look so nice on me. At school, I can put on just a touch, like Irene let me do at the concert. Old Sister Marie is near-sighted and will never notice. Then after school, I can make it darker. Maybe that good-looking chap on the road crew will finally notice me." She strutted out the door, swishing her skirt as she walked down the steps.

The school day was perfect. Coletta never felt so pretty. Henry, the cutest boy in the class, winked at her. Even snooty Cecelia lent her the big hairbrush she always combed her own hair with. The hours dragged on. Was the day ever going to end? Finally, Sister Alice, the principal, rang the brass bell and school was out.

Coletta hurried out to the barn. Wendell had already hitched Old Ben to the wagon. She took his feedbag off, then put a bucket of water in front of him. The horse took a long, slow drink.

"Just right," she mumbled. Everybody else had already left, and Esther was still playing hopscotch. Fishing in her skirt pocket, she pulled out the tiny mirror and the red case. With a steady hand, she outlined her lips and pressed hard. Red, her lips were rosy-red. "Very pretty," she said as her smile reflected back to her.

Esther came running in the barn. "Are we going home, Coletta?" She stopped dead. "What did you put on your lips?"

"Shush," demanded Coletta. "Go get Wendell. Tell him we have to go now, or Pa will be upset."

"Wait until Ma sees your lips," sneered Esther. "She is the one who is going to be angry."

"Quiet now. Go call Wendell."

"He left, with cousin John." The girl started to cry. "He turned around to me and yelled, 'Tell the folks I am going to live with John.'"

"So, he is running away again." Coletta stomped her foot. "Pa is really going to be mad this time." She grabbed the horse by the reins and led him outside. "Climb in. It is just the two of us today."

"Oh, good." The older girl brushed her hands over her dark curls. "The highway crew is working right by the corner of the road to our farm. Maybe the good-looking one will notice me today. I am so glad Wendell took off. Now is my chance." She straightened her back and sat tall on the wagon bench.

As they got closer to the construction area, her coy looks darted back and forth over the men. "One last look to check my makeup." She put down the reins and pulled Irene's small mirror from her pocket. Coletta pursed her lips and took in the admiring glances of some of the young fellows.

Old Ben plodded along slowly, easing up to the work crew. The horse and wagon threaded through the center of the men. A quarter of a mile down the road, a huge pile driver was pounding pilings down for the new bridge. Just as the steam-driven engine revved up, an earsplitting "swoosh" rushed through the cool September air.

The poor old horse had never heard such a noise. His front feet rose off the ground two feet, and he was off and running. The wagon bounced over the rough, uneven, new roadway. The wheels rattled and bumped over the ruts on the dirt road leading out into the country. Old Ben's ears leaned way forward and his nostrils flared.

Coletta's and Esther's knuckles turned white. "Hang on," yelled the older sister. The lip rouge case bounced at their feet. Shiny splinters of broken mirror littered the wagon floor.

Old Ben quickly left the noise of the machinery and the laughter of the road crew far behind. Meadowlarks sang from the tops of fence posts. Rooster pheasants and quail strutted across the road. Cottontail bunnies stopped to chew on young grass. Old Ben's flanks were wet with sweat. His breathing finally slowed and his long brown ears relaxed.

"Coletta, your face is so white and your lips are so red." Esther doubled over in laughter. "Do you know how funny you look?"

"Hush, hush, you bratty kid. You better not tell Ma and Pa, cause if you do, I will get even with you."

"You do not have to worry about me. Old Ben will tell them. Look at him, Coletta. You about killed the old horse."

"Yea." Coletta pinched her cheeks to bring some color back. "I guess we are lucky. The wagon did not tip. Now if Old Ben just does not lay down and die on us."

"Wipe your lips off, so Ma cannot see them. You will really be in trouble."

Coletta took her embroidered white handkerchief and rubbed and rubbed. Then she pitched it in the ditch. "I sure cannot take this home. Ma would never get over it."

Old Ben turned in the driveway just as Joseph walked back to the house. "How come he is so wet?"

Coletta gave Esther a stern look. "Oh, Pa, it was so scary. When we crossed over the highway, the loudest noise from the construction went off. It scared Old Ben out of his wits and he took off running. I never knew he could run so fast." She gave her sister another "be quiet" look. "Pa, we were so scared. All we could do was hang on and hope he would not run in a ditch and tip the wagon. I do not know about

Esther, but I was really praying."

"Where is Wendell? How come he was not with you?"

"When I was watering the horse after school, he left in the wagon with cousin John."

"Yea, Pa," Esther hastened to add. "He yelled back to tell Ma and Pa he was going to live with cousin John."

Joseph turned white and gritted his teeth. "This is about the fourth time Wendell has tried that." He took Old Ben's bridle. "You girls go in the house. Tell Ma I am going to Uncle Frank's place and bring that boy home again." He shifted his old felt hat around on his head, but just could not seem to get it right.

"Get in the house, Esther," Coletta hissed. "When Pa cannot get his old hat to sit right, he is mad."

"Giddy-up," shouted Joseph. Poor Old Ben about stumbled going out the yard. He half turned his head around to see who was whizzing the whip past his ears.

"Hello, Ma." The two girls put their books down on the sideboard. Coletta put her finger to her lip to shush Esther. "Come on." She grabbed Esther's hand and pulled her to the stairway. Up two steps at a time they went, and closed the door as fast as possible.

Together, the sisters flopped down on their old iron bed. The springs squeaked and sagged. Pillows were pulled over their heads, but the girls' giggles could not be silenced.

"We came out of that all right." Coletta hesitated, and then burst into guffaws, "Thanks to Wendell and cousin John." The laughter hurt their sore sides even more and a river of tears ran down already wet cheeks.

Esther rolled over and over. "Thanks to Wendell and cousin John."

Joseph's face was red with anger when he jumped out of the wagon. He stormed through the yard gate at his brother's farm and banged on the door.

"Why, Joseph, I did not expect to see you." Lizzie, Frank's wife, wiped her hands on her apron and opened the screen door.

"Where is Wendell? I came to take him home."

"He is fine here with my son, John. Let him stay."

"I want him home."

"But he likes to come here. He is having a hard time at your house with your wife. The boy told us everything."

"What?" demanded Joseph.

"He told us how she makes him read and study for hours. And then, makes him do work that is too hard for him. His back is so weak, Joseph, and Wendell has twisted it doing what she orders him to do."

"Get him out here." Joseph tried hard to keep his anger under control. "There is no truth to that. He comes over here to get out of work and do nothing but play. Play, just like your son, John. All the time, play."

"Agnes is too hard on your children, Joseph. Everyone knows that."

"She is no harder on them than on herself. Now, where is my son?" He noticed Wendell and John peeking around the corner of the house, teeth showing in large grins. "Get over here, Wendell, you are going home." The boy sauntered toward his father, a cocky smirk on his face. "Get in the wagon." Joseph climbed in and slapped the reins hard across Old Ben's flanks. "Why do you keep doing this, running away?"

"I would rather live here than at home. I do not like your wife."

A shocked look clouded the father's face. "What did you just call Ma?"

"Your wife. Nobody likes her. Ellen sure does not; she always made her work too hard. William and my sisters do not like her either. Aunt Lizzie says she is proud and bossy, and makes all of us work too hard." Wendell squinted his eyes and frowned at Joseph. "Uncle John and Aunt Minnie told me your wife is not nice and has no right making Katherine's children do what she demands. Aunt Minnie says your wife thinks she is better than everybody else because she came from the old country. She also said your wife wastes too much time reading when she should be working."

Anger creased Joseph's face, for he knew only too well how lazy Katherine's sister was. He wanted to punch his son's face, but that was not in his manner.

"My wife is now your ma. Do not forget that. She is working hard to make all of us a nice home. And Ma does not like to see you run away. That hurts her."

Joseph wiped a speck of dust from his eye. Wendell smirked under his breath. "Good, I have him thinking now how terrible she really is."

"Your ma is a smart woman who does read, and has her own views.

I am proud of her for that. That does not make her lazy otherwise. No other woman around here keeps a neater house, cooks better or works harder that Ma."

"That woman is not my ma," snarled Wendell. "She is only a step-ma. And I hate her. I hate her, do you hear, Pa?" To add further insult to his father's wounded heart, he lashed out, "Aunt Minnie says she does not treat you as nice as my real ma did. All your wife does is boss you around, just like the rest of us."

"Oh, Son," Joseph uttered softly. "Someday, maybe you will realize what she has come to mean to me, and know how hard she has worked to make you a nice home. Wendell, you disappoint me so much."

"Well, Pa, that is the way it is with me. She will never be my ma, or ma to any of the others either, no matter how hard she tries.

"Oh, Son, please do not believe everything your aunts tell you about Ma. They do not know." His voice ended in a whisper and his thoughts wandered off for several minutes.

Then Joseph looked at his son with sadness. In a raspy whisper he said, "They do not know what it was like for me before she came."

32

TARGET PRACTICE

"COME HERE, CHILDREN," Agnes called. She handed each of them a bucket. "I talked to Mrs. Gretchmer, and her pink mulberries are ripe now. She said to send you over and we could have some."

"But it is hot, Ma," Coletta complained.

"If you hurry before the sun gets higher, it will not be too hot. And you know how your pa likes mulberry pie."

"So do I," chimed in Robert.

"Just like your father." Agnes smiled at her son.

"I do not like that kind of pie," moaned Coletta again.

"Whether you do or not does not make any difference. Now go. I will expect you back in an hour. It will not take you long to walk over there, and it is a beautiful day."

Esther and Robert ran on ahead, while the older girl moaned and groaned to herself. "Why doesn't Ma go get those mulberries herself? She knows how much work they are to pick up. I just hate that job." All at once she looked up and saw how far the two younger ones were ahead of her. "Crazy kids, they are walking right down the middle of the road." She lifted up her skirt and ran after them to catch up. "Get off to the side of the road," she yelled. "What if a car or a team of horses comes past? You will get run over."

"Ahh, good morning," said Mrs. Gretchmer cheerfully. "A lovely morning to pick plump, ripe mulberries. I know how much your pa likes them. And your ma makes such good pie, especially when she mixes them with gooseberries."

"Oh, I guess," muttered Coletta. "Ma said we had to be back home in an hour. That will not give us much time to fill these buckets."

"Come now, wipe off the long faces, children. I know just how to take care of that. If you wait just a few minutes, I will be right back." The neighbor lady was hardly in the house, when she came back out, carrying a bed sheet. "Help me spread this under the tree, and I will show you how our family picks mulberries. No climbing and very little stooping, I guarantee it."

Esther and Coletta each took a corner, and the woman took the other two corners. Together, they spread the sheet out on the ground. She looked at them and laughed, "Now we will shake some of the branches as fast as we can."

Reaching up, the woman grabbed a branch and pulled it down close to her. "Here is a branch that is just loaded with ripe mulberries. I think they are the fattest ones on the tree." She looked at Coletta, who took hold of the branch. Then Mrs. Gretchmer pulled down two more branches, and handed one each to Esther and Robert. "Hang on to them and do not let go. If you do not hang on tight, that branch will jump right back up and pull you up into the tree with it." They all laughed.

She grabbed another branch and tugged at it. Her eyes twinkled as she looked at the three youngsters. "Now, when I say shake, everybody shake. This old tree will drop its mulberries faster than a bird flies."

The children laughed, and waited expectantly for her command. She hesitated just to build up the suspense.

"Now shake." The mulberries dropped to the cloth in bunches and built up little mounds of large reddish-pink fruit.

"Don't we have enough to fill our buckets yet?" asked Robert.

"Just a few more shakes." The children shook the tree with all their might.

"Enough, enough," she laughed. "Now everyone down on the sheet, and let us see how fast you can fill those buckets." The children scooped berries like mad, and in just a few minutes, every bucket was filled to the rim.

"What time is it?" she called to one of her children in the house. "Nine-thirty, did you say?" She looked at the neighbor children and proudly announced, "It took us exactly ten minutes to fill your buckets. You tell your ma that has to be a record." She stood up to fold the sheet. "And if she needs some more, come back. We all know how to beat the birds to the mulberries, don't we?"

The three strolled leisurely home and munched on the luscious, sweet berries. Large purplish-pink rings formed around their mouths. The girls looked for pretty wildflowers. Robert picked up rocks and things that moved, if he could catch them.

"Look at this great bug." He held it close to Coletta's face.

"Stop it, you little pest." She put down her bucket and took out after him.

"Try and catch me if you can," he taunted her.

"Just you wait," she jeered. Picking up the buckets, she hurried home. The youngsters almost ran to keep up with her.

Agnes opened the porch screen door for them. "Look at those mouths," she said gaily. "And look at the size of those berries."

"They are so good," mumbled Robert through a mouthful. Purple juice ran down his chin.

The summer passed much too quickly for the family.

"Soon school will start again," said Joseph, one day at the dinner table. "Are you all ready for that?"

"I am," answered Coletta. "I love school."

"I hate it," growled Wendell. He stopped to think for a few minutes. "On the other hand, I am ready to go back. I think Mr. Brown will make me one of the starters on the eighth grade football team. My friends, Jake and Henry, should also be on the first string."

"From what I hear," Joseph said, "the talk in town is that the public grade school should have a very good team this year. Some of them are saying the team might win the championship."

"I hope so." Wendell puffed up his chest and stuck out his chin. "We had a good team last year, Pa, and you know we will only get better during the summer." He looked at Coletta and smirked, "Our fellas are going to beat the socks off every team we have to play."

Now, Son, do not get too big a head," Joseph said amused. "Bragging on yourself beforehand can sometimes backfire. Then you will have to admit you are not as good as you think you are."

"Aw, Pa, Jake and Ben are fast, and Henry is a hard hitter."

"I know, I know." Joseph's hazel eyes twinkled.

Serious practice for the football team began right after school started. Helmets clashed, shoulder pads buckled and cleats slid through the muddy playing field. "Let's go," shouted the coach every day right after school was out.

One day, Joseph asked, "How does the team look this year, Son?"

"Good, Pa, real good." Wendell shuffled around and looked down at the floor. "But school is not going too good."

"Not getting your homework?"

"I guess," muttered Wendell. "Coach Brown told me if I did not get better grades, I would be put off the first string."

"Why, Wendell, what is going wrong?"

"I do not know, Pa. It is just not going right. I do not know why."

He turned and walked away before Joseph could question him further. The boy never did like the structure of the classroom.

"I can not understand that boy." The father watched him walk away. "Where is he going?" He kept his eye on Wendell. "Looks like he is going out behind the barn. That is his hideout if he is in trouble."

"This year the teasing is getting worse than ever." Wendell half-walked, half-ran behind the barn. "Step-Ma, I hate her more every day. Why did she ever have to come into my life?" He hit his fist against the side of the barn. "I am getting fed up with all the cracks the other fellas are making."

He heard Coletta call his name, "Wendell, Wenn-dell."

The boy did not answer. "I sure do not want to talk to her right now, or to anyone else. I do not even want them to know where I am."

But she kept up, "Wendell, Wenn-dell."

Finally, her whining voice got to him, and he forced himself to answer, "Back here, back of the barn."

She came running around the corner of the building. "What are you doing back here?"

"Just be quiet and leave me alone," he growled.

"But you are acting so funny, what is wrong?" She sidled up to him and tried to look into his eyes. He kept his face down so it was hard for her to do that. "Why are you being this way?"

He finally lifted his eyes to meet hers, and they were filled with tears. "Wendell, I have never seen you cry before. Are you all right?" His sister pressured him for an answer.

"No, I am not all right. I hate Step-Ma. I hate her, I hate her." He wiped his runny nose on the back of his hand. "All the other fellas do is tease me about her. They call her the German spy lady, and wonder why she is living in our house. They laugh at me and ask if our family was rooting for the Germans a few years ago, during World War I. They said we could not possibly have been wanting America to win over there, when a German was with us. They even asked me how it felt when we saw boys from here go into the war."

He flopped down on the ground, and propped his knees up close to his chest. "They just do not believe I hate her so much. Ever since that crazy woman stood up in church and talked back to the priest about that Kaiser, or whatever he was, they have razzed me. They just will not quit, no matter what I say."

Coletta slumped down beside him and put her hand on his arm. "I know what you mean. I get teased, too, but not so much. Those in my class hear it from the older ones, and they think it is fun to call me names. Yesterday, one on the big boys called me 'German lover.'" She took a stick and scratched it around in the dirt for a while.

"What did you do?" asked her brother, looking at Coletta.

"I just turned away from him and tried to act like I did not hear it." Little piles of dirt formed as she brushed it together with the twig. "I told Irene what he said to me, and she said people still whisper behind her back. She can hear them saying things about Step-Ma, too."

The girl leaned against her brother's shoulder, "I hate Step-Ma, too. She is so mean to us. All the work she makes us do, and she does not let us go anywhere unless she is along. I talked to Ellen about that, and Ellen told me they never had to do all that before she came."

"I am going to get even with her," mumbled the boy. "Just you wait and see. I am going to get even with her; then maybe, she will get tired of us and leave." He stood up and banged his fist against the barn boards. "Just you wait and see. She will be sorry she ever came here." He stomped his foot hard on the ground and dust flew up around his shoe. "She will be sorry."

He twisted his shoe around in the dust. "I will make her so sorry she came, she will be only too glad to pack her bags and get out of here." He was quiet then, shuffling his feet around and around. Finally, he looked at Coletta, "I know what I will do."

Wendell ran around the corner of the barn and to the house as fast as he could run.

Coletta sat there for a long time thinking. "What will he do?" She said out loud, "Wendell can be so mean sometimes."

Coletta was almost afraid to come out from behind the barn. When she eventually did, she saw Ma taking clothes off the wash line. Pa was walking out to the garden. Just then, she saw Wendell run into the house.

The boy hurried into the parents' bedroom and tore down a picture from the wall. As he rushed through the kitchen, he threw the picture frame on the table. "Now, we will see how she likes this when she finds it."

He stopped in the porch to take down Pa's old rifle. The door slammed shut loudly as he came running out.

"What is he doing with that gun?" Coletta stopped in terror and watched him. "I hope he does not see me out here, who knows what he is going to do." The girl held her breath, "Please, God, do not let him do anything really foolish. I am scared now."

Wendell ran out to the board corral fence south of the barn, and put the gun down beside one of the posts. He stuck a piece of paper on a nail near the top of the big square corner post. Then he backed up about fifty feet and took aim.

"Thank heavens, he is only practicing. Wendell likes to hunt rabbits, and he probably just wants to see how good his aim is."

Pow, pow, bang, bang, bang! He shot the gun again and again until the paper hung in shreds. "Now there, Step-Ma, we will see how you like that." He turned and walked proudly back to the house. His swagger grew more pronounced the closer he got to the porch.

Agnes had walked into the porch just as the boy started shooting. Joseph was close behind her, as she entered the kitchen. "What is this frame doing out here?" She looked at her husband with a questioning look. Then she rushed into the bedroom and saw that her picture of Kaiser Wilhelm the Second was gone. She turned just as Joseph followed her into the room. "Oh, Joseph." She slumped down onto the bed.

"What is it, Agnes?"

"My picture of the Kaiser is gone, and the frame is on the table. Where could it have gone?"

Joseph got a horrified look on his face. He had heard Wendell shooting his old gun. He turned to go back into the kitchen just as Wendell sauntered back in, with a more than satisfied look on his face.

"Wendell, where have you been?"

"Out target practicing, Pa." His cocky look warned Joseph there was more to the shooting.

"What did you use as a target, Wendell?" Joseph's tone was surprisingly calm, yet angry. "What did you use?"

Just then Agnes came into the kitchen, and looked at the two.

Wendell laughed wickedly, "I used Step-Ma's favorite picture from your room." He laughed more and more. "She thinks more of that wicked Kaiser than she does of you, Pa."

"You did what, Wendell?" Agnes screamed at him. Then she lunged for him, but Joseph caught her and held her back.

"Agnes, Agnes, sit down, let me handle this." Joseph guided her to a chair.

Joseph grabbed his son by the shoulders. "What is the meaning of this, Wendell?"

"You know, Pa, you know how I feel."

"Right now, you go out and get that picture."

"There is nothing left of it."

Joseph shook him soundly. "Go get that picture, now."

"Aw, Pa." But the father did not budge. The boy looked into Joseph's face and saw a look he had never seen before.

"Now."

"Yea, yea, Pa." He wiggled himself loose from Joseph's grip, and ran out the kitchen door, banging the porch door as hard as he could.

In a few minutes, he stomped back into the house and threw the tattered shreds on the table. "Here is your picture. Now, are you satisfied?"

"Wendell, Son, why?"

The boy just shrugged and laughed hysterically. "It is no use telling you, Pa, you will never understand. You believe everything that woman tells you. You never listen to us. If you did, you would have gotten rid of her a long time ago."

Joseph stood there in shock, and looked at his son in total disbelief. "Wendell," he muttered pleadingly.

Agnes put her head down on the table and wept uncontrollably. For a long time, her cries went unheeded, while the father and the son stood there, no one offering her any consolation. When the last tear was spent, she raised her head and looked at her husband. "What do you say, Joseph?"

"Yea, Pa, what do you say?" snarled the son.

"I am sorry," he answered, so softly Agnes hardly heard him. "I am sorry." He turned and walked out through the kitchen and porch doors. With long, quick strides, he found his way to the white rock building and leaned against the inside wall.

Coletta tiptoed close to the door and peered inside. She saw her father standing there, heaving with heavy sobs. In between his gasps of deep breaths, she heard him cry out.

"Why, Son, oh, why?"

33

GRADUATION

THE EIGHTH GRADE boys hurried to put on their helmets and football gear. The coach was yelling at them to get out on the practice field.

Then Jack, the scrawniest one on the team, looked at Wendell. "If I could just get Wendell riled up and mad, then maybe Coach would bench him and put me in to play."

He cleared his throat and in a loud voice called out, "Hey, Wendell, is that German spy woman going to come watch the games, or has she decided you are not good enough to play?"

Wendell stopped in his tracks, and whirled around to grab the little guy by the jersey. "Look here, you weasel of a kid, you get one thing straight. That woman does not tell me anything to do." The others stopped to turn around and watch. He thumped his chest, "I want all of you to know she is not even my Step-Ma anymore. I had that old witch in tears last night." His raucous laughter lashed out. "I took her precious picture of the German Kaiser and used it for target practice. All that was left was shreds." He put his hands on his hips and gave all of them the mean eye. "I am a good shot, and I tell you, there was nothing left of that picture for her to hang up anymore."

Enjoying the spotlight, he pranced around the team, "I even had Pa trying to figure out what to say." He bent over and laughed hard and loud. "That was something to see. Poor old Pa. Did not know which way to turn. I even had him over a barrel." The gleam in his eye became more evil. "Yea, I even had old Pa almost begging for mercy. I just hope he sees what she really is now." He strutted some more.

"Maybe then, he will get rid of her once and for all."

Some of the boys said weakly, "Yea, yea." The others stood there in disbelief. None of them wanted to counter Wendell and be on his bad side. He would beat them up without thinking twice about it, and he was strong enough to do it.

"Are you men coming or not?" yelled the coach. "Get out here." The boys quietly ran out to get in line. "What is the matter with all of you?" Every one of you looks like you saw a ghost except Wendell." Not one of them dared say a word. At the moment, they were more afraid of Wendell than they were of the coach.

When Wendell's friends, Jake, Ben and Henry, finally got off by themselves, they gasped, shocked and totally amazed. Then Jake spoke, "I never thought Wendell would be that mean."

"Me, either," countered Ben.

"He scares me," said Henry, visibly shaken.

Several weeks later, Agnes' neighbor lady, Daisylue Peppen, came over to visit. Their light chatter centered around the everyday chores of life.

Then, the visitor could contain herself no longer. "Oh, Agnes, I heard what Wendell did to you. How awful that was."

"What are you talking about?" Agnes looked at her questioningly.

"It has been the talk of the town. I am surprised no one said anything to you before."

"Whatever do you mean?" Agnes leaned to the front of her chair and looked at her neighbor intently.

"About your picture of the German ruler. Wendell was bragging in school not long ago how he used your picture for target practice to get even with you."

Agnes was silent for a long time, her face twisting in surprised anger. "He was, was he?" she finally said. "He told others what he did?" She bowed her head and put her hand to her forehead, "I never thought he would stoop so low. He actually bragged about that?"

"I am sorry," the lady went on, "I thought you knew he had told everyone about that."

Agnes looked at her, then closed her eyes to try and curb her hurt feelings and rising hostility. "No, I did not know."

"Oh, Agnes, no wonder the boy acted that way. Joseph's children have been teased so much the last years about having a German woman in the house." She reached out to take Agnes' hand. "You know how cruel people can be. Anyone that is a mite different from them, they make fun of. You are so much smarter than most of the other women around here, they cannot begin to compete with you, so they try and tear you down to their level." She rubbed Agnes' hand tenderly. "All that talk has certainly not been fair to you or to the children. It has caused hard feelings here in your family. Oscar and I have seen it more than once."

Agnes stared at the woman, then pulled her hand away and put it on her lap. "So, Wendell bragged about that, did he?" She pursed her lips together for a long time, then spoke more to herself than the other. "In time." Her eyes narrowed. "He will never forget he did that. I will not let him."

"Now, Agnes." The other looked at her with compassion. "Do not do anything rash."

Agnes' face curved into a wicked grin. "I think Wendell will be more than a little surprised one of these days." Her voice rose in a sneer, "Yes, and when he is least expecting it, I will remind him." She looked directly at Daisylue, "I am so glad you told me this. It will make things much easier for me."

The weeks and the football games flew past in a rush, and soon the season ended. The eighth grade football team played up to the community's expectations and, without any losses, they earned the championship.

"Sam Stone told me you were the best player on the team, Wendell. Without you, the others could not have won all the games." Joseph patted Wendell on the back. "I am real proud of you, Son. William would always explain the games to me." He laughed, somewhat embarrassed, "I just never quite understood the game." He hung his head, "I should have taken the time and come to some of the games, I guess."

"Ah, Pa, that was all right. Very few of the other pas came either." He punched Joseph on the shoulder, "It would have made me nervous if you were there."

The boy sauntered around the house with a new importance. Out of the corner of his eye, he made sure Agnes was close around whenever his place on the team was mentioned. She acted like she did not hear the discussions.

Throughout Wendell's last year in school, he took off several times with cousin John. Joseph would go over to get him and bring him home again.

Each time, it was the same discussion on the way home. "I do not like living there with Step-Ma, she is so mean to us." Joseph would listen to him patiently. Secretly, he hoped the boy would soon change his attitude. But Joseph's hopes were dashed, for that day would never come.

The end of April was fast approaching and graduation was near. Wendell became more and more cocky around the house, and especially in Agnes' presence. He was going to show her how important he really was. He kept repeating the coach's words to himself.

"You are going to get the top football award this year, Wendell," the coach had told him. "Without you, we would never have won the championship."

He strutted around like the old farm rooster, mentally spreading his wings to show his stuff. Everyone seemed to be accepting of his new station in life, everyone, that is, except Agnes. To her the whole idea of sports, and football in general, was a waste of precious, productive time.

She could also see Joseph beginning to fail physically. Even though he was only fifty-one, he appeared to be slowing down considerably. Agnes detected a slight side-to-side movement of his head that had not been there before. When that occasional happening occurred, it seemed to catch Joseph by surprise, and he would try desperately to control the involuntary movement. Trying not to alarm him or embarrass him, she did not mention it.

Still, it angered her that Wendell kept running off from home, trying to distance himself from the help that his father would need. In just a few years, William planned to marry and move away from the farm. When that time came, Robert would still be too young to carry much of the farm work. Joseph would have to depend on Wendell. But the idea never seemed to enter Wendell's mind. His sole purpose in life appeared to be freedom from the responsibility of his father's farm.

The boy came into the kitchen the second to the last day of April, stomping as loudly as he could. He flopped himself down at the breakfast table, his defiant countenance challenging Agnes. "Ham and eggs," he ordered her.

She added more ham to the skillet, and broke several eggs in a bowl to scramble. Without saying a word to him, she put his breakfast on a plate and served it. He opened his mouth wide, smacked his lips together and made a great show of chewing his food with as much noise as he could. When he finished, he slammed his knife and fork down on the table. "Just let her say something to me about table manners this morning." The look on his face said it all.

Still, Agnes was silent. He banged his cup down hard and watched for her reaction. But there was none. "Now is the time to let her know how important I really am."

He looked at her for a long time before speaking. "Today is the last day of school. Tomorrow will be my graduation. I will need my suit pressed, and my white shirt washed." Then he waited for her reaction. He knew she had always kept his clothes very presentable, but he had to show her he was now in command.

Wendell stood up from the table, put his right hand on his hip and stared at her. "I need to look my very best. The top football award will be mine, and I do not want to look sloppy." He turned to leave for school, but paused at the kitchen door. "Make sure, my shirt collar and cuffs are scrubbed white, starched and ironed without any wrinkles."

Agnes bit her lip. "That foolish boy. If he thinks he is going to get by with this." She gathered his dishes from the table. The smirk on her face became more pronounced. "He will learn his last lesson tomorrow."

Early the next morning, Agnes put a big breakfast on the table for Joseph and the family. He looked at the children and smiled in his nice, quiet way. "Your first day out of school, huh?" They smiled and nodded their heads. "I looked outside this morning, and it is a good day to go out and pull weeds in the garden."

He took a large serving of fried potatoes, ham and eggs, then passed the platter on to one of the children. "That shower we had the other night was good for the vegetables, and also, too good for the weeds." He winked at the younger ones. "If the rain could just tell the difference between the plants we want to keep and the plants we do not want to keep, it would sure save us a lot of backbreaking work."

They all chuckled along with him. Joseph buttered one of Agnes' fluffy biscuits. "So, if every one of you comes out to help, it will go much faster. Ma has some work she wants to do here in the house. If we all work out there, it will also help her."

They pushed back their chairs, grabbed their thin, little old jackets and slipped on their wooden shoes. Esther and Robert laughed as they tried to see who could make their shoes clomp the loudest.

"Now, children," admonished Agnes. "Those shoes are to keep your feet dry from the damp grass and weeds, not to see who can make the most noise with them."

Joseph reached for his old hat. "Wendell, go take care of the livestock first. William has to cultivate the kaffir corn before the weeds outgrow those young plants."

"Sure, Pa. But I need to get dressed about eleven. The awards and graduation ceremony is supposed to be at three this afternoon.

A disappointed look passed over Joseph's face. "I forgot about that, but if you must go, you must go. The work around here will still be here tomorrow, although it would be better to get those weeds today."

Wendell made a face. "Pa, those weeds are not going to shoot up that much in one day."

"They grow much faster than we would like for them to do, even in a day," answered his father. "But you go. That is more important to you than weeds." Joseph rubbed his hands together, and then brushed along the back of his neck. Just then, Agnes noticed, again, the slow side-to-side movement of his head. Then it stopped as suddenly as it had begun.

"Just a nervous twitch, I hope." She began to gather the dishes from the table.

Agnes hurried around so she could get to the job she had planned for today. Joseph had gone into town the day before and brought home a quart of varnish and a new paintbrush. She wondered how long it had been since the steps had been refinished. During the last ten years, she had painted, papered and varnished the downstairs. The upstairs needed to be cleaned up, too.

At ten-thirty, Wendell came in. He threw his jacket down on the kitchen table, looked at Agnes and then demanded, "Do you have my suit and my shirt ironed? I need to get ready." His challenging look was not wasted on Agnes.

"Your clothes are ready in your bedroom, but you are not going upstairs to get anything. I just finished varnishing the stairs, and they will not be dry for another six hours." She turned back to the stove to stir the soup she was making.

"What did you say?" he yelled.

"I just told you, the stairs have been varnished, and you can not go up there for another six hours," she replied calmly.

"How dare you. You knew I needed my clothes for today." He stomped his foot hard on the floor. "You are about as wicked as other people say you are." He whirled around to grab the broom and swung it at her.

"Put that down, you obnoxious boy." She glared at him hard. "You want to be treated like you are some kind of king by your pa and me. Your father may do that for you, but I will not." She wagged her finger at him. "You have absolutely no respect for him, or for anyone else, but especially not for your father." Her eyes narrowed and her brow creased in deep angry ridges. "He needs your help so desperately now, and in the years ahead, but all you think about is running off and having fun."

She stepped closer to him, "Fun, not work, but fun. No wonder you want to run off all the time to Frank and Lizzie. They do not make their sons do anything, and that is the way you want it to be."

He put his hands on his hips and stared at her. Hissing like a viper, he snarled, "You are a mean woman. You are not my step-ma and never have been. You are just some woman who came in here and wrapped Pa around your finger. Well, woman, you are not going to do that to me."

"I have no intention of doing that. You are only ruining yourself with all this play. Next thing you know, it will be more and more parties. I have seen what it did to my pa, and, Wendell, it wrecked his life. You do not want that to happen to you. But it will if you are not careful." She turned back to stir the kettle.

He made a fist at her and growled, "I am finished with you, old woman. If you think I am going to stay here and listen to you preach, you are wrong." He was getting more and more angry. Grabbing his jacket from the table, he yelled, "I am not staying in this house one more night with you, you old witch. Aunt Lizzie is where I am going to live from now on. She is now my mother." He shook his fist at her again. "Try and explain that to Pa, will you? Just watch what you say. I am stronger than you. You do not scare me, no matter what you say."

The boy stomped to the door, then turned around. "I am still going to the graduation, you cannot stop me from doing that. Aunt Lizzie has a suit over there that will fit me, so I will still go and get my football award. Maybe you do not think much of me, but somebody else does." He slammed the door as hard as he could.

As he walked out the porch door, he was yelling over and over, "You old witch, you old witch!"

Joseph heard the boy scream, but kept pulling weeds. "Ah, my, those two," he said to himself. His head swiveled harder, sideways.

Coletta heard her brother ranting and raving mad. She ran around the house to see what was going on. "Wendell, Wendell." He just kept walking down the driveway. "Wendell, where are you going?" He hurried more, and she had to run to catch up with him. "Wendell, what is going on?"

He stopped to face her, and snarled, "That old woman had to varnish the stairs, and would not let me get my suit, but I am going to show her. Aunt Lizzie said I could wear cousin John's if Step-Ma gave me any trouble. So that is what I am going to do."

"But, you cannot leave this way." The girl grabbed for his hand. "Wait, Wendell, I will get my jacket; you can wear my jacket."

He put his hand on her shoulder, "I do not think your jacket will fit me."

"But my sweater, I will go get my sweater, Wendell. It stretches." She clung to his hand, as he started off down the driveway again. "Please, Wendell, wear my sweater. Do not go this way, please do not go."

"I have to, Coletta, I will not live in this house one more night with her."

"But what will I do?" She hung on, as he dragged her down the dirt drive.

"You will be fine. You have Esther and Robert here for you. I have nobody. William is too good, and I am not like him at all. He is her pet. He and Irene, neither one of them can do anything wrong, according to Step-Ma." He stopped to look at her, "Take care of Pa, Coletta. He needs your help so he can live with that old witch." Shaking her hand loose from his arm, he growled at her, "Let me go. I need to get over to cousin John's."

His stride lengthened as he walked off down the road. Coletta sank down to the ground and sobbed, "Wendell, Wendell, come back, come back."

That evening, Joseph made another trip to his brother's house to get Wendell. His sister-in-law met him at the door. "I do not think he will go home with you anymore, Joseph. He is really angry with your wife."

"Get him out here." Joseph stepped past her and into the kitchen. "Wendell, Wendell, get out here. You are going home with me now."

The boy stepped out of the dining room into the kitchen and stood with his feet wide apart. "I am not, Pa. I will not." He walked closer, "I am sorry, Pa, but this is where I stay from now on."

"But, Uncle Frank and Aunt Lizzie do not need another mouth to feed. They have their own large family."

"Aunt Lizzie said she always has room for one more, especially someone who has been as mistreated as I am." Wendell turned to go in the other room. "I will not go."

Joseph's head drooped and began to swivel from side to side violently. He tried to stop the motion, but could not. He hurried out the door, past Lizzie, and crawled on the wagon. With hot tears filling his eyes, he could hardly see the road. The horse knew the way home.

Two weeks later, the boy returned for just a few minutes. "Pa, could you get my other clothes for me? I will not go in that house."

"What is the meaning of this, Wendell?"

"Uncle Frank said I could work for them, they need the help." Wendell rocked from one foot to the other. "They said I could live there with them until I am eighteen, if I want to."

"They do not need your help as much as I do, Son. They have three sons and some girls who can help with the farm work." He put his hand on Wendell's arm. "I need you here."

"Sorry, Pa, but I will not work here for you as long as that woman is on this place. If she goes, I will come back, but not otherwise."

"Ah, Son." Joseph turned to go in the house and gather up his son's things.

34

A NEW DAUGHTER

"COME ON OVER again," neighbor Peppen told Joseph. "'The Major Bowes Amateur Hour' is on tonight."

"I will have to mention it to Agnes. She has been busy sewing school dresses and shirts. Maybe a radio show would give her a chance to think about something else."

The November evening air was crisp. The last of the leaves rustled in the slight breeze. A Great Horned Owl sang his mournful song, *Hoo, hoo-hoo, hoooo-hoo.* A heavy comfort was tucked around the youngsters to keep them cozy.

"Listen, Robert, listen. Somewhere out there is that big huge owl just waiting to pounce on you. He has his long, curved beak and claws all sharpened up, ready to take a hunk of curly hair out of your head." Esther's naughty giggle filled the air. "Listen to that. He knows just where our buggy is now, and he is flying through the night faster and faster."

"He cannot see me," the brother snarled.

"Oh, yes, he can. His eyes are so sharp he can see a mouse from way up by the clouds. So he sure is not going to miss your big head." In the darkness, the boy did not see her hand coming under the cover. When she grabbed his shoulder hard, her frightened brother jumped up and screamed, "Ma, the owl, the owl got me."

"Quiet, Robert, you will scare Old Ben."

"But, Ma."

Esther clamped her mouth shut hard to stifle the giggles.

"You keep on like that, we are turning around and going home. I cannot have my children acting up at the neighbors."

"I promise, Ma," he whimpered. Robert slid back down under the blanket.

"Scaredy-cat," sniffed Esther under the covers. "Scared of a little bitty owl."

"Esther, my warning is for you, too."

The neighbors' dog heard the buggy coming up the road and set off the alarm in his yard. "Did you ever hear a dog bark so loud?" Agnes asked Joseph.

"It just seems louder since the air is so clear and cool."

Mrs. Peppen was silhouetted in the doorway against the lantern light. "Shush, Bruno." A beat-up shoe flew through the air and hit the dog on the rump. *Yipe, yipe*. He sailed off the porch and high-tailed it around to the barn. "Silly old dog. He should know your buggy sound by now."

Joseph helped the children down and led them up the steps onto the porch. "Now you know, Daisylue," he laughed, "dogs will be dogs."

"So glad you came." She took Agnes' arm. "Oh, Agnes, I have so much to tell you." Then she giggled, "And ask you."

Daisylue took their wraps and put them in the dark bedroom. "I hope Oscar's radio works better tonight. He is so proud of that thing. I call it his toy for the winter. You know men; he just had to be one of the first around here to get one of those things. I do not know if it was worth the money, but at least it keeps him from falling asleep so early on winter evenings."

Joseph looked at Agnes and grinned, but Daisylue never noticed. She just kept up the chatter. "Not only that, it keeps his hands from getting full of gout. All that twisting of the dial to get the sound clear must do some good. His fingers do not seem to stiffen up so much any more." Picking up a pillow from the divan, she fluffed it up, then threw it in the corner. "This old thing anyway." She patted the seat, "Come sit, Agnes, we can talk better. The men can fool around with that silly contraption."

Oscar pulled his chair closer to the radio. Joseph sat down in the big rocking chair and propped his feet up on the footstool.

"Will not be long now and the talent show will start."

A deep voice filled the room, "And now, ladies and gentlemen." The radio crackled and wheezed and popped. The voice faded in and out of the racket. Just as Oscar got up to try and tune in the reception better, the radio would clear. When he sat down, the static started all over again.

Daisylue whispered to Agnes, "I am not sure, but Oscar seems to be the aerial for the radio." Amid giggles, she leaned closer to her neighbor lady. "He just needs to stand there all the time if we are ever going to hear anything." Oscar kept turning first one dial and then the other. "Just look at that old man of mine, that contraption is making a fool out of him." Daisylue lifted the corner of her apron up to hide the smile on her face.

"And now, the best talent of the evening … " *Crackle, sputter-sputter, pop-pop.*

Oscar shook his head, "Maybe the next show will be clearer. Joseph, you should hear this some nights. Why, we sit here glued to this radio set and just listen to the world come right into our parlor, show after show. It has to be the greatest thing ever invented by man."

Joseph nodded in agreement.

Oscar kept trying to get the knobs just right so they could hear the talking and the music. "And the comics, the music, the actors. You have never heard such good actors. You can almost feel yourself being right in the story with them."

"Come, Esther and Robert, come in the kitchen and help me put out some divinity fudge. There is still some chocolate fudge with walnuts left from the other night, so you can have your pick."

Esther jumped off her chair, followed by Robert. They were by the woman's side in a split second, eyeing her huge pans of candy.

Esther started to carry the bowls back to the parlor. "Robert," she whispered, "grab a handful of each kind for us. We cannot pass this up."

The boy smacked his lips. "This is good, sure wish Ma would make this." He stuffed another big piece of fudge in his already bulging cheeks."

"Too sweet, too much sugar. You know Ma," whispered Esther.

"Agnes, I hear William has a sweetie."

"It seems so."

"Is it serious?" Daisylue winked. "I need to know, I am ready to go to a wedding."

Agnes smiled. Her eyes twinkled. "William has not mentioned how serious this is getting to be, but she does seem like a very sensible girl. Thank heavens, she is not one of those wild things that drink and smoke and carry on. Or, at least, I hope she does not do those things."

"Oh, Agnes, William would not notice anyway. Love is one of the blindest things there is, especially to a man." Daisylue held her hand up to her lips to stifle her laughter.

"Not William. He is one of the most straight-laced young men I know."

"Well, then maybe he needs a wild one to bring a little excitement into his life."

Agnes laughed, "I would rather not suggest that to him. He may not take that too kindly."

"And now, ladies and gentlemen, this is Radio coming from the heart of Times Square, signing off for tonight." Oscar got up to turn the knob off. "We just did not hear much tonight. Maybe another night. Come over again, Joseph, and we will have a few good laughs. Some of those comedians are really sharp."

The air was a bit frostier than it had been when the family drove to the neighbors. "I always enjoy talking to the Mrs." Agnes tucked her hands a bit farther under the flaps of her long coat.

"The fudge was worth the whole evening," Esther whispered to Robert.

Every two or three weeks, Oscar drove over to Joseph's farm to visit. Soon, he would get around to the real reason he stopped by. "Come on over, Joseph, there are some good programs on tonight."

Robert and Esther were only too happy to hear the words, "Pa wants to go to the Peppens' tonight, and listen to the radio."

Every time they went, Mrs. Peppen piled a large bowl full of her mouth-watering fudge. The children never missed the chance to eat their fill.

Looking forward to the good radio shows, the family was hardly aware of the passing of the weeks.

The harsh winter snows of early 1924 eventually melted. The potatoes were planted and mulched. The garden was all worked and ready for planting.

William pushed his plate off to the side and finished his coffee.

The early April sun was setting, casting long, shadows through the west kitchen window.

"Ma, Pa," his eyes lit up. He stood, cleared his throat and looked at his beloved. "Since it is Easter, and most of the family is here today, I have something important to announce." He shifted from one foot to the other, and then cleared his throat again. "Last Sunday, I asked Alvina's father for her hand in marriage and he gave us his blessing. Alvina has said yes, she will be my wife."

"A wedding, a wedding. We are going to have a wedding," Coletta chanted.

"Can I have a pretty new dress, Ma?" Esther looked at her with imploring eyes.

"What do I get to do at this wedding?" asked Robert, wide-eyed. Esther gave Robert a cross-eyed look. "Nothing, you are a boy."

William laughed. "Do not get discouraged so fast, little brother. Maybe I can set it up for you to be a Mass server. No promises, you understand, since the wedding will be in the bride's home parish."

Robert made a crooked face at his sister. "See, Esther."

"How much home brew and moonshine do you have to come up with for this?"

"Wendell, you are always the first to worry about the booze." William punched him on the arm. "Why is that?"

"One has to take care of oneself," heehawed the other.

Joseph stood and reached across the table. "Congratulations, Son. Alvina is a very nice young woman. Very sensible."

The young lady lowered her eyes demurely.

Agnes walked around the table and put one hand on his shoulder and the other on Alvina's shoulder. "The two of you will make a fine couple."

"Thanks, Ma. Thanks, Pa."

"When is the wedding?" Ma asked as she sat back down.

"October 2, 1924, this fall."

"That gives us time to plan, William. I hope our garden will do really well this summer. Then we will be able to can extra jars of vegetables and make some jelly for your pantry. When Pa butchers the hogs and the steer, we can fry down some pork sausage and cure a ham or two. A few jars of canned beef will help, too."

"I would really appreciate that," nodded William.

The summer rushed past, and the leaves turned to their fall colors. A bright blue October sky heralded the wedding.

The groom was handsome and his bride beautiful. The demure young lady was all aglow as she and William walked down the aisle to be married.

"I love her dress, so stylish; and that mid-calf length skirt is just right. That is the kind of wedding dress I want someday." Coletta danced around in circles and pretended to be much older.

"I want a long veil just like Alvina's," added Esther. "And that pretty band she has across her forehead with all those beads. Do you think she will let me wear it someday when I am a bride?" She danced around with Coletta. "Weddings are so pretty."

Joseph, Agnes and the two youngsters were once more at the neighbors, trying to hear one of Oscar's favorite radio shows.

Agnes leaned over to Daisylue, "We have a lovely, nice, modest, new daughter-in-law. We are so happy with the choice William has made."

The snows began to fly, and the excitement of Christmas was upon the household again.

The two youngest daughters watched Agnes baste the Christmas goose. A mouth-watering aroma filled the house. Wendell tried to teach Joseph and Robert a new card game that was popular among the young men of the town.

"Are they ever going to come?" moaned Esther.

"I hope it is soon. The front of my stomach is meeting my backbone." Coletta began to put plates and silverware on the table. "It will be so much fun today with Alvina and William here. I just love her, she is so sweet."

"Me, too." Esther looked out the kitchen door. "Agnes Marie has come with August, Ellen and their babies." Esther rushed out the door, "Merry Christmas, everybody."

Several minutes later, the newlyweds drove in. Before they even got out of the car, Esther was there to greet them. "Oh, Alvina, your hat is so pretty."

Coletta had come out behind her. "It is a cloche," the older sister corrected her. Both girls held Alvina's hands and escorted her into the house.

"What a lovely welcome I have received. Merry Christmas, everyone." Alvina's smile lit up the room. She slipped off her long black wool coat to reveal a red silk, low-waisted, sleeveless chemise dress. The short skirt ended above her knees. Silk white stockings ended in a roll right below her pretty knees. Strands of white pearls embraced her neck and cascaded to below her waist. William looked at her and beamed. He could not hide his pride at how lovely his new wife looked.

"Oooh, Alvina, your dress, your beads. You are a vision of loveliness." Irene had just walked into the kitchen from the parlor. She leaned over and gave the other a big hug.

"And you got your hair bobbed," added Agnes Marie. She laughed, "So, have you and William learned to do the Charleston yet? Have you taken up smoking with a long, jeweled cigarette holder?"

Everyone laughed, everyone that was except Ma. Joseph happened to look her way and noticed the disapproval on her face. She cringed and bit her lip. His breath caught. Long ago, he learned that Agnes always voiced her opinion at some time. "I just hope she holds her tongue today."

The goose, and apple and raisin dressing were piled high on huge platters. Mounds of mashed potatoes and candied sweet potatoes filled large bowls. Pumpkin and gooseberry pies sat on the sideboard. The clatter of silver on Agnes' china added to the delight of the feast. The food quickly disappeared. Chairs scraped across the floor as the family moved back to rest and wait for the serving of pie and fresh coffee.

Joseph glanced around his table and smiled in happiness. Ellen and her husband, August, took good care of their three little girls and young son. William and Alvina were well settled on their farm and acted so happy. Wendell had come home for the day.

Then he looked at his second daughter, Agnes Marie. "How much longer in nurses' training do you have?"

"Another six months or so. Oh, Pa, I really do like being a nurse. There are so many exciting advances in medicine coming up all the time." She shrugged and sighed, "It is a real challenge just keeping up with them."

The older Agnes smiled at her. "You will make a good nurse, Agnes. One has to be organized to do that, and you, my dear girl, are that." The two women smiled at each other in understanding.

Agnes Marie nodded in agreement. She was so like Step-Ma, organized, ambitious, punctual and outspoken."

The happy hours passed quickly, and the time came for the guests to depart.

"Thanks for everything." William held the coat for Alvina. "Thanks, Ma, the meal was delicious."

"Yes, Ma, you must teach me how to roast such an excellent goose."

Agnes glanced down at the short skirt and the long beads, but held her tongue. Half smiling, she looked at the young bride, "Yes, someday I must."

Joseph breathed a quiet sigh of relief. Agnes had held her opinions today, but at some time, he knew. "I just hope that does not happen. Alvina is much too nice a girl."

35

THE KILLER CAR

JOSEPH HITCHED PRINCE to the buggy. How he missed Old Ben. "That horse just knew his way all around this country," the farmer mused. "I always felt so safe with him. He just knew to be extra careful when the children had the reins."

He straightened out the horse's bridle, and checked the buggy hitch. "But old horses deserve a rest when their time comes, too." He patted Prince on the flank, then brushed along his silky brown nose. The horse turned his face to Joseph, "You are a pretty horse. Be gentle with Coletta, will you? She has to take Esther and Robert to school now." The horse whinnied softly, and Joseph grinned. "So, does that mean I can count on you to take special care of the children?"

"Is it all ready, Pa?" The three, Coletta, Esther and Robert, came out, loaded down with books, syrup bucket lunch pails and heavy sweaters.

"What are the sweaters for?" Joseph laughed, and tugged at Robert's ear.

"Aw, Pa, you know Ma. She thinks it might be snowing by the time school is out this afternoon," the boy frowned.

"Yes, I do know that is how your Ma is, always worrying about something. Sometimes she is much too careful, but that is her way. She never wants anything bad to happen to anyone. Most people do not know that about her, but that is her secret."

"It will take me a little longer this morning, Pa." Coletta climbed into the buggy. "Ma asked me to stop at the store. She needs more sugar."

Joseph smiled, "Now you know, if it takes you too long, you can pick these two up after school, too. But then I do not suggest you do that. Ma will have me coming into town looking for you."

"I know, Pa, I know. I promise to save you that trip."

The three waved as they went out the yard. Joseph could hear their happy laughter through the clear fall air, even though they were near the corner about a quarter of a mile from the driveway. He smiled in warm happiness, "What fun those three have together. A stranger would never know they are not blood brother and sisters, but that is the way it should be. They are mine, regardless."

He walked out to the barn to check the animals. How quiet it was around the farm with William married and Wendell still off working for Frank and Lizzie. "How I could use that boy now," Joseph spoke aloud. "All these years over there. I just cannot figure out what went wrong with him and Ma. Both of them are such stubborn people."

He pulled open the barn door and walked into the shadowy hall-way. "Wendell said he would stay there until he is eighteen, so in a few more months, I suppose he will try and get a job in the city. So many of our farm boys are doing that instead of staying on the farms."

Joseph put his oldest cow, Gert, in the stanchion, and then sat down on the milk stool beside her. His fingers tightened and pulled at her udder, and the white foamy liquid squished into the bucket. While he milked the cow, his mind wandered restlessly. "But then, the young boys leaving the farm is no different that it used to be. Most of my older brothers did the same thing." He shrugged, "Just the ways of youth growing up, I guess."

He put the full bucket of milk close to the door. The cow turned her head in the stanchion, waiting for the hay. Joseph dropped the slab in the feeder in front of her. He brushed Gert's back gently. "Gert, you do not mind Coletta being around you, do you? She has really become my right hand. She tries so hard to fill Wendell's place. I must thank her for that some day."

It was not long when he heard Prince come in the yard again. He looked out the door and called to Coletta. "You did not waste any time this morning."

"No, Pa, Prince just pranced right along." She waved and went into the house.

"I hope she and Ma are both in a good frame of mind today. Some days they do not seem to get along very well." He patted Gert absentmindedly. "Coletta is growing up, too. She is getting to be more independent, and sometimes that is not too good." He smiled, "But again, the ways of the young."

The school year was going well, six weeks had already passed. Every day Coletta took the two youngsters there in the morning and, in the afternoon, went back to get them.

"I really get tired of doing this," she sighed. "It was more fun when there were girls there my age, but they are all working now at home or helping the neighbor ladies. They are better off than me, they have brothers that come to school and get the little ones." She looked from side to side, watching for the fall flowers in the pastures and fields. "Ah, if Pa would just ask the neighbors to take Esther and Robert along, it would make it much easier on me." She shrugged her shoulders, "But I doubt that will happen at all. He does not trust some of them. So, it looks like it is up to me."

One late October afternoon, she walked out to the yard where Pa had Prince and the buggy ready to go.

"I really do not like going over the Cannon Ball Highway very much, Pa," she said.

"Why is that, Coletta?"

"Some of those people drive so fast, it is hard to see them coming. And all those black cars, they just blend into the background. I really have to look both ways several times."

"Just take your time and be careful." He put his hand on her shoulder. "I know some of them drive too fast. They forget that those newfangled cars travel much faster than a horse can cross the highway." He smiled at her, "But I know you will be careful, you always have been."

"Thanks, Pa."

Esther and Robert were playing in the schoolyard when Coletta got there. They were both having so much fun with other students, they pretended not to see her.

"Come on, Esther, get Robert, we need to go."

"What is the hurry, Coletta?" The girl turned back to talk to one of the other girls.

"There are clouds building up in the northwest, and it looks like it could rain. I do not want to get caught out on the road in a storm."

"Robert, Robert, come on, we have to go." Esther ran over and grabbed him by the arm. "Coletta says it looks like a storm is coming."

"Aw, all right," he growled, as he leisurely walked over to the steps of the school.

"Robert, come on," called Coletta, "or you will be walking home. And you know how mad Ma would get if that happens."

The youngsters climbed in the buggy and settled on the seats. "Giddy-up, Prince, we need to go." Coletta tugged at the reins.

"School was so much fun today, Coletta," gushed Esther. "We jumped rope and I went the longest."

"We had races today, and I was the second fastest." Robert patted himself on the back.

By the time they got to the Cannon Ball Highway, their chatter overlapped that of the other. The clouds had moved in and the wind had changed to the northwest. Coletta stopped Prince to look both ways on the road.

Just as Prince stepped onto the cement road, Esther shouted, "Coletta, a car, there is a car coming."

The older girl turned and saw the car speeding from the east. "Whoa, Prince," she yelled and pulled hard on the reins.

The horse stopped in the middle of the narrow road. But the car kept coming, faster and faster. "That car is heading right for Prince," Coletta screamed. "It is going to hit our horse."

The horse turned its head to the left, but the top of the car windshield caught Prince right above the eye and knocked him hard to the side. The children saw the three men shake their fists and heard them laugh as they hit the animal. The driver slowed down a little, but then speeded up and kept going. Prince tried to stay upright, but staggered and stumbled to the ground. The buggy rolled over with him.

"Are you all right, Esther?" called Coletta, as she picked herself up off the ground.

"I think so." Esther rolled over in the ditch, then slowly managed to stand up. "I jumped out of the buggy."

"Robert, Robert, where are you?" Coletta could not see the boy on the other side of the buggy.

"I am still here, in the buggy." His voice rose in a quiver, then broke into tears. "I am not hurt, Coletta."

The oldest girl felt her body begin to shake hard. She had to think what to do. Prince still lay there, stretched out long on the pavement. "Oh, no," moaned the girl, "Now what will I do?"

She stood back and watched him breathing hard. Finally, Prince raised his head slightly and tried to look at her. One of the neighbors came up behind them with his team, and stopped beside the buggy.

"Looks like you could use some help here, Coletta."

Another buggy pulled up behind and a second neighbor hopped down. "We will unhitch your buggy and put it upright."

The first farmer pulled at Prince's reins. "Your horse will be all right, Coletta, you will just have to give him some time to rest. He has been shaken up quite a bit, but you can walk him home real slow."

When they got the buggy unhitched, Prince struggled to his feet and stood there, looking at them.

Robert laughed nervously, "Look at him. He is trying to figure out what is going on."

"You mean he is trying to decide what hit him." Coletta slowly walked up to him and stroked his bloody nose. "You are a good horse, Prince, you tried to stop."

The men hitched the buggy back up. "What really happened anyway?" asked the first one.

Coletta told them how the men hit the animal, then laughed loudly as they drove past and did not stop.

"Sounds to me like they were all drunk," said the second neighbor. "Anybody else would have stopped to check on you. Too bad someone else did not see it happen, so they could have gone after them and stopped them."

"I just hope Pa does not get too angry," sighed Coletta, " or Ma, either."

The three children walked home slowly, taking their time beside Prince. Joseph was waiting for them when they arrived there. "The neighbor stopped and said you had trouble, but that you were coming soon." He walked up to Prince and patted him on the neck. "What a terrible thing to happen to you, tangling with a car."

Agnes came rushing out of the house and looked at Prince's bloody face. "What happened?" she screamed. Then she looked at Coletta and wagged her finger in the girl's face, "And you, what are you trying to do, kill my children?" She stomped closer to the older girl and kept on, "Irene would never have let this happen, she is more careful. You are not careful, not like her."

"Now, Agnes." Joseph rushed to her side. "The children are not hurt. It could have been worse. Just calm yourself, calm yourself."

"Come here, my children." She held out her arms to Esther and Robert and hugged them when they came. Giving Coletta a dirty look, she turned and hurried them into the house.

"No more, Pa, no more will I take them to school. I tried. I did not mean for this to happen, that car just came so fast, Pa, I did not see it. Esther and Robert did not see it either."

Joseph gathered Coletta in his arms, "I know, I know. Those cars just go too fast."

"Why does Ma think I did that on purpose? I did not." The tears built up and bubbled over. "She always thinks Irene would do better than me. Nothing Irene ever does is wrong, she is Ma's favorite." The girl sobbed.

He hugged her tightly, "I have worried about you taking the others to school since the new road was built." Releasing her from his grasp, he held her back and looked into her eyes. "You did your best, and I do not blame you. That is a lot to ask of a young girl." Hugging her again, he muttered, "I am sorry, Coletta, I should have known better."

Brushing the tears from her eyes, he continued, "This evening I will go ask the Winters to stop by and take Robert and Esther along when they take their children to school. Then you will not have to worry anymore."

"Thanks, Pa, thanks."

"Now, into the house. Ma will be calmed by now, and it is time to get supper. So, go help her. Let me see your pretty smile first."

Agnes and Joseph on the front porch of their farm house.

A friend joins the family photo; Sam, Joseph, Agnes, Irene and Coletta, and Robert and Esther in the front.

36

HARSH WORDS

THE FALL DAYS melted into the early days of the twelfth month. On a clear, cold December day, Esther ran to the door. "Ma, William and Alvina and their baby are here." She pushed open the door, hurried through the porch and outside without a sweater.

"William, William, you brought Baby Dorothy. Has she grown? Can I hold her? Can I see her, Alvina?"

"Slow down, little sister," laughed William. "It is too cold out here to talk much, or to show her to you. Let us go inside, then she can have her covers off."

They trouped into the warm kitchen and put the baby on the table. Joseph and Agnes and the children all gathered around to look at her.

"Look how much hair she has," giggled Esther. "Is she big enough to play with us?" added Robert.

"Now, children," Agnes admonished them, "you have to wait a while for that. Dorothy is only four months old, and she has to get much bigger before she can play." She took the child's hand and stroked the tiny fingers. "Our fifth grandchild, our 1925 grandbaby. This is a good year for us." She smiled at Alvina, "Our family has been blessed."

The afternoon wore on. Soon it would be time for the couple to go back home. William and Joseph walked outside to check the cattle and their feed bunks. "There is enough feed here for another day or so, Pa," William said.

Alvina was sitting at the table, gently rocking back and forth to put the baby asleep.

Agnes had frowned at her short, stylish dress when she came in, but refrained from saying anything. But now she looked at her again. As Alvina held Dorothy, her skirt slipped higher and higher up on her thigh. Finally, Agnes could contain herself no longer.

She walked around and put her hand on Alvina's arm. "We are so glad you came. But next time, Alvina, dress more conservatively."

Alvina's breath caught and her face turned white.

"I know that is fashion, but you are a married woman now, and should not be going around showing your bare knees to other men. That is disgraceful. You come in dressed in too short a dress, and with your pretty hair bobbed like a loose woman. It makes you look like some kind of …." Agnes sighed loudly in disgust.

Alvina gasped, as she tried desperately to pull her skirt closer to her knees.

"If you just do not take up drinking, or flinging one of those long cigarette holders around, it will be a wonder. And your painted red lips. Alvina, if I did not know better, you would impress me as nothing more than many of the other women who have no respect for themselves." Agnes paused to catch her breath. "What are those bold women called? Flappers, is that right?"

"Ma, Ma, I meant no harm." Alvina struggled to put the baby on the table and stand up. When she was able to, she rushed into the bedroom and grabbed her coat. Bundling up the little one and grabbing the diaper sack, she headed for the door, looking back just long enough to say, "I am sorry."

The young mother rushed out the door, "William, William, come, I have to go." He turned to see her half-running to the car. "Come, I can not stay here."

William ran to her, "What is it, Alvina, what is it?"

Leaning against the fender of the car, she blurted out, "Ma called me a flapper; she called me a flapper, William."

"What?"

"She called me that terrible name."

"Why?"

"Because my dress is too short. Oh, William, get me out of here."

Joseph hurried over and heard the last part. "Agnes is at it again," he muttered.

Just then, Agnes came to the porch door. "She should know better."

"Enough," thundered William. "Ma, you had no right." Opening the car door, he took the baby while Alvina scooted in. "Come, Dear, it is time for us to go."

"This is my house and I can say what I like," retorted Agnes.

The silence was deafening, until the porch screen door banged behind Agnes as she stormed into the house.

"William, Son, William, please."

The younger man crawled in and banged the door shut. Alvina put her head down on her baby's blanket and sobbed loudly.

Joseph opened the door and leaned in. "Please, do not go like this."

"It will be a long time before we return." William's face was ashen and lined in anger. "Why don't you get rid of that woman? She is never satisfied with anything."

"Please, listen to me," pleaded Joseph. "I know she is outspoken, and you know Ma is outspoken, but she is my wife, William, no matter how you feel right now." He put his hand on his son's shoulder, "I did marry her for better or worse, just like you did your wife. And sometimes I get the worst, but most of the time, I get the better." He squeezed William's shoulder. "You will understand after you are married a long time. That is the way it is."

"But, she never gives up. There is always something wrong with one of us." William wiped his face with his white handkerchief.

"Please understand, Ma did not mean to hurt anyone. She admires both you and Alvina so much. She just did not want Alvina to make a spectacle of herself now that you are married."

Joseph looked across at his daughter-in-law. "Please try to understand, Alvina, she does not want to hear others speak unkindly of you because of the clothes you wear. She was only trying to spare your feelings in the future."

"I am sorry, Pa. You tried hard to explain, but Alvina is now my wife. If I approve of what clothes she wears, then it should be of no concern to others. She is my wife and I will be there for her and protect her from others." He tugged on the door handle. "Please, Pa, move so I can close the door. We must go. My wife is too upset to stay longer."

Joseph held the door open forcefully.

"Please, please, William."

"I can not, anymore, I can not," emphasized the oldest son.

Joseph shuddered. "Please, Alvina, she is worried what others will say. She knows about that. She knows about the vicious lies people tell." Joseph choked back the sobs building in his throat, waiting to erupt. "Please, Alvina; Ma knows how it feels to have others make up lies about her. It has happened to her many times." He pulled his big, red handkerchief from his pocket to blow his nose. "Ma knows, and it hurts. Others hear only the bad stories. They do not want to listen to the good side." Joseph's voice broke. "Please, she does not want that to happen to you."

"It is no use, Pa. You can say all you want; it is no use. Ma has spoken, spoken too much this time."

Joseph stepped back. His skin turned ashen. Violently, his head began to shudder from side to side. He tried to stop it, but to no avail; he just could not.

"Maybe I will see you one of these days, Pa." William slammed the door shut, started the car and spun the wheels as he drove out the driveway. Slushy snow and mud flew everywhere.

"Good-bye, Son." Joseph stood there in shock. "Good-bye, Son."

37

FAVORED CHILD

THE WINTER MOON filled the February sky with silvery light. Irene's latest beau slid across the seat of his new Model A.

"Did you notice how shiny my car is?" He snuggled up close against her. "Irene, you know how you have stolen my heart, don't you?" He tried to kiss her, but she pushed back hard, up against the door.

"Why do you do that?" the young farmer asked. He stretched over to stroke her cheek. "My dear, I am ready to take a wife, and I have had my eye on you for years. You are just what I need on the farm I bought."

"Oh, come now," Irene laughed. "What you need on a farm are cows, pigs, horses, chickens, ducks, geese, turkeys, guinea hens and all those other animals, maybe a few goats or sheep. I do not think I quite fit that category."

"Ah, but you are wrong, my dear," gushed Arthur. "You are exactly the kind of farm wife I need to take care of all those animals."

"Just why do you think that?"

"Because you have them on your pa's farm. And if any young woman around here has learned how to take care of all those animals, it is you. With a step-ma like yours, you could not help but learn."

"Ohh," she laughed. "You mean more like forced into it. Step-Ma never let any of us get off without work. I never met a woman who could demand so much of another person."

"See, you get the point I am trying to make." Arthur slipped his arm around her back as much as he could. "You know all the things you need to know to raise those animals and a big garden besides." Then he laughed, "And, maybe even, a whole houseful of little ones."

He chuckled more, "And if you have learned to cook like your step-ma, there is nothing more I could ask for." He pulled his slender fingers through her long, dark hair.

"That does it," Irene snorted. "All you want is a hired man, a housekeeper, a cook and a baby producer, so you can have help later on in years. The more babies your wife produces, the easier it will be on you in your old age."

Arthur nodded his head in agreement, "You do get the picture. Now, can I count you in or not?"

"Definitely not," she insisted. One of these first days, I am going to pack my bags and head for the city."

"Well, I wonder then, Irene, what has kept you around here this long?"

"The neighbor ladies have been so busy having babies that I just have not had the time. They all need a good helper." She smiled, "And even though Step-Ma is a hard task master, she needs the help, too. She raises such a big garden, and has all those eggs from the chickens. Every week, we collect dozens of eggs and all kinds of vegetables. The folks take them into Wichita to sell to one of the hospitals." Irene paused, "And I do like working with her. She and I are so much alike. I know that sounds strange, even though she is my step-ma, not my real ma. It would have been interesting, however, to know my ma better, and see how much I would be like her."

"Are you planning on moving soon?" Arthur tried to steal a kiss. "'Cause if you are not, I plan to keep knocking on your door to see if I can change your mind."

"Arthur, to be honest, you are wasting your time with me. I suggest you start looking elsewhere. There are many girls around here that would love to become a rich farmer's wife." She giggled, then added, "And have lots of little ones hanging onto their skirts."

Irene sighed, "And if I am to make my way in the city, I need to do it now. In just a few months I will turn twenty, and you know what they think about twenty-year-old young ladies out here in the country? If you are not married by that age, you are destined to be an old maid, and that I do not intend to be." She rubbed her hand on his cheek, "Nor do I intend to be a farmer's wife."

She could barely see her wrist watch in the moonlight, but just enough to read the time. "Oh my, I did not know it was this late. Step-Ma will have a fit." She sighed again, "No matter how old we are, or just how much she thinks of us, she still runs our lives, it seems."

Irene pushed the car door open before Arthur could even think about walking her to the door or collecting a goodnight kiss.

"Squeak, squeak," the porch door sang out, when she opened it. As it closed behind her, another rasping squeak filled the cold night air. She shuddered, "It never sounds like that in the daytime." Giggling, she muttered, "Step-Ma does not need a watch dog, she has this noisy, grating screen door spring to announce our comings and goings."

Slipping off her shoes, the kitchen linoleum felt icy cold on her feet. Going barefoot was the only way to get past her folks' bedroom door and not make all kinds of noise. On tiptoes, she slipped upstairs, and carefully sat down on the squeaky bed. She breathed hard. "Everything in this house makes a sound at night. I cannot believe it." Pulling the thick featherbed up over her head, she was soon fast asleep.

Agnes rapped on the stairway door early the next morning. "Time to get up and get dressed to go to Sunday Mass."

Irene heard the younger ones and Pa get up and move around. But her throat felt scratchy inside. "Too much night air," she decided. "Think I will just stay under these warm covers. The Lord will never miss me this morning."

"Irene, Irene, get up." Agnes stood at the bottom of the stairs calling. "Can you hear me?"

Irene made sure her voice sounded really bad when she answered, "I can hear you, but I can hardly talk this morning."

"You should still go to Mass." Agnes put her hands on her hips. "Come down here, let me check your throat."

"Aw, Ma, it hurts so much."

"No wonder, when you came in, it was almost daylight." Agnes raised her voice, "You thought I did not know when you came in, but I did. Now, get down here."

Slowly, Irene struggled to get out of the warm bed, and even more slowly, she went down the stairs. "I just do not feel good, Ma. And riding in that cold buggy. If Pa had a car, it would not hurt me so much."

"That is no excuse, young lady."

"No, Ma, I will not go this morning. I can pray here at home."

Agnes growled and carried on, but she could not persuade Irene to get dressed and go along.

Once the others were out of the yard, Irene knew what she had to do. Finding several boxes Ma had stored in the pantry, she carried them upstairs. She stood there looking in her wardrobe for a long time, then finally decided to begin folding her clothes. "It is time for me to go, now." Dress after dress went into the large box. "I need to call the Gretchmers. They will come get me and take me to William and Alvina."

Being careful not to slip down the steps in her haste, she rushed to the telephone and rang up the neighbors. "Mrs. Gretchmer, could someone from your family come get me in thirty minutes? I need to go to William's place today."

"Sure, Irene, what is the trouble?"

"It is just time for me to leave home, and I know if I ask Pa, it will be too hard on him, and too hard on me."

"We will be there."

Just then, Irene heard the horse and buggy come in. "They cannot possibly be home already. I did not expect them so soon." She hurried back upstairs to finish folding her clothes. Then she heard them come into the house.

Agnes came up the stairs. "Irene, Irene, how are you feeling?" She walked in the bedroom door. "What is going on here?"

"I am packing, Ma, I am leaving."

"Why, where are you going?"

"I want to go to the city."

"But how are you going to get there?"

"The Gretchmers are coming over in thirty minutes to get me and take me to William's house. From there, I can go into Wichita tomorrow or the next day and look for work."

Agnes grabbed another box and started throwing some of Irene's other things in it.

"Please, Ma, understand, I am almost twenty."

"But I could use you here, Irene; you are such a help to me."

"But, Ma, I need a life of my own. I have some money saved up from helping the neighbor ladies. I have talked to some of the girls from town. They are going to business school, and maybe I can, too.

Then I can get a job in town and support myself. That way, I will not have to depend on you and Pa. And maybe, I will meet a nice man."

Agnes huffed, but did not say anything. She just kept pitching Irene's belongings in the box.

"Please, Ma, try to understand. Agnes Marie is going to nurses' school, and you and Pa helped her out. So, give me a chance to go to school and make something of myself, too."

She stood up tall, then put her hand on Step-Ma's shoulder. "In an off-handed way, Arthur asked me to marry him last night. But, Ma, I do not want to be a farmer's wife and live on a farm all my life. There is more out in the world for me, I feel it."

Agnes was silent. When the boxes were full, she called Robert to come help take them downstairs. As Irene walked through the kitchen with the last box, Agnes whispered, "You have always been my special one. I will miss you."

The neighbors were already parked by the walk, and Irene quickly carried her boxes out to their car. She turned around to wave to Pa and the younger ones, but Agnes was not to be seen. "Tell Ma good-bye for me," she hugged her father.

Coletta walked back into the kitchen. "Why did Irene leave?" she demanded of Agnes.

Agnes threw her coat on the table, and hissed to the girl, "One more devious, demon Fraulein has left this house."

Sixteen-year-old Coletta shrank back in horror. Then, in a defiant voice, she answered, "You do not need to worry, Ma, I will not be here much longer either." She turned and stomped through the parlor and up the stairs to her bedroom.

Joseph walked in and stood in front of Agnes. "What caused Irene to go?"

"It was time for her to leave, Joseph. She could not stay here all her life, she needs to get out in the world." With that, she went into the pantry and brought out several potatoes. With defiance in her eyes, she roughly peeled them.

The weeks rolled around slowly for those at home. Then one day, Joseph came in with a wide smile on his face. "Agnes, Agnes, a letter from Irene was in the mail."

Agnes came into the kitchen from the bedroom and sat down at the table. "Read it to me, Joseph."

"You read it, Agnes, you are better at that."

She tore open the flap and began to read. "Dear Ma and Pa. I am fine. I just want you to know that I have an apartment with some other girls, and am taking care of some children, when I am not in school. I am going to business school, and will learn to type and to take short-hand. I will tell you more about that when I come home in a few weeks for a weekend visit. William will bring me home."

Agnes wiped a tear away and whispered, "She is coming home to see us, Joseph. Irene is coming home to see us."

"I knew she would, Agnes," he spoke quietly. "I knew she would. Both of you are so much alike, you understand each other."

Christmas of 1926 was a happy time. Agnes had prepared all the favorites of the holiday, and everyone was coming home to spend the day. Coletta, Esther and Robert were excited. "Do you think there are more gifts from Aunt Martha in Germany this year?" Coletta laughed. "One of these days we will be too old and she will not have to send any more."

"Just do not ever tell her," giggled Esther.

The family all gathered around to share their stories. Wendell spoke first. "I have a job in Wichita now." He paused, then chuckled, "And I met a girl. Do not know how it will work out, but I hope it does."

"Wendell is getting married," sang out Esther.

"Not just yet. Do not rush me. Remember, I am only young once, and I intend to make the most of my freedom while I can."

A handsome man had come in with Agnes Marie. She stood up and motioned to him. "Pa, Ma, this is Wilbur." Blushing a soft pink, she continued, "He is very special to me, and since I am now a full-time nurse, who knows what will come."

Everyone laughed. Wilbur raised his eyebrows and looked at Esther and Robert with amusement, then winked at them.

Joseph turned to Irene, "Are you learning anything interesting in business school?"

Irene graciously folded her napkin and placed it beside her plate. "Another organized daughter," Joseph noticed. "So like Ma, and so like her sister, Agnes Marie."

Irene smiled at him. "My typing skills are improving every day, and I can file alphabetized folders faster than anyone else in the class. And," she paused to look around the table, "my shorthand speed is 120 words per minute, and sometimes more than that."

"What does that mean?" Wendell leaned forward on his chair.

"That means, Dear Brother, that you can speak 120 words a minute, or talk faster than that, and I can take down everything you say in shorthand, then read it back to you."

Wendell winked at her, "Nah, I will bet money I can talk faster than you can write it down."

"The bet is on. Later today, perhaps, Brother." She lifted her fork to cut off a bite of pie. "More great news. I have an interview after the first of January for a possible secretary position with one of the largest real estate firms in the city of Wichita."

Joseph bowed his head and smiled. Agnes touched her arm thoughtfully. "Good luck" and "Congratulations" echoed around the table.

The year passed quickly. Everything seemed to be working out for each member of the family. Ellen's and William's families were growing; Agnes was a nurse in one of the largest hospitals in the city; Wendell had a good job and a steady girlfriend, and Irene was the secretary for the growing real estate firm. On weekends, Joseph and Agnes held summer picnics under the big trees in their front yard, and invited neighbors and cousins to join them.

Agnes and Joseph were kept busy delivering eggs and fresh vegetables from their big garden to the city hospitals. With the extra hired men Joseph had to hire now to help with the farm work, Agnes and Coletta were kept doubly busy in the kitchen.

It was soon fall, then Christmas time again. The family gathered together once more around the large kitchen table.

"I have special news to tell you," Agnes Marie announced happily. She lifted up her left hand and showed off two fancy rings. "Wilbur and I were married the end of November in Wichita."

"But where, why did you not tell us?" asked Ma, in surprise.

Agnes Marie looked at Joseph to gauge the reaction on his face. "We were married by a county judge at the courthouse." She was silent for a few seconds, "We thought it would be better that way."

There was total silence in the room, until finally Wendell lifted his cup, "Toast to the new couple. Long life to you both."

Laughter erupted as each tried to question them at the same time.
"He is so handsome," gushed Esther to Coletta.

Robert, seated next to her, elbowed his sister in the side and whispered, "What is so handsome about him? He is just another middle-aged man."

"Oh, you," giggled Esther as she jabbed back at him. He is Agnes Marie's husband. That makes him special."

That evening in their bedroom, Joseph tossed and turned in his bed. "Why are you so restless, Joseph?" Agnes asked.

"Why did Agnes Marie get married that way? I do not understand."

"I do not know for sure, Joseph, but I did overhear her tell Ellen and Alvina that he had been married." She added then, "Maybe his wife died."

"But that should not be a reason for them to get married by a judge."

"Perhaps, Joseph, there are other reasons. It sounded like that."

"I never thought one of my daughters would do that."

"Joseph, they are grown women, and their lives are their own to live as they choose."

He was silent for a long time, until finally he answered, "You are right, Agnes, although it is hard."

"Joseph, it is always harder for a father to understand these things than a mother. Every woman has a need for self-fulfillment. For that reason, a father must understand."

He was so quiet then, Agnes became worried. "Joseph, are you all right?"

"I am. I was just thinking about what you said." Then, in a soft voice, he said, "Thank you, Agnes, thank you." He turned over and quietly relaxed until he fell asleep.

38

THE LEAVE-TAKING

JOSEPH AND WILLIAM walked around the farm. "I need to make some changes, I think."

"What do you mean, Pa?"

Joseph smiled, "I have been thinking about investing in an automobile. Oscar Peppen told me the Ford dealer at Cheney is going to have a Model A over there in a few months. Thought I might go over and at least look at it."

"That sounds like a good idea, Pa. I heard that model is easier to drive than the Model T. It is also coming out with an electric starter, so you do not have to crank it every time you want to go somewhere."

"That is what Oscar was telling me. And if I do not need to crank it, that would be a real advantage. Cranking much of anything is getting too hard on my old bones." Joseph smiled at his son. "With all the garden produce Ma sells to the Wichita hospitals during the summer, it would make it so much handier. The horses are getting old and all those noisy cars in the city make them real edgy. I am afraid one of these days Prince will bolt and we will have a runaway."

"Why don't you quit hauling all that produce to the city?"

"We need the extra income. The price of calves and the wheat just do not cover everything. And with Robert and Esther growing up, that takes money." He sighed, "Ma is willing to do all that work, and as long as she can manage it, I will not discourage her." He looked at William, "I have never seen a woman who is so willing to work as hard as she is. But, I always have to remind myself that she had a hard life as a youngster, and had to go to work when she was only fourteen, so their family could eat. So, that has always been with her from early on."

"Once you get used to driving, Pa, you will wonder why you ever put up with horses as long as you have."

"I do not know about that. Driving around here will not be too hard, but in the city might be different. Those drivers are so reckless." He bent over to pick up a bucket to take back to the barn. "If it gets too much for me to drive in Wichita, Esther and Robert can do it. Esther will be fifteen in two years and she can drive then." Joseph chuckled slightly, "That girl is not afraid of anything, it seems. Has the nerve of her ma."

"When the cars come in, would you like me to go with you to look at them?"

"I sure could use some advice, if you do not mind, Son." Since Wendell is not around here, I have to depend on you. Robert is too young yet."

"I sure do not mind, Pa, any time."

"Wendell told Uncle Henry that he is thinking about getting married in the spring. So, he must be getting serious about that girl."

"He is only going on twenty, Pa. Is he really ready to settle down and make a life for himself and a wife?"

"He seems to think so. She will have to be a special kind of woman to put up with him, though. He is different from you, William. His thinking on life is not like yours, but that is the way he is. Wendell is a good worker, that much I have to say, although he likes to party a little too much, as far as I am concerned."

"I do not think you have to worry too much, Pa. I know Bertha and her family, and none of them are afraid of work. Bertha is a strong girl in her own way. They will get along."

"Coletta is getting restless, too. She and Ma always seem to be at odds. There is hardly a peaceful day around here between those two."

"She is nearing that age, Pa, when she needs to get out on her own. I have watched other girls who have left home to work, and it does them good. They need to see how things are for other people before they settle down with a husband and a houseful of children." William laughed, then continued, "It just is not good for a young girl to go directly from her bed in her parents' house to her husband's bed. If they are out on their own, even for a few months, they at least learn a little about managing their own money."

"I know that, William. Ma could use Coletta's help, but you are right, it is about time for her to go. Esther is getting to be good help now."

"I need to be going, Pa, but whenever they get that Model A in at Cheney, and you want to go look at it, let me know. I will be glad to go with you."

"Thanks, Son."

As Joseph walked to the house, he could hear Coletta and Agnes arguing loudly. "Why they cannot get along, at least part of the time, I just do not understand. Ma thinks Coletta is not particular enough, and Coletta thinks Ma is picking on her." He sighed loudly. "If both of them would just learn a little patience, it would be so much quieter around here. I do not like getting in the middle of them."

His head suddenly swiveled hard from side to side. "What is happening to me? I cannot control the movement of my head." He put his hands on either side of his jaws and held tight, but he could not stop the shaking of his head. "My years are catching up with me," he whispered. As he walked into the house, their yelling was too much for him. "Stop it, stop it, you two." They stopped to look at him in surprise. "Enough, enough, I can not stand your arguing anymore."

Agnes noticed his head shaking violently, and walked over to him. "Joseph, are you all right?"

"I do not know for sure. Something is wrong, but I do not know what it could be."

"Come sit down here, Joseph, and rest awhile." She looked over her shoulder at Coletta and motioned for her to leave the room. "I am sorry you had to hear all of this again. I will try to be more patient with her."

"Please do, all this is too much for me."

The next day, Coletta found her father at the barn. "I need to talk to you, Pa. In a few weeks, I will be eighteen, and I think it is time for me to leave home." She hesitated, while he stood there silently. "Agnes Marie and Irene left home, and I need to do that, too."

Joseph was so silent, she could hardly go on. "I saw Wendell the other night at the wedding dance in Garden Plain, and he will be getting married two days after my birthday, the middle of May. He said Bertha will be giving up her job in Wichita, and they are looking for another girl to take her place. If I want the job, he said he would tell her, and maybe I would have a chance to take it."

Joseph just stood there, looking at her. "Oh, Pa, I know Ma needs the help, but Esther is already a good worker. And Ma never did like any of the rest of us very much. So, it is time for me to go."

Her father moved close to her and put his hand on her shoulder. "It is not that she did not like the rest of you, it was just that she wanted so to teach you all the value of work, and that was hard for some of you to see. Your aunts and uncles did not make it any easier for her, or for any of you children, either." He squeezed her shoulder, "But it is time for you to go. If all you two are going to do is gripe at each other, then you need to be apart. And the only way is for you to go."

Joseph leaned back against the barn door. "I will miss you around here, Coletta. I will miss all the laughter I hear from you and Esther and Robert. What fun the three of you always seem to have. That I will miss." He sighed heavily, "But I understand. When the time comes for you, call William and have him come get you. I know he and Alvina will take good care of you." He reached into his pocket and pulled out a ten dollar gold piece and gave it to her. "This will help you for a few weeks, at least until you find work."

She put her arms around him and hugged him for a long time. "Thanks, Pa. I will miss you, too." With tears brimming in her eyes, she turned and ran to the house.

Joseph walked into the barn and leaned over a feed bunk. He cried and cried until he thought his heart would break. "Why, oh why, Lord, could things not have been easier?"

Several weeks later, the buggy was loaded with potatoes, early peas and onions from the garden. "Are we all ready to go, Agnes? Is everything in here that the nuns wanted this week?"

"We need to get the eggs from the cellar. Robert, go get them, will you?"

"Sure, Ma." He hurried down to carry up the two large egg cases they wanted. "The hens are really laying good, aren't they, Ma?"

"Yes, and the nuns will be glad. They use many eggs there at the hospital." She climbed up in the buggy and turned to the boy. "Robert, go see if Esther is about ready to go. We will visit your grandfather while we are at the hospital."

"Oh, good," laughed Robert. "We will see if he has any empty chewing tobacco cans for us this time."

Coletta watched as they drove out the yard. "Now is my chance. I am leaving this farm once and for all." She danced around the kitchen and sang as loudly as she could, "No more will I go out and pick up the eggs from a mean old hen. No more will I help clean all those chickens and pull all those feathers from those geese and ducks. No more weeding in the garden. I am going to be free, free from all of this. Let Ma do it all for herself, if she wants it taken care of, because I am leaving, leaving for good."

She picked up the phone and called her brother, William. "Come get me as soon as possible. I am leaving this farm. I will not put up with Ma any more."

"Does Pa know about this?"

"Yes, he does. We talked about it."

"I will come, but first, I want to drive into Wichita and check with Pa. I just do not like coming in there and taking you away without his permission."

"He gave it, he told me to call you when I was ready to go."

"But, I still want to check with him."

"Oh, all right, but I will be ready when you come. I do not want to get caught here like Irene did."

Coletta found several boxes Agnes had put back for storage and carried them upstairs. She was in such a nervous hurry, she did not even take the time to pull the hangers out of her dresses. "I will need those wherever I go. Ma has enough hangers around here. She will never miss these.

Half falling down the stairs, she lugged the heavy boxes out through the kitchen and into the porch. Then she went down in the cellar, cut a large hunk of homemade butter out of the crock and wrapped it in a clean cloth to take along.

"This one last time," she muttered as she hurried out to the chicken house. "This is going to be the last time I will reach under a feisty old hen to get her egg. No more pecking for me, I am finished with that." Gathering up the skirt of the apron she had put on, she filled it with

265

two-dozen eggs. "These will help Alvina while I stay there."

Coletta found a box in the kitchen for the eggs, and then sat down to wait. It was so still in the house, she never realized how quiet it could be there. "I guess I just did not notice before." The longer she sat there, the more she thought about the day Irene had left, and the angrier she became. "I will never forget what Step-Ma said to me that day."

Jumping up, she searched in the cupboard for a piece of paper and a pencil. Leaning over the table, she looked at the paper for a few minutes, then scrawled, "This last demon Fraulein has left home to keep peace." She put it right in the middle of the table where she knew Ma would find it. "There, that is done."

After thirty minutes or so, she heard a car come in the drive. "It has to be William, it just has to be, so I can get out of here before Pa comes back." She raced to the door and looked out, "Oh, yes, it is." Rushing out into the porch, she pushed the loaded boxes to the door. "I am so glad to see you." As he lifted them into his car, she grabbed him by the arm, "Wait just a minute, there is one more thing."

"What is that, Coletta?"

She ran out to the chicken house where the young roosters were, and grabbed for the wire hook that hung on the gate. "These are going to be the last roosters I am going to clean, but Ma is not going to eat them, we are." Chickens squawked and scattered everywhere as Coletta ran after them and finally snared two of them by the legs with the curved hook. With them hanging upside down by the feet, she held them away from her so they could not peck her.

William laughed, "Coletta, I do not think I have ever seen you run that fast."

"Quit laughing, let us get out of here before they come back."

"We better put those chickens in the trunk. I sure do not want the inside of my car dirtied by them. Alvina would not like that."

"Put them wherever you want them, but let us go," she shrieked.

Several hours later, Joseph and Agnes returned from their trip into town. Esther and Robert ran in the house ahead of them, and saw the note in the middle of the table.

"Ma, Ma," called the girl as she ran back outside. "Coletta is gone. She left this note."

Joseph grabbed the note from her and read it, then crumpled it into a tight wad.

"What did the note say, Joseph?" Agnes asked as she walked up to the porch door.

"She just said she had called William to come get her, and she was going to be there for a while."

Esther looked at Robert, but held her lips tight together. Later, she whispered to him, "That is not what she wrote."

When the family returned home from Sunday Mass a few days later, Agnes spent the afternoon carefully reading every page of the paper. "Oh, Joseph," she said to him as he came into the kitchen from his afternoon nap, "Here is Wendell's and Bertha's marriage license listed. Did you know they were going to get married?"

"Henry mentioned it to me about two months ago, and I asked William the last time he was here. He said he had heard that, and he knew Bertha. Her family lives close to William.

"What kind of family does she come from?"

William said they were hard workers, and he thought she would be a good wife for Wendell."

"I hope so. He will need a very understanding woman." She paused to think for a few seconds, then added, "That is probably why Coletta left, to go to their wedding. It will be in the town where William lives, will it not?"

"Yes, I think so."

"Did Wendell not ask you to his wedding?"

"I am not sure just when it will be," Joseph answered. "But no, he did not invite me. Ever since he has been at Henry's and Lizzie's, I do not know much about what he does."

"His day will come, Joseph, when he realizes just what an injustice he has done to you. Until then, we can only be patient with him."

"I suppose." Joseph turned away from her so she could not see his face. "I need to go for a walk outside," he mumbled as he hurried out the door.

"Poor Joseph," she thought, "those children just do not know what he has been through all these years. But they will know someday, they will know."

39

THE SCHOOL STOVE

ON A SUNNY but very cold day, William and Joseph took the ten-mile trip to the car dealer in the neighboring town of Cheney. Joseph walked around the Model A on the dealer's showroom floor and stroked the shiny headlights. Looking inside, he marveled at all the room and the leather seats.

The farmer looked at his son, "I am almost too old for this much change, but then, I guess progress means progress." He grinned at William, "The time is now, I think. I need a horseless carriage."

Right then, before the Christmas week, Joseph placed his order for a brand-spanking-new black Model A.

"Wait until Robert hears about this. He has been badgering me about a car for months now."

William laughed, "He will probably be one speed demon if he ever gets behind the wheel."

His father grinned, "If that happens, I will just tie this thing to a hitching post and make him take a horse."

The younger son wasted no time in celebrating his father's purchase.

"What a birthday present that is going to be," Robert boasted to all his friends at school. "Pa is finally getting a horseless carriage." He punched his fists through the air in a mock boxing match. "That will make me one of those fellas who cannot wait to learn how to drive a car. What a day that is going to be. Our very own Model A."

"Robert, come in here," called his fifth and sixth grade teacher, Sister Mary Hildegard. "I heard you say your birthday is soon. When?"

"December 29, 1928, Sister. I will be 12."

"Good, you will be old enough then to be on the stove group. You will train with some of the older boys so you can learn how to start a good fire in our classroom wood-burning stove. Can you come early on the mornings you are assigned? We need the classroom warm when the pupils all get here after morning Mass."

"Oh, yes, Sister. Ma would like for me to be on the stove group." Under his breath, Robert breathed a sigh of relief. To be on the stove detail was a much better assignment than being on the blackboard and eraser cleaning detail, or cloakroom monitor and, more especially, the sweeping detail. Those jobs were boring and took so much more time. "There is nothing to carrying an armload of wood and emptying the ash pan every morning," he decided.

"The grates have to be inspected once a week to make sure they have not cracked. I think you know that, Robert."

"Oh, yes, Sister, how soon can I start?"

"As soon as I make up the list."

He could not wait to tell Ma and Pa, and anyone else who would listen, that Sister had put him on the stove group. That was considered the most responsible and important job any student in the school could have. The boys vied for the honor of being on that list, and they wore a silent code of honor and dignity.

The school day seemed so long to him, but eventually, it was time for school to be out for the day. He could not wait to get home. Esther and Robert rushed into the house, and headed for the kitchen wood-burning stove. They held their cold hands over the warmth coming from the big stove.

"Where is Pa?" asked Robert. He looked at Agnes with a special gleam in his eye, "I have something very special to tell the both of you."

Agnes set a plate of cookies on the table for the two. "Pa and William went to the car dealer in Garden Plain to pick up Pa's new Model A."

"He got it, he got a car." No longer was the stove detail important. Nothing could compare with getting a car. Robert jumped up and down and hooted, then ran out the door and around the house, scattering chickens, ducks and geese as he went.

Esther followed him outside. "Goodness sakes, Robert, slow down, you will run these chickens to death." His sister reached out to grab him as he sailed around again. "Robert, stop, here they come."

He slowed down and stopped at the end of the walk, beside Esther. The two youngsters beamed when Joseph and William drove in the driveway. Joseph parked the wagon and hitched the horse to the fence.

Agnes came out of the house and stood near the door. She had to smile. If Joseph learned how to drive that thing, it was certainly going to have its advantages. She could already visualize trips to see other places in the state.

"Can I learn to drive, Ma?" begged the boy.

She walked up and ruffled his head of dark curls, so like her own father's black curly hair. "Do not be too anxious. You are a mite young yet, I think. In a year or two, perhaps." She put her hand on her son's shoulder, "Why, Robert, I doubt you are tall enough to see over the steering wheel."

"I could stretch real tall."

"Are you going to learn to drive, Ma?" Esther had grown as tall as Agnes by then.

"I rather think I will leave that to Pa. William will be a good teacher."

Robert snickered, "Pa might forget himself and yell 'Giddy-up.' Or he will run in a ditch looking for the reins."

Esther giggled, "That was not very nice to say, Robert, but that is probably what you will do."

The car stopped near the house. William got out and went around to the passenger side. "Now is the time, Pa, for your driving lesson."

"I may be a bit old to learn this. You realize, Son, on my last birthday, I turned 57."

"Oh, Pa," William laughed, "that was just last week. You are just in the prime of your life." He grinned. "First, you turn the key, then push this button on the floor. That is the starter." He chuckled, "If you do not do these things, Pa, you will not go anywhere no matter how hard you try to get this car moving."

The Model A zigzagged down the drive and out onto the road. Agnes put her arm around the girl's shoulder. "Esther, in a year or so, Pa had better teach you to drive."

"I am ready now, Ma."

By the summer, Joseph had mastered the Model A, at least to drive in the country. Agnes was always interested in history, and with this new car, the chance to see more of the state whetted her interest even more.

"One place in Kansas I would really like to visit is Caldwell, where the Oklahoma Run began," she told Joseph. "Just to imagine all those covered wagons thundering across the plains must be beyond belief." So, one summer weekend, the four of them headed south to the little town, on the Kansas and Oklahoma state line.

Agnes had read so much about that area, it was as if she had been there before.

"This woman never ceases to amaze me," thought Joseph. "All the reading she does and the information she knows." He smiled to himself, "She has even aroused my interest in Kansas history, and it is good for Esther and Robert, too."

Caldwell was like a step back in history for Agnes. Every shopkeeper and older person she met, she quizzed, digging for any additional bit of colorful history she could find. At the end of the day, the family settled into the town's only hotel.

"We must get started early this morning," Joseph reminded her. "It is a long drive, and the day looks like it could get very warm." He started out the door to go check the water and oil in the car.

"Robert, carry this luggage down and help Pa put it on the rack. Hurry now. As soon as he gets that finished, we will eat breakfast in the dining room. A good meal will keep us more content on the ride home."

It took all of the boy's strength to lift the valise. "Wonder what Ma has stashed in here? It weighs a ton." Down the steps and out through the lobby, he struggled. Pa had parked the car by the curb the night before. "Sure glad I do not have to lug this any further."

Right next to the car sat a little white dog, with black spots on his face, black ears and one stray black spot on his side.

"Hey there, dog, whatcha doing here?" The dog just sat there and looked and watched every move Joseph and Robert made. "Look at that nice little dog, Pa. I think he needs a boy like me."

"That pup probably already has a home and belongs to someone here in town. Leave him be."

"But, Pa."

"Time to go eat with Ma and Esther, Son." They were already seated and ready to order.

"Oh, Esther, you should see that cute little dog that is sitting by the car. He just watched Pa and me." Robert looked at his father. "I think that puppy needs a boy."

"Who?" Agnes grinned at her son.

"Me. That dog needs me."

"He has probably run away by now." Joseph stirred his coffee.

Esther made a face at her brother. "He was watching you 'cause he has never seen such a strange-looking boy before."

But the little mongrel was still there, sitting right by the car door. Robert opened the door to get in, and before he could, the little animal jumped in and sat down in the middle of the back seat as if he owned the car.

"See, he does need a boy. Me." Robert threw his arms around the small dog and hugged him hard. "Noodle, he looks like a noodle. That will be his name."

"Maybe he is a stray." Agnes saw how Robert's eyes lit up as he hugged the dog.

Joseph looked at her out of the corner of his eye, "Now, Ma, we can not take this dog."

Agnes smiled at him warmly. "But, Joseph, since Shep died, the place seems so lonesome. Every farm needs a dog, and this one looks like he needs a farm and a family." She looked more closely at the scrawny little mutt. "He acts like he has already adopted us. Look at those bright eyes."

"I guess we could use another dog." Joseph shook his head in resignation.

"Ma, I will take good care of him," boasted Robert. He will be my dog."

All the way home, the boy and the dog were silent in a newfound friendship. Agnes glanced back now and then and caught both of them with their eyes closed. She whispered to Joseph, "Those two just look like they match each other."

When they arrived back at the farm, Robert carried the pup into the house and put him down on the kitchen floor. The animal sniffed his way around the room, then claimed the space behind the huge wood cookstove for his own.

"I am not sure about a dog in my kitchen, but he seems to be a housedog. We will try it for a few days. If he messes up anything, he will have to go outside."

"Yea, Ma." Robert bent down to reach under the stove to pet the dog.

After a few days, even Joseph consented to having the dog around the house.

"I cannot get over that dog and how he has taken to us and this house. He acts like a good watchdog, too. He just does not miss anything that goes on around here," marveled Joseph.

Agnes laughed. "He is a smart dog, too. The other day, I mentioned to the children a big pot of chicken and noodle soup would be good. Noodle crawled out from behind the stove, stretching and yawning, and just sat there. He looked at me for the longest time, wondering what I wanted."

Esther tugged at her father's arm. "Oh, Pa, you should hear Noodle bark at Ma when she gargles so loud every morning. It is so funny, he just raises his front feet off the floor and barks and barks."

"That dog has very poor manners," giggled Agnes. "One of these days, I will just have to sit down and explain to him the reason for my gargling ritual every day. Maybe he will be able to understand I lost all my teeth from a gum disease when I was only seventeen. My gums have to be very clean before I put in my false teeth." The children giggled when she added, "The only way he will stop barking at me is if I teach him to brush his teeth."

"Where can we find a dog toothbrush?" Robert slapped his knee and heehawed until tears rolled down his cheeks.

September rolled around much faster than the youngsters wanted, but soon the summer was over. School bells rang out, and Esther and Robert were back in the classroom.

"What a year this has been for me," Robert bragged to his friends. "Pa got a Model A, we picked up a funny little dog this summer and Sister Mary Hildegard just told me I would be in charge of the stove group this year."

That evening, he explained how important his new job was to his parents. "I will make sure all the other boys fill the stove right." He beamed, "Sister also said I have to teach the new boys who will start doing it this year."

Cold weather descended on the plains. The north wind and snow whipped around the old wooden schoolhouse. Snow sifted in around the weathered window frames and piled up in the corners of the sills. Robert and the other boys carried armloads of chopped wood into the classroom every day. Kindling had to be chipped so fires could be started more easily. After a few weeks, the chore became more boring, until Robert had an idea.

The boy looked around in Pa's garage until he found what he was looking for. "A little excitement will make this detail more interesting." An ornery grin spread across his face. "Just wait until tomorrow."

The classroom was cold and empty the next morning. Robert shuddered in the January chill. There was no time to waste. The pupils would be coming in soon from Mass.

He packed several armloads of wood into the stove. In the front of the pile, he stuck in sticks of kindling and some scrap paper. The boy looked at the small, shiny object in his hand, polished it on his shirtsleeve and then tossed it in the stove. It clinked against the cast iron side of the stove as it slid down to the bottom of the wood chunks. Robert had to strike several matches before the paper and kindling caught the flame and roared into a good fire.

The fifth and sixth grade students settled down in their desks. Robert joined his sixth grade classmates in a spelling exercise. The room got warmer and warmer as the wood chunks started to burn. The snow on the windowsills began to melt and run down the wall to the floor where it collected in little pools. The jacket of the stove was glowing bright red. The pupils closest to the stove started to wipe the sweat from their brows. Those farthest away still blew on their fingers to warm them.

"Spell the word 'geography.'" Sister Mary Hildegard pointed to one of the girls.

Kaboom, zing, boom! The door blew off the front of the stove. The jacket was blazing red-hot, hot enough to melt. Black soot and smoke filled the room.

"Help, help," choked the girls as they fell to the floor.

"Where is the door?" The boy closest to the entrance groped around the wall looking for the door.

"The stove blew up," another screamed.

The loud explosion brought the seventh and eighth grade boys running from another classroom. They yanked the door open and ran into the room to open the windows. "Anybody hurt in here?" one of them hollered.

"Let me take roll call. Pupils, answer with 'not hurt' or 'hurt,'" the nun called over the noise, the screaming and moaning. "Susan, Mary, on and on. Robert." No answer. "Robert," Sister demanded, "answer me."

"Not hurt, Sister." He doubled over in laughter. "That was a blast."

"What is so hilarious, Robert?" She grabbed him by the scruff of the neck.

The air had cleared enough for all to see. "Look, there are puddles all over the floor. They wet their bloomers, ha-ha-ha."

Sister Mary Hildegard yanked him right up out of his desk. "Your parents will hear about this." She threw him back down in his seat. "The priest will deal with you later. As of now, you are no longer on the stove group. I have a new job for you. From now until school is out, you will clean the outhouses every day and keep them neat."

"But, Sister, there is no outhouse cleaning list," he boldly stated.

"There is now, young man, there is now. There will be no arguing or excuses; you will keep the outhouses cleaned. Once a week, no matter how cold, you will scrub every section of the outside toilets with soapy water. Is that clear?"

"Yes, Sister," his suddenly meek voice quivered.

"Now, go get a mop and bucket of water and scrub under every desk in here."

She caught Esther before school was out for the day, and handed her a note. "Please take this to your parents."

"Dear Mr. and Mrs. Linnebur," the note read. "I am thoroughly disappointed in your daughter and son. Esther has been caught, along with some friends of hers, sampling the priest's wine stored in the church sacristy. They have also burned some of the altar cloths Father uses for Mass, trying to hide the evidence.

"The worst is Robert. He caused a terrible confusion because of his irresponsible stunt. We are fortunate no one was hurt when the shotgun shell he dropped in the classroom stove exploded. Your son will never be on the stove group again. He is not trustworthy." Signed, "Sister Mary Hildegard."

Tears filled Agnes' eyes. "My children, how could you?"

The two meekly walked out of the kitchen and into the porch. Esther pushed Robert up against the wall, "You show-off. Just because of you, I also got in trouble. I will never forgive you for this."

"Sorry," he whimpered. Then he brightened, "But, Esther, you should have seen all the puddles under the desks. It was so funny."

Agnes and her 15-year-old daughter, Esther, prepare for their trip to Breslau, Germany, in 1930.

40

THE JOURNEY

"AGNES, MY LOVE." Joseph walked up behind her and wrapped his arms around her waist. She turned to return his embrace.

"I have been thinking a lot lately about you and how you came into my home and raised my children and ours." He rested his cheek against hers for a long time. She felt a tear trickle down his cheek and come to rest on hers. "I owe you so much. There is no way I could have managed without you coming into my life."

They stood there for a long time, relishing the warmth of the other's arms about them. No words were spoken, for words could never replace what their closeness to each other had come to mean.

"Agnes, for all these years, I know you held in your heart the desire to visit your homeland."

She mumbled, "Uh-huh."

"The last years have been good years on our farm. I would like so much for you to go back to Germany again, and visit your family."

She lifted her face to look into his eyes, so pleasant. Those hazel eyes that conveyed such goodness and kindness.

"Robert is thirteen now and quite a good help. Esther will be fifteen in February. I would like for you to make plans to go. The last of April, May, June and July would be good months for you. Spring in Germany would be nice for you, too. You have always talked so much about the beauty of the Mai Luft."

"But, Joseph, the garden and the spring chickens. Three months, Joseph, that is too long to be away."

"Agnes, my older daughters, and Alvina and Bertha can help clean the chickens." His eyes sparkled, "To help make them a little more willing, I will share the young fryers with them. We just will not order so many this spring."

"But the garden."

His rough, strong finger traced her cheek gently. "A small garden this year, I promise. Not much more than Robert and I need."

"Joseph, will you go with me, please. I want so much to have you meet my sister, Martha, and brother, Conrad."

"I had not planned to go, Agnes, only you, and Esther and Robert."

"Oh, Joseph, please say you will go."

He held her tightly for a long time. "I will think about it then."

The next few days went past in a blur for Agnes. Her feet barely seemed to touch the floor, her heartstrings hummed with joy. Thoughts tumbled one upon the other in her mind. The excitement of it all was almost more than she could bear. At 50 years of age, the happiness, and also concern, were almost too exhilarating. So had she dreamed of a return trip to see her loved ones, and now it was a possibility. What pleasure filled her soul.

"Please, Joseph, will you go with us?"

He stirred his coffee slowly, absentmindedly. His innermost thoughts whirled in confusion. The farm, he hated to leave the farm for so long a time. Certainly, he had sons and brothers who could, and would, manage it for him. But it was never in the nature of any farmer, and especially Joseph, to entrust the upkeep of his beloved land to anyone other than himself.

"The ocean, all that water," Joseph mumbled, distracted. He became aware of Agnes, Esther and Robert all gazing at him, waiting for his response.

"I was just thinking about all that water," he confessed. "You know, I have never seen a body of water wider than the Mississippi River. But it was the worst during the years it met with the Missouri River to flood all over Portage de Sioux. It rampaged for days over my papa's farm, and was so frightening. All that water rushing past in a mad whirl. It swirled and tore at the soil. Big trees were uprooted and twisted around like small sticks of wood." The farmer shuddered.

He looked around the table and into their eyes. "No, I have no desire anymore to see the power of so much water. And the ocean, I cannot imagine being in a place where there is not even a speck of land in sight for days on end." For a long time, he was again lost in thought until, finally, he had made his decision. "I am sorry not to go, Agnes, but I would rather die on dry land than drown in the ocean."

"But, Joseph," she pleaded.

"If Pa stays, so do I." Robert looked at her with anxious eyes. "I will stay and help Pa."

The disappointment showed clearly on her face. Surely, she would not be going alone. Fear crept into her heart. Esther had not yet answered if she wanted to go.

Esther's eyes brightened with excitement. "I will go with Ma to keep her company. The big ocean does not scare me." She jumped up and threw her arms around Agnes. "Oh, Ma, what a good time we will have. How soon can we go? What kind of clothes do I take? Does my hair need to be trimmed?"

"Gracious, child," laughed Agnes, relieved and happy, "one thing at a time. First, I must find out the ocean liners' schedules, then make reservations for our ship passage going to Cuxhaven, Hamburg. Also, we have to find out about the train schedule, and how long we have to leave before embarking. The Leo House, I have to contact my old friends at the Leo House in New York City, so we can room there with them until the day the ship departs."

"What else do we need?"

"Passports. We will need passport photos, and then apply for passports."

Joseph leaned back in his chair and chuckled. "Robert, if the ladies of this house have to make all those arrangements and shop for different clothes, too, you and I might be batching and doing all our own cooking faster than we thought."

"I can boil coffee, the best coffee you will ever taste." Robert jumped up and pretended to get the big blue and white enamel coffee pot ready to put on the stove.

The days sped by quickly. "The birth certificates for our visas came, Ma." Esther danced around the table. "Did you notice, Ma, we have always celebrated Pa's birthday on January 20th, but it says on his birth certificate he was born January 12th. I wonder why that is?"

"You might ask him and see what he says." Agnes stirred a large pot of chicken and noodle soup on the stove."

Joseph came in, damp from an early March shower. "Another calf was born during the night. That should be about the last of the cows to calf. In two months, we can put them out to pasture." He dried his face and neck. "That is always a good feeling to see the young calves scamper after each other. Does my heart good."

"Pa, according to your birth certificate, you were born on January12th instead of January 20th. Did you know that?" Esther handed the paper to him.

He studied it for a long time, and then laugh lines formed across his face. "Do you know why that is, Esther? With all of us children, my mother was bound to forget someone's right birthday. And since I was the youngest, it looks like it was mine." He fell silent for a few minutes. "For whatever reason, my folks always celebrated my birthday January 20th. Since I am so used to that date, there is no need to change it." His lips curved up in a smile. "I sure do not want anybody to get it mixed up, or there will never be any presents for me."

"Will you drive us to the Union Depot in Wichita, Pa?"

"I have talked to William. He gets along so much better driving a car in the city. All those stop lights and trying to shift gears makes me really nervous."

Esther came around and put her hand on his shoulder. "Especially when all those crazy drivers lean on their horns as soon as the light turns green. They get so mad when the person in front of them does not shift gears quick enough to shoot off down the street." His daughter leaned over and kissed him on the cheek.

"When we get back, I will drive the car for you in Wichita, Pa. That way, you will not have to turn off the Model A when some silly fool behind you honks like mad." Her soft giggles fell gently on his shoulder.

He looked up at her and smiled, "Sounds good to me. After that last trip into town, I never want to drive there again." Joseph squeezed her hand gently.

The day arrived much sooner than they anticipated and planned for. Adventuresome Esther was eager. Agnes was anxious. After all these years, she had lost some of her youthful braveness.

They stood on the platform at Union Depot, not knowing how to say good-bye. Joseph's eyes filled with tears, as he put his arm around

Agnes' shoulder. For a minute, he brightened. "When the two of you get back, we will plan one of our big summer picnics under the front lawn trees. Robert and Coletta can help contact all the neighbors, and all my relatives and children."

"Alvina can help too," added William. "We can get in touch with Ellen and her family, and Irene and Agnes and Wilbur, and some of the others who live away from Garden Plain."

"That would be very nice, Joseph. That is one thing I will really miss in Germany, those Sunday afternoon picnics." She brushed his cheek with her fingertips. "We will look forward to that on our return."

A soft, early April shower passed over the city just as Agnes and Esther boarded the train for New York City. "All aboard," the conductor called out. Joseph, Robert and William waved until the train passed out of the depot.

"Auf Wiedersehen, Agnes. Come back to me," Joseph whispered.

For three days and two nights, the railroad car clattered over the rails, *clickety-clack, clickety-clack.* "What a relaxing rhythm that is," said Esther, "almost like a song."

Agnes watched the landscape of her adopted homeland go past from the window of the dining car. "I never dreamed I would be able to take this trip again, Esther. When you and Robert were mere babes, I wanted so to take you to Germany and to show you to my mother. To see you cradled in your grandmother's arms and rocked by her at night was my wish. But she discouraged me. Now, I realize how really wise her advice was."

She sipped the heavily creamed, strong coffee from the fine china cup. "It would have been so difficult managing two small children for all this time on the train, and then on the ship." A smile lit up her eyes. "If I had taken the two of you so young, I would have spent the entire ocean voyage just trying to keep Robert from slipping through the rails and falling into the ocean."

"You still would, Ma." Esther put her hand on her mother's and laughed. "I am so happy to go with you."

"We will change trains in Chicago. It is disappointing we do not have more time there, so we could see the city. Oh, but Chicago is nothing like New York City or Breslau. Now, those are cities with a life all their own. There is such excitement, such energy in those cities. It will be like nothing you will ever experience again."

The two walked into the huge train station in Chicago and found the Harvey House. "In two hours, we will board the train for New York." Agnes sipped the strong black coffee and leaned back to relax and watch the other passengers. "Just look at some of those people," she said to Esther, "Where must they be going?"

Esther smiled, "Maybe the same place we are."

The train roared through the night, nearer and nearer the eastern states. The conductor walked through the cars on the long passenger train. And then, he spoke the words they waited to hear, "Pennsylvania Station, New York City."

Esther felt the blood course through her at a more rapid pace. Goosebumps rose mysteriously on her arms. "Ma, oh, Ma, New York City, to be here is like a dream."

The two walked along the seemingly endless length of passenger cars and emerged into the cavernous main hall of the train station. The girl craned her neck, "Pa and Robert would never believe this."

The multitude of bodies, the strange sounds of the city and its people engulfed them. "The streets, Ma, and the buildings. I will have to tell Robert about all of this. If only he had come."

The cab driver put their heavy suitcases on the steps of the Leo House. Agnes lifted the carved brass knocker and rapped it several times. A young, full-faced nun with happy eyes opened the door and ushered them into the sitting room. "I will tell Sister Mary Anthony you are here."

A stooped, aging nun came shuffling into the room. "Agnes, my friend, Agnes Puder. You came again to New York City, all the way from the Plains of Kansas."

"We have, Sister, my daughter, Esther, and I."

Just then, another acquaintance of past years walked in. "Sister Mary Bernard, hello."

"Agnes, my friend," the nun laughed, "the one we thought would never survive out on the Great Plains." Her brown eyes twinkled, "And your daughter, your prairie rose. Look at those cheeks, blushed with the sun of Kansas."

The older nun pointed to the chairs, "sit and tell us everything we want to know, and more. We have waited so long to know how your life has gone."

"You will stay a few days with us?" Sister Mary Bernard leaned forward on her chair. "Tell us all about this farmer who lured you away from the big cities."

"We will stay until the ship embarks for Europe. There is something you may find interesting." Agnes took off her hat and put it on another chair. "The round trip train fare from Kansas to here was more expensive than the round trip passage fare to Germany."

"Blame it on the greedy railroad enterprises," chuckled Sister Mary Anthony. "They will wrest the last nickel out of the likes of the rest of us."

"However, the train is quite an improvement over the horse and buggy age," agreed Agnes chuckling.

The April morning sun made the buildings of the city sparkle like so many colored jewels. Spring flowers lined the walks in the parks. Off in the distance, the sound of tugboats rocked the stillness of the day. Esther and Agnes found empty chairs in the White Star terminal building.

"It will not be long now, Esther." Agnes wiped tears of joy from her cheeks. "I feel like we are living a dream, a dream I could never dare to let myself think about."

The stevedores rolled cart upon cart of baggage off to the ship's cargo hold. Women in fancy fur coats watched as mountains of their luggage were lifted up by the strong-armed men. "I am glad we do not have so many valises, Ma."

Agnes smiled, "We do not even have enough clothes to fill one of those wealthy ladies' trunks. And it will be more fun for us to shop in some of the German stores. If we dress like our relatives, we will not be so obvious as Americans."

Esther glanced down at the water when she and Agnes walked up the passenger gangplank. From the second-class deck, she looked down at the throngs of people, and up at the city's skyline. The deep-throated whistle sounded, and the tugboats tightened their cables. Brawny dockworkers loosened the thick ropes holding the ship and uncoiled them. The anchor clanged against the side of the vessel when it lifted.

"The ocean and my Fatherland await us." Agnes bowed in respect to the Statue of Liberty as their ship, the *S.S. Deutschland,* sailed past.

"She is the most beautiful lady in the world. How I wept when I first saw her. And now, I weep, seeing her once again."

The orchestra played hour after hour, night after night. Dancing feet swayed to the tempos of the waltz, the foxtrot and the Charleston. The admiring glances of suave European men and wealthy, nattily dressed, Eastern-bred ivy-leaguers made Esther's pulse race. Her hazel eyes and long brown curls turned even the heads of the most reserved aboard the ship. An aura of Kansas innocence emanated from her like the brilliance of the sun upon the snow. She caused others to wonder and to delight in her joys.

Late evening parties and the masquerade ball were filled with flirting and lively encounters. The fifteen-year-old could not even remember the staid life she had left only days before.

The Atlantic churned and caught the ocean liner in mid-voyage. The spring storm flopped huge waves across the decks and tossed the vessel about like a small toy. Foghorns blared every few minutes to warn passing ships of their presence. Thick fog cut visibility to only ten feet or less. Its moisture permeated every space of the ocean liner.

"All ship's passengers must stay off the decks today," the Captain commanded. "We do not want anyone washed overboard."

The young girl did not mind the weather. A day spent in the lounge was filled with as much excitement as a day on the deck. Agnes envied her daughter's stamina and remembered her own some 20 years before, when she was younger. But the ocean took its toll on her, and she spent the day in her cabin, too seasick to move. She stayed in their outside cabin and endured the pounding of the ferocious waves against the ship's sides. "I may never see my daughter again," she thought. "Any minute now, our cabin wall will surely split and I will be floating in ocean water."

The door opened and Esther came in. "Feeling any better, Ma?"

"I do not feel too bad when I stay down, but I do not feel I could stand up long if I tried. Just listen to those waves hitting the portholes and the walls. It sounds like someone has been throwing bricks at our cabin all day." Agnes rolled over to her side. "Would you please bring me some bread and a cup of soup when you come back? Maybe if I eat something bland, my queasy stomach might settle down."

The eight-day journey was about to end. Only a few more hours and the port would be visible. "The White Cliffs of Dover are so pretty." Agnes showed them to her daughter. "They look just as they did the day I left here for America. Only, then I was sad. Now I am happy, happy to see my family again."

They crowded onto the train bound for Breslau. "Not many hours now and we will be there."

The train slowed and came to a halt outside the large depot. Agnes and Esther walked through the surging crowds. "I hope they have come," Agnes whispered softly to herself.

Then, off in the distance, she heard a familiar voice, "Agnes, Agnes, over here, Agnes." A white handkerchief waved above the crowd.

Her sister, Martha, pushed through the passengers and the carts of baggage. "Oh, Agnes, I can not believe you actually returned to see us."

Tears slid down their cheeks and dropped like a spring shower of raindrops.

"Meine Schwester," Martha whispered in the other's ear.

"My sister," Agnes whispered in return.

"You have come, you have come. Oh, thank the Lord, you have come." Martha hugged her tightly.

"All the way from America, Agnes. You have come. All the way."

A friend, the Captain, Esther and the First Mate aboard the S.S. Deutschland. Destination: Breslau, Germany, April 1930.

41

THE SLOGANS

HER BROTHER HELD her at arm's length, with his hands on her shoulders.

"Conrad, you have aged a bit since I last saw you."

"Talk about yourself, Sister. You do not look quite as young either." He pulled Agnes into a tight embrace. "How wonderful to see you, to have you travel so far to come back."

"Thanks to my kind and loving husband. I brought a Kansas map along, so we could show you just where we live. And pictures, lots of pictures of Joseph, his family and our son, Robert. There are a few photos of the farm, and his cows and pigs, and," she paused to giggle, "my chickens, geese and ducks. Can you ever begin to imagine your city-bred sister raising farm animals?"

Conrad, Martha and all their families erupted in guffaws, knee-slapping and snickers. " 'Tis true, 'tis true," she teased. "I am now a full-fledged farm wife." Her eyes sparkled, "But I love the life. And to think I swore I would never live anywhere but a good-sized city."

She looked around Conrad's immaculate bakery and saw the shelves piled high with loaves of bread, cake, cookies and rolls. "One thing, Conrad, what you do for a living sure smells good." Agnes turned to his wife, who handed her a huge pecan roll. "Do you bake these delicious rolls or does he?" She grinned at her brother, "You never liked to clean up the dishes when you were young. It is rather hard imagining you doing all this."

"Our bakery has done very well all these years, thank you." He winked at Agnes. "We were able to buy this entire three-story building, and now we rent out all the apartments except for the one we live in." Conrad handed her a steaming cup of coffee. "To go with the pastry, my dear sister." He sat down on the chair next to her. "Mama lived in our apartment the last years. It was a joy having her here with us."

A good-looking, blond young man of fourteen walked through the bakery's door. "Agnes, Esther, my son, George, just home from school. "Son, meet your Aunt Agnes and her daughter, Esther. They have come all the way from America to see us." He looked at Esther, then George. "You two young people should have a good time getting acquainted."

"We hear you are quite a talented and accomplished pianist." Agnes took her nephew's hand in hers. "Someday, very soon, you must honor us with a concert."

His father beamed as he looked at the boy. "Esther likes to sing, Son. Perhaps the two of you could arrange a few selections to entertain us."

"Yes, but Uncle Conrad, I am not so good as George." Esther smiled at her cousin. "You already give piano lessons. I do not even know a boy who can play a piano, much less give lessons." She grinned and tossed her head to make her brown curls bounce around her rosy cheeks. "All the boys around where I live are only interested in cows, pigs, horses and Model A cars." Her happy, light-hearted laughter endeared her instantly to her cousin.

"Conrad, there is something I would like to do as soon as it is convenient for you."

"Anything you ask for, we will arrange." Elsie nodded yes to her husband.

"I am anxious to visit Mother's grave."

"Tomorrow morning, we will do just that. The cemetery is near the church and close by. We will stop and take Martha with us. She likes to go too, but it is hard for her to go alone."

The early morning sun caused the dewdrops on the new spring grass to sparkle like a multitude of tiny rainbow-colored jewels. Old, old tombstones, many of them sinking to one side, filled the tiny, ancient lot.

"Mama was one of the last to be laid to rest here." Conrad pointed out her marker. "There is no room for any others."

Conrad and Martha stood at the wrought iron entrance gate and waited respectfully for Agnes to go to her mother's grave alone. Esther stopped a short distance behind her mother. On the tombstone, the girl could read, "ANNA PUDER, Geboren Sept. 30, 1850, Sterben Nov. 27, 1919." She bowed her head and asked for eternal rest for Anna. "This is the grandmother I have learned to love through Ma's memories. If only I had known her before."

Agnes knelt down on the soft earth, close by the granite stone. With slow, measured touch, her fingers rubbed over each etched letter and stone, time and again. She relived the day the black-edged letter came, and finally, the tears could be contained no longer. The sound of her heavy sobs carried over the small burial ground. Anna's daughter doubled over and wept uncontrollably, "Meine Mütter, Meine Mütter. How I long to hold you close once more, and hear your voice, and show you my babies. Oh, Mütter, now that will never be."

Esther went to kneel beside her mother. A young, strong arm encircled the other's shoulders. A thick crown of long dark curls rested against the dark head of older hair, swept back and rolled tightly in a bun.

"Meine Mütter, meine Tochter. My mother, my daughter." The two knelt in silent reverence there, until the tears dried and the emotions of loss were spent.

Conrad and Martha walked slowly to the grave. Agnes leaned hard on Esther's strong arm and rose to her feet. The four of them clung together as a family in long overdue mourning.

The thick, pungent fragrance of the spring flowers floated through the streets, carried by the soft breezes of the May month.

"Tomorrow morning, early, we must gather to walk in the Mai Luft, the May air," declared Martha.

Agnes smiled at her daughter. "Now you will experience the real ecstasy of the flowers. The blended fragrances will descend upon your senses. With each breath, the perfume of the blooms will be a pleasant surprise."

Esther put her hand upon her mother's. "The Mai Luft of Kansas is sweet. Can that of Breslau be any sweeter?" Her hazel eyes twinkled mischievously. "Ma, if you are not careful, you may make a poetess of me yet. And what would my friends back home say? They would no longer know me." Her young fingers gently squeezed those of Agnes.

At five the next morning, Conrad, Elsie, Martha, their sons and families joined Agnes and Esther for a very early stroll. Huge, beautiful trees towered over the city's parks and hid the sky from the ground below. Branches of flowering bushes thick with blossoms, hung like draperies of heavy silken tapestries. The varied hues of nature's colors filled the eye with unimaginable beauty, more picturesque than an artist's palette.

"Ma, I never knew there were so many beautiful flowers in the world." At every turn, another floral surprise awaited Esther. "Now I know why you always talked so of the Mai Luft. It is unbelievable."

But there were ominous signs amongst the flowers. For written on the cement walls along the Oder River bank and on bridges and buildings were sinister messages, scribbled there, most likely, by the young military faction loyal to the rising fascist movement.

The messages were chilling, written in huge letters so no one could miss them. "Down with Jesus Christ," was scrawled in various places. Another message, "Down with the Jews," was meant to strike terror in the hearts of others.

Agnes gasped when she saw the first one. A gray, ashen color broke across her face. "What does it mean, Conrad?"

Her brother waited until there were no strangers around them before he spoke. "We are not exactly sure what the writings mean, but we are worried, afraid for our country and scared for ourselves." He moved her away from the others. "Others feel, and so do I, that something really bad will soon happen here. No one seems to know just what, but there is a tremendous unrest in our ruling parties and the government."

He motioned for her to sit down on a nearby park bench. "About ten years ago, our country was almost on the brink of economic collapse, but it has stabilized, at least for the present. There is a very forceful leader now in the Nationalist Socialist German Workers Party. He has had quite an impact on Bavarian politics, but we do not know much about him."

"Conrad, why not consider coming to America? The government is so different there. America does not have the military attitude of Germany. And," she tugged at his sleeve, "you could start a bakery anywhere and have a good business. Your pastries would have people crowding your door shortly after you open."

"But, Agnes, this is our Fatherland. We have seen hard times before, and surely our life will not be as difficult as after the last war."

"I hope you are right, Conrad, how I hope you are right."

The anti-Jewish and anti-religious slogans unnerved Agnes. The writings were all over the city, everywhere. When she saw them, she forced her mind to blank them out. "Esther and I will be here for only a few more weeks, and then we will return to the safety of America," she often thought. "Please, Lord, keep my family safe here."

Agnes could not speak to her loved ones of her strong intuitive nature, for she did not want to frighten them needlessly. But she saw signs in Breslau she had never seen in America. "The difference of our two worlds," she thought.

Martha Puder Neumann, Agnes' sister.

Konrad Puder's bakery in Breslau. Konrad was a brother of Agnes. To the left on sidewalk is Anna Puder, Agnes' mother.

Middle row: Elsie and Konrad Puder with his sister, Agnes. Behind his right shoulder, his niece, Esther. Others unknown.

42

THE SECRET

"YOUR DAYS ARE getting fewer," Martha told Agnes one day. "We have been so busy, going here and there, that the two of us have not really had a whole day just to sit down and visit."

"You are right, as usual," laughed Agnes. "I want to hear in your own words, every little detail of your life since I left here."

Early the next morning, Agnes rapped on Martha's apartment door. A freshly brewed pot of coffee and an assortment of pastries from Conrad's bakery were on the table."

"I see you serve the finest pastries in all of Breslau," chuckled Agnes.

"There is good reason for that, dear Sister. Agnes, you will never know what this has meant to me, to see you again after all these years. Why did you have to go to America? I have missed you so much."

"You know the reason, Martha. All the promises Wilhelm and I made to each other, to be faithful, to be true. But it seems that as soon as the train left the station and I was out of his sight, he forgot all about me." She hated to have that part of her life brought up again. Those memories had been stored in the bottom of her subconscious. "Tell me about you, Martha. I would rather listen to that."

"Yes, yes, I must go back years and relive memories. You remember how many children I lost those first years of marriage? Thanks be to God, two of my sons lived."

"Alfred and Ervin are such fine men, Martha, and with nice families."

"It was so hard for the two boys when their father died so young.

And then, when we got word Constantine had died in World War I, it was not only hard on our mama, but also my small sons. After my husband passed away, Constantine had become like a papa to them. It took me several days to have the courage to tell them their special uncle was not coming home again.

"His body came back much later, in a narrow wooden box. Mama asked that he be buried in a country cemetery. There were hardly any men left in the city to dig the graves." Her tears came in a rush and dropped onto her lap. "Conrad was not around here much either. He had to work for the war effort here in the city. When we did see him, he was so good to the boys."

"How did you support yourself and the boys all those years?" Agnes touched her sister's hand tenderly.

"With my sewing. I even helped mend soldiers' uniforms when they needed repair. Much of my sewing was used in hospitals for the wounded men. Then, after the war ended, it was hard to find customers for my handiwork. So I would barter things I made for food. Fortunately, I had some ladies who liked my embroidery work and crocheted things. A few of them were from wealthy families. They recommended me to their friends and relatives who wanted extra fine crocheted lace collars or pillow tops. Occasionally, they ordered crocheted tablecloths or bed covers. Over the years, my client list increased, and I was able to provide a steady income for us."

Her thoughts wandered for a few minutes. "As Alfred and Ervin got older, they would do odd jobs to help out." Martha smiled at Agnes, "I am so proud of my boys. Conrad helped them and gave them business advice when they decided to try operating a dry goods store." Her light chuckles filled the room. "They really made some bad mistakes at first, but they learned. Their store is now one of the finest in this area of Breslau."

Martha stood and walked across the room. "I still have here an assortment of my handiwork that is ready for them to take. Anymore, everything I make goes into their store. It is so much easier for me. They handle all the money from my sales."

"Would you show me some of these items?" Agnes picked up the top piece and began looking at it. "I just always like to look at your work, Martha. You are so particular." Agnes smiled at her sister. "Never a stitch out of place."

"I try," she giggled like a young girl. Then she became serious. "Oh, Agnes, do you remember the hard times we had growing up? Papa was always away, but when he came home, how good it was to see him. He always spent his money on liquor, but we were too young to know. But, still, he was like our great angel from heaven." She smiled, "Remember all the silly trinkets he brought and the scowls Mama would have on her face. He had never saved any money for food for us."

"I remember only too well. And how Mama did not have enough money to bring him home to bury him, and only she could go to his funeral. Mama certainly did not have an easy life with him, Martha, not at all."

Martha unfolded each piece of her beautiful handiwork and put it out on the table for Agnes to admire. "How I always envied your patience and pride in your work, Martha. My patience runs thin with this kind of work."

"But you liked to read and dream of faraway places, Agnes. My nose was never in a book, but bent down threading a heavy crewel needle or counting crochet stitches."

They leaned forward to each other and clasped hands in a warm and loving embrace. The two sisters gazed into each other's eyes for a long time. They spoke not, because the need was not there. Martha tightened her hands upon Agnes'.

"Dear Sister, there is something I must tell you." Martha hesitated. A strange and frightened shadow passed over her face. She lowered her eyes to focus on Agnes' wedding ring. What a lovely ring Joseph gave you, Agnes. Treasure it always."

Agnes' eyes twinkled, "Come now, Martha, what was it you thought I should know? It was hardly about my wedding band."

"No, no, that is not it."

"Then what? Do not keep me in suspense, Martha. You know my patience is nowhere as long as yours." Agnes pinched the other's fingers. "Tell me soon." A soft ripple of humor escaped her throat. "Do we have an unknown rich uncle somewhere who has willed us his fortune or castle?"

"Wilhelm did write to you," Martha blurted out.

"What?" Agnes was shocked completely. "What? Did I hear you

right?" Her body wrenched upright. A dark look crossed her face.

"Yes, Wilhelm did not forget you. He wrote many letters to you."

Agnes loosened her grip on Martha's hands and let them fall into her sister's lap.

"Say that again. Repeat what you just said." The sound of anger trembled in her voice.

Martha's eyes searched for Agnes' eyes. "Dear Sister, I am so sorry. Why did I think I had to tell you after all these years?"

"You knew. You knew all these years?" Agnes' voice rose in pitch. "What did you know all these years?"

"About the letters."

"Wilhelm wrote to me, you say?" Agnes' face was turning livid. "What happened to his letters? Why did I never receive them?"

"Because of Mama and me," muttered Martha in a weak voice.

Agnes stood up and looked down at her. "What did you and Mama have to do with it? Tell me now, right now," she demanded.

Martha's voice was barely audible. "We burned his letters." She dared not look up at Agnes, she could feel her sister's fury rising.

"You burned his letters," shrieked Agnes. "My mama and my sister burned the letters from my betrothed." She stomped her foot hard. "Why? Why?"

"Because he was not Catholic. Mama did not like that he was not of our religion."

"That is it, because he was not Catholic? What did you have to do with it?"

"Mama asked me to help her get the letters before you received them. We did not know how to keep you from finding them, so we burned them."

Agnes wanted so to put her hands on Martha's shoulders and shake the woman to pieces. Instead, she walked to the door of the apartment and turned back to her sister. "I can not believe this. All these years, I faulted him. All the tears I shed when he was innocent. All the wonderings of why? Trying to figure out what made him change his mind." A gasp caught in her throat and her voice choked back a sob. "And it was not Wilhelm at all. It was my own mama and sister." The tears came faster. "Dear God, forgive me. What anger I felt toward Wilhelm." Agnes felt weak and leaned against the nearest chair.

"Mama cried so many times. She suffered more than you will ever know for doing that to you." Martha stood and walked to Agnes. "She just never thought you would go to America. She hoped, that in some way, you would forget Wilhelm and find a nice Catholic man to marry. Nothing would have made her happier."

"So Mama suffered. She should have. To think, a mother doing that to her own child. What she did was cruel. What you did, Martha, was cruel." Agnes wiped tears of anger from her cheeks. "And I cried so when she died. Had I only known, there may not have been any tears."

"Agnes, you can not let this anger eat at your heart. Mama was really trying to protect you. Mixed religion marriages are difficult. Mama saw it in her family and knew."

"She did not trust my judgment, and neither did you. Neither of you had any right."

"Dearest Sister, when you decided to leave all of us and go to America, Mama agonized for months over your decision. She wanted to tell you, but could not admit what she had done. She knew she had broken your heart, but at that time, she had no idea how to mend the hurt."

"So, neither of you did anything. How convenient for your feelings. Let Agnes go and we can forget the entire situation."

"You are being cruel now, Agnes. After you left to go to America, your mother cried many tears. Her agony soon affected her, and her health started to suffer. To save you further heartache, she begged us to say nothing to worry you." Martha reached for Agnes' hand. "Mama loved you so very much, Agnes. You will never know how much."

Agnes sat down on the chair and put her hands up to cover her face. Her silence was deafening. But then, a feeling of peace settled upon her heart. The face of Joseph flashed before her eyes. Then she knew in her soul, that her mother's wish had been fulfilled. Joseph and she were of the same beliefs.

"Did Wilhelm ever know?" Her eyes pleaded with Martha.

"I do not think so. But he never married."

"The poor man. What must have been his thoughts of me all these years?" More tears etched their way on her face. "What a horrible person he must think I am."

"He lives not far from here, Agnes. Would you like to see him again?"

The vision of her sweet Joseph filled her thoughts. For a long time, she did not answer. But when she did, it was with finality.

"No, my life is now in America."

The Linnebur family gathers to celebrate Esther's wedding in 1936. Back row: Joseph, Robert, William, Irene, Wendell and Agnes. In the front: Agnes, Coletta, Elnora (Ellen), Esther.

Agnes and Joseph stroll down a Wichita, Kansas street, in the 1940s.

EPILOGUE

AGNES AND ESTHER returned to America and the farm in Kansas in July of 1930. In September of that year, the economic stability of Germany faltered and the onslaught of a terrible depression followed. Adolf Hitler was making a greater impact upon the country's politics.

The families of Conrad Puder and Martha Puder Neumann survived the horrors and bombings of World War II in their beloved city of Breslau. As the end of the war approached, it became evident that through the Potsdam Declaration, Germany would be divided between the three Allied Powers – Russia, Great Britain and the United States. Breslau became part of Poland and the city was renamed Wroclaw.

Russia would control Germany east of the Elbe River, including the Oder River and Breslau. Many residents of the city and the area feared the atrocities of the Russian soldiers and leaders, and escaped by whatever means was available.

The Puders and Neumanns, like many other residents of Breslau, chose to make the trek out of the designated East Germany area, by way of an underground network. The walk, through forests and heavily guarded areas, was treacherous and dangerous. Fear of detection was persistent. They were allowed to leave their homes only with what they could wear. The only other things they were allowed to take were a bowl and a spoon, necessary if food was offered to them. Because the two items were so vital to their well-being and their continued health on the journey, they had to be very careful to protect them, so they would not be lost or stolen.

The families were able to get to the Allied sector before the Russians entered Breslau. The city had been damaged extensively during the bombings, and the Russians destroyed and flattened what was remaining of the beautiful city.

Eventually, Agnes' family was able to contact her, to tell her they were safe in the Karlsruhe area, but without anything. She and her husband, Joseph, sent them bolts of wool material, flat leather pieces that could be fashioned into shoes, coffee beans, beans, rice, sugar and any other things the families could use themselves, or use to barter for other necessities. Many of the staples they requested were also hard to obtain in the United States, but Agnes and Joseph were persistent in their search, and sent several thousand dollars' worth of goods to them. That was also quite a financial burden on the Linneburs, by then retired and living in the city of Wichita, Kansas. The couple, by then quite elderly, was living on a small income from their farm.

The shaking of Joseph's head worsened through the years. The dear, patient man had to endure the constant side-to-side motion. The condition, most likely, was Essential Tremors, a hereditary disorder. Medication to control the effects was not yet available at that time.

Agnes' staunch individualism was evident even as she rested in death. Black and navy blue were the colors of burial. Agnes had, however, instructed Esther to bury her in the favored white eyelet dress, accented with a silk nosegay of yellow and brown blossoms at the collar.

Agnes loved to wear white, and was well remembered for her all-white dressy summer attire: the eyelet dress, the large-brimmed straw hat, purse, gloves and shoes. She occasionally added a touch of color, a silk nosegay of her much beloved violets. Hence, the sprigs of "Violets for Agnes" sprinkled about within this book.

Joseph lived to be 79, and died January 22, 1950. Agnes, 75, followed him in death, September 27, 1955. Joseph is buried between the two loves of his life, Katherine on his left, and Agnes on his right.

Joseph's and Agnes' daughter, Esther, lived to be 83, and died November 22, 1998. Their son, Robert, passed away July 22, 2001, at 84.

Biography of

ROBERTA AGNES SEIWERT LAMPE

IN THE MID-1990s, Roberta Agnes Seiwert Lampe's family battled an on-slaught of health, accident and personal problems. The outcomes swirled around the author as she struggled to be the main-stay of support for each of them.

Over the six-year period, her husband fought cancer and chemo treatments; her mother had feet and knee amputations, ending with her eventual death; her daugh-ters faced stressful turmoil and trials, and the youngest was the head trauma victim of an unusual accident. Seiwert Lampe's fortunate good health allowed her to provide emotional stability. Eventually the hardships pressured her. That inspired the impetus to put her stories on paper.

Seiwert Lampe was raised in rural Kansas, Garden Plain, the small town where the story, *AGNES,* took place some 90 years previous. A high school journalism teacher, Bobbi Booth, and Floyd and Norma Souders, editors of a local newspaper, were her inspiration to write.

In 1956, she enlisted in the Women's Army Corps and graduated from the U.S. Army Public Information School, Ft. Slocum, New York. She then served as a newspaper reporter at the Armor School Head-quarters, Ft. Knox, Kentucky, and later, at the Northern Area Com-mand Headquarters, Frankfurt am Main, Germany. In later years, she graduated from correspondence courses with the Newspaper Institute

of America and the Institute of Children's Literature. She also re-searched, wrote and edited a local historical book, *100 YEARS, 1880-1980, St. Joseph's Parish, Ost, Kansas*. Other works have been published in *Country, Country People, KanHistique, Capper's, Brave Hearts*, and various newspapers.

In 1959, she returned to her hometown. There she met her husband, Roman Lampe, and settled down to be a farm wife. The couple raised two daughters, Mary and Ramona. Without sons or brothers, the Lampe ladies spent summers driving tractors, plowing and doing other field work, hauling wheat and working with the cattle, to help Roman with his farm operation.

She also worked in the Garden Plain Elementary/High School libraries. Being surrounded by others' literary efforts, her thoughts kept focusing on someday doing serious writing of her own.

Several story lines brewed in Seiwert Lampe's mind, especially the one of her grandmother, Agnes, and another based on the Lampe family's landlady, whose family crossed the prairie in a covered wagon to homestead in Kansas. The time to write those stories never seemed quite right.

In the midst of the family crisis, Seiwert Lampe awoke one morning to hear her subconscious say, "The time is now." She lifted a worn business advertising ballpoint from the desk drawer, grabbed a wad of scratch paper and set about following the directive. Wherever she went, the old pen and paper were handy. With a few minutes here, or a half-hour there, she turned to the stories.

The short pen, its advertising logo already dim, appeared to be almost out of ink when she began. However, it was a magical pen. Whenever it touched the paper, Seiwert Lampe's subconscious asserted itself. The words came in torrents, and what appeared surprised even her.

After two and a half years, the author had penned her two intended 60,000 and 70,000-word novels, plus another nine short children's stories, all in long hand.

The magic of the pen lasted on. It was only after the last words of the many stories were written that the old orange and black pen finally ran out of ink and gave up the ghost.

The pen, paper and words had helped the author through all the trials her family faced and gave her the emotional stamina to carry on.